Magnolia

CAROLINA GARCIA-AGUILERA

For information, go to www.booksandbooks.com

Published by B & B Press

Publishing Consultant Ausbert de Arcé
Project Director Petra Mason

Cover Design by Jeff Griffith Creative
Interior Designed by Kaile Smith

Library of Congress Cataloging-in-Publication Data
Magnolia by Carolina Garcia-Aguilera
Library of Congress Control Number 2012947196

For information about special discounts for bulk purchases,
Contact www.booksandbooks.com

First Edition

ISBN: 978-0-9839378-4-5

This book is dedicated to my three daughters: Sarah, Antonia, and Gabriella, the loves and passions of my life. And, of course, to my beloved Cuba, may she be free soon!

Miami, August 2012

It probably hadn't been a brilliant idea to go to a bar for a drink when the one credit card in my possession had a good chance of being declined, but I was desperate, and my options were running out. I also had a fifty folded into a tiny square in my wallet but I had sworn to myself that I would only use it in a life-or-death situation.

"Would you like another one?" the bartender called out.

I looked down at the empty glass in front of me, and the image of the dead president popped up in my mind. I was about to accept when he spoke again.

"On the house." I watched as in one swift motion, the bartender placed a fresh glass of rum and Coke in front of me. He had been watching me on and off during the hour I'd been nursing my drink, so he'd probably figured that I couldn't afford another. Either that, or I was the slowest drinker in Miami.

I wondered what he thought of me, dressed in my khaki cargo pants, black cotton T-shirt and red Converse sneakers, no makeup, and long hair pulled back in a braid. Whatever his conclusion, I sure as hell didn't look like I was there to pick up men. And, then, of course, there was the fact that I kept drying my tears and blowing my nose with several of the stack of paper napkins on the bar. No man in his right mind would want to hook up with a clearly depressed, drippy, weepy woman. I hoped he wouldn't ask me to leave, claiming that I was bad for business, hanging out there with such a dark cloud hovering over me. Just then, at that point in my life, I had bad juju—the last thing I wanted was to spread it around.

"Thanks." I tried not to sound as desperately grateful as if he'd tossed me the last life jacket on the Titanic.

I took a small sip of the drink and returned his smile. It was possible that, in spite of my sad state, he had some interest in me, but maybe it was standard procedure at the bar to treat new patrons to a refill. I didn't have a clue, nor, just then, did I particularly care. I was used to having men hit on me, so it would not have surprised me if he had been doing that. My four older brothers used to tease me that I looked like a milkmaid from a Scandinavian farm, that all I was missing to complete the image was a three-legged stool and milk pail. I hated to admit it but they were not so far off the mark, as with my long, wavy blond hair, light blue eyes, and fresh, slightly freckled face, I did look about as wholesome as could be. More than once I had heard the comment that I looked so innocent men wanted to seduce me at first sight.

I'd never in my twenty-two years gone into a bar alone in the middle of the afternoon during the workweek to have a drink, so I wasn't quite sure what to expect. As I looked around the huge, empty room, it occurred to me that if the goal of the designers of the Miami Sports Bar had been to create a setting so generic that it could have been located anyplace in the country, they had been spectacularly successful. There were no windows anywhere so that once inside, a customer would not have known if she were in Minneapolis, with a blizzard raging outside, or in Miami, with a hurricane blowing through. With its traditional woodsy décor, the place made me feel safe and protected, exactly what I needed just then. There were no clocks either, so patrons, unless they were wearing a watch, had no sense of time, kind of like a Las Vegas casino.

Sitting on the barstool, sipping my drink in the dim light, I could see why people became alcoholics—the real world was completely blocked out. With its paneled walls, tables, and booths strategically placed in front of the dozen or so flat-screened televisions suspended from the ceiling, and extra large bar in the middle of the room, the place offered an anonymous environment in which to spend a few hours.

Even though the bartender had not asked for an ID, I knew that I still had that "just out of college" look about me, not exactly surprising given my age and what I was wearing. It could have been also because he was curious to find out what I was doing, blinking back tears as I nursed a drink, alone and apparently not waiting for someone to join me, at three o'clock on an unbearably hot August afternoon in Miami.

Miami—the reason for my predicament.

The hell with acting like a lady—my mother was thousands of miles away—what she didn't know wouldn't hurt her. I picked up the glass with the fresh drink and drank the contents in one huge gulp. For someone who had taken a full hour to consume her first drink, I must have become awfully thirsty all of a sudden.

"Rough day?" The bartender looked at me with a sympathetic expression, his eyes so kind that they persuaded me to talk.

"Yes, very." The room had started to spin a bit, not exactly surprising. I hadn't eaten since breakfast.

The bartender noticed my reaction to the second drink, quickly reached under the bar, and brought out a small ceramic dish filled with an assortment of nuts. "Here, help yourself. I keep these hidden for my special customers."

I moved the dish closer and took a handful. "Thanks again."

He waited until I'd finished chewing before speaking again. "Want to talk about it? I'm a good listener."

I took a deep breath and blurted out. "I have less than twenty-four hours to decide whether to stay or go back home to Minneapolis."

The bartender looked at me as if I were a nutcase. "Sorry, I just don't understand your dilemma." Shaking his head, he took some peanuts from the bowl, tilted his head backward, quickly tossed them one by one into the air, and, in a practiced motion, caught them all in his mouth. "All I would have to think of would be of winter in Minneapolis, wearing six layers of clothing, with the snow up to my ass, versus one in Miami, where I would be lying out on the beach, where the most important decision I would have to make was which strength sunblock to apply, and there would be no contest."

"I hate the cold, too, and the endless, dark winters. They really depress me. But it's not quite that easy a choice." My pride was at stake, and I placed a very high, probably too high, price on that. I couldn't deal with the inevitable "I told you so" from my family and friends if I were to give in, and go back to Minneapolis. I began to think back on the events in my life that had led me to be drinking rum and Cokes, alone, in a sports bar in Miami.

"I have just enough money to last one more day here," I confessed, thinking of the fifty in my pocket. Fortunately, I'd had the foresight to buy, even though it had been very expensive to do, a round-trip airline ticket from Minneapolis to Miami, valid for one year. Thankfully, I didn't have to worry about how I was going to get home.

"Maybe you could wait tables or hostess or work in retail."

The bartender folded his arms. "Until your luck changes."

I took a sip of my drink and shrugged my shoulders. "I suppose I could." I'd already considered doing that but had dismissed it. I'd waited tables in college and hated it. I'd been living here for three months, ever since my graduation with a degree in art history from the University of Minneapolis, not exactly the kind of academic credentials that excite human resource departments on job applications. I'd known when I'd chosen my major that jobs in my field were few and far between, but still I had persevered. Most importantly, though, I may have been down and out, but I hadn't given up on getting some kind of a job in art history. I didn't want to take even a temporary job because I needed to concentrate on my searches.

I'd envisioned using some of the money I earned in the art field to open a school for underprivileged children, a place in which they could be empowered by art while learning about it. I'd helped teach art appreciation classes as a volunteer for years, and I loved how the kids' faces lit up when they looked at a work of art, as if they were looking not just at the paintings and sculptures, but at life itself. I had witnessed the healing power of art.

My parents had hinted that through their connections they could get me a job at one of the museums in Minneapolis, but I had demurred. My pride, what was left of it, would not let me. I was definitely in between a rock and a hard place. How did I get myself there? As the youngest of five children in a close, conservative Catholic family, I'd always figured that after college I'd marry (probably one of my brothers' friends, someone I'd known since we were in diapers) and settle nearby. I'd go to Sunday Mass with my spouse and children, and then head over to my parents' house for a family lunch.

But it was not to be, as love (or, more correctly, lust) interfered, and right after graduation, I had followed Fred Lumkins, my college boyfriend, to Miami. We'd moved here because Fred, who had a degree in marine biology, had been offered a terrific position at the University of Miami as a research scientist. At first, I'd been hesitant about leaving Minneapolis—I'd never really been away from home before—but Fred had assured me that getting a job in Miami would be a breeze.

As graduation grew near, the prospect of staying in Minneapolis without Fred had become unimaginable; I had not been able to see myself returning to the relatively unexciting life I'd had before him. Other aspects of my life had been going very well, so it wasn't as if I'd had to leave: I treasured my closeness with my family, but the pull of Fred and Miami had been just too strong. I'd always had an adventurous streak in me, and I was ready for the next chapter in my life. Fred, knowing how important he had become to me, had heartily encouraged my accompanying him. The fact that the job offer had come during a particularly brutal day in February, with the snow piled up seven feet high, helped reinforce the logic of our going together.

Every member of my family, both sets of grandparents, my parents, as well as my four brothers and their wives and children, had begged me to stay in Minneapolis, telling me to let Fred go off by himself, that if we were meant to be together, then we would find a way. I had dismissed their advice, and two weeks after graduation, with the ink still wet on my diploma, I had boarded a flight to Miami to find fame and fortune with my hunky, charming, brilliant true love by my side.

Fabulous Fred, as my friends called him—a misnomer I found out, if there ever was one—turned out to be a complete asshole. Back home, he'd mostly been a serious, studious guy;

true, every so often a bit of a wild side would come out (he frequented strip joints, but that was only when he was out with the boys), but nothing that alarmed me. His wild and crazy side emerged when we had sex, but since I was a participant as well, I wasn't overly concerned. In Miami, though, that part of his personality took over, and he started getting way too fabulous, "too big for his britches," as my mother would say. Not only did Fred let his hair grow out, he stopped washing it. He stopped shaving, and began nurturing stubble (that took him two weeks to grow) something that, rather than making him look like a tough guy, made him seem as if he had dirt smeared on his face.

That first weekend here, Fred purchased a brand new wardrobe: out went the Dockers and Polo shirts, and in came the baggy clothes that rappers on South Beach wore. He threw away his white cotton briefs and wore, instead, two-sizes-too-large paisley boxers that showed over the waistband of his pants. He retired his closed-toe leather shoes and Top-Siders, and began sporting extremely large, blindingly white, unlaced sneakers. He switched from beer to brandy. I suspected it was just a matter of time and money before he got rid of his reliable Swatch and began wearing oversized crucifixes (in Minneapolis, he had been an atheist) and diamond earrings. He thought he looked hot; I thought he looked ridiculous.

What kind of scientist looks and acts like a rapper wannabe? In Minneapolis, Fred had been quiet and unassuming, a perfect gentleman, polite and considerate of others. Marine biologists were down-to-earth types, and Fred fit that bill. In Miami, though, he wasted no time developing a kind of macho swagger, an attitude as if he was God's gift to humanity, a mindset that, unfortunately, especially applied to the women here. He could not get over the bevy of beautiful Latin love-lies who could be found in every nook and cranny of the city, becoming so smitten by the sight of all those staggeringly hot, sexy women that he set out to meet as many as he could.

Soon Fred began going to events after work, joined a trendy gym, attended wine and cigar tastings, signed up for sailing classes. He even took up yoga, for God's sake! He began to fool around. In the beginning, he had tried to be discreet about his dalliances, but subtlety had never been Fred's strong suit, so in time he didn't bother to hide them. He'd stagger home at ungodly hours, stinking of perfume, cheap liquor, and cheaper sex. A couple of times, his clothes had been ripped—slashed, really—but I hadn't allowed myself to dwell on how that had happened. By then, we were barely having sex. The thrill was definitely gone, so I found myself torn between hoping he wouldn't get an STD (the Catholic in me), and hoping he would (the jealous girlfriend in me). I was so angry and repulsed at how he was behaving that I wasn't even hurt that he was being unfaithful.

So neither the job nor Fred was working out. Sex, hope, and idealism weren't enough to make a relationship work, nor did they pay the bills. All the help he had promised me, all the networking he had assured me would succeed, all the contacts he'd told me he had, well, none of those material-ized, either.

I should have researched the job market myself before coming down here, but as the saying goes, "love is blind," although it was more like "lust is blind." It didn't take long to discover that Miami was not a mecca for Impressionist paintings or painters; there was no Louvre or Metropolitan Museum in Little Havana or South Beach. There was Art Basel, the one-week convention that brought in artists and dealers from all over the world to Miami, but that took place in December. And it was May at this point. This blatant failure that was so out of character showed how skewed my thinking had been, how hooked on Fred I had become. Fred had become like a drug for me; the sex was so exhilarating that I could not see staying in Minneapolis without him.

Before Fred, the limited amount of sex that I'd experienced had been pretty much the vanilla variety: missionary with the occasional bit of oral stuff thrown in. Fred had made me become more adventuresome, and I found I liked experimenting with various positions, and later on we dabbled a bit in domination. It did not take long for me to look forward to spending time with Fred as much in the vertical position as the horizontal one, to the point where, even while having sex, I would imagine what we would do during our next tryst. Sort of like the way I'd heard the French felt about their meals: while eating, they discuss the meals they'd had in the past, comment on the one they were currently enjoying, and contemplate the one they will next have. Fred, of course, took full advantage of this transformation, and I became an increasingly willing participant in our encounters, to the point where I would initiate them the majority of the time.

We weren't doing well financially, either, not after Fred went on his wardrobe shopping spree while we were staying in a Motel 6–type place near the airport, an establishment that I soon determined was a "hot sheets" motel, given the amount of activity that took place at all hours and the cacophony of weird grunts and noises that I could hear as I paced up and down the hallways. The fact that the establishment did not accept credit cards and charged by the hour was a dead giveaway. There were vending machines in the lobby that dispensed sex toys, bondage items, and lubricants.

I didn't consider myself a prude, but I had no idea twelve-inch-long, four-inch-wide penises that lit up in different colors existed. The infinite assortment of lubricants (scents, consistency, hues, etc.) was also an endless source of curiosity. The machine that sold feathers especially fascinated me.

Not surprisingly, I couldn't wait to get out of there. So after a cursory search of rental properties, we signed a one-year lease for a modest one-bedroom apartment in the Coral Gables area of Miami. As he would be getting a paycheck every few weeks, Fred was in a much better financial position than I was. His job included a nice cushion of benefits: great health insurance, dental and vision, IRA, 401K, etc. I, on the other hand, had emptied out my bank account to finance my move to Miami, so my situation was truly precarious.

In the beginning, though, I have to admit, life in Miami had worked out well for us. The city was fascinating, so vibrant and lively and blessed with mind-boggling beauty. The color of the waters that surrounded it was enough to send me into raptures. I could not get enough of its mix of cultures; rapid-fire Spanish spoken everywhere; strong, heart-attack-inducing coffee sold on street corners; salsa music blaring from live bands or boom boxes located in expected places; the aroma of garlic sizzling from open flames. I had never felt so alive.

Every aspect of our lives was so interesting and exciting that we were able to overlook problems that were beginning to surface in our relationship. As the days passed, however, and Fred's metamorphosis into his new persona began, he would spend longer hours away from home, claiming to be at the lab, a flimsy, laughable excuse that I did not believe for a nanosecond. Not surprisingly, the situation between us became increasingly strained. Not having physical relations did not help either. I was stuck in an apartment with no job, little money, and no reliable means of transportation. Fred took the car to work, which meant, given that Miami had no public transportation system to speak of, that I was pretty much stranded unless I could reach my destination by bicycle.

Our apartment was in a residential neighborhood blocks away from any main streets, so getting around was not easy. The oppressive heat made walking or even riding the fourth-hand bicycle I'd bought quite unpleasant. I tried to stay optimistic, and would read the Miami Herald and the New Times every day, scouring the help-wanted ads of which, given the dismal state of the economy, were few and far between. My laptop, the MacBook I'd had since my first year at college, finally gave out, and not even the guys at the Apple store could get it to work. Without my computer, I felt more lost than ever.

I spent my days at the Coral Gables library, competing with others who were unemployed or homeless to use the computers to job search. I didn't speak Spanish, something that severely limited the choice of available jobs. On the plus side, though, I was in the country legally, so I had a leg up on many of my fellow job seekers. And then one day, my bicycle was stolen.

One month after arriving in Miami, having made the rounds of the handful of schools and museums with my admittedly slim resume, the realization hit me that I was going to have to forget finding a job in the arts and broaden my search to include all areas. By then, I was almost broke, discouraged, depressed, and, worst of all, very lonely. Fred was gone all day and most nights, and, when he was home, all we did was fight.

Perhaps the worst part of my Miami experience was

that, for the first time in my life, I had not been able to be honest with my family about my situation. Given how I had left home, there was no way I could tell them how miserable I was. If I were to even hint about my circumstances—Fred was a world-class shit, no money and no job—they would tell me to forget Miami and come back home. However lonely, broke, and unhappy I might have been, I was not going to throw in the towel and return to Minneapolis with my tail between my legs. I loved Miami and was not prepared to give up on the city just yet.

The darker my job prospects became, the worse my relationship with Fred became. For the first time in my life, I did not like myself: my self-esteem was in shambles and my self-confidence had taken a serious beating. Late one Friday night in July, after a huge fight, Fred and I decided to split up; it was either that, or we would kill each other. Fred must have felt guilty about how he'd behaved, because he gave me his car, a Ford Taurus with over 100,000 miles on it as a going-away present. Less than fifteen minutes later, I had packed my belongings and moved out of our apartment, heading for Little Havana, where I had seen buildings with "for rent" signs in the windows of several buildings. Using eight hundred dollars of my fast-dwindling cash, I put down two months' rent on a studio just off Calle 8, in a neighborhood that was geographically only five or so miles away from our apartment in Coral Gables, but emotionally, thousands.

The building was so decrepit that I was surprised it had not been condemned. As I handed over the cash (no checks accepted) to my landlady, I consoled myself that at least I would have a roof over my head. This was only temporary, I vowed, as I inserted the key in the rusty lock.

I might have been finished with Fred, but I was not yet done with Miami, a city where, in spite of my dismal experience, I had actually come to increasingly feel at home. I didn't really even mind the relentless, stifling heat, or the threat of hurricanes that set everyone's nerves on edge. I wanted to give this sexy, tropical city another chance. Now Fredless, I resumed my job search with renewed vigor, but, unfortunately, with few results.

A month later, in spite of all my efforts to find a job and having gone through almost all my money, I came to the conclusion that I had no other choice but to return to Minneapolis or take a job that required no language skills or experience. I could try my luck working as an exotic dancer or a stripper. There were lots of jobs like that available. But I'd never in my life done such a thing—guess my values were too Midwestern. At best, I'd get up there on one of those stages and look like an idiot—a naked one. Even I, in the depths of my depression, realized the absurdity of presenting myself as an exotic dancer from Minneapolis. The term alone was an oxymoron. I even considered taking a job at the Miami Seaquarium, performing with the whales and dolphins, but even though I was a reasonably good swimmer, I wanted a job in which I wouldn't be in danger of drowning. I wanted to spend the money I'd earned, not use it to pay for my funeral.

The dancer/stripper possibility kept coming back to me—I was that desperate—no Spanish required for those positions. After all, in Miami, tall, long-legged, blue-eyed natural blondes with their original body parts are as rare as winter snowstorms, so I shouldn't have had too much trouble getting a job in one of the hundreds of strip joints in the city. And that's what I was thinking about when I walked into this bar.

I turned my attention to the pair of sports commentators

on the nearest screen that were discussing a preseason football game that had just taken place. I said, "The guy on the right knows what he was talking about, but the other is a complete idiot, the one with the hairpiece."

"Yeah—he's full of shit—always has been. Don't know why he's a commentator." The bartender and I began a lively discussion about the exhibition game that both of us had watched the previous Saturday, one that I had spoken of at length the day before with my brother Peter. I had just begun quoting several of the players' statistics—it seemed that quite a few of the players were injured, and the season had not even started—when I heard a voice behind me.

"Excuse me, miss, is this seat taken?"

I'd been so occupied discussing the show with the bartender that I hadn't noticed the woman who was now standing next to me. Not happy with the interruption, I slowly turned to look at her. She seemed to be about forty years old, elegantly dressed in a well-cut, expensive-looking suit, black stiletto high-heeled shoes, and she had an attractive, self-assured air.

Not wanting to encourage her, the last thing I wanted or needed at that point was to have to make polite small talk with a stranger, so I simply shook my head no. I hoped that she wouldn't sit too close to me.

The woman slid onto the barstool one seat away and began to watch the television screens, slowly, one by one just as I had done earlier. The bartender and I continued with our conversation about the commentators, agreeing or disagreeing with certain of their pronouncements. We even got into a lively discussion as to which team might make it to the Super Bowl, premature for sure, as it was August, but fun nevertheless to speculate.

"Do you think it'll be the Giants and Patriots again?" I

wondered. As I'd long had a crush on Eli Manning, I fervently hoped that would be the case.

"Maybe. Depends on their season, of course." The bartender wiped down some glasses. "That Brazilian model wife of Tom Brady's was right when she complained the receivers couldn't catch."

"Next year, the Super Bowl will be in New Orleans. Serious party town. I wonder if the players will even show up for the game."

The bartender chuckled. "Yeah, there's that possibility. Whenever the game's held here, it's a sure bet that several of them will be arrested for partying too hard on South Beach. Too many distractions."

As we spoke, I sensed that the customer sitting next to me did not have a casual interest in the events being televised; she was watching the screens as I was. The woman must have been a regular because a few minutes after her having sat down, the bartender brought her a drink, a scotch or Jack Daniel's—some kind of golden liquid over ice—without her having ordered it.

"Cheers." The woman tipped her glass in my direction and then took a sip. Noticing my empty glass, she asked, "May I treat you to another of whatever it is you're having?"

I didn't hesitate to accept her offer. "Thank you."

The woman waved to the bartender and pointed to my glass. "I didn't mean to eavesdrop on your conversation, but I couldn't help but overhear you speaking to Frank about the game and some sports statistics." The woman took another sip of her drink. "Please don't think I'm being condescending or offensive or anything like that, but if I may ask, how is it that you know so much about sports? My personal experience has been that most women aren't so knowledgeable. I noticed you were discussing the plays, quoting statistics, things like that. By the way, I agree with you about which team you think will make it all the way to the Super Bowl. Giants all the way again. Eli's the best quarterback in the NFL. No question. I like how you came up with your picks." The woman chuckled. " A lot of times women watch the games just to look at the athletes, at least I know I do. Usually, they're a bunch of good-looking guys with great bodies, fun to watch, but you—you know your sport. It's not just about the athletes that marry supermodels even though Tom Brady did. I'm impressed."

"I like following sports, I do." I laughed. "I have four older brothers—and they're all jocks, so in order to keep up with them, I had to learn about sports. That, plus I have strong survival instincts!" I picked up the glass in front of me and took a tiny sip. "But I have to confess, just like other women, I do look at the good-looking guys just a bit longer—that's true." I was drinking on an empty stomach, so I had to be careful to pace myself. "And you, how is it that you know so much about sports?"

"It's my business to know." The woman reached into her purse—a Chanel quilted black leather one, I noticed. She took out a business card and, with a flourish, presented it to me. "My name is Oona O'Ryan. I'm a sports agent."

I vaguely knew what sports agents did; I had seen the film Jerry Maguire. By the confident way Oona acted, and the expensive way she was dressed, she clearly expected me to be impressed. My Midwest manners kicked in. "Hi, I'm Magnolia Larson. Pleased to meet you." We shook hands. "If you don't mind telling me, what exactly does a sports agent do?"

"I'll be happy to, if you'll tell me how a young lady with your upper Midwest accent came to be called Magnolia—if that's your real name."

Chapter 2

Two hours and four rum and Cokes later, I knew exactly what a sports agent did. Oona's primary responsibility was to keep the athletes she represented happy, which she accomplished by making sure they were offered the best contracts and by seeing that their each and every need, personal and professional, was met to their full satisfaction.

Coming from a family of men who were obsessed with sports, I knew the different games as they were played on the field. However, as none of my brothers had ever chosen to play professionally, I was clueless as to the business side of it and I found myself becoming increasingly interested in what Oona was telling me. No doubt helped along by liberal amounts of Jack Daniel's, Oona became quite informative, even hinting at what keeping her athletes "happy" meant. She hadn't exactly spelled out what she meant, but as I listened, I was getting a pretty good idea what that was.

Although Oona was a lawyer, she said it was not necessary to be one to become a sports agent and that she had become one almost by accident. She had been practicing criminal law when one of her partners, an attorney who handled civil matters, asked her for help when a client faced a criminal charge. A well-known soccer player, a Venezuelan called Mario—no last name needed—had been accused of shooting and killing his wife's lover, her personal trainer. After playing in the World Cup game in Buenos Aires, a game his team had lost by just one goal, Mario had returned home unannounced, a day ahead of schedule. He found his wife and her trainer frolicking in bed. His bed.

The prosecution, knowing it was facing an uphill battle to convict Mario in soccer-crazy Miami, had offered him a sweet deal—manslaughter, probation, no jail time—but he turned it down, and on Oona's advice, insisted on going to trial. Oona had made sure that each and every one of the jurors selected to hear the case was either a soccer player or fan, and Miami's being an overwhelmingly Hispanic city made her job easy. Mario's entire defense had been that he had shot his wife's lover in a fit of passion, an explanation that might not have played well in Peoria, but was accepted and understood in Miami. After acquitting him—the jury deliberated for thirty minutes, if that—Mario stood outside the courtroom autographing jerseys with his number (Oona had ordered hundreds, in anticipation of the verdict).

Soon, Oona had begun advising Mario on other legal matters, and she was so successful at it that the athlete had begun referring other players to her. First, it had been players on his team, then others who played different sports. Oona soon began to have a steady stream of clients, representing them not just on criminal matters but also in the drawing up, writing, and reviewing of their contracts.

Oona enjoyed being a sports agent a lot more than being a criminal defense attorney. And the perks were better: she got to attend her clients' games and sit in VIP sections, and she was invited to amazing parties. And then there were the hot men who hung around the clients, and who, if they couldn't hook up with athletes, were okay with going with the lawyer/agents. Oona clearly had no qualms about that.

As I listened to Oona, I had the feeling something was bothering her. True, I had only just met the woman, and I was on my fourth rum and Coke (not exactly perfect conditions for lucidity) but, still, I sensed that the picture was not as rosy as she was painting it.

"So how long have you been doing this kind of work, being a sports agent?" Although Oona had made it seem as if it were perfectly normal for a woman to be in that line of work, common sense told me it was very much a man's world there. As I listened to her, ever so slowly I was getting a presentiment that Oona O'Ryan was going to somehow have influence on my life. I usually scoffed at anything to do with psychics, thinking it was a bunch of mumbo jumbo. However, in spite of the liquor I had consumed, I could not shrug off that feeling.

"Ten years this month." She picked up the fresh glass of Jack Daniel's that Frank had placed in front of her and raised it to her lips. "To your health, Magnolia." She took a sip. "By the way, you were going to tell me about your name."

I certainly did not look, act, or speak like most people's preconceived idea of a Southern belle. "Magnolia's my real name. My mother was reading Gone with the Wind while she was expecting me and got caught up in the whole Southern thing."

"It suits you. You're a beauty, that's for sure. An interesting mixture of innocence and sexuality." It was strange the way Oona was scrutinizing me in such a detached manner, almost as if she were in a store, deciding whether or not to buy me. I didn't mind; I was happy for the company and the rum and Cokes.

Oona O'Ryan was not a tall woman, but she had such

erect posture that she seemed much taller. Her dark brown shoulder-length hair was expensively cut and styled, with layers that framed her face, discrete highlights catching the light as she moved. Even though it was dim in the bar, I could see that her caramel-colored eyes had green flecks in them. She did not have on much makeup, but what she did have brought out her cheekbones. She had clear gloss on her lips.

The dark blue, beautifully cut two-piece suit that she was wearing was made of gabardine and fit her body like a second skin. Apart from the small diamond studs she was wearing, the only other piece of jewelry that she had on was an ultra-thin gold square-cut watch with a band made out of some kind of black reptile skin.

Interestingly, Oona was quite pale, no mean feat in Miami where one could get a tan from just walking across a parking lot. Although by any measure Oona was an attractive woman, she did not come across as being sexy, and, true, I had only spent a limited amount of time with her, but I could not tell whether she was gay or straight. She had said she'd appreciated that a perk of being a sports agent was that she got to spend quality time with male athletes, but for some reason that had not convinced me that she liked only men. It could be that she had said that in order not to put me off, fearing that she might hit on me. After four drinks, I was not thinking very clearly, so I was not in a particularly strong footing to make those kinds of determinations. Still, there was no question that I found her very interesting—but she had ordered Jack Daniel's, traditionally a man's drink.

"So enough about me. Tell me about you, Magnolia." Oona smiled with her mouth, not her eyes. "I'll bet you a pair of Miami Heat floor seat tickets you're not from here."

"That's right. I'm not from here. Far from it," I replied.

"Minneapolis."

Oona was so easy to talk to that, almost before I realized it, I told her the story of my life, beginning with my background in Minneapolis and ending up with my sitting there, next to her, having twenty-four hours to make the decision to leave or stay in Miami.

Oona seemed so sympathetic that I even told her my dream—quite unrealistic, really given my current impoverished state—to bring the world of art to underprivileged and/ or at risk children.

I glossed over the sad, tawdry tale of my falling out with Fabulous Fred, only alluding to the fact that my family and friends had warned me that coming to Miami with him would be a mistake. I told her of my futile job hunt experience, and how bleak my prospects were. I even told her how I had graduated with a degree in art history with a concentration on the Impressionists. I ended my tale of woe by telling Oona that I needed to make money fast if I were to stay in Miami, and that my MacBook had crashed, leaving me without a computer.

I could feel my eyes mist over slightly as I looked down at my bare wrist, where my watch—a high school graduation present from my maternal grandparents—had been. It was now sitting in a pawnshop in Little Havana.

"The only way I can stay is if I take a job waitressing or stripping or exotic dancing, where I get paid at the end of every night. I need cash, and I need it like yesterday," I explained. "I've worked as a waitress and wasn't good at it, but if I had to, I could learn to do it well; I'm a pretty quick study. "

Oona reached into her purse and bought out a clean, white stiffly starched handkerchief. She held it out to me, and watched as I wiped my tears.

"I'm broke, but I'm not yet really desperate. I know I could take one of those jobs. I could work at them until I can get back on my feet."

Oona was looking at me intently, not saying anything, but her calm presence was comforting, so I kept going.

"It would only be temporary, if I were to do that. That's all. It wouldn't be a career." I seemed to have developed a severe case of verbal diarrhea, but I couldn't stop. "I would still be looking for a job in an art-related field. Something would turn up in time, right?"

"It's true you can earn fast money by working at any of those jobs until something better turns up. But when is that going to happen? Look, Magnolia, I don't want to be depressing and burst your bubble, but the harsh reality is that you've already spent a considerable amount of time looking, and nothing has come your way. The kind of job you are interested in is not posted on Craigslist or in the Miami Herald. Your field—the Impressionists—that's tough anywhere, but here in Miami, close to impossible." Oona shook her head. "Also, with the economy, lots of places are not hiring. They just don't have a budget. They're all cutting back, not just the ones in the art world; it's bad all over. Plus, remember, it's August. Anyone who is in a position to offer you a job is on vacation. And even if you were to apply for waitressing jobs, remember this month is dead tourist season. Restaurants are not hiring now. Sorry."

I blew my nose in Oona's handkerchief. As I did so, I realized that I had turned it into a soggy mess. Oona, thank God, did not seem to notice.

"And you need enough money to fulfill your dream of helping kids. But first, you need to get some cash, right? Get a steady income stream going, as you said."

I felt so stupid that I hadn't realized how the fact that it was August would impact my job search. In Minneapolis, where no one really went away for the month, that wouldn't have been such a problem, but here in Miami, where August was the hottest, most miserable, least touristy, and most hurricane-ravaged month, clearly it was.

It was time to stop fooling myself into thinking that if I just waited a few more days, something would turn up. I had to face reality, ugly as it was. I blinked back tears hard. It wouldn't do to have Oona think I was a sloppy drunk—she seemed so well put together. "I should have listened to my family. I should have done my homework and had a job lined up before coming here."

"Listen, Magnolia, don't beat yourself up too much over this. We all make mistakes that we can learn from. It's called experience." Oona put her hand over mine, and patted it softly. "I don't want you to think I'm hitting on you or anything. You seem a bit lost, that's all, and in need of some human contact. I met you... what?" Oona looked at her watch. "Less than three hours ago. Isn't that right?"

"Something like that."

"I've told you I'm a lawyer who is a sports agent." Oona suddenly turned crisp and businesslike. "Didn't you wonder what I was doing, going to a bar like this, a woman alone, to get a drink at three o'clock in the afternoon? I'll tell you why. I'm here because I've been given some really bad news. Two of my best clients, brothers, guys who played in the NBA whom I've represented for five years, told me this morning they don't want me to be their agent anymore."

"Did they say why they were leaving?" It was clear that the news had been devastating. "Did they give you a reason?"

"Not exactly, but the implication was I had gotten stale, and it was time to move on." Oona slammed a fist on the bar. "Stale! Total bullshit!" She was almost shouting, frightening me a bit, as she been in such control before. "Magnolia, these are guys that I got multimillion dollar contracts for, when they were playing in podunk colleges located in West Bumfuck, with one-way tickets to a league in Transylvania."

I thought about what Oona had just said. "Is there anything you can do to stop them from leaving you? Don't you have a contract with the brothers?"

"The athletes I represent can drop me at anytime, that is, if they continue to honor the terms and conditions of any contract that I negotiated that they signed while I was their agent. Which is pretty much my own legal position as far as my representing them. I can stop being their agent as long as I keep sending them the money they earned under any contracts I negotiated for them." I must have looked perplexed. "What I just said means that as long as we don't screw each other out of any money, yes, both parties can cut their ties anytime, for any reason."

"Well, I'm sure that's a blow to you, but you have other clients, right? And you'll get new ones, won't you? To replace those?" I wondered.

"True, but the world of sports is really quite small and people talk a lot. Word gets out that the brothers took a hike on me. Who knows what might happen?" Oona chewed on her bottom lip with such force I was afraid she'd draw blood. "Athletes have a kind of herd mentality. One goes off the cliff, the others follow."

"What makes you suspect that the reason the brothers left you was because they thought you might be getting stale?" I tried to phrase the question as delicately as I could.

"You said that they didn't express that, so why would you think that?"

Oona gave me a sad smile. "Look, Magnolia, I've been in the business for ten years. I hate to admit it, but I just had my fortieth birthday last month. In my business, that's old, really old." Oona was now tapping the top of the bar. "Remember, these athletes are just kids really; some are still teenagers. To them, anyone in his or her thirties is senile almost. As far as they're concerned, I have a foot in the grave." Oona took a sip of her drink. "It's not just the brothers; they were the last of four athletes that have dropped me in the past six months. That makes six that have left me. Six in six months! That's not good, not good at all. I have to stop the stampede, I just have to!" Oona's hands, with perfectly manicured nails painted in French style, were shaking.

"So what are you going to do?"

As I sat there, I began to think that the situation I found myself in was so typical of me. I'd come to the bar to make a difficult decision, and not only had I not accomplished that, I had become involved with the problems of the stranger beside me. And now I was on the verge of being drunk without having solved anything.

"I have to get an edge, something that no other sports agent has: an edge. I need an edge. Something that allows me to keep the clients I have, plus represent new ones without my age being a factor."

"An edge? What's an edge?" I had no idea what she was talking about.

"I don't know exactly what that is right now, but I will, soon. I guarantee it." Oona spoke with conviction. "I knew coming to the sports bar was what I should do and you see,

I was right. I met you, and, thanks to you, I am figuring out what it is that I need to stay on top!"

I wondered if Oona was hallucinating, or if it was the Jack Daniel's. If thinking that I had helped her figure out an answer to her problem made her happy, then I was happy for her. Maybe, hopefully, I'd be next.

Oona stood up and signaled to Frank for the check. "Listen, I know I haven't been much help to you with your situation, but I will do something for you. I promise. You've helped me more than you'll ever know." Oona turned to me, took my hands in hers, then looked into my eyes, and said. "I want you to do something for me. Please."

"What is that?" I was instantly on my guard. Oh, God, please don't let her proposition me. Please don't ruin the past few hours by her hitting on me, just as I was beginning to like her.

"I want to ask you to postpone making your decision, whether to stay or go, just for twenty-four hours. Please." Oona reached for her wallet, inside her purse, searched through it, and peeled off three hundred-dollar bills. From the pocket of her suit jacket, she took out a business card and along with the bills, laid them on the bar in front of me. "Please, Magnolia, come to my office tomorrow; we'll discuss your future. Solve your predicament. You helped me. Now, it's my turn to help you. I know I can. I just have to figure out how. You have to trust me."

I looked at her like: What are you smoking? I knew what she'd been drinking. Maybe it was my Midwest upbringing, but where I came from, a total stranger certainly didn't give women cash, and not expect something in return. It just didn't happen. And a lady didn't accept the money, but just then I didn't have the luxury of doing that. The three hundred would buy me time—time I desperately needed. Besides, all Oona wanted in return was for me to go to her office in the morning—she wasn't asking me to meet her in a hotel room or in a seedy bar or anyplace like that. I glanced at her card and saw that her office was located on Brickell Avenue, the main downtown road with tall office buildings where many businesses were located. Besides, I wasn't clear on how, exactly, I had helped her. I'd just listened; that's all I had done, really. Certainly not worth three hundred dollars. It was all so weird, having a woman give me money.

"Please, I'm asking you, as a favor to me. I really, really feel that you are going to bring me luck. I just know it. You can't leave me at a time like this. I know we just met, and I'm asking a lot of you, but please help me out. I'll help you, too. I know people; I have connections; I have money. You have to trust me. Don't leave Miami yet, please. Give me a chance. Wait a day," Oona pleaded, her eyes locking onto mine.

"Okay, I'll stay one more day, but I'm not sure how I helped you. I don't think I earned this money, really I don't. But I give you my word, I'll be at your office tomorrow," I replied. What, I asked myself as I pocketed the bills, did I have to lose? At the very least, I could get my beloved watch out of the pawn-shop before returning home. "What time tomorrow?"

Chapter 3

It had been so long since I'd had any cash, so it wasn't surprising that the three hundred dollars that Oona had given me were burning a hole in my pocket. I set aside fifty dollars to pay the pawnshop, so I could retrieve my watch. For now, though, I would treat myself to a good meal. I was tired of eating cheaply. I would throw up if I had to eat another peanut butter and jelly sandwich, tuna salad, or greasy Cuban and Latin American food from the restaurants in my neighborhood. I needed to have some good, healthy food, the kind my mother fixed for the family at home.

It was amazing what having some money was doing for my frame of mind. For the first time in months I was upbeat, hopeful and optimistic about the future. I'd been given a lifeline, one that I'd gratefully accepted. Three hundred dollars wasn't exactly a fortune, but I felt as if I'd won the lottery.

By the time I left the Miami Sports Bar, my stomach was growling something fierce, so I got in my car and headed directly for the Spanish Rose, a fancy restaurant I had been yearning to visit, but which I had thus far been unable to afford, located just a block from my studio apartment. And which now, thanks to Oona, I could. I knew the menu by heart, having read it from where it was posted outside the front doors. I probably should have gone back to the studio and changed my clothes, but I was just too hungry.

It was only seven, early to be having dinner in late-night Miami, so I wasn't particularly worried that I wouldn't find an empty table. The Spanish Rose was popular; on week-end nights the crowds would spill into the street, a reliable indication that the food was good. I loved to eat, always had. I could be dying, in the hospital ICU, hooked up to an IV, but I would never even consider skipping a meal. I never exercised—it was a blessing that I did not have to worry about getting fat. I had inherited my father's metabolism—the man could put away a five-thousand-calorie meal at lunch, take a nap, and still look forward to dinner. My brothers were the same. My mother, unfortunately, was cursed: she just thought about food and she packed on the pounds. Totally unfair.

The delicious smells that greeted me as I opened the front door of the Spanish Rose confirmed that I had made the correct choice in having my first good meal in months there. The restaurant was only half full, so I pretty much had the place to myself. I requested that the maître d' seat me at one of the booths that lined the back wall, a location that would give me privacy but would still allow me to see the whole room.

After giving the waiter my order, I began to relax, sipping red wine and munching on the garlic bread. The restaurant began to fill up. I watched as the tables around me were taken, but mostly I observed an attractive black-haired man as he moved smoothly and confidently around the room. Every so often, I would catch him glancing over at me.

The mystery man was forgotten as soon as my dinner came, and I turned my full attention to the delicious food that the waiter set down in front of me. I had my priorities straight, right? I began with an enormous Caesar salad, and then moved on to the specialty of the house, a steak Florentine, accompanied by an enormous baked potato, which, of course, I slathered with sour cream and butter. After all those rum and Cokes at the bar, I really didn't want to drink much more, so I had settled for half a carafe of the house red wine. For dessert, I inhaled a sinful chocolate cake that the waiter had assured me was homemade, the perfect finish to a wonderful meal. After paying the bill for the dinner, the food and wine plus the generous tip for the waiter, I was pleased to see that I still had $150 left.

I vaguely wondered if prisoners on death row felt the same way I was, when, hours before they're about to be executed, they're granted an unexpected reprieve. I had no idea what was going to happen the next day at Oona's office, but whatever it was, I would face it better on a full stomach.

I had eaten and drunk so much that, even though it was still quite early, my eyes were getting heavy. I was about to go into food coma. At that point, really, there was nothing left to do but leave and go back to the apartment. I took the last sip of wine left in the glass, and reached for my purse.

I was about to get up when the tall, dark, and handsome—a cliché, for sure, but that's literally what he was—man that I had been observing earlier moving around the room hurried over to my table. "Not leaving so soon, are you, señorita?" He gave me a devastating smile.

"Yes, actually, I am."

"Well, the restaurant will lose the presence of a beautiful woman. Here, let me help you." He pulled out the table so I could slide out from behind it more easily. "I hope you enjoyed your meal."

"Yes, very much, thank you," I replied, standing up next

to him. The man must have been someone important at the restaurant; otherwise, he wouldn't be pulling out the table for me with such authority. "Everything was delicious."

"My name is Max Martinez. I am the owner."

The owner! A pang of disappointment went through me. So he was only interested in me as a customer. Oh, well.

"Congratulations, your restaurant is terrific," I told him, as I began to walk away. "Wonderful meal. Especially the chocolate cake."

"It's my mother's recipe." Max took my elbow and guided me towards the front of the room. "Next time you come, and I hope there will be a next time, you must be my guest. It would be an honor to welcome you back." He reached into his pocket, took out a business card, and handed it to me. "Please let me know when you plan to come again—I'll make sure to be here, and take care of you personally."

"Thank you." I took the card and slipped it into my purse. His eyes, which I would have expected to be dark, were a startling shade of blue—the exact color of the deepest part of the ocean.

"I look forward to that... Miss...?" Max asked.

"Larson. Magnolia Larson," I replied.

"Magnolia! A beautiful name for a beautiful woman! And a beautiful flower, as well." He nodded approvingly, a slight smile on his face.

"Good night, and, thank you again." I stepped outside into the hot, sultry Miami night. The restaurateur may have been super-attractive and very nice, but his enthusiasm, just then, was a bit overwhelming. It had been quite a day, and meeting Max had certainly topped it all.

Although I was drop-dead exhausted, I still had one more place to go before heading home—the 24-Hour Pawn Shop where I'd dropped my watch off ten days before. I hated the place. It smelled of dried sweat, stale cigarettes, and broken dreams; to describe it as being seedy was giving it a huge compliment. I headed towards the bulletproof counter and pushed the ticket I had been given over to the clerk through the small opening, plus the fifty dollars. As soon as I had my watch back, I put it on my wrist, where it belonged. Oona O'Ryan had helped me more than she'd ever know.

That night, for the first time in months, probably helped by all the delicious food and wine, I slept like a baby. My brief meeting with Max Martinez must have had a deep influence on me as every so often his face would appear in one or another of my dreams: I was dreaming of a man I had only met once and for a couple of minutes at most. Clearly, I must have been lonelier than I thought. Or Max Martinez might have made more of an impression than I'd realized.

After a quick breakfast, I left my studio apartment, got into Fred's Ford Taurus, and headed toward Oona's office. I had no idea what to expect. I had already checked the availability for flights back home to Minneapolis for that night.

It would not take a full hour to drive from my apartment in Little Havana to Oona's office, but because I didn't want to risk being late, I gave myself plenty of time. I should be punctual for such an important meeting. At the parking garage under Oona's building, I drove up the endless circular ramp until I found an empty visitor spot on the eighth floor.

I still had close to half an hour before the meeting, so I used the time to visit the ladies' room on the ground floor of the building to do a final check of my appearance.

In contrast to my outfit from the day before at the bar, this morning, knowing I would be going into an office, I was much more formally attired and was wearing my one suit—khaki colored, slightly safari style, but still office appropriate, with cream-colored sling-back shoes and matching purse. Although I did not normally wear much makeup, this morning I had made an exception and put on eye shadow, eyeliner, and mascara. A bit of blush, lipstick, some perfume, and I was ready. I'd left my long hair loose, with the hope that the oppressive humidity would not do weird things to it.

After touching up my makeup in the ladies' room, I hung around the newsstand in the lobby of the building until just after eleven o'clock. I did not want to seem overly eager and arrive too much ahead of time. Oona's office was located on the penthouse floor of the building, so I had to take two elevators to get there.

As the doors of the elevator opened directly into the reception area, I had no time to look around the room before going over to the gorgeous, olive-skinned receptionist who was seated behind the long S-shaped glass desk. The dark green carpet I had to walk on was so thick that I felt myself sinking a few inches as I made my way across the room.

"Good morning. My name is Magnolia Larson." I tried to sound as if coming to such an opulent office was something I did every day. "I have an appointment with Ms. O'Ryan at eleven o'clock."

"Ms. O'Ryan is expecting you. Please take a seat. I'll tell her you're here."

The receptionist stood up and led me to a seating area resembling a mini living room, right in front of the huge picture window with an enormous view of Miami that took up an entire wall. She was very formally dressed, wearing a chic, navy two-piece designer suit, with stiletto heels and stockings.

Stockings! I hadn't seen anyone wearing a pair in the four months I had been here. What torture it must be, to be so uncomfortably dressed in the steamy, muggy, intensely humid month of August in Miami. Either Oona paid her a fortune to work here, or she was a masochist. I had to admit that she looked terrific, though.

"Would you care for anything to drink? Coffee, tea, a soda, water, anything?" The receptionist was very solicitous.

I shook my head. "Thank you, no. I'm fine."

I sat in one of the oversized armchairs and began to look around the room with its American-interpretation-of-English-country-taste décor. Either that or the designer had gone to a Ralph Lauren store and bought the entire display and had it transported to the offices of O'Ryan and Associates. The overstuffed sofas and oversized armchairs were upholstered in rich green paisley fabric; dark wood tables polished to a high sheen were scattered around; there was an enormous Oriental carpet on the floor, and dozens of hunting prints hung on the walls. Not very "Miami" in terms of style but likely the perfect decoration—masculine and sporting—for rich athletes.

Less than a minute later, the double doors to my right opened and Oona walked out, arms outstretched, greeting me in a hug. "Magnolia!" Oona held me so tightly that I was enveloped in the cloud of very strong, expensive perfume that wafted from her. She took my elbow and guided me back toward the double doors from where she had come. Her overly effusive expression made me suspect that she might have had some doubts that I would actually show up. As had been the case yesterday afternoon, Oona was wearing a beautifully cut suit, this one a light gray, with a cream silk shirt underneath. She had on a double strand pearl necklace with matching earrings. On her feet, she wore mid-heel cream-colored sling-back shoes. She radiated confidence and success from every pore, an impression that differed from that of yesterday afternoon at the bar.

Once inside the doors, we walked down one corridor after another, turning so many times that I thought we must have retraced our steps. On one side of the hallway were dozens of cubicles occupied by very busy young men and women; on the other side were the larger offices, with spectacular views of Biscayne Bay. Oona's office was at the end of the last hall.

"Please, come in. Make yourself comfortable." She pointed to the sofa against the wall.

I sat where she indicated; she sat in the armchair to my right. Then, suddenly, like a child who has been guilty of neglecting her manners, Oona asked in a stricken voice, "I'm sorry, would you like anything to drink?"

"No, thank you. I'm fine." I smiled. "Your receptionist already asked me."

We sat in silence, like two strangers who had been brought together by a series of strange events. I could have made an effort to diffuse the awkwardness of the moment with chitchat, but I was running short on time, and if this mysterious offer wasn't going to work out, I had errands to run if I was going to be catching the flight to Minneapolis at five-fifteen.

"Magnolia." Oona sat at the edge of her chair, and fixed those eyes of hers that missed nothing on mine. "I'm going to be open and honest with you. You told me you came from a family that played and watched all kinds of sports, a family of jocks, remember?" I nodded. "And I told you about the two brothers, NBA players, who left me because I supposedly was getting stale? And that the sports world was actually quite small, so if the brothers were going to leave me, it was a given that sooner or later my other clients would follow?"

"Yes, I remember all of that." I sat up a bit straighter on the sofa.

Oona sensed that she'd better get to the point or I might bolt. "Please bear with me, Magnolia."

"Okay, sure." This was getting a bit strange, but I was here, so I might as well see it through. "I'm listening."

"Please, I don't want you to be offended by what I'm going to say." Oona had begun speaking in a hesitant tone of voice. She took a breath and continued. "Remember yesterday I told you I needed an edge?" I nodded yet again. "Well, Magnolia, you're going to be my edge!"

How could I be her edge? What did she mean? I felt a tiny quiver of excitement. Was my presentiment of the day before at the Miami Sports Bar about Oona being an important person in my life being realized?

"I believe in Fate! You and I, Magnolia, we met for a reason." Oona stood up and began walking around the room gesturing wildly. She looked like Glenn Close playing the demented Alex in the movie Fatal Attraction. Was she crazy? Obviously, I didn't know her well enough to be sure of that, but she was certainly acting weird.

Stopping in front of the bay window, Oona looked out at the view for a moment then turned to me with a serious expression on her face. "There were too many coincidences, Magnolia, for our meeting to be just by chance. I stayed up all night thinking about it, analyzing all the factors. Early this morning, I figured it out! You're going to be my edge! That's the reason we met."

"I'm not quite sure what you mean. Where do I fit in?" I had to admit I was curious.

"Because of you, the athletes I represent will not leave me. And new ones will come to me. It's a win-win situation!" she declared triumphantly, and then continued with her explanation. "If the athletes who are my clients leave me, they lose you." She looked off in the distance. "And, not just that, but ones that I don't represent realize that if they become my clients, that means that they can become acquainted with you—become good friends with you, enjoy your services."

"Become friends? Enjoy my services?" I repeated. "I don't understand." Although, I thought that I was beginning to. And it wasn't something I liked.

"By becoming my edge, you not only will be able to stay in Miami, which means, of course, that you can avoid having to return to Minneapolis, broke and defeated, a failure. Plus, you will be living very, very well." Oona beamed at me. "You will make more than enough money to realize your dream: by agreeing to become my edge, you can easily fund your art school for underprivileged children. You will be able to do that, and, on a grand scale, do more than you ever thought possible."

Now, by bringing up my school, Oona had my undivided attention, as she knew she would. I could already visualize my life here: Cuban coffee in the morning; sun and fun year-round; no snow or overcoats or boots or Chapstick; a school full of kids I would be helping. But what exactly would I have to do to get that? Oona was certainly not running a charity. What did "become acquainted with me" and "enjoy my services" mean? Was it what I thought? Was I going to become like Julia Roberts in Pretty Woman? Could it be? No!

"Oona, I'm sorry, you're way ahead of me; please slow

down. I don't follow what you're telling me," I protested, hoping that I was mistaken in what I thought she was saying. "Can you explain what it is, exactly, that I'm supposed to do for you?"

"Your job is going to consist of making my boys very, very happy. So happy that they'll never leave me. They'll love you! One look at you, and they'll fall in love with you! You're gorgeous, you're classy, educated, beautiful, and very knowledgeable about sports. Athletes love to talk about sports—not just the one they play, but pretty much all others, too. I heard you in the bar yesterday talking to Frank. You really know and like sports, it's very obvious. It's genuine, not like the kind of women they normally meet who are just starstruck and can't wait to tell the world they fucked a professional player. Star fuckers. Not you—you're the whole package, Magnolia." Oona was beginning to sound positively giddy at the idea. "You'll start by dating them, becoming friends with them, getting to know them, and then see where that leads."

"Becoming friends with them? Seeing where it leads? I'm not sure I understand. You mean like a sports escort? I go to their games and cheer them on, sort of like a cheerleader?" I wasn't Einstein, but I wasn't exactly being fooled by what Oona was explaining; she was sugarcoating what she wanted me to do, what I had to deliver as her edge. I moved to the edge of the sofa, ready to leave at a moment's notice if necessary. A woman wanting to pimp out another woman? Was I hearing right?

"Wait, Magnolia, let me describe what I mean." Oona hurried to calm me down. "Well, you'll start off by meeting the clients, getting to know them, and they you. Before you first meet with them, you'll have background information about them. I'll give you that before so you're prepared, so you know how to treat them, deal with them, know their likes and dislikes."

Then, her fears of offending my sensibilities obviously forgotten, Oona proceeded to describe in detail exactly how I was expected to bring such joy into his athletes' lives. It was pretty much as I suspected. I had no problem with hanging around with a bunch of jocks, but being some sort of an escort to them didn't sit well with me. I still had trouble believing what I was hearing.

As I listened to Oona explain the job requirements, I couldn't help but notice the irony that my one and only job interview in the three months that I'd had in Miami was for the position of a sports geisha. When I thought back to all the time, energy, and money I had invested in conscientiously and diligently filling out applications in the hopes of acquiring a position, any position, in an art-history-related field (as an assistant to the curator of a museum, working in a gallery, teaching art in schools) it seemed as if Fate had decided to play a joke on me and, instead of landing a reputable, respectable job, had given me Oona, with her proposal that I act like some kind of sports hooker.

Oona had told me last night how difficult it was to be a sports agent and how especially difficult it was for a woman to succeed in that field. But even so, for her to offer me a job as a hooker for her clients? It was really, really weird.

Chapter 4

During the meeting Oona often lost her focus; the woman obviously had ADD—but a couple of very important facts stood out in my mind: I would be able to remain in Miami and not have to return to Minneapolis that afternoon as a loser; I could make lots of money; and it had a finite time period—at the most, two years. Oona had made it very clear that I was not locked into this arrangement indefinitely, which made it more attractive. It had taken me a while to realize that Oona had, in fact, been deadly serious when she suggested that I become a sort of in-house call girl for her.

Although she had not explicitly mentioned the kind of sexual relations I would be having with her clients, I likened what she expected of me to a sort of a modern-day sports geisha, one who was rigorously trained to give pleasure to clients who were elite athletes. Oona had a natural talent at selling ideas, no matter how outrageous and outlandish. I had no illusions about her—the more I listened, the more I saw that she was an immoral person. After all, she was suggesting I become, in effect, a prostitute, a very expensive one—for a very specific purpose, to be sure, but a prostitute nevertheless. But then I had listened to her, so I wasn't much better, was I? For some odd reason, though, something pulled me toward her; perhaps built into that was the fact that she was the only one to reach out and offer help at the time when I most needed it. Still, I could not get over the fact that it was a woman making the suggestion. Did women pimps exist? Did that mean that Oona was a man in woman's clothing? It was all so very surreal.

The downside of the deal—I'd be selling my body for money, what I'd be doing was illegal, how becoming a high class hooker would affect me—she glossed over. Of course she knew that what she was suggesting was something completely alien to me, a nice Catholic girl from the Midwest, by all appearances. At least that's how I'd presented myself to her. I suspected that my innocent appearance would be a real plus in the eyes of her clients, so she'd better do a damn good job of convincing me of how I'd benefit from the experience.

Oona was clever in her approach. At no time did she try to disguise what she was proposing, but she didn't have to, really, as we both knew that I was smart and desperate enough to understand what she meant. The longer we discussed his proposal, the more logical it sounded, kind of shocking, really, but true, and Oona, brilliant and calculating woman that she was, knew that. As for me, it was crystal clear that by accepting, I wouldn't be joining Mother Teresa's order any time soon, but then again, I wasn't planning on doing so anyway.

Oona was very clear on one matter—one that she said was completely nonnegotiable. A condition of my accepting the job was that I not have a relationship, any kind of a relationship, with a man other than her clients. A boyfriend would be a distraction from the job, and in order for me to be successful, I had to give it my full commitment. Then there was the fact that prostitution was illegal, and the fewer people knew about what I was doing, the better. Loose lips sink ships and all that. It made sense that I not get involved with a man while working for her. But was that purely for business reasons, or did Oona want me for herself? The question nagged at me.

Last night, at the Miami Sports Bar, Oona had asked me if I had a boyfriend. I replied that my breakup with Fabulous Fred had been so painful that it would be a while before I even contemplated being with someone again, so the "no boyfriend" requirement did not particularly bother me. Besides, if I accepted her proposal, I wouldn't be working for Oona as her edge for the rest of my life, so it wasn't as if I'd never be able to have a serious boyfriend again. Sure, meeting Max Martinez last night had sparked an interest in me, confirming that I had not turned into a nun, checked into a convent, committed to a life of celibacy, or started liking girls, but that had been a fantasy. Five minutes with an attractive man—not exactly the stuff of a long-term, serious, committed relationship.

The way my relationship with Fred had ended had been so painful that I hadn't looked at another man in the month since I had moved into the studio in Little Havana. I had been hibernating—kind of like a bear that retreats into a cave for the winter, waiting for spring, before venturing out again.

However, those few minutes I spent with Max at the Spanish Rose last night had rekindled the possibility that, at some point in the future, I might be ready to venture out into the world of dating again, meaning that maybe, hopefully, the healing process had begun. Clearly, I was getting way ahead of myself; after all, I'd only spoken to the owner of the restaurant for five minutes. Still there was no harm in speculating, and although I certainly wasn't against making the piles of money that Oona assured me would be coming my way, the Max factor—as I was beginning to think of the "no men" condition—was something that I would seriously think about.

For all her fancy law school degree and plush offices, Oona's offer meant that she would be playing an active role as my pimp. Astonishing that, without knowing me at all, she would drop such an offer in my lap. But maybe the question I needed to ask myself more was: Why was I not all that shocked at her proposal? Had we both subconsciously known what role I would play in this edge business? And was the fact that I'd accepted the three hundred dollars a sign that I was willing to entertain what she was proposing? Especially one coming from a woman? During the three months I'd been in Miami, had I turned into the kind of woman who could be approached so easily? I knew that my dismal experience with Fred had changed me, made me a bit harder, less trusting, but had it affected me to such a degree that I could have sex with a man for money without having second thoughts about it? Where the hell was my conscience? My morals? My Catholic upbringing?

"Magnolia, I realize all this is quite a lot for you to absorb at one time. Although, I must say, you're handling all this with aplomb, and it's apparent you have quite a bit of self-possession, a very important character trait, in my opinion. I know that I've thrown you for a loop with my proposal."

I nodded. "Yes, you certainly have." What an understatement.

"If you accept my proposal, your entire life will change. That may seem quite obvious, but it bears repeating, so you know exactly what you're getting yourself into. I would not want you to say you'll do it, then when the realization of what you've actually accepted doing hits you, back out."

"Don't worry about my backing out," I said. "You've made it crystal clear what the job entails. If I accept, I would be doing it with my eyes open."

"Good. I don't want there to be any misunderstandings. We are in this together, and I would be investing heavily in you. I would really, really hate to throw away my investment." Oona wagged the index finger of her right hand to make the point.

I felt a shiver go down my spine as Oona's words registered. Was she threatening me? Or was she just making sure I fully understood the implications of her offer? "No, that would not happen. When I commit to something, I see it through."

"Okay. Just so we are clear, I will sum up what your duties would entail. I know I'm repeating myself, but I don't want any confusion, none." Oona spoke crisply. "You will satisfy the needs of whatever athletes I send your way. These needs will most likely be physical, but they could be emotional, too. Some hand-holding, a shoulder to cry on, but I anticipate that would be rare. These are not normal men; they are elite athletes, with specific tastes. You are expected to satisfy their requests to the best of your ability, but, of course, that does not include getting injured or doing illegal acts. Only do what you feel comfortable doing, but make sure they are pleased with your performance."

"Yes, I understand." I was beginning to feel uneasy. What the hell was I considering getting myself into? Oona made it sound as if joining the Special Forces would be a breeze compared to this job.

"You are not allowed to have any kind of personal relationship during the time you work for me: not with the clients, not with a man or woman you may meet. If you do break that rule, our arrangement will be immediately terminated, and you will have to reimburse what I've invested in you."

"Got it." An image of Max flashed across my brain. I shook it away. "As you describe my duties, I'd be like a professional girlfriend with benefits, providing services that go beyond sex, kind of like a sex therapist?"

"That's exactly right. You will be making a great deal of money in a short period of time, so maybe that won't be so bad, right? Keep your eye on the prize and all that. I expect after some time has passed, you might even enjoy yourself." Oona softened a bit, sounding almost motherly.

"Could be," I agreed. "You never know."

"Okay, then." Oona seemed pleased with my reaction. "Let's keep going."

Of course, there was also the all-important matter of how could Oona be so very certain that I would be so successful at sex that men would be willing to pay big bucks for having sex with me? I could turn out to be a total dud in that department, but then again, one could always learn from practicing. I'd heard that no porn stars were born with great skills; such abilities were acquired over time.

I still couldn't believe that was discussing having sex for money with a woman I'd met less than twenty-four hours before, and that was doing so with a kind of detachment as if I'd been discussing a straight business deal. I'd read someplace that that was how prostitutes were able to have sex with strangers—they removed themselves from the actual act. I was no prostitute, well, not yet, anyway, but there was no sugarcoating what Oona was proposing. As I listened to Oona explain the terms and conditions of the job, why had I not turned her down flat, and gotten out of her office? Why was I not in a taxi, heading to the Miami airport to catch the afternoon flight back to Minneapolis?

I tried not to think how the members of my family

would react were they to learn what I was contemplating doing in Miami. Had the heat gotten to me? The provocative Chamber of Commerce posters inviting tourists to visit here proclaimed: "There are no rules in Miami." Clearly, I hadn't taken that as seriously as I should have.

As Oona continued to explain the terms and conditions of her offer, she would look at me intently, gauging my reaction to what she was saying. "They're all young guys with great bodies, the best in the world. You'd enjoy being with them, Magnolia."

"Oona, how do you know that your athletes will want me?" I was curious that she hadn't wanted me to audition for the job, although by what means I did not want to speculate. "What makes me so different from another girl you might approach for this job?"

Oona bit her lip and smiled. "Magnolia, look, you may know a lot about art history, but sports and athletes are subjects with which I am intimately familiar. You are an intelligent, very attractive woman who is both genuinely knowledgeable about and interested in sports. I've told you that several times already. You have to trust me on that just as I'm trusting that you will be successful. During my career, I've signed rookies without ever having seen them play. I work on instinct. I've learned to trust it. Maybe that comes from being a woman in a man's world. I just know that you posses that unique combination that will appeal to my clients. Sort of like the perfect storm of Magnolia Larson."

Oona stood up and walked over to the picture window, where she stood and stared out over the magnificent view of Biscayne Bay. By then, after two hours of intense discussions, apparently realizing that she had said just about everything that she needed to, she gave a final pitch. "My dear Magnolia, think of this little adventure as a means to an end—keep your eye on the prize: opening your school for kids—and you'll be financially independent in a relatively brief amount of time. No more Fabulous Fred and guys like that. Sex and sports—that's a powerful combination, Magnolia, one that's unbeatable. Plus, you get to stay in Miami, something you said you really want to do."

"All true, Oona," I agreed. "If your plan works out the way you're convinced it will, you'll gain from my accepting the offer, too." I let her know that that fact had not escaped my notice. "You'll keep your clients—and your reputation and make lots of money, too," I emphasized. "You'll be the most successful woman sports agent—maybe of all sports agents—after this."

Oona smiled at me and then opened the large, square, highly polished wooden box on her desk. She inspected the contents and took out one of the cigars that were lined in neat rows inside. "Don't worry, I won't light it—I just want to smell it. I learned about cigars from my clients. They don't smoke cigarettes—they can't really—but every so often, they do enjoy a good cigar, and they taught me about them. In the beginning, I went along, pretending to like them, and then I did develop a taste for them. But only the good ones." Oona held the cigar up under her nose and breathed deeply. "If I were to light it, the fire alarms would go off, and the sprinklers would come on automatically and we'd be soaked. Less than ten minutes later, the fire department would be charging down the hall."

"Sounds like you know that from personal experience," I commented.

"Yes, unfortunately. My Cubans, Montecristo Number

Ones, which one of my clients gave me, were ruined. Fucking embargo. Can't get them in this country. What a shame. But I learned my lesson, and I've never made that same mistake again." Oona pointed the cigar at me. "I learn from my mistakes, Magnolia."

There was a very important aspect of the job that needed to be addressed. I took a breath and said, "Suppose I were to accept your offer, Oona—remember, I said 'suppose'—what exactly, and I mean exactly, would I be expected to do, and how would I get paid for doing it? I know you spoke about it before, but I need specifics."

"I was getting to that. Let me begin to answer your questions by explaining about the money you would stand to make." Oona got a mischievous look in her eyes. "I've found out that when contemplating a new business venture—one that will reap lots and lots of money for those involved—it's always much more fun talking about money first."

"Okay." I was fine with that; after all, that's why I would be doing it.

"First of all, your living expenses would be paid—for six months at least—to get you started. After all, you couldn't be expected to plunge right into this without training and preparation. I know you're broke—that's very clear—no shame in that." Oona looked rueful for a moment, so fleeting I might have imagined it. She then waved her hand around the office. "Don't be fooled by all this. I know what it's like to be poor. Dirt poor. I earned every penny I ever made." She shook her head slowly. "Maybe someday I'll tell you my story."

"I'd like to hear it." I thought that would go far toward my understanding her motivations and behavior.

"No, not today." Oona almost snapped the words. "Now, to get back to what I was saying. You're going to have to work hard in the beginning. Really work hard. It only seems fair that you receive financial help until you start working for me, that you don't have to concern yourself with finances. After all, you'll be training for the job, schooling yourself. The plan is for you to live in the penthouse apartment in one of the high-rises on Brickell Avenue, in an apartment that belongs to a very wealthy client of the firm. The client bought it years ago as an investment but has never lived there. We manage it; we've done that for years. I've been there, so I can assure you it's a very nice place."

"A penthouse apartment on Brickell Avenue?" I had a flashback to the roach-infested studio I'd been living in for the past month. The place was indescribably horrible, and becoming increasingly uninhabitable. I didn't know which I hated the most: the snowy black-and-white twelve-inch television set (no cable, naturally) haphazardly placed on top of the rickety bureau; the twin bed, only an extra-hard mattress, no box spring; the thin, worn sheets on it; the caked-on grease stains on the Formica countertops; the cooking smells that permeated the studio through the cracks in the windows and doors; the paper-thin walls through which I could hear my neighbors fighting or having sex; or, worst of all, the roaches that had become inured to the healthy squirts of Raid that I would regularly attack them with. By now, I swear, I could identify several of them as they scurried around the room.

"That sounds very nice, but would I have to entertain your clients there?" The idea of living in the same place where I would be meeting with the clients was not very comforting.

"That apartment is private, only for you to live in—remember, it belongs to a client of the firm. No business will ever be transacted there. Ever."

As I listened to Oona, I became increasingly convinced that getting in would be a hell of a lot easier than getting out. Sort of how it was joining a gang, or the Mob, only instead of getting brutally beaten, I'd probably end up broke, ashamed, and exposed... or in jail.

Oona stood up, walked over to the bookshelf on the far wall, and began looking through the rows of books that were stacked there. She pulled out what looked like a magazine and walked back to the couch where I was sitting. She leafed through the glossy pages of South Florida Architect Home and Design, a high-end magazine much along the lines of Architectural Digest, until she found what he was looking for.

"Ah! Here it is!" Oona turned the magazine over to me so I could look at the pages she was holding open. "Look, Magnolia, at the apartment where you will be living."

"It's gorgeous, absolutely gorgeous." The photos showed a very modern apartment done almost exclusively in white, and that was fine because it was so high atop the building, the only color it needed came from the brilliant hues of blue ocean reflected off the wide terraces. The living room was enormous, with an open plan that made it seem even larger than it probably was. All the rooms faced the terrace, with a breathtaking view of Biscayne Bay, and beyond that, the Atlantic Ocean. The photographer must have been as mesmerized as I was by the view, for most of the photos were angled to show it. Only in my dreams could I ever have imagined living in a place like that.

"What are the other terms, please, if I were to accept the offer?" I forced myself to look away from the magazine and continue the conversation.

"You would get a very generous clothing allowance; I

certainly don't expect that you would pay for the clothes
you're going to need to do your job correctly out of your earnings. You're going to need high-end designer clothing, and
lots of it. You have to look and dress the part—a stylist will
help you with that. You have to dress expensively, quietly sexy
but not too flashy, then after you start making serious money,
which should not take too long, you'd be responsible for your
personal expenses and clothing."

"Yes, that seems fair."

Now that we were discussing concrete things, the enor-
mity of what I was contemplating doing was starting to hit
me. I really had no idea what I was saying; at that point, I
would have pretty much agreed to just about anything.
I had so many questions, but my head was starting to spin
after all that time, so they would have to wait. For example,
as a lawyer, wouldn't she be breaking some law by setting me
up as her edge? I mean, I wasn't too familiar with how lawyers operated, but it seemed to me that Oona was acting in
much the same way a pimp would. She was trading me out
to her clients for money and contracts. Why would she take
such a risk?

Oona's motivation for setting me up didn't make much
sense—the risk she was taking, her betting on someone she
had just met—seemed enormous. Plus, I had absolutely no
experience, no track record whatsoever in what she was
proposing; surely she could come up with another way of
retaining her clients. Was bringing me on board one more
tool she would use to stay on top? Kind of like using steroids
to improve performance. I knew it was tough for a woman to
be successful in such a competitive business, but it was hard
to believe that setting me up as a hooker was the only way,
really, that Oona could stay on top.

I told myself to stop speculating about Oona's motives and concentrate on what she was saying. The penthouse, clothes, etc., were great, but I wanted to know more details about my salary, even though "salary" did not seem the right term to use somehow, but I had no idea what else to call it, so that would have to be it for now. I mean, I didn't think I would get the normal array of benefits—health insurance, vacation time, participation in her firm's 401K—that came with regular employment. Come to think of it, absurd as it sounded, was I an employee of O'Ryan and Associates, or was I an independent contractor? And who were these associates?

Oona sniffed the cigar she was holding in her hand again. "And I almost forgot. This is important. You'll be dealing with quite a few Latino athletes, so you will need to learn to speak Spanish. Yesterday you said you spoke French, so picking up Spanish should not present too much of a problem; after all, they're both Romance languages, with many of the words having the same roots. You'll take a total-immersion course at a language school, which we'll pay for, of course. That's all right with you, learning Spanish?"

Actually, that was more than all right. I was thrilled that Oona would be paying for my classes. Almost the minute my flight had landed in Miami I'd seen firsthand that it was close to impossible to land a job here if one did not speak Spanish. Miami was a predominately Hispanic city, so much so that English was a second language here. Some businesses had signs posted in their windows that stated, "English spoken here." If the association with Oona did not work out, I would still have learned another language. I knew how expensive those courses were; I had looked into signing up on my arrival here. My parents, sensible folks that they were, had always taught me that someone could take everything away from you, really, at any time, but your education was something that no one could take away.

"Yes, I think that learning Spanish is a terrific idea," I replied.

"I'm pleased you agree," Oona said. "Now, as far as the actual dollars that you would be paid for your services, I think you'll find that I am prepared to be very generous. I expect you to work hard, and you'll be paid accordingly."

I leaned forward in my chair. "I'm listening."

"I make fifteen percent of whatever my clients earn. That may not sound like much, but I'm not only talking about their actual contracts for playing. That fifteen percent also applies to endorsement deals, appearances, any kind of ads—print, television, radio, Internet, everything. It adds up," Oona explained. "I'm prepared to offer you five percent of my fifteen—with a bonus for every client that I acquire and retain as a result of your services. Five percent is a really high number—no agent I know would willingly give up that much for anything—but I want you to work hard, and that would be a good incentive. Besides, it would be for two years at the most, and the returns that would come from that would more than make up for it. We could see how that works out and, of course, modify the arrangement as needed. And, of course, you'd get other bonuses if the clients were particularly pleased with your services. However, whatever I charge them for legal work will not apply to you; that's not part of our deal."

My mind was reeling. Five percent? Bonuses also? Although Oona had not disclosed the actual amount of dollars and cents that I would stand to make, the way she had presented the deal implied that we were talking about a significant amount of money. I would be taking my life in a direction I never expected to, and I had to be properly compensated for that. I knew that once I embarked on this road, I would never return to being the kind of person I had been. Sort of like losing your virginity—once lost, it was gone. I knew that there are surgeries to stitch one's hymen back, but that was like putting lipstick on a pig.

"Approximately how much would I be able to make in a year?" Ever the accountant's daughter, I wanted to know the exact amount, but knew that Oona could not give me such a figure just yet. "A ballpark figure."

"I can't tell you exactly as that would depend on a lot of factors, but in your first year, if you work hard, you're good at it, and, of course, if the clients like you, you could make a couple of million. Naturally, that figure would fluctuate. Remember it would be based on my clients' earnings. Some years they make more, others less, and, of course, you wouldn't be getting together with all the clients—only the ones that would be appreciative of your services and who would need them. But, yes, I think a couple of million is pretty much a realistic number. You wouldn't declare it to the IRS. So most of it would be tax free. We could use creative accounting—there are lots of loopholes for the self-employed or contract employees. Not sure yet how best to declare your earnings. It would be up to you how you want to handle your payments."

Millions? Had I heard right? Millions? Almost tax free? Not only would I be in the sex business, I'd be in the tax-dodging business, but then again, things work differently in Miami, I had to get used to that. My father, an accountant, would be completely appalled if he ever found out that I would not be paying taxes on my income. He and Mom declared their income down to the last penny. This tax situation was one more thing that would be going against what I had been taught all my life. I would be betraying my back-

ground and upbringing on all counts, not to mention breaking various laws. My father had a heart condition, and this
could cause him to go into cardiac arrest.

I had to snap out of my guilt-ridden Catholic funk. My
parents were thousands of miles away, and, realistically, the
only way they would find out about my adventures in Miami
would be if I tell them myself. Plus if my conscience were
to bother me too much, I could always go to confession and
repent my sins, then be forgiven, a perk of being a Catholic.

"Oona, this is all very strange for me. I have to think over
your proposal very carefully. It's a huge decision." I figured
that, if I was careful, the hundred and fifty dollars that I had
left over from the three hundred that Oona had given me last
night at the bar would hold me over for a couple of days, maybe
three. And I still had the "life or death" fifty in my wallet.

"Of course. Take your time. I'm well aware that this
is an important, life-changing decision for you. But I'll tell
you this one more time, if you accept my proposition, there's
no backing out. I can't stress that enough. You can see how
much I'd be investing in you. To have you take a hike—I
couldn't let that happen. Also remember, the life you will be
leading would be private—no one, not your family, not your
friends, are ever to find out. This is totally confidential. All
the world will ever know is that you've worked for this agency.
We'll think of a good cover for you, with the highest of recommendations," Oona reassured me.

"That would be the only condition under which I would
accept," I quickly agreed.

"Trust me, Magnolia, for obvious reasons, it wouldn't
benefit either of us if that were to get out," Oona stressed.
"You have my contact information; if you want, you can text
me or send an e-mail. I'll receive it instantly on my Black-

Berry, and I'll get right back to you, I promise."

The only way I could send Oona an e-mail was by going to the public library and using one of the computers at the terminals there. My cell phone had been turned off for lack of payment two days ago, so I could not call or text her. It had been so long since I'd used a pay phone that I didn't even know how much a phone call cost. Oona, of course, was very aware that I was in difficult financial straits, as she had so delicately put it, but I was not about to let her know exactly how bad the situation was.

"I promise I'll let you know my decision by tomorrow." I held out my right hand and shook hers, a stupidly formal act, seeing as how the intimate the conversation that we had been having had been and how she'd kissed me in greeting me outside in the reception area. "Until tomorrow then. Thank you."

That night I ate a tuna sandwich for dinner; I was back to being frugal. Then, needing to clear my head, I went out for a walk and found myself strolling past the Spanish Rose. I noticed that there were several couples standing outside, apparently waiting for their tables. I lingered for a minute, in the hopes of catching a glimpse of Max Martinez, but when I didn't see him, I continued walking.

Chapter 5

In contrast to the previous night when I had slept like a baby, the next night I'd tossed and turned. Images of the photos in the magazine of the drop-dead gorgeous apartment kept coming into my brain, with me in them. It was a bit shocking how very natural and comfortable it was for me to envision myself living there, almost as if it was already my own place. Visions of sitting on Oprah's couch, answering her questions about how a nice, family-oriented, good Catholic girl from a conservative Midwest family could become a high-priced call girl to elite athletes kept coming into my mind. This interview would take place, naturally, after I'd written a best-selling "tell all" book about my experiences, and probably after I'd done some kind of time for prostitution and tax evasion, of course. My family would have disowned me, and I would have been excommunicated from the Church.

I had to weigh whatever I decided to do very, very carefully, as there would not be any turning back, that Oona had made very clear. The way she had kept emphasizing that point made me fearful. I understood why she kept hammering that home, to make sure I understood, but still... In the past, I'd found it helpful to make lists of the pros and cons when having to make a decision, so I thought I would do so now.

I turned on the lamp on the night table, and after the roaches scattered, got out of bed and walked across the small room. From my purse, I took out a pen and a notebook, poured myself a glass of water, and made myself as comfortable as possible on one of the two chairs next to the dinette in the kitchen. I took a deep breath and opened the notepad to an unused page.

First, I drew a line through the middle of the page, and labeled one column "Pro" and the 'other "Con." Under "Pro" I listed, in order of importance, all the reasons why I should accept Oona's offer, beginning with the obvious one that I could make a lot of money in a short period of time—two years max. And even though I knew I was probably being delusional imagining that it would ever really happen, I listed the fact that having that kind of serious money would let me open my art school for underprivileged and at-risk children or maybe even start a foundation. Was I kidding myself by thinking I would actually do it? How much of that was a rationalization?

Could I really and truly have sex with strangers for money? How would I feel that first time when one of Oona's clients put a hand on me and began touching me in an intimate way? Would I brush it off and run out of the room? That was not an option. They had paid for me, and I'd committed to satisfying their requests, so I had to deliver. I'd have no choice but to see it through. More troubling, almost, than having sex was, how would I feel? These were questions for which I had no answers and wouldn't until I actually had to do it.

Next, I wrote down that I would be learning Spanish, a skill I could keep for the rest of my life, and which would not only serve me well in Miami but also down the road. I had never thought of myself as being particularly materialistic, but the idea that I would suddenly be catapulted into a much higher standard of living had an undeniable appeal for me, so I listed improving my standard of living next. I couldn't ignore the fact that my days of living in a studio in a dilapidated, dirty, smelly, roach-infested, walk-up building in Little Havana being instantly over was very attractive.

I began to imagine myself in the very fancy penthouse apartment on Brickell Avenue. Although the photo spread in the magazine had not shown the bathrooms, surely a place as grand as that one was likely to have wonderful ones. At the very least, it would certainly have a tub. Baths had always been my weakness, and on any given day, I would have sold my soul for a long, luxurious soak in a steaming hot bath filled with sweet-smelling oils.

I couldn't deny how very tempting it was that accepting Oona's proposal would allow me to be able to wipe out the debt—my three credit cards were maxed out—I had amassed while being with Fabulous Fred. I had been brought up in a household where debt was considered to be a four-letter word. Our parents had always told us that if we couldn't pay for whatever it was with cash, then we couldn't afford it. All that debt was a constant reminder of what a fiasco it had been to follow Fred to Miami. By erasing the debt, I was also erasing Fabulous Fred, a very appealing prospect.

For the next hour I continued writing, listing all the positive things about this daring, lucrative, but also immoral and illicit adventure. Another really important reason why I should stay in Miami was that I wouldn't have to endure another winter in Minneapolis; even spring back there wasn't as warm as I liked. In Miami, there weren't any dark, dreary days, no biting wind, no layers of thick clothing, no snowdrifts, no frozen cars in the morning, no pale faces, chapped lips, or runny noses.

I would never have to hock my watch again. I would never have to suffer the humiliation of having to walk into an establishment such as the 24-Hour Pawn Shop, my heart beating loudly, putting up with the owner's snide comments, to pawn an item dear to me to get cash to eat or pay rent.

I wouldn't have to go crawling back to Minneapolis admitting that my brief stay in Miami had been a mistake, that following Fabulous Fred down here had been a disaster. The Bible says that pride is a deadly sin, and I had more than my share of it. I may have been broke and desperate, but I still had that. My family would take me back, no questions asked, as they loved me unconditionally. My reasoning may have been all fucked up, but at that low point, I would rather have sold my body than admit I'd made a huge mistake in coming to Miami with Fred.

If I was going to be brutally honest in an assessment of my situation, I had to include one very important reason why I would accept Oona's offer: I was depressed by how my life was at the moment. On the job front, I was disheartened by the search that, although I had expended a lot of energy, had yielded no results. The sad, hard truth was that I had no prospects: I was not waiting for a call back from anyone from a company's Human Resources; I had no resumes on someone's desk waiting to be read; I had no connections in Miami who might offer me a job. Not even my natural optimism could raise my spirits, nor could the sunny days and soft balmy nights. It was difficult to believe, but at that low point, I was even unmoved by the in-your-face natural beauty of Miami. If my situation did not improve, and fast, I could see starting the day by pouring a shot of vodka in my orange juice.

At that point, sad and pathetic as it was, I had to admit that at twenty-two, I was bored with my life. For the past month, the days had evolved into a sameness that made even getting up in the morning a chore. I, who used to look forward to each day, now found the hours dragging. Every day I would force myself to come up with something new to do, something to look forward to: exploring a new park, visiting a museum on the days the entrance was free, going to the beach, attending readings at the different bookstores, enjoying outdoor concerts, but after a while, even those only supplied a temporary respite from my situation. I considered volunteering, but I didn't really think I had much to offer in my current frame of mind. Plus, if, by some miracle I were to land a job, I would have to quit.

I was becoming increasingly consumed by my job search, so much that I had become obsessed with it. I realized that my problems were minor and self-made—certainly not on a level with cancer, world hunger, jihad, nuclear war—but still they loomed very large in my mind. And, unlike those situations, there was an easy, simple solution: all I had to do was hop on a flight back to Minneapolis, and they'd be over.

I was very aware that I was in danger of falling into a depression, if I wasn't already in it. At the very least, I was becoming neurotic, not an attractive quality. As much as I hated to admit it, even Fred, as much as I loathed him at the end, had evoked emotion in me. Well, I'd cried at the Miami Sports Bar the day before, so maybe all was not lost, a thought that briefly comforted me. However, that had been after six rum and Cokes, so maybe that did not count. Still, those had been real tears.

I did not want to get to the point when I stopped liking

myself, stopped believing in myself. Where was the happy, adventurous girl from Minneapolis? The one who was always up for a challenge? The fearless one? The one who had left her safe, comfortable life back in Minneapolis for the unknown wilds of Miami?

The fact that I was seriously contemplating accepting Oona's offer indicated that that Magnolia was still there— buried deep, true, but still there. The offer, even with the many risks that it contained, would make me feel alive again, something I desperately needed.

Under "Con" I began by listing that I would be work- ing as a prostitute, high-class, of course, and under the aus- pices of a sports agent, but as a hooker nevertheless. Was I delusional in thinking that I could actually do that? I was so modest that to go swimming I still wore one- piece bathing suits! The nuns back in Minneapolis had done such a good job during sex education classes that, except for having sex with Fred, I had trouble showing certain parts of my body, both in public and in private. On a practical level, what if I was to contract an STD? AIDS? Get pregnant? These things happened even if one took great care to prevent them. My other eight reasons—two through ten—in the Con column were the same as the first. I'd listed a lot of different ways of saying the same thing: me, a high-priced hooker.

For reason number eleven, I listed the fact that Oona would be my immediate boss. I really did not know the woman, so I would be taking a risk. So far, she had been very nice to me, but that could change; after all, we were ven- turing out together on what was unquestionably an illegal scheme. Oona hadn't gotten to where she was in life by being nice to everyone all the time—she had made it very clear to me that this was an extremely cutthroat business, especially for a woman. Which explained why she needed an edge. At times, in her office, Oona had frightened me, the way she told me that once I accepted the offer, I could expect to pay a huge price if I were to back out, that she would deal with me harshly. I would be working for someone who had the ability to hurt me, even if she was another woman. Did I really want to put myself in that position? I had heard that women, in certain situations, could be even more cruel and tough than men.

I wrote "Family" even though "Family" should have been at the top. To begin with, Oona had made it perfectly clear that I wouldn't be able to see them for a long time. I missed each and every member of my family terribly, so I knew that being without them would become increasingly difficult. Even though Oona would sympathize with how I felt, it was highly unlikely she would allow me to visit them so soon after I had begun working for her. I had not seen any family pictures in Oona's office. Did she not have any? Or if she did, was the reason she did not display any because she did not want anyone to know she had family ties, therefore possibly appearing soft? Oona had not divulged anything about her personal life, had made no references at all to any kind of partner, man or woman. Clearly, this was business for her. She would be making a very expensive investment in me, and she would want to recoup her money as quickly as possible — and she made it clear she did not want to waste any time in starting. A critical component of "Family" was that I would be lying to my parents, grandparents, brothers, and friends about what I was doing professionally. How could I possibly justify the fact that I was staying in Miami so I could make millions of dollars by having sex with athletes? Oh, God! What if I were to get caught? What would become of me then? The rewards, true, were enormous, but so were the risks.

The "Con" list was becoming longer and longer, an indication that I should not accept Oona's offer. The situation had somehow seemed less complicated in her office, something that definitely was not the case in my cramped studio, with me suffering from sleep deprivation.

And apart from lying to my family and possibly killing my father in the process, complicating matters was the fact that I had just met a potentially nice man: Max Martinez. He hadn't acted as if he was attached, but maybe that had just been professional interest in me. After all, as the owner of a restaurant, he met his customers every day, and to be successful, he had to make them feel welcome. Now I wouldn't be able to pursue any interest I might have in him.

I knew Oona was manipulating me into accepting her offer, so she had presented it as a positive, while warning me that once I accepted, I could not walk away. I closed the notebook, put it back in my purse, and got back into bed. I closed my eyes and tried to sleep, but my mind was whirring around at a million miles an hour. Finally, I began to drift off, but just as I was about to fall asleep, I would awaken. I decided to let my mind float wherever it wanted.

I had lost my virginity late in life—well, anyway, late in comparison to my friends—at age twenty, to Sven Martins, my brother Peter's closest friend. It had not exactly been planned out. Actually, Sven and I had not even been dating, yet my first time was with him, late one night in his off-campus apartment at the University of Minneapolis.

Although I had known Sven pretty much all my life, I had never considered him to be a potential boyfriend. First of all, he was my brother's friend, which made dating him seem like incest, and second, although he was certainly good-looking, I had never been that attracted to him in a sexual way. We'd been in the same classes together all six years of elementary school, for God's sake! Even so, as we got older, I had to admit that there had always been a kind of sexual tension between us.

That night, when it happened, we had been studying for a test, a final exam—we were both in the same psychology course. One thing led to another, and during one of the ever-more-frequent breaks, we ended up discussing our relationship and how we felt about each other. No doubt helped along by the several beers he had consumed, Sven revealed that he had always been in love with me, but because I'd made it clear I was not interested in him, he had never made a move. After Sven made his confession, I began to look at him in a totally different way. In retrospect, it was more than likely that the couple of beers that I had drunk as well during the study session helped change Sven's status from that of my brother's friend to that of a possible love interest.

Whatever the case, the night had ended with me lying on Sven's unmade bed and being relieved of the burden that my virginity had become. At that time, the fall term of my junior year in college, I hadn't been seeing anyone—actually, I had not had a steady boyfriend in over a year—so it wasn't as if legions of guys had been banging down my door. My brothers claimed that was because I projected an ice-queen image: beautiful, but cold and unapproachable. I wasn't exactly a wallflower—I'd gone out on dates, but not with any guys that I had the slightest interest in, which was probably why I had gone out with them. I didn't want to be involved with anyone just then.

Most of my friends had steady boyfriends, ones they were contemplating marrying. For some reason, girls married young in Minnesota, a fact that I personally attributed to the weather—it was just too damned cold to sleep alone. I really didn't want to get married at that point—I just slept with my dog, a hundred-and-twenty-pound chocolate Lab called Fluffy, so my bed was warm. But my single status, a social stigma in Minneapolis, was beginning to weigh on me. That, plus the fact that I was still a virgin, was not doing much for my self-esteem.

So when Sven declared his love for me, I decided it was time to be deflowered. Also, I have to admit, I wanted to satisfy my curiosity about what the experience was all about. So for all of the above, I gave in to Sven, and was soon lying naked on the bed. I was fortunate that Sven was loving and gentle with me, but to this day, I wished that for such an important, life-altering occasion, the sheets on his bed had not smelled as if they needed changing.

Sven and I dated for a couple of months after that, even though our hearts weren't really into it, at least mine wasn't. It was more along the lines that we had had sex, so we should be involved with each other for a bit, to validate the experience. I dated several other guys after Sven, but none of them on a steady basis, until Fabulous Fred.

Fred, for all his boring scientific training—or perhaps because of it—had turned out to be a very enthusiastic fan of exploring new sexual frontiers, so we had indulged in some practices that I certainly would not have done otherwise. Compared to Fred, my previous boyfriends had seemed very boring. Fred brought a level of excitement to my life that I hadn't encountered before. Too much, as it turned out. Occasionally we used sex toys, patronized strip clubs, role-played, watched porn videos, and on one very memorable occasion, participated in a threesome with a girl he had picked up in a bar. I may have been very modest in my dress and demeanor, but I was quite adventurous as far as sex was concerned. Given those experiences with Fred, the sexual part of Oona's offer, a bit surprisingly, did not put me off that much—it was getting paid for sex that bothered me. I suppose more than the immorality of becoming a prostitute was the harsh reality that the risk of getting caught was uppermost in my mind. The price would be high. I could go to jail for prostitution, for income-tax evasion, or I could contract an STD. And what, God help me, if I were to become pregnant? I may not have attended Mass recently, but I was still a Catholic. What would I do then?

After much soul-searching I decided, as had perhaps been inevitable, that I would accept Oona's offer. It made sense, in lot of ways, and not just because living in that fabulous apartment was part of the deal. Though I had to admit, it did kind of factor into my decision. I had never run away from a challenge, and although working with Oona would certainly be the highest risk I had ever taken in my life, it was one I thought I could handle.

Ultimately my decision had been based on the answer to one question: Could I live with the "what if" if I turned down Oona? I knew I would go through the rest of my life wondering, "What if I had accepted her offer?" Even if I were to lead a perfectly satisfying, happy, fulfilled life, I knew myself well enough to be rock-solid sure that the "what if" would have endlessly plagued me. I didn't want to be a person who could turn down what promised to be a hell of an adventure. At the very least, I would learn a lot about myself. Of course, I was scared shitless; anybody in my situation would be. But I just had to chance it.

Early the next morning, using part of the money that remained from the three hundred dollars Oona had given me, I went to the Verizon Wireless office near my apartment and paid the bill to activate my phone. Oona had said I could text her my answer, but I didn't think that was the right way to respond. I would speak with her. Do it properly.

"O'Ryan and Associates. Good morning." I recognized the receptionist's voice on the other end. I told myself I'd better learn her name, now that I was coming on board, as I would no doubt be in frequent contact with her. I asked to speak with Oona. Less than thirty seconds later, I was connected to her.

"Magnolia, good morning." Oona's voice came through the line, loud and clear. "How are you?" Oona didn't wait for an answer. "Happy to hear from you. And, hopefully, I'm going to be a lot better if you're calling to give me good news."

Oona's warm, friendly, welcoming voice gave me confidence. I could easily picture her in her office, impeccably dressed in yet another a beautifully tailored suit, perfectly coiffed and manicured, seated in her big, black leather chair, probably looking out the window at the beautiful view of Biscayne Bay.

"Well, Oona, I do think you're going to be feeling better. I've spent the better part of last night thinking about what you said," I declared. "And, yes, I will accept your offer."

"That's terrific news! You'll not regret it, Magnolia, I know you won't." Oona was almost beside herself with glee. "Where are you right now?"

"I'm at my apartment," I answered a bit warily.

"Give me the address. Pack your belongings, please. I'll send Anita Fernandez, my assistant, to pick you up. She'll be there within the hour. And Magnolia, don't worry about any details—notifying your landlord, paying any outstanding charges. We'll take care of all that. Just pack your things."

"I'll do it right now." Oona never heard me, as she had already hung up the phone.

Although I was more than happy to move out of the roach motel, I was a bit taken aback that things would move so very quickly. Clearly, a period of transition to my change in status was not a luxury I was going to be given, which may have been a good thing, as it would prevent me from backing out.

According to what Oona had said, Anita would be arriving very soon, and the last thing I wanted was for her to climb up the stairs to the studio and see how I'd been living. Packing my meager belongings took only a few minutes. Before closing my bag, I put into it photos of my family and the eight-by-ten photo of my beloved Fluffy that I had in a silver frame. As I looked through the studio one last time to make sure I had not left anything behind, I realized that it would be a while before I'd have to worry about such mundane things as having to deal with landlords, paying rent, the electric bill, etc. I loved my independence, but I hated the day-to-day hassles of everyday living. Oona was already taking charge of me, which was reassuring. I was tired of struggling.

I had just finished closing my suitcase when my cell phone rang. "Ms. Larson?" A woman's voice—tough, competent, no-nonsense—came on the line. "This is Anita Fernandez, Ms. O'Ryan's assistant. I'm outside your building, waiting for you."

"Oh, hi, Anita. I'll be right out." Well, I was about as ready as I was ever going to be, but I was not going to let her know that. I picked up my suitcases, squared my shoulders, waved good-bye to the roaches, and, without a backward look, walked out the door to my new life.

Chapter 6

The minute I laid eyes on the apartment that was to be my new home, I thought I had died and gone to heaven. Just as the photo in the magazine had shown, the whole place was decorated in various shades of white, making it seem positively ethereal and giving the impression that it actually was in the sky. I loved it on sight, which helped to soothe my anxieties. I was still waiting for a feeling of guilt to seep over me, or maybe a tinge of regret, but, thankfully, so far nothing. The apartment was just so beautiful that it did not allow for bad thoughts.

I could have stood there longer in the foyer of the apartment, savoring my first impression of the place, but Anita was having none of that. "Come on, Ms. Larson, let's go inside," she urged in an authoritative, efficient-sounding voice.

Anita Fernandez was scarily skinny, with the familiar gaunt, unhealthy look that individuals who suffered from some kind of eating disorder had. Standing next her was like standing next to a corpse. She was cold and emotionless. The short-sleeved, severely cut white cotton shirt she was wearing showed collarbones that were so prominent that they protruded half an inch from her neck. Her scrawny, bony legs were especially noticeable in the short, tight, dark blue skirt that she was wearing. Her black hair was pulled back tightly in a bun, so much so that in some places her scalp was visible. I noticed that she needed to touch up her roots. She wore no makeup—well, at least none that was noticeable. In sharp contrast to the receptionist at the firm, who put herself together in the most attractive and flattering way possible, from what I could tell, Anita did nothing to improve her appearance or hide how frighteningly skinny she was. She was the same size from the side as she was from the front. My mother would have wanted to feed her the moment she saw her.

The last thing I wanted was to annoy the woman; Anita was, after all, Oona's personal assistant, and it was likely she would be reporting back every detail of what had taken place this afternoon, so I picked up my suitcase, and followed her into the enormous living room. "What a beautiful apartment. What an amazing view!" I said as I immediately headed for the terrace.

"Yes, it is nice," Anita replied, without even giving it a glance. The woman was all business. "The apartment is completely stocked with whatever you might need. There's food in the refrigerator, dry goods in the pantry, cosmetics in the bathroom." Although I'd met her less than one hour before, it was becoming crystal clear that we would never become friends.

"Oh, thank you. That's very nice and thoughtful of you," I replied sweetly.

"I was told to get the place ready for you." Anita was not going to budge. "You can take your things into the bedroom, if you want." She pointed to a room to the right of the living room. "Or if you prefer, I can go over your schedule with you now, and I'll leave after that."

"Let's go over it now." I didn't have the slightest idea what Anita was referring to, but I wasn't about to let her know that.

I could be all business, too. "I'm sure you're very busy, and I've taken up too much of your time as it is."

"Here, I typed up your schedule. You begin tomorrow morning, bright and early at eight o'clock sharp. You can do what you want the rest of the time until then." She held out a navy-blue folder, about an inch thick, that was bound at the side with black plastic. I noticed that my name was prominently printed across the top in gold letters. The pages of the various sections were marked with colored tabs.

The minute Anita had said she'd typed up my schedule, I knew why she had been behaving in such a cold, dismissive manner with me. It had probably taken her less than a minute to figure out my role in the O'Ryan organization. Either way, Anita made obvious who and what I was: the high-paid hooker her boss had brought in to entertain her clients. I was clearly beneath her, someone that she had to tolerate as part of her responsibilities at O'Ryan and Associates. With any luck, Anita would probably have minimal contact with me, something that clearly would please both of us.

"I tried to make it as easy for you to follow as possible," Anita explained. "It's all quite simple. You should be able to understand it." She implied that I had single-digit IQ.

I took the folder and opened it to the first page, which had the heading of "Table of Contents." I flipped through the book and couldn't help but be amazed at what my schedule was going to include. Not just that, but how fast Oona had managed to have all the arrangements made: Anita fetching me, the schedule drawn up, the apartment ready and stocked, etc. Even if Oona were to have moved at top speed, things still took time to arrange. Yet again, the thought occurred to me that she had planned this quite some time before, and had just been waiting for the right edge to come along. I would probably never know unless I asked Oona directly, and even then I suspected she would not give me an answer, but the question kept nagging at me. I also wondered who the wealthy client was, the owner of the apartment. Was it kept fully stocked in case he or she would decide to drop by unexpectedly? I might never know, but that really didn't bother me.

"One more thing." Anita reached into her briefcase and brought out a laptop, which she handed to me. "Here, a new MacBook Air for you. Ms. O'Ryan said yours broke so you should have a new one. All the programs have been installed. You just have to chose your user name and password."

"Thank you." I took the computer and hugged it to my chest. It felt so light, not like the heavy ones I had before. I could hardly wait to open it, but that would come after Anita left.

Anita walked toward the front door, and as she passed by me she handed me a business card. "Here, Ms. Larson. These are the numbers where you can reach me: my direct line at the office, plus my cell phone number. I always have the cell phone turned on so you can call or text anytime." The way she said that implied I'd better never call her after office hours, unless, of course, there was blood on the floor.

We stood in the foyer, looking awkwardly at each other for what was quite possibly the longest thirty seconds of my life.

Suddenly Anita spoke. "That's what I forgot! The keys. I still have to give you your set of keys." For a moment, she looked so stricken that I thought she had made some colossal mistake, her attitude revealing to what degree she prized her efficiency and competence. Still shaken, she reached into her briefcase and brought out several key chains, which she held out, one by one, in front of my face. "These are for the apartment, the elevator. You need keys to get to the top three floors, the security gate that leads to the pool area, your car. There's a Mercedes, a new one, for your use, parked in the spot that corresponds to this apartment."

A car? I didn't know there'd be a car. Good-bye, Fred's Ford Taurus with a million miles on it; hello, Magnolia's new Mercedes! It was all I could do to stop from jumping up and down from excitement. Instead, though, I kept my cool and just smiled as if it was every day that I was given keys to a luxury apartment and a Mercedes. "Thank you very much." I put my hand on the doorknob. "I appreciate all your help."

She had just pressed the button when she turned to me. "Your day starts at eight o'clock sharp tomorrow morning," she reminded me again. "Don't be late."

"Good-bye." I immediately went back into the apartment and bolted the door. I wasn't planning on going anywhere. All I wanted to do was enjoy my new surroundings and, of course, play with the MacBook. Finally alone and eager to inspect my living quarters, I raced through the apartment, first heading to the bedroom. Never in my wildest dreams had I ever imagined that a bedroom could be so humongous. I'd always had a tendency to exaggerate, but even taking that into consideration, the size of the bedroom alone was easily over a thousand square feet—and that didn't count the dressing room I could see through the archway at the far end, or the walk-in closet the size of the studio where I'd been living in Little Havana.

And the art! Was this an original David Hockney? I stepped closer until my nose was practically touching it. It had to be. And the print on the wall in the living room—I dashed back into the other room—not one, but two of them in this room were his trademark tropical scenes in his sherbet colors.

Dressed as I was in jeans, white cotton shirt, and sandals, I felt out of place, an imposter from the wrong side of town. As I looked at my reflection in the mirror that covered the entire east wall of the room, I sure as hell didn't feel I belonged there, yet deep inside, I suspected I would in time. And if the bedroom was this outrageous, I could hardly wait to check out the bathroom.

"Oh, my God!" I gasped out loud upon entering the bathroom, a room the likes of which I had only seen on the History Channel or in movies set in the Roman era of Julius Caesar. Three walls of the bathroom were painted from the floor to ceiling with murals showing Roman bathing scenes. There was a white marble bathtub—well, it wasn't really a bathtub, more like a small swimming pool—in the center of the room. In the four corners of the tub were statues of roly-poly cherubs holding urns, apparently ready to pour thin streams of steamy-hot, perfumed water. Assorted glass bottles in various colors, filled with wonderful-smelling oils and gels, lined the ledges of the tub. There was a large-screen plasma television built into the wall across from the bathtub. As I marveled at it, I hoped I could manage to work the complicated controls that were placed in a clear plastic box next to the tub.

The only wall of the bathroom that didn't have a mural painted on it was completely covered by a mirror. Two over-sized sinks with faucets in the shape of dolphins that looked as if they were made of sterling silver were placed in a marble countertop that ran along the entire wall. The shower, a square enclosure made out of clear glass, had a shower-head coming out of the ceiling that measured at least a foot in diameter. Extra-thick white towels were stacked in various piles here and there around the room. And, just in case those dozen or so towels weren't enough to dry myself with, a terry-cloth bathrobe hung on a hook behind the door. I sensed I would be spending quite a bit of time in there.

I was tempted to immediately jump into the tub and try it out. As there had only been a shower in my former studio, I hadn't soaked in a bath for two months—the last time had been in the apartment in Coral Gables when I had lived with Fred. But I held back. There would be plenty of time to do that. Anita had told me that the kitchen was fully stocked, so I decided to check out what provisions had been procured for me.

One peek inside the refrigerator—a very expensive-looking two-door aluminum Sub-Zero—and I came to the conclusion that Oona either thought I was underfed or that I had the fastest metabolism on earth, because the fridge was stocked to the gills with every kind of food imaginable. There was no way on God's earth, even if I were to eat non-stop for the next month, that I would be able to consume all that was in there. Four kinds of milk, all in gallon jugs: skim, whole, two-percent fat, and soy. Outside of a grocery store, I had not seen that much milk at one time since our fifth-grade teacher Mrs. Johansson had taken us on a field trip to a dairy farm outside Minneapolis.

On the second shelf were containers of deli foods with several types of salads plus assorted breads, fruits, cold cuts, etc. The drawers were filled with fresh produce, salad greens as well as vegetables. Dozens of cans of sodas had been placed in neat lines on one of the counters. On the shelves of the door of the fridge I saw an assortment of condiments, including two jars of mayonnaise, regular and fat-free, capers, pickles, and half a dozen different kinds of salad dressings. There was a huge bowl filled with mangoes and papayas, as well as apples and bananas, on the center island of the kitchen counter.

Overwhelmed, I closed the door of the refrigerator and turned my attention to the walk-in pantry. I wasn't exactly surprised to find out that there was the same overabundance of products inside. The small room was filled from floor to ceiling with an eye-popping variety of dry goods, from pastas to crackers. For a second, I thought I was in a very, very upscale deli.

In the cabinets, there were two different sets of dishes: everyday, all-white ceramic plates, and another, the more formal china, plates rimmed with what looked like real gold. The cutlery was so heavy it had to be real silver. Who the hell lived here?

On the far wall by the pantry door, I found a second fridge, a tall thin one, specifically for wine. Rows of bottles of wine, beer, and champagne lay side by side inside. Nearby, a dozen or so bottles of red wine were stacked in a wine rack on a shelf over the countertop. Did Oona think I was an alcoholic? I know I'd had several rum and Cokes at the Miami Sports Bar, but still!

I had saved the best for last. I walked across the living room and out to the terrace to look out at the view. To the east, I could see the blue waters of Biscayne Bay, to the west, the city of Miami. and although it was only noon, the hottest part of the day in this brutal month of August, a nice breeze cooled the terrace.

As I stood there, looking out, my arms resting lightly on the railing, I could not help but wonder yet again who the owner of the apartment was. According to Oona, it belonged to "a wealthy client of the firm's," but she hadn't volunteered much more information than that. The place, although beautifully furnished, was quite impersonal, even to the degree that it was impossible to tell if the owner was a man or a woman or a couple.

I was about to turn back to walk into the apartment when I felt my cell phone vibrate in the pocket of my pants. I took it out, and my blood ran cold as I read "home" on the screen. At this time of the day, it could only be one person calling. I took a moment to compose myself before answering.

"Hi, Mom, how are you?"

"Hi, Maggie. Haven't heard from you for a couple of days." I could hear the concern in her voice. "Are you okay?"

"Sorry I haven't called." I walked into the apartment and locked the sliding glass door behind me. "I've been busy going out on job interviews." Well, it was sort of the truth.

"Really? Anything promising?" My mother perked up.

"Actually, yes," I replied. "A good job." I paused. "With benefits."

"Oh, Maggie, that's great. What kind of a job? Does it have to do with art history?" My mother, understandably, was eager to hear the details.

"I don't want to jinx it by talking about it." I deflected her questions. My mother was very superstitious, so I knew the questions would stop. Although I was manipulating her, I was not ready to begin lying to my family. "I should hear back soon."

"Oh, okay. I'll say a prayer for you to get it," she volunteered.

"Thanks, Mom. I appreciate it." I felt like such a shit. "I'll let you know."

"Oh, Maggie, I almost forgot to tell you. That's another reason I was calling. Your father has vacation time coming. Three weeks. We've been discussing coming down to visit you."

"Here? To Miami?" I almost choked. "But you never leave Minneapolis. You always go to the lake with Uncle Mike and Aunt Sophie."

"I know, but we haven't seen you for over three months, and we miss you," my mother explained. "And now, if you start a new job, you probably won't get vacation for a while, so if we want to see you, we'll come to you instead."

"Of course I'd love to see you." My eyes filled up with tears. Oh, God! What was I doing? What had I done? "But with a new job, I'm probably not going to have much free time to be with you."

"We can take care of ourselves, entertain ourselves, your dad and I. You don't have to worry about us," she assured me.

"I know, but I'm going to want to be with you a lot. And with the job... " I protested.

"Look, Maggie, please don't think about that now; it was just a thought that your dad and I had, to come and visit with you. Just concentrate on the job. Think positive thoughts. You'll get it, I know you will."

"Thanks, Mom," was all I could manage to say. "I'll let you know."

"Maybe we'll just show up, surprise you," my mother teased. "Not tell you that we're coming, so you don't worry about us."

"Surprise me?" I repeated rather stupidly. "Not tell me in advance that you're coming?"

"I'm not going to say another word." My mother sounded quite pleased with her plan. I could picture her sitting at the kitchen table, an ever-present mug of coffee in front of her, doodling on the pad that she kept next to the phone so she could sketch as she spoke. "Call home when you hear back about the job, okay? We think about you, Maggie, wondering how you are doing. You're so far away. We don't know anything, really, about your life down there in Miami." My mother pronounced it Mhyahmiah.

"I know, I think about the family, too." I was seconds away from breaking down. "I miss you a lot. But I'm okay. Please don't worry about me."

"We'll see for ourselves soon how you're doing," she added a bit mysteriously.

I gripped the phone tighter. What if they did show up? Would they really do that? What would happen then? The implications were too dire to even contemplate.

"Mom, I have to go now." I had to get off the phone before I totally lost it. "I'll call real soon. I promise."

After hanging up, I stood in the middle of the living room and looked around me. The pleasure I had felt at being in the apartment earlier was gone. The conversation with my mother had been a wake-up call as to the danger I had put myself in by accepting Oona's offer.

Eating usually comforted me, so I decided I would fix myself something for lunch. Once in the kitchen, however, the pull of the bathtub was just too strong, so I decided that I would take a bath first and eat later. On my way to the bathroom, I picked up my suitcase from the living room and carried it into the bedroom to unpack.

I burst out laughing when I saw how small a part of the walk-in closet my clothes—all I owned in the world, really—took up. It didn't take long to arrange my belongings. I began by placing the photos of my family, starting with the one of my parents on their wedding day, continuing with the one of Fluffy, next to the bedside table. Then I went back out to the living room and picked up the folder with my schedule to look over while I soaked in the tub.

Back in the bathroom, I stripped off my clothes and placed them in the dirty clothes hamper to be washed later. Although I had not yet found it, the apartment was so fully equipped that it was bound to have a washer and dryer somewhere. Next, I carefully inspected each of the bath oils to see which one I wanted for such a special occasion: my first bath in the apartment. I settled on one made from rose petals. I turned on both faucets, adjusting the temperature to my liking, watching steam rise. When the tub was full, I gently eased myself into it, and lay, without moving, with my eyes closed, for close to half an hour. Every so often I would relive the telephone conversation I'd had with my mother, and I would feel a great sadness come over me. I told myself to concentrate on the present, and not to speculate on what might have been if I stayed in Minneapolis close to my family. There was no upside to doing that.

Only after I was totally relaxed did I reach for the folder that contained my schedule and started reading through it. One look told me that Oona had made good on her promise that she was going to work me hard. The woman was going to get her money's worth out of me. No wonder she wanted to be positive I would not back out.

As I had suspected, Oona intended to turn me into a type of geisha: a woman of many talents and abilities, my only job being to bring pleasure to athletes, men she intended would be thrilled in my company. After reading the schedule that I was to follow, I had no doubt that I would be impressively prepared for that job. If the preparation and training didn't kill me first, that was.

My time was going to be very tightly controlled; there was practically no free time built into the schedule and it was quite likely that today would be the last day for a while when I'd be able to soak in the tub in such a leisurely fashion. I poured a bit more rose-scented oil into the tub, added some hot water, and soaked for another five minutes. By then, my skin had begun to wrinkle, so, with some regret, I wrapped a towel around myself and got out.

I walked back to the kitchen and opened the wine fridge, then took out one of the bottles of champagne, Dom Pérignon, a brand I had heard about but never drank. I reached for one of the tall flutes from the cabinet and carried the bottle of champagne and the glass back to the tub. After carefully opening the bottle, I poured myself a glass. I spent a minute or so admiring the golden bubbles as they floated to the top of the glass before taking the first sip. Next I turned on the television, channel surfing until I found a show I wanted to watch.

I lay back, sipping champagne, soaking in hot water, smelling the aromatic rose oil as I watched television. All thoughts of Minneapolis banished from my mind.

Chapter 7

*I*n the distance, a church bell had just finished tolling eight times when the intercom buzzed. I had been expecting the call; still my heart was racing as I pressed the "talk" button. "Yes?"

"Ms. Larson?" There was so much static on the line that I could barely hear the man's voice as he spoke. "Good morning. I am Ramón, your driver. I'm here downstairs in the lobby to take you to your appointments."

"I'll be right down," I replied.

Well, no backing out now, I told myself as I picked up my purse. Of course, I'd known from the moment I stepped into this penthouse apartment yesterday that my training was actually starting, but the fact that there was a driver downstairs, waiting for me, was a wake-up call as to what I'd agreed to do. I felt a thrill of excitement go down my body as I prepared for the day.

After making sure everything was in order, I picked up my purse and walked out into the foyer. No sooner had the door closed behind me than I remembered that I hadn't set the alarm and that the sheet of paper Anita had given me with the instructions to do so was inside the apartment. I would simply have to take the risk that everything was going to be okay. Surely, I simply could not have such bad luck as to have the place burglarized the first day I was there.

I hadn't been sure how I should dress for the day, but I'd settled on the Miami interpretation of business casual, a pair of dark blue cotton pants, a blue-and-white-striped cotton tailored shirt, and black leather ballerina flats. I had braided my hair to keep it as frizz free as possible for the long day ahead of me.

In the lobby, I was met by a very young-looking man. "Ms. Larson?" He addressed me in such a formal fashion that I had to control myself from laughing. "I am Ramón, your driver." He actually bowed to me as he introduced himself.

Ramón could not have possibly been older than fifteen. From the smooth look of his cheeks, I doubted that he even shaved. He was dressed in a black suit, black string tie, and white shirt. He seemed so very nervous that I suspected I might be his first client. God! I hoped he had a valid driver's license, and not a restricted one. Great!

"Good morning, Ramón. How are you?" I smiled, trying to be as reassuring as possible. "Should we go? We have a busy schedule." I didn't want to offend him by speeding things up, but we were going to be late for sure if we kept inquiring about the state of each other's health. We'd already established that we were both fine.

"Oh, yes, right away, Ms. Larson, yes." Ramón led me outside to the driveway where a black Lincoln Town Car with tinted windows was parked. "Please." Ramón opened the back passenger-side door for me.

I made myself comfortable in the soft leather seat as I watched Ramón walking around the car to get to the driver's seat. I thought back to my great-aunt Tillie's funeral in Minneapolis last year when the driver was dressed in an undertaker's black suit while driving a black Lincoln Town

Car. Although I had never been particularly superstitious, I hoped that vision was not a bad omen.

"Ms. Larson, last night Miss Anita faxed a schedule of where I am to take you today. You probably have one, but I made a copy for you in case you didn't."

I scanned the sheet of paper Ramón gave me. According to the schedule, our first stop that morning was to be a language school in Coral Gables, a fifteen-minute ride from my apartment building. I hoped that the fact that it was the first stop of the day—eight o'clock was brutal, in my book—didn't mean that my classes would be at this hour every morning. My brain didn't normally start functioning until around ten o'clock, and then, just barely.

The Best Language School was located in a three-story, nondescript building with dark tinted windows off Ponce de Leon Avenue. Ramón turned into the driveway and stopped the Town Car as close to the double glass doors as possible without actually driving through them. He had barely put the car in park before hurrying out to open my door.

"I'm not sure how long I'll be." As it was the first day of classes, I didn't know if the teacher would keep us for the full four hours.

"No problem, Ms. Larson. I'll be here in the parking lot, waiting for you." He bowed yet again, something he did so easily. I wondered if he had ever spent time in Japan.

The schedule had not specified exactly where I was to go or what I was to do at the Best Language School. Inside, I walked over to the front desk, a long, minimalist slab of glass in the middle of the lobby. The receptionist, a Courtney Love look-alike, though a bit younger, sluttier, and more fragile looking, was so busy she didn't notice me standing in front of her. I watched admiringly her skill at multitasking: The girl was simultaneously talking on her cell, listening to her iPod, typing away—sending and receiving texts, all at nanospeed. I had considered myself to be pretty good at being able to accomplish several tasks at the same time, but this babe left me in her dust.

"May I help you?" The receptionist reluctantly acknowledged my presence a full five minutes after my arrival, and even then, she didn't look up from her telecommunications empire.

"I hope so. I was told to report here to start Spanish classes this morning, but unfortunately, I was not told exactly where to go. Would there be a list showing where students should report on their first day?" I asked politely.

"So what's your name?" She still hadn't looked up from the computer screen.

"Magnolia Larson."

Finally, I had caught her attention. She actually looked up at me. "No, I mean, your real name."

"That's my real name." I dropped the smile. "Now, can you please tell me where I'm supposed to report? I don't want to be late for my class."

Courtney opened one of the drawers of the desk, took out a clipboard, and started flipping through it. "Magnolia Larson. Here you are. You're supposed to go to Mr. Ramos' classroom, room 202. He's expecting you."

I waved her a half-assed thanks and headed for the stairs, hoping that I wouldn't be late for my first class; that would not have been a good start. However, the moment I entered Mr. Ramos' classroom, I saw that my fears were misplaced.

Mr. Ramos, wearing a name tag, was standing in the corner of the room, busy pouring thimblefuls of what smelled like industrial-strength Cuban coffee into tiny little cups, which he then handed to the half-dozen Japanese men who were clustered around him. The men were all formally dressed in dark suits, black ties, and white shirts. Even their hair was combed the same way, with the parts on the right. In sharp contrast to them, Mr. Ramos, in his surfer-type out-fit of shorts, loose cotton shirt, and flip flops, looked as if he had just returned from Margaritaville, still under the influ-ence of his recreational drug of choice. A slight, stale odor of weed emanated from him.

He looked up, and, when he saw me, his eyes lit up, and a huge smile spread across his face. I immediately liked him. "Señorita Larson! Buenos dias! Welcome!" Mr. Ramos put down the coffee and made his way across the room. "We've been waiting for you. Come, come, have some coffee. Here, I made it myself, so I know what it'll do to you: open your eyes, make your heart beat fast, and maybe even make you fall in love." I suspected that, in addition to the weed, Mr. Ramos was also on Adderall.

"Muchas gracias." With those words, I had just exhausted my entire Spanish vocabulary.

"Señorita Larson, welcome to Introduction to Span-ish Conversation I. We have a small class this session, just you and these six gentlemen. It'll be fun!" Mr. Ramos posi-tively beamed as he made the introductions. The man was higher than a kite. His pupils were so dilated that I couldn't tell what color his eyes were. Classes with him were sure to be interesting. "Mr. Tanaka, Mr. Hirai, Mr. Yamamoto, Mr. Suzuki, Mr. Mora, and last but not least, Mr. Takahashi."

The men all bowed deeply as Mr. Ramos introduced them. I bowed back in return and instantly thought of Ramón, and how at home he would feel here, dressed in his dark suit and bowing continuously.

"I'm looking forward to it." I took a sip of the coffee. The hot, sweet brew was so strong that I almost gasped out loud.

Mr. Ramos, who had been watching and waiting for my reaction, broke out in laughter. "Good. Look, this class is way too early. Let's take a vote on moving it back to ten o'clock for the rest of the session, okay? Let's vote!" He raised his right hand. Watching him, the Japanese gentlemen raised theirs as well. So did I. "Good. Ten o'clock it is."

The teacher leaned over to me and whispered, "Señorita Larson, these gentlemen don't understand a word of either English or Spanish. They only speak Japanese, so I guess this will really be a total immersion course." Mr. Ramos got a twinkle in his eye, and added, "You might even pick up some Japanese—at no extra charge, of course—that's okay with you?"

"If you don't mind my asking, why are they learning Spanish? I mean, wouldn't it be more practical to learn English?" I was curious.

"You probably thought they were businessmen, right? From their looks, business suits and all that? Well, they're not—they are masseurs. As soon as their Spanish is fluent enough, they're going to Buenos Aires to set up a Shiatsu massage parlor there," Mr. Ramos explained.

I'd been worried that Mr. Ramos would ask me why I had signed up for the course, but thankfully, he didn't. In spite of the industrial-strength coffee that was flowing through my veins, I began to relax. Mr. Ramos indicated we should take our seats. Our first class was about to start.

The teacher may not have spoken a word of Japanese, but somehow he was able to communicate with his students. He was so good, so funny and nice that he actually made learning Spanish fun. I suspected that it was because he was such a good instructor and so popular with his students that the Best Language School let him get away with the flip-flops, the mid-morning starting time and, of course, the fact that he was constantly high.

A few hours later, I was back in the Town Car with Ramón, heading for my next appointment: a session with Dr. Bernstein, a sports psychologist. Oona had explained that the reason for that was that if I were going to be effective in dealing with her athletes, I should be knowledgeable about all aspects of their profession—and psychology was a huge part of that.

Dr. Bernstein wasn't half as fun as Mr. Ramos that morning, but he was quite interesting. He was formally dressed in a dark suit and tie—and he didn't smell like weed, nor did he seem to be high. Dr. Bernstein's office was in Coconut Grove, in a three-story, concrete-block building just off U.S. 1. Like the outside of the building, Dr. Bernstein's office was spare and businesslike, and even though I conducted a fairly in-depth inspection of it, I couldn't find anything personal: no photos, no knickknacks, and no books (apart from shrink-type ones) in it. There were two boxes of Kleenex, though.

Dr. Bernstein must have been around fifty years old, with the kind of bland looks that made it hard to tell for sure. Thin, with bright blue eyes, round wire-rimmed glasses, and slightly balding with dirty-blond hair, Dr. Bernstein looked as if he spent all his time indoors. Whenever he looked at me, his gaze was so piercing that I swear he could look directly into my brain. I knew I wouldn't be able to get away with anything.

I had just made myself comfortable on the small two-seater sofa placed across from Dr. Bernstein's desk when he addressed me. "Ms. O'Ryan explained why she thought you and I should meet." Dr. Bernstein looked intently at me. "Would you like for me to tell you what she said?"

"Yes, please." I was curious to know how, exactly, Oona would describe my role, and what she expected that Dr. Bernstein do for me.

"Ms. O'Ryan told you that I'm a psychologist, right? My specialty is counseling elite athletes, helping them with their problems, addressing their concerns, doing whatever is necessary to improve their performance, making certain they behave in an appropriate manner not only on the field but off it as well."

"Oona did tell me that I would be meeting with you, but she did not go into specifics, only that you would be giving me tools so that I can do my job better." I realized I was being vague, but the truth was that I honestly did not know much more than what I was telling Dr. Bernstein.

Dr. Bernstein smiled, an action that made him look younger, softer somehow. I instinctively liked him. "Well, Magnolia—I can call you by your first name, right? I've taken care of Ms. O'Ryan's clients for over ten years, but, I confess, this is the first time I've ever had a young lady such as yourself—an 'edge' as she referred to you—as a patient." I must have looked perplexed, for he quickly added, "But I still know what to do. How I can help you carry out your responsibilities in a way that you will be successful."

"This is a new role for me as well," I told him. "Did Oona tell you how we met, and how this all came about?"

"She told me about the clients leaving her, how she feared that an avalanche might start, how she had to come up with something to stop the defections. An 'edge,'" he explained.

"That would be me." I filled in the rest. "I'm the edge."

"Right. I got that from what she told me." Dr. Bernstein chuckled. "I'm not here to judge you in what you are doing. Although Ms. O'Ryan did not go into specifics, I have a pretty clear idea what your job is working for her. My responsibilities are to make sure you have a very thorough understanding of what life is like for an elite athlete; how much pressure he is under to perform both in his private as well as professional life. It's unbelievably stressful for those men, and some of them are barely out of their teens. Unless you understand that kind of pressure and stress, you cannot be of any use to Ms. O'Ryan or to them. I've been treating professional athletes at the elite level for over twenty years, so I feel confident I can help you look into their world."

I took in what Dr. Bernstein said but was not at all reassured by it. I hoped his confidence was not misplaced as my success as Oona's "edge" greatly rested on what the good doctor could do with me. "Their lives seem quite complicated, really, the way you describe the pressures these men are under. I hope I can be successful."

"For the next few weeks, as I understand it, we'll be meeting daily, which should give us time to get into it," Dr. Bernstein pointed out.

Great. I was going to absorb twenty years of Dr. Bernstein's knowledge in a few weeks. Pressure much? And, of course, become fluent in Spanish as well.

After that, we didn't discuss anything personal—rather, for the half hour I was with him in his office, he explained to me how he intended to conduct our sessions. Dr. Bernstein said that not only would we be discussing the psyches of athletes, he also intended to delve into my background, an approach he considered necessary for his counseling sessions to be successful.

Dr. Bernstein explained that athletes were not like the men that I might have been involved with in my life, because at that elite level, not only was much required of them to maintain themselves at their peak physical state—the training was brutal, for example—but they also had to make themselves available to the media for interviews, help promote charities, integrate themselves into their communities. True, they did they make enormous salaries, but they were treated like kinds of gods, and that went to their heads. Dr. Bernstein told me that he would explain about all those kinds of pressures in such a way that I could relate to them, understand them, and successfully interact with them. He finished by telling me that the athletes' lifestyles impacted their sexual lives in large and small ways. Sometimes the athletes' failures in the bedroom had a direct detrimental effect on how they performed on the field.

I had taken several psychology courses in college, classes I had actually done quite well in, but they weren't very helpful in this first session with Dr. Bernstein. At the end, just as I stood up to leave, Dr. Bernstein handed me a shopping bag full of books—Sport-Specific Performance, Applied Sport Psychology—lots of others in that vein. "You will need to read all of these by the time our sessions are concluded," he instructed as he walked me to the door.

By then, it was close to lunchtime. I asked Ramón to stop at a Subway, my favorite of the fast-food places. I had never skipped a meal in my life and was not about to do so now. Even though I offered several times to treat Ramón, he politely declined my invitation, so I ate my tuna on whole wheat and drank my lemonade alone.

Next on the schedule was a visit to a private gym on South Beach, where I was to meet with the personal trainer with whom I would be working. The Workout Place was a state-of-the-art gym with rows upon rows of gleaming, shiny, brand-new equipment just begging to be used. Looking them over, I could just visualize leaving the place with toned muscles and a six-pack.

My personal trainer, Brandi, was a perky blonde, so friendly and enthusiastic that I would have bet my bottom dollar that she had been head cheerleader in elementary, middle, high school, and college. Brandi was wearing a yellow spandex unitard, a garment that was cut so tight to her body that it was possible to see her blood pulsating in her veins and arteries. There was not one ounce of body fat on her. Cellulite was not and would never be a word in her vocabulary. Or at least only as it applied to her.

With frightening efficiency, she weighed and measured me, (I immediately regretted having stopped at Subway) and pinched my flesh with enormous pincers to determine my body fat content. She drew blood and made me pee in a cup. After that, she strapped a heart monitor on me and had me run on one of the treadmills while she recorded the results.

Before I left, the last thing Brandi did was to give me a tour of the gym, beginning with an explanation of what each of the machines was for and ending with a visit to the ladies' locker room. I had never, ever imagined a locker room in a gym could be as luxurious as the one there. I honestly did not know that towels that fluffy existed; eight people could easily fit in the sauna at one time.

While that first day I hadn't worked out at all, when I staggered out of there, three hours later, I was as exhausted as if I'd run a marathon. Brandi had assured me that she would review the results of my tests and that, by the time I returned the following day, she would have my workout schedule all planned out. I would only need to bring a pair of sneakers, as any other items of clothing I might need would be supplied.

According to the schedule, after the gym I was supposed to return to the apartment, where a stylist would be meeting with me to look me over and determine which style of clothing, hair, and makeup would suit me the best for different occasions. Then, later on in the week, after deciding on an appropriate look for me, Stacy, the stylist, would take me shopping.

At that point, it was early in the afternoon and rush-hour traffic was just beginning. Ramón stuck to back roads, so the return trip to my building didn't take very long. Before splitting up, we made a plan to meet the next morning, my first official day of training. Just as I was getting into the elevator, I snuck one last look at Ramón and saw that he was still bowing to me. I couldn't help but smile.

Once back upstairs, I was very relieved to see that no one had broken into the apartment while I'd been gone. I had not been inside for five minutes before I promptly collapsed on the sofa and fell into a sound sleep. Less than an hour later, the intercom buzzer awoke me, announcing that my guest had arrived and was waiting in the lobby. I was so groggy that I ran to the bathroom and splashed freezing cold water in my face. I had barely finished drying myself when the doorbell rang.

Stacy was a twenty-something, frighteningly fashionable-looking woman. She was wearing a pencil-cut, knee-length black skirt; a tight, white T-shirt; and sling-back, pointy, low-heeled shoes; and had tortoiseshell dark glasses perched on her perfectly highlighted blond hair. She was holding an over-sized tote bag, and next to her were two huge, almost trunk-sized suitcases. I don't know what spooked me more—Stacy or the suitcases. What I did know was that I felt like a frump.

Stacy air-kissed me on both cheeks, then stood back and checked me out. "Good. You're tall enough, good body, thin but not skinny. Boobs could present a problem, though, with some outfits, but we'll just stay away from those. If not, we'll tailor, easy fixes. They're your boobs, right?" She reached out and touched them. "Too bad. Fake boobs are easier to fit. Oh well, what size bra do you wear?" She examined my breasts again. "Thirty-four C, right? I can work with that although a B would have been easier. I'll bring your linge-rie on the next visit. La Perla, Agent Provocateur, Wacoal. A selection of each."

I had no idea what Stacy was talking about. La Perla, Agent Whatever, Wa-something or other, but I just stayed quiet and let her assume I knew. Stacy kept looking me over as if I was a specimen on a slide under a microscope. She seemed perfectly comfortable standing there in the doorway and continued to inspect me as carefully as if I was for sale. Once satisfied, she then turned and pointed to the suitcase that was closest to her. "Here, help me with this, would you?"

I had no idea what she had been told about me, but I had a sense she couldn't have cared less. A total professional, she was there to make me as attractive as possible.

Stacy wasted no time in getting to work. She set up her suitcases in the living room—better light, she claimed—and proceeded to have me try on every single item she'd brought in my size: casual, business, cocktail, evening clothes. Some were quite nice, others I wouldn't be caught dead wear-ing, but all were from well-known designers. Stacy's fears notwithstanding, my breasts weren't a problem, thankfully, as I fit into just about everything selected for me. Not once did Stacy ask for my opinion on any outfit, something that I found quite interesting as well as most revealing. It was clear that my preferences did not count.

After having gone through the contents of the suitcases, Stacy measured every square inch of me, from my head to my toes. Last, she took a digital camera from her purse and snapped a dozen or so photos of me. As I stood there in my underwear, striking the poses she asked me to do, I wondered if she would put them in a "before" and "after" file.

Stacy had taken everything—dresses, skirts, pants, bathing suits, shoes, purses, and assorted accessories—out of the suitcases so the living room looked like a hurricane had ripped through it. When we finished, I helped her pack everything up again, then escorted her to the elevator. I was quite proud of myself that in spite of my exhaustion, I'd somehow managed to get through the appointment, though the truth was that she hadn't needed for me to put forth any effort. I had been more of a mannequin than a live person. Never, not even once, did she ask for my opinion on anything. Was this what my new job would be like? Would the clients treat me this way? I was too tired to speculate.

I crawled back into bed and slept for three hours, only waking up because I was hungry; the tuna sandwich from Subway that I ate for lunch was just a distant memory. I fixed myself some pasta with tomato sauce for dinner, took a bath and, still tired, got into bed again. I had planned to read one of Dr. Bernstein's books, but in spite of my best intentions, my eyes closed after just a few pages, visions of the lingerie that Stacy would be bringing me on the next visit dancing in my head.

Chapter 8

The next morning, the minute I opened the double doors from the lobby of the apartment building that led to the driveway, Ramón sprinted over, stopping just inches away from me.

"Buenos días, Miss Magnolia," Ramón greeted me, bowing so low that he was almost horizontal to the floor. As before, he was formally dressed, wearing an undertaker-style suit identical to the one from yesterday. Discreetly, I looked it over, in an attempt to determine if it was the same suit, or its twin brother, but I couldn't tell.

"Buenos días, Ramón," I answered. "Cómo estás?"

Ramón beamed with the type of pride normally associated with parents when an offspring has made some particularly brilliant comment. "Ay, Miss Magnolia, your Spanish is perfect! You have no accent!"

I wasn't quite sure how, after hearing me say all of four words in Spanish, Ramón had determined I had a career as a linguist, but his attitude certainly lifted my spirits. The boost from him helped give me an extra bit of self-confidence that I would need to tackle Mr. Ramos' class.

"Muchas gracias." On a roll, I had continued speaking Spanish. The brief exchange with Ramón had put me in a good mood. I was smiling as I got into the back seat of the car.

Since I didn't know how much longer I would be given the use of a car and driver to get around Miami, I began to pay attention to the route Ramón took as we drove to the Best Language School. After all, although I had not yet gone down to see it, there was a Mercedes parked in the building's garage for my use. Unlike yesterday, when he actually obeyed traffic laws and didn't run red lights or tailgate, this morning Ramón drove like a regular Miami driver, which needed no further explanation given the city's kamikaze breed of motorists. Maybe now that we had connected by speaking to each other in Spanish, Ramón felt he could be more himself, an image that, from what I could see, was an aspiring NASCAR driver.

For me, probably the most difficult aspect of becoming acclimated to living in Miami had been getting used to the traffic here, where driving entailed breaking almost every rule of the road. Laws were flouted to such a degree that the only way to get anywhere safely was to ignore red lights, not signaling when making a turn, weaving in and out of traffic, and, last but not least, ignoring the posted speed limits. In Miami, if a motorist were to follow traffic laws, two things were likely to happen: he or she would cause an accident, or he or she would be pulled over by the police on a charge of acting suspiciously, under the influence of something.

The driving habits of motorists back home in Minneapolis were the polar opposite of those of their Southern counterparts. Up north, reckless drivers were looked upon with derision, lawbreakers so loathed that they were almost shunned by their fellow Minnesotans. Although I had driven in Miami—the few occasions when I had tooled around in Fred's ancient Ford Taurus—I couldn't really say that I was experienced in getting around on my own, so the prospect of being let loose on the streets of the city both terrified and excited me.

I knew that, inevitably, the sad day would come when Ramón would no longer be waiting for me downstairs, dressed in his undertaker's suit, bowing to me, ready to whisk me around town. Being adventurous by nature, although not exactly eager to brave Miami's murderous traffic and homicidal motorists, I was prepared to do so when necessary. All I could do was hope that Oona had insured the Mercedes up the wazoo.

That morning, because of the way that Ramón was driving, the trip from my apartment building to the Best Language School took less than fifteen minutes, so I arrived there in plenty of time before the class. As before, the Courtney Love look-alike was at her post, still multitasking. This morning, however, she was even busier than the day before: Not only was she talking on the phone, listening to her iPod, typing on her computer, but she was also plucking her eyebrows. I could only stare at her with amazement and, I hated to admit, admiration. Even though I'd been standing in front of her for a couple of minutes, waiting to greet her in a friendly fashion, she didn't look up from the magnified mirror into which she was peering intently, about to pluck out a deviant hair.

I knew from personal experience that mistakes while plucking one's eyebrows could be disastrous (with waxing, catastrophic), so one should dedicate one's total attention to that all-important task. I really couldn't hold it against her that she hadn't greeted me when I stood in front of her waiting to wish her a good morning; still I called out a cheery hello as I passed her desk on the way to the stairs.

Although class was not scheduled to start for another

fifteen minutes, I found Señor Ramos already in his office, taking sips from the dark blue ceramic mug filled with coffee so hot that steam, thick as fog, was rising from it. Dressed much as he had been yesterday—he still looked like an escapee from Key West—Mr. Ramos was holding on to the mug with such a tight grip that it looked as if his life depended on it. As before, I could detect the faint aroma of marijuana emanating from him, confirming yet again that Señor Ramos was a firm devotee of all things Margaritaville. As his pupils were less dilated than they had been the previous day, I could see he had hazel eyes.

"Buenos días, Señorita Magnolia. Cómo estás?" he greeted me. Yesterday, Señor Ramos had addressed me as Ms. Larson, and today Señorita Magnolia. Did that mean anything? Was I making progress? Ever the optimist, I interpreted the change as an omen of good things to come.

"Muy bien, gracias," I replied.

Señor Ramos, apparently deciding that continuing our conversation in Spanish with me took way too much effort at such an early hour, switched to English. "Ready to work hard?" The teacher took an enormous gulp of coffee. I expected him to be scalded, but he showed no reaction. Did marijuana have anesthetic properties, too?

"Yes, I'm looking forward to it," I replied.

As I watched him take another sip, I remembered that he'd said yesterday he wasn't a morning person, so maybe he was too asleep to notice that he was risking third-degree burns in his mouth; yes, I decided that weed had the effect of anesthetizing him. "We have a lot of ground to cover. Making sure you are all fluent in conversational Spanish in six weeks is going to be a challenge, but if we all work hard, we can do it."

Six weeks! That was the first I'd heard how long the course would last. I was going to have to work my ass off to learn Spanish that fast. I was about to start worrying about the challenge that presented when the classroom door opened, and my six Japanese classmates trooped in. Just looking at them, so solemn, dressed in their formal dark suits, made me feel guilty. I suspected learning Spanish was going to be much more difficult for them than for me; at least I spoke French, a Romance language, so I wasn't starting from scratch. I decided that the Japanese masseurs would be my inspiration to work hard.

With fresh conviction, I walked over to the same desk where I sat yesterday and opened up my textbook to the first lesson. My fellow classmates were busy taking their seats and doing the same. I had just finished looking over the chapter when I glanced up and caught sight of Señor Ramos popping several pills in his mouth, which he then proceeded to wash down with the coffee. Caffeine, weed, and pills? I had a feeling it was going to be a long six weeks for him.

That second day, we were so busy that the four hours in the classroom whizzed by. Señor Ramos was a natural teacher, and even though the subject matter was, at times, by definition, tedious—how exciting can grammar for beginning students be?—he still somehow managed to make it as fun as possible. Well, actually, as fun as someone, while high, can make a course in which six of the students (the Japanese) spoke only their native language, and neither of us spoke theirs. Part of the time, to understand each other, we were reduced to communicating by using a form of sign language, moving our hands and bodies in sudden and bizarre ways.

In spite of those challenges, somehow my Japanese classmates and I managed to progress. However, not all was fun and games, for, just as Señor Ramos had warned us, we had to work hard. For all his laid-back Jimmy Buffet–style demeanor and drug habits, Señor Ramos was a surprisingly tough teacher, and a firm believer in the power of homework. As a result, the six Japanese masseurs and I left class with hours of assignments to do before the next day.

I suppose piling on the work was the most efficient way that Señor Ramos could accomplish the goal of our becoming fluent in Spanish in six weeks. Still, given the schedule that I had with my other subjects, keeping up with the homework assignments was going to be tough and if I was not going to slip behind, I was going to have to learn how to manage my time better.

Unfortunately, as far as Dr. Bernstein was concerned, I was already behind in the reading he had assigned. Although I'd had the best of intentions of at least beginning to go through some of the books he'd given me, the truth was that I'd barely been able to look over a few pages of one of them. I hoped he wouldn't give me too hard a time about it, nor report my lax ways to Oona.

The best defense, I decided, would be to take the offense and tell him the truth: that I'd intended to read at least one of his books last night, but that I'd been so tired that I'd fallen asleep instead. My strategy must have caught him by surprise, for Dr. Bernstein didn't lay into me, but, instead, told me to get to it whenever I could, the books were a supplement to our sessions and I would benefit much by reading them.

That second session soon became more interesting than it had been the day before, when basically all he had done was to give me the books and tell me what he expected from our meetings. Maybe the fact that I had been honest with him from the beginning had sparked some kind of respect, but whatever the reason, Dr. Bernstein was definitely not as dry and colorless as he'd been the day before.

Never having been in therapy, I was unfamiliar with what exactly happened during a session with a psychiatrist, so I wasn't sure what to expect from my meetings with Dr. Bernstein. That afternoon, he started the session by telling me that in order to counsel me on working with the athletes, we should begin by talking about me: my background, history, expectations of my association with Oona, etc.

At first, the subjects that Dr. Bernstein wanted to discuss were pretty simple—mostly they focused on my background (parents, siblings, education, life in Minneapolis) and as we spoke, I began to suspect that I could learn at least as much about myself from these sessions as about Oona's clients. At the very least, I might start to understand what my real motivation had been for having accepted Oona's offer. After the session, I decided I would read as many of the books Dr. Bernstein had given me as I could manage.

I'd always considered myself to be in relatively good shape, physically and mentally, but Oona's schedule was wearing me out. This was only the second day and if I'd ever thought I was going to fully participate—do all of Señor Ramos' homework, Dr. Bernstein's reading, train with Brandi, etc.—well, I was going to have to work way, way harder. The sleepless night, the four hours of classroom, and the session with Dr. Bernstein had left me so drained that by the time I reached Brandi's gym for my workout, much to my embarrassment, I was so tired that I was pretty much useless.

Brandi, bless her heart, having been a trainer for over

twenty years, instantly recognized the fact that I was tired, sore, and emotionally fragile and quite likely to hurt myself if I attempted to do anything strenuous. She took pity on me and told me she would, instead of making me work hard, put me through a light workout. She lied.

The workout that Brandi had called "light" had me huffing and puffing so much that anyone watching me would have thought I smoked three packs of unfiltered cigarettes a day. At the end of that endless hour, I, who hardly ever perspired, was sweating as profusely as if someone had turned on a spigot inside my body. By the end of the workout, I wasn't doing much more than staggering around the gym, looking like a drunken sailor who was missing his sea legs. After the class, Brandi (I swear she was a Marine drill sergeant in her previous life) made sure to let me know I had barely accomplished anything more than just stretching. Harder sessions were in my future.

I was so exhausted by the time I left the gym that I briefly considered asking Ramón to buy a Coke to revive me. I reached into my backpack and brought out the agenda with my daily schedule in it and almost kissed Ramón when I saw that there was nothing planned for the rest of the day. Had there been, my next appointment would have probably thought I was on drugs, that's how zombie-like I was at that point—totally worthless. I, who had always been in great shape with much energy, during the months in Miami, much to my embarrassment, had turned into a lightweight, one with no stamina. That would surely change.

This way of life was completely different from anything I had ever known before, and I needed to find which way would be optimal for me to do the best job possible: to diligently work on Señor Ramos' assignments so as to be prepared for class; to read Dr. Bernstein's books, so as to get the most out of our sessions; to be physically fresh so I could give my all to the workouts with Brandi, and still have time to work on my appearance.

That day, the activities had been so tightly scheduled that I hadn't even had time to stop for lunch, so I was ravenous by the time we reached the building. For me, food definitely was fuel, and without it, I did not function well—hell, I didn't function at all.

On the plus side, there was an advantage to being so busy, as I would not have any time to be lonely—a good thing. Still, though, every so often, an image of Max would pop into my brain, and I found myself smiling. One negative of being constantly occupied meant that I would not have the time to volunteer anywhere, which was not good. In any case, just then, I was too damned tired and hungry to worry about that. My body was screaming for food and a bed.

Ramón and I said our good-byes and agreed to meet the following morning at the unholy hour of seven-thirty. Ramón must have been tired as well, for, when he said good night to me, I noticed that his bows were not as low as they had been in the morning.

I dragged myself up to the apartment, dropped the backpack on the sofa, and went into the bedroom, where I was asleep before hitting the bed. I immediately began to dream and images of Max came into my brain. I pictured myself with him, in his restaurant, laughing and talking with him.

"Magnolia, mi amor!" Max reached for me and kissed me low on the right cheek, barely missing my mouth. He then took my hands and squeezed them in his. I was surprised to feel how warm he was, even in the freezing cold restaurant.

"You look perfectly beautiful, just like your namesake flower."

One look at the obvious pleasure on his face and I knew I'd made the right decision for our dinner date by wearing the rushed tight black satin Dolce & Gabbana dress that Stacy had picked out for me. Although the dress looked outwardly simple, it was so beautifully constructed that it fit me like a glove. I felt like a supermodel in it, experiencing the high that women get when they have on the kind of dress that tells the world they are fabulous. The "fuck me" black lace and satin four-and-a-half-inch-high shoes by the same designers, although they might have been a bit much for the Spanish Rose, complemented the outfit perfectly.

Max did not look so bad himself, formally dressed in a navy blue suit with a pale pink shirt and gray tie. He vaguely smelled of some kind of citrus scent that brought fruit orchards to mind. "Thank you. Thank you also for having invited me to join you tonight." I took his hand, and followed him to the back of the restaurants where the booths were. "I'm very happy to be here."

"Please." Max pulled out the table so I could slide into the red leather booth. "Now, Magnolia, please let me order for you." His blue eyes twinkled. "You will not be disappointed." He reached for the bottle of wine that was on the table and began opening it. "I remember the night we met, the first time you were here, that you ordered half a carafe of red wine, the house wine." Max poured a couple of inches of wine into his glass, swirled it around for a few seconds, and took a sip. Next, he served me. "Now, I know our house wine is quite good, but, for my opinion, this is one of the best bottles we have." He showed me the label of the bottle he had just opened. "Gevrey-Chambertin. Wine produced in the Burgundy region of France."

Max watched me closely as I tasted it. "It's absolutely delicious. I don't think I've ever had this before. I definitely would have remembered."

"I agree. You would have." Max thought for a moment. "Are you familiar with the English writer, W. Somerset Maugham?"

I thought for a moment. "Yes. Of Human Bondage, right?"

"A great writer. That's my favorite book of his. Anyway, he had a reputation as a drinker. He once said something like 'There are few ills in the world that a hot bath and a bottle of Gevrey-Chambertin cannot cure.'"

Good to know that, given my predilection for hot baths. "I'll keep that in mind," I replied as I finished the wine in my glass. "The wine selection was terrific. I can't wait for the meal now—I'm starving."

Max smiled. "Good. I like a girl with an appetite."

The rest of the dinner was as spectacular as the wine had been. If I recalled correctly, none of the items we ate had been on the menu: asparagus mousse as an appetizer, rack of lamb with potatoes au gratin as the main course, and crème brûlée for desert. I speculated that Max had gone French all the way in honor of the wine, or it could be he wanted to impress me with his worldliness. Whatever the reason for his choices, they were hugely successful, as I thoroughly cleaned each and every dish that was placed before me. I even polished off the entire contents of the basket of breads.

The hours we spent together raced by as we talked and talked pretty much nonstop, learning about each other, divulging enough to keep the other interested but still retaining the mystery. Even though we came from totally different backgrounds, Max and I connected on a level I had not done with another man, even with Fred when we were getting along. It was as if, in another life, we had known each other. Really bizarre but true, and I was feeling so happy that I was not about to question it. Oona and my deal with her about no relationships were totally forgotten, as was my new role as sports geisha. I was living, or rather dreaming, in the moment, and nothing could take that away from me. The dream was so vivid that when I woke up, I was not sure whether it had actually taken place, but I fervently wished it had.

Three hours later, in spite of my best intentions to adhere to Oona's terms and conditions, I looked for the business card Max had given me two nights before, then picked up the phone and called him.

Chapter 9

It was late Friday afternoon and Ramón had just dropped me off, dead tired, at the apartment. I'd just spent three hours at the hair salon, getting my hair cut, highlighted, and blown dry. I'd never been one to spend hours at a salon, but I had to admit, the folks at Oribe, where I'd been sent (Oribe, the owner, was best known for doing J-Lo's hair) were experts. For the first time in my life, I had highlights. I looked and felt terrific.

It was six o'clock, and as nothing was scheduled for me, I had the next two days all to myself. I planned on not going out of the apartment much that weekend, intending to stay in and catch up on my assignments all day Saturday and Sunday, maybe even work ahead. In spite of my goal to read every night, I'd barely started any of the books that Dr. Bernstein had given me, and he'd given me a couple more today. Señor Ramos had piled on the homework as if we were going to become interpreters at the U.N. For a stoner, he was quite demanding.

It wasn't just any Friday night however. I had a Friday night date: I couldn't remember the last time I'd been on one. When I'd called Max earlier in the week, he hadn't sounded surprised in the least to hear from me, and it was as if he'd been waiting for my call. Vivid images of my dream kept flashing in my brain, showing up at inopportune times, for example, when I was in class or at the gym. Once even during a session with Dr. Bernstein, which thoroughly threw me off. I wasn't used to going out; that fact, coupled with my exhaustion, were unknown factors, so I hoped I wouldn't fall asleep at the table. Just in case, though, I drank a can of Red Bull I'd bought that afternoon. Thankfully, that had done the trick, so even before I finished it, I was as wide awake as if I'd slept for twelve hours. My heart was beating twice as fast as normal from all the caffeine; I hoped I wouldn't go into cardiac arrest—well, at least not until after I'd had dinner with Max, anyway.

After taking a bath, I stood in the closet, trying to decide what to wear. Stacy had left a few outfits for me, so I had several to choose from, but after trying pretty much all of them, I still couldn't pick one. I passed on the Dolce & Gabbana black one from the dream; it would have been too much déjà vu. I decided on a simple dark blue Diane von Furstenberg wraparound dress—not blatantly sexy, but it still showed off my body—and, on my feet, a pair of black leather pumps. I was as nervous as a schoolgirl going out on a first date.

Even though I hadn't yet driven the Mercedes, I wasn't afraid to take it out, but I had to be extra careful, as the last thing I needed was to get into an accident while sneaking out on a date. As I drove over to the Spanish Rose, I kept telling myself that there was no reason to feel guilty, that by having dinner with Max I wasn't breaking an important condition of my agreement. It wasn't as if I was going to have sex with him in spite of the implications of the dream I'd had about him. Accepting a dinner invitation from the owner of a restaurant, a man I'd known for just a few minutes, was hardly what anyone would call "having a relationship."

Max was waiting for me by the front door, looking just as sexy—maybe even more so—than I remembered from that first time I had met him.

"Magnolia!" He greeted me by taking me into his arms and kissing me on both cheeks, French style. As he had in my dream, he smelled clean, crisp, and citrusy. "It's so wonderful to see you." He took a step back and inspected me, then took me by the arm and effortlessly guided me into the room. "Come, let's sit. We're at the back of the restaurant where hopefully no one will come looking for me."

Max and I talked for three hours. It was so very strange to be having a conversation with him in which I told him again about myself, repeating the same information I'd given him in my dream of a few nights before. Even though it had been very vivid, I wasn't sure exactly what I'd told him then, and what I hadn't, which confused me. I made a mental note to ask Dr. Bernstein about the significance of dreams, especially to get his thoughts on whether or not events that took place in them were ever realized.

"So I'm interested to learn what brought you to Miami from Minneapolis." Max was understandably curious to learn that important fact.

I froze a bit as the implications of such a seemingly innocent question hit me. If Max and I were to have any kind of relationship, I was going to have to level with him about certain facts regarding my life, especially as I was going to have to keep silent about the Oona situation which, just then and for the foreseeable future, would comprise a great deal of it. Keeping such a huge secret wasn't an ideal way to get acquainted, and I felt extremely duplicitous doing so, but given the realities, the best I could do. On our first date, I sure as hell could not come outright and volunteer that I was training to be a high-priced call girl for elite athletes. "I came here to be with a boyfriend."

"A boyfriend?" Max's right eyebrow arched just a bit.

"Oh, we're not together anymore," I hurried to assure him. "Our relationship broke off, but I stayed here. I wasn't ready to go back home."

"So you like Miami?" Max was curious. "I've been to Minneapolis; it's a wonderful city, but the two places could not be more different."

"Yes, especially in winter." I laughed. "I've signed up for Spanish classes. The course just began this week, and I'm really liking it." I proceeded to tell Max about Señor Ramos and my Japanese classmates, stories that he seemed to enjoy.

Max had not been able to spend the entire time with me during the dinner because as the owner, he did have to make sure everything ran smoothly, and it was Friday night, the busiest night of the week for his restaurant, he told me. Still, I was able to find out a few personal things about him, including the three most important ones: he was neither married, nor engaged, nor involved with anyone.

"Because I haven't met the one woman who I wanted to spend the rest of my life with. My parents were happily married for forty years. They set a great example. I intend to follow in their footsteps," he explained.

I learned Max was an only child, that his father was Cuban and his mother, who had passed away five years before, was American, a Miami native, a rarity in this new town. His father had been in the restaurant business in Havana, and had immigrated to Miami when the Castro government had confiscated his restaurants. Even though everything he had worked so hard for had been taken from him, all had not been lost, his father always claimed, because it was in this country that he'd met his wife, Max's mother.

Max told me that had never been interested in running a restaurant—while in college he had studied architecture—but he'd ended up doing so because his father had, unfortunately, developed Alzheimer's, and kept insisting to him that his only wish was that he keep the business going. "So, of course, it is my duty, and I'm proud to do this for my father. It's just the two of us now. Once my father passes away, and I will have fulfilled my promise to him, I will take up my true profession and become a practicing architect."

When it was my turn to discuss my situation, I commented that, at the present time, college graduates with a degree from the University of Minneapolis in art history, with a concentration in Impressionist painters, were not exactly in hot demand in Miami, one of the reasons I was taking Spanish classes. I wanted to use the time in a productive fashion while, hopefully, a job opened up. Max told me he'd keep his eyes and ears open in case he came across anything—at the restaurant, he met a lot of people, and one never knew.

As had been the case in my dream, the hours flew by. Very mindful of the fact that I was not supposed to be out at night, especially with a man, I decided that I should not push my luck further, so at ten I told Max I really should be going. "It's been a wonderful evening, really delightful. Thank you very much."

"Why? It's still early. It's Friday night. Surely you don't have classes tomorrow," Max protested.

"No, you're right. I don't have classes, but I do have responsibilities. I'm staying at an apartment of some friends of my parents, professors at the University of Miami, while they're away on a three-month sabbatical in Chile, and I'm taking care of their two dogs. I have to get back to them and walk them," I lied, hopefully convincingly.

"Yes, it's important you get back. The dogs are waiting for you, and you can't disappoint them. I'm a dog lover, so I know how that is. Well, then, you'll have to promise me that you'll stay longer next time. I'll let you go on only that condition." Max put my hands in his. Yet again, I was a bit taken aback by how warm they were.

"Definitely." I stood up. "Thank you again for the lovely evening. The meal was wonderful, very special." And it had been. The wine, also, although it was not the Gevrey-Chambertin of my dreams.

Max walked me outside and waited with me until the valet brought the car around. I noticed his surprised expression when he saw what it was. "My parents' friends left me their Mercedes. Nice, right?" I felt I needed to give him an explanation for the expensive car.

"Very nice." Max kissed me again on both cheeks. "Drive safely, Magnolia. I'll call you."

I drove to the apartment with a big smile on my face. Surely Oona hadn't meant that I couldn't be friends with a man. Kisses on the cheek did not make a romance. It had been wonderful getting away from my responsibilities for a while, but my day wasn't over. Although I had two full days of weekend left, I had all kinds of homework, and as I was still feeling the effects of the Red Bull, I figured I might as well take advantage of that.

I'd come to the conclusion that the only way to get as much accomplished as possible was to develop a schedule and stick to it, a plan which so far, I'd been able to follow successfully. After getting dropped off at home by Ramón,

I would take a quick nap followed by dinner, then tackle the assignments that were due the following day. Tonight, though, instead of taking a nap, I'd treated myself and had gone out to dinner.

After getting home from my date with Max, I wasted no time making preparations to begin to do my assignments. First, I took off my clothes then I washed my face and brushed my teeth. I was wide awake, but my mind kept drifting back to Max, so I wasn't focused enough to tackle the first of the many assignments that Señor Ramos had given us for the weekend. Instead, I decided to begin by reading one of the books that Dr. Bernstein had given me. Suddenly, a thought occurred to me. On Monday, would Dr. Bernstein notice anything different about me? He was pretty sharp. I'd picked up on that right away. Would he be able to tell I'd been with what he would call a "normal" man?

Oh, God! Already, a complication! Well, there was nothing I could do about that. I lay on the bed, and picked up the book at the top of the pile on my night table. I opened it to the first page, but try as I might, I couldn't absorb anything.

My thoughts kept turning to how my life had changed in just five days. On Monday, I'd been living in a roach-infested studio in little Havana—my only worldly possessions apart from my clothes were a credit card that probably didn't work, fifty dollars in cash, and a plane ticket back to Minneapolis. And now here I was, living in a luxurious penthouse apartment with all my expenses paid, a car and driver at my disposal, taking Spanish language classes from which I would benefit for the rest of my life, improving my body, mind, and appearance. My outfits, designer clothes for the most part, were being put together by the best stylist in town.

Focusing on Dr. Bernstein's reading was impossible as

well, so I decided that maybe if I relaxed, I might be able to get something accomplished and that taking a hot bath would surely do the trick. I got out of bed and headed toward the bathroom. There I chose my favorite oil, the rose one, and poured a healthy amount into the bathtub. After it had filled up, I slowly lowered myself into it, letting the hot water do its thing and relax my muscles. Once I was immersed up to my chin, I closed my eyes and inhaled the sticky-sweet scent of the rose petals. I thought back on what Max had said in my dream about a hot bath and a bottle of wine. Well, just then I did not have any "ills" in my life, but I sure as hell would not have turned down a bottle of Gevrey-Chambertin if W. Somerset Maugham had offered it to me. The schedule I had planned for the night was not going to happen, so I would have to just work twice as hard in the morning. I lay in the water, eyes still closed, letting the stress of the day leave me.

Although at times I did feel overwhelmed, the truth was that I really did enjoy the different activities that I had been participating in. If I had to choose one, the clear favorite was Señor Ramos' class—hands down, he was the best teacher I'd ever had. I was convinced that if he hadn't been such a stoner, he would have been brilliant in academic circles. I had been getting so involved in his class that not only was I learning Spanish, but I was also picking up a few Japanese phrases from my classmates. True, that had come about from sheer necessity, as we'd had to try to learn a bit of each other's languages just to be able to communicate, but still it was happening. Although it had never been openly acknowledged, we'd all quickly realized that it was easier and more efficient for me to pick up some Japanese than for them to learn English. Spanish was so difficult for them to learn that it was almost painful watching them attempt to grasp it.

In the beginning, I'm embarrassed to admit, I'd thought of the six masseurs as being kind of interchangeable; after all, not only did they have a striking physical similarity to each other, they all dressed alike. However after a couple of days, I began to think of them as individuals. I got along the best with Mr. Tanaka, the leader; he had a wicked sense of humor, even if I didn't understand most of what he said. His eyes had a sparkle, and he was almost always laughing, making him look like the pictures I'd seen of the Dalai Lama.

Something that was quite amusing and which pleased me greatly was that lately Señor Ramos had started to rely on the rudimentary Japanese I had learned from my classmates to get them to understand him when he taught them Spanish. If anyone had told me back in Minneapolis that I would be translating phrases from Japanese into Spanish and vice versa, I would have assumed that they'd been drinking or taking drugs.

I made up my mind to open up to Dr. Bernstein and discuss my issues, figuring that, as a practical matter, the sessions were paid for, so I might as well take full advantage of them. One of the subjects I wanted—needed, actually—to discuss with the good doctor was why I was such a perfectionist in certain matters but a bit lax in others. On the one hand, being that way had served me well, as throughout my life, I had been an outstanding student, winning awards and prizes and earning a full scholarship for college. On the other, I would drive myself to the ground, working way harder than was probably necessary in order to do a job perfectly. For my training here in Miami, I could already see that I had to pace myself so as not to burn out. My disastrous relationship with Fabulous Fred was a telling example of how lax I could be, and with what serious consequences could come from my not studying certain situations as thoroughly as I should.

And then, of course, there was the insight I was supposed to get from Dr. Bernstein for my work with Oona's
clients. Because I had taken all those psychology courses in
college, I was somewhat familiar with behavioral problems;
however, none of those classes covered how certain sexual
situations/problems/preferences impacted the performances
of professional athletes. I'd already discovered from a couple
of our conversations, that Dr. Bernstein, for all his nerdy
appearance, was very knowledgeable about sexual preferences, deviant behaviors, and fetishes.

As he began to discuss the situations I was likely to
encounter, Dr. Bernstein went into minute details about
the subject that he had touched upon during our first meeting: that athletes of the caliber of Oona's clients did not, for
a variety of reasons, lead what would be considered normal lives. Because of that, they tended to have "special and
specific" needs in their sexual lives.

"Now, Magnolia, so far in our sessions, I know that we
have not examined your sexual history. You may not want to
discuss it, but if I'm to help you, I have to ask you about it. I'm
especially interested in knowing if you've been involved in
an intimate relationship with an elite athlete." Dr. Bernstein
brought up the subject almost as an aside.

"No, I haven't. I don't even know any elite athletes," I
replied. "My sexual experiences have been kind of limited."
I proceeded to tell him about losing my virginity to Sven
Martins, my brother's friend, not out of any love for him, but
because I was curious about the act, and the opportunity had
presented itself.

"So your first lover was your brother's friend, someone
you knew well and were comfortable with, but there was no

real lust or passion involved." Dr. Bernstein wanted to be sure he understood.

"Well, it was time." I shrugged my shoulders, as if to indicate it was not something I was particularly proud of having done. "There were a couple of other guys, classmates, mostly one-night stands after parties where I'd had something to drink. Nothing really. Until Fred."

"So talk to me about Fred. You've told me in our previous meetings that you had come to Miami to be with him, then the relationship deteriorated and you moved out. He had changed to the point where you almost didn't recognize him," encouraged Dr. Bernstein.

I hated talking about Fred. He was like a dark cloud in my past, but if Dr. Bernstein thought it necessary that I do that, I had to. "Okay." Speaking slowly in a monotone, I gave him the story of my history with Fred, from our meeting at college in Minneapolis to the bitter end in Miami when I moved out.

After I'd finished, Dr. Bernstein sat quietly, taking in what I'd said. "You said you'd been adventurous in some of your sexual encounters. How did you feel during those?"

"They were fun," I admitted. "I mean, I didn't want to have sex that way all the time, but, yes, I liked it."

"As I told you the very first time we met, Ms. O'Ryan was quite clear in what she expected of you, why she contracted you to work for her in this capacity, as her 'edge.' You've already experimented having sex in different, nontraditional ways with Fred. He was just one man, one with whom you were involved. Do you think you'll have trouble doing those same acts, and other ones, too, with multiple partners, men you really don't know—in effect, with strangers?"

I noticed that Dr. Bernstein leaned a little closer to me

in his chair as he asked that question. It sounded so tawdry the way he put it, but it was the truth. There was no point in sugarcoating it. "No, not really. I mean, I agreed to do it, right? That's why I'm here, to learn more, to make it easier for me."

"Okay. A little while ago you said you've not had relationships with elite athletes, so you don't have any real familiarity with them, right? Maybe I should start by explaining in detail the three characteristics that the athletes you will be meeting with have in common. Studies have been done that have determined that these traits apply to all sports. First of all, for these men to have reached such heights, they all possess extreme self-confidence, which comes from having put in endless hours of training. Second, in order to work that hard and for such long periods of time, they've had to make huge sacrifices, so they are all highly motivated. And last but not least, they have what's referred to as 'low performance anxiety.'"

"That's very interesting," I commented. "So do most of the patients that you treat come to see you because of that last one, the low performance anxiety? I mean, they've developed high performance anxiety, and you have to help them recover their extreme self-confidence?"

"Very good, Magnolia." Dr. Bernstein seemed pleased I'd caught on so quickly. "They all have several coaches, so that's not what I'm here for. I help them with their mental preparation and have them visualize how they will be successful while competing. I teach them to run tapes in their heads of how they want to act, and once they've mastered that, then they will be successful."

"I get that. And my role? I mean, besides giving them great sex, what part do I play?" I smiled. "Am I to be their sex coach? To make sure they focus on their performances, to be in the best mental state possible during competitions because they've had their physical needs satisfied?"

Dr. Bernstein was quiet. "I guess if that's what you want to think of yourself, then you could call it that. You are to satisfy their needs, both physically and psychologically. My job is to show you how to help them cope with pressure and anxiety using sexual methods."

"And what about the ones that don't have performance issues, the ones that just want to have fun with me?" I teased him.

"Those are the easy ones, and you have fun with them, too." Dr. Bernstein chuckled. "I'm sure you know how, but I'll help you with those, too."

Then Dr. Bernstein began giving me a crash course in how to be a sex therapist. However, in my case, instead of having my clients lie on a couch (with me sitting on a chair opposite them) as they divulged their deepest, most intimate sexual longings, I would be expected to be lying right alongside them on the couch, probably naked, helping them act out those fantasies: a sort of hands-on approach to therapy. Mostly, and perhaps most importantly, he taught me to be nonjudgmental.

If an athlete was to request a special service—as unappealing as it might be to me—I was not to let my feelings be known. If a client wanted me to dress a certain way (nurse, teacher, policewoman, and the like), or speak in a kind of voice (babyish, threatening, accented, whispering), the absolutely worst thing I could do was to ridicule them, something that was not exactly news to me. I discussed with Dr. Bernstein if it would be appropriate for me to suggest to my clients that I use props from the athletes' particular sport to satisfy them during our encounters. In other words, if the client was a soccer player, could I hand out red cards or yellow cards according to their performance with me, and stop during halves, things like that? I could blow a whistle like the referees did, penalizing him for certain plays then rewarding him for scoring a goal. I could dress appropriately for the encounter, maybe as a cheerleader or as an umpire. On certain occasions, and when the client was very important, we could even meet in the place where the client actually competed: Marlins Park (baseball); Sun Life Stadium (football); American Airlines Arena (basketball); Jai-Alai Fronton (jai-alai); Calder Race Course (horse racing). Dr. Bernstein thought that was a splendid idea, but only if the client was enthusiastic, naturally.

Of course, I was not to stand for physical abuse—my agreement with Oona did not require for me to submit to any kind of sadomasochistic practices, or anything that caused me pain. If that were to happen, I was to excuse myself politely and leave. So far, I'd found the sessions and the reading material that complemented them intriguing.

As far as the workouts with Brandi, even though I'd only trained with her four times, I could see my body changing. It could have been my imagination, but I swear I could detect a bit of muscle definition, something that had not been there before. I'd been in shape, but I'd never been ripped. Perhaps even more important than the visible changes was that I had developed quite a bit more endurance, which, if Dr. Bernstein's sessions on the athletes' sexual preferences were correct, I would be sure to need.

Recently, Brandi had begun to incorporate yoga into our workouts, claiming it would give me much needed flexibility. According to the schedule she had provided, she would regularly be adding other activities to our training sessions: aerobics, gymnastics, boxing, martial arts, even belly dancing, all of which I was looking forward to.

The beauty part of my regime was another sort of education. Except for the thought that I might be a bit too voluptuous, I had always been pretty much satisfied with my appearance, so I had never really exerted much time or money to my looks. I would go to the hairdresser when I needed to get my hair cut, bought makeup when I ran out, and shopped when I needed a new outfit or for a special occasion, but those had been about the extent of my normal female pursuits.

At first, the appearance-improvement part of the routine put me off a bit; I certainly hadn't been used to being pampered to such a degree. There had not been any extra cash in the Larson family budget for that but, I have to admit, after seeing the results, I took to it like a duck took to water, and I'd happily indulged myself in the manicures, pedicures, facials, waxing, and massages that were offered. Coming from a family of four boys, such pampering was considered totally indulgent, almost immoral; besides, no one I knew in Minneapolis did that. And, not surprisingly, I became even more enthusiastic about those kinds of appointments when I saw how much better I looked as a result of all those professionals helping me.

The one beauty treatment that I could have easily done without was the Brazilian bikini wax. Being a natural blonde and fair-skinned, I didn't really have much hair anywhere on my body, and the hair that I did have was not very noticeable; however, the beautician that I was sent to, one of seven Brazilian sisters whose specialty was in waxing, had disagreed with me. On my first visit there, I found myself, lying on a narrow bed in a room in her salon, wearing only a T-shirt, with my panties on a chair, face down, my legs spread wide apart, with my butt-naked ass up in the air while she poured hot wax on my most private of parts. I was so shocked at what was happening to me that I didn't even cry out as she pulled the hair off with little strips of cloth. The notion of retaining any semblance of dignity during this process was but a forgotten dream. I emerged from her room half an hour later, with my body as smooth and hairless as a baby's bottom. Even though I was fully dressed, I felt naked as a jaybird. What the hell had just happened to me?

As I limped out of the salon, I thought yet again, how different Miami was from Minneapolis, which surely didn't have seven Brazilian sisters there whose goal in life was to make sure no one, man or woman, had a single hair on their bodies, especially their private parts. My life was never going to be the same after having been Brazilian waxed, that was for sure. It took me three days to get used to the feeling of being totally bare.

All in all, even though it had taken hard work on my part, there was no question that I was personally benefiting from all that Oona had been offering me. I made up my mind that I was going to work hard and keep my mouth shut. As the long-ago prime minister of England, Benjamin Disraeli once famously said, "Never explain, and never complain." I was going to live by those words.

Oona, with all the classes, sessions, workouts and physical improvements she'd provided, was giving me an Ivy League education on becoming a sports geisha. And I was determined to take full advantage of it.

Chapter 10

Apart from the three Friday night dinners I'd had with Max during the past three weeks, perhaps the most pleasant aspect of my new life was the friendship that was slowly developing between my Japanese classmates and me. At first, because of language difficulties, we were not able to communicate much; however, as the days passed, and we became more attuned to each other, we were able to understand one another more.

Although I would have liked to have been able to also learn to read and write kanji, as the written language is known, given the time constraints and the difficulty, I was limited to only picking up conversational Japanese. Still, I was beginning to think that if I continued to learn the language at my current rate, by the time the course with Señor Ramos concluded I might be fluent enough to be able to carry on a conversation with a Japanese person other than my classmates. Learning to speak that language was coming so easily to me that I began to suspect maybe one of my ancestors had fooled around with someone from Japan, a liaison that might have resulted in a couple of drops of Japanese blood flowing through my veins.

And it wasn't just the language that intrigued me. I was starting to be interested in all aspects of Japanese culture:

art, films, flower arrangements, food, etc. It was actually quite bizarre, but then, nothing about my life just then was normal, so I soon stopped analyzing my sudden interest in all things Japanese. Even Dr. Bernstein couldn't offer any reasonable explanation. I reasoned that if I were to seriously examine my love for Japan, then I might wind up analyzing all other aspects of my life. I mean, how did saving money for an art school for underprivileged and at-risk children fit in with an obsession with Japan?

The methods I used for learning Japanese weren't exactly sophisticated, but they were effective: I would mostly point to objects in the classroom, and Mr. Tanaka or one of the others would tell me the Japanese word for whatever I was indicating. I would then say the word, while they, trying to keep straight faces, would correct my atrocious pronunciation. I would play close attention to the way they said the word, and then repeat it, doing my best to imitate their accent and inflections.

My vocabulary increased to such a degree that I purchased a notebook to write down—phonetically, of course—the words I'd learned. Flush with success and confidence, one afternoon I went to a bookstore and bought an English-Japanese dictionary. Within weeks, much to the surprise of all, I was actually speaking in short sentences. Mr. Tanaka and his fellow masseurs were very pleased with my progress and treated me as if I was their star pupil.

Next, I found myself going to my neighborhood Blockbuster and renting Japanese films. I also joined Netflix. I spent the little spare time I had watching these movies, trying to match the dialogue on the screen with the English translation at the bottom of the page. Not surprisingly,

Blockbuster didn't carry a huge selection of Japanese movies, and the ones they did have were mostly about life in
eighteenth- and nineteenth-century Japan. After spending
hours watching those films, I would have bet my last dollar
(yen?) that I knew more about the lives of samurais than
any other twenty-two-year-old American female.

It was at the end of the third week of classes that Mr.
Tanaka approached me and, in a very shy way, asked me,
using the peculiar combination of Japanese and Spanish we
had developed, if I would be interested in joining him and
the five other masseurs for dinner at a Japanese restaurant
located close to the school. Mr. Tanaka had been looking
at the floor the entire time he was speaking to me, so I had
trouble understanding him; however, I was able to learn that
the particular restaurant was in a nearby shopping mall, and
that it was one that they had frequented often.

Apart from the various fast-food places where Ramón
drove me to during the course of our daily rounds — exclud-
ing my secret dinners with Max at the Spanish Rose — I
had really not been to many restaurants the last few weeks.
Though Max and I always intended to go out somewhere,
instead, we always ended up eating at his restaurant — his
was a twenty-four-hour job. I didn't really object to sticking to the Spanish Rose. I felt safe there and didn't have to
worry about being caught by Oona; the servings were more
than plentiful and the food was delicious, so continuing
to see each other at the Spanish Rose, really, wasn't a problem. I could have done without the constant interruptions
of the staff or the patrons, but I understood those were an
ever-present reality of his life. The truth was, I enjoyed seeing Max at work, watching him as he went about his business.
He had an unmistakable air of quiet authority, a trait that I

have always liked and admired.

Although I knew Max wanted to make love with me, as I did with him, so far, he hadn't pressed the point. True, our good-byes had become more physical, more urgent, but so far, three weeks into our dinner dates, nothing had really happened. Of course I knew that eventually our relationship would become sexual, but I figured there was no point in agonizing until that happened, as I would deal with it when the situation arose. I was living on borrowed time, and I was very aware of that. Because Max and I had not yet had any kind of physical relations, that meant that I was still in compliance with the terms and conditions of my agreement with Oona. Still, though, what I was doing did trouble me greatly. Also I was running great risks—someone could see me at the restaurant, maybe Anita or Oona, and I would be busted. A scene would, no doubt, ensue, and Max would find out about me in a truly terrible manner. And Fred? What if Fred were to show up with a date? I had not seen or heard from him since I stormed out that night from the apartment in Coral Gables.

I was delighted at Mr. Tanaka's invitation, and I was touched that my classmates had done me the honor of inviting me. I knew that the Japanese were very fond of fish, so wherever my classmates decided to take me, I could be assured there would be seafood, which was fine with me. I loved seafood, any kind, really. Also, I could practice my very rudimentary Japanese, something that simultaneously thrilled as well as made me apprehensive.

My friendship with Mr. Tanaka and his countrymen was curious, to be sure, but it was genuine. The more I thought about it, the more convinced that I had met Mr. Tanaka and his colleagues for a reason, much as Oona had been convinced that she and I had been at the Miami Sports Bar at the same time that Monday afternoon for a reason. I was coming to the same conclusion as far as Mr. Tanaka and his fellow masseurs were concerned, that we were meant to meet.

I read in the schedule that Anita had prepared for me that, as of next week, my sessions with Dr. Bernstein were going to be cut back from five days a week to three, then two. I wasn't particularly surprised by that as by the end of the second week we had pretty much exhausted the topic of athletes and the situations I might encounter during my sessions with them. I did read all the literature he had assigned me, material that I found to be interesting and illuminating, subjects such as performance anxiety, stress—and how to deal with weird requests.

Because I wanted to further develop my idea of specializing in having sex with the clients using props from their individual sports, and possibly conducting those encounters in the venues where they competed, I would discuss with Dr. Bernstein different ways to make that happen. The more I delved into that, the more I thought it would work and Dr. Bernstein agreed, which increased my confidence. In the end, it would certainly help me be more unique, and make my encounters with the athletes more successful. Plus, it would be fun.

During our sessions, once we'd finished with business, Dr. Bernstein and I would discuss politics, religion, me—anything, really. My relationship with Max, though, was something I had not brought up, thinking that doing so would complicate matters and put Dr. Bernstein in a difficult position. I didn't know how far the doctor-patient confidentiality agreement went in a situation such as ours, and thought it best not to test it. Even though I was still very interested in discussing the vivid dream I'd had of Max and me having dinner at his restaurant, I thought better of it in case Dr. Bernstein became suspicious. Now I was even suppressing information from my doctor.

I suspected I'd miss meeting with Dr. Bernstein. I really didn't have too many people to talk to, and the hours we spent together had become more like conversations between two friends than between a therapist and patient, so it was appropriate that they wind down. Dr. Bernstein had been invaluable in helping me deal with my family, giving me advice on how to call or e-mail them by giving them just enough information so that they wouldn't worry. In that regard, I followed Dr. Bernstein's gentle guidance to the letter, but, as much as I tried to pressure him, he never would come out with any concrete directives. He was of the school of thought that patients should figure out on their own what path they should take. I, of course, completely disagreed with him on that. I wanted answers—and not just more questions. It was frustrating.

"Dr. Bernstein, I hate to say it, but it annoys me when you won't answer me when I ask about my relationship with my friends and family." Because the subject was important to me, it took a bit of self-control for me to keep my voice even. "You answer any and all questions I ask you about how I should behave with Oona's clients during sessions with them, but when I ask for guidance about how to handle my family, you just tell me to figure it out by myself."

"That's very true, Magnolia. But you're talking apples and oranges. That's not a valid comparison. You know your family best, and the nature of your relationship with them, so you're the one who has to work through how to deal with them. The encounters you'll be having with Ms. O'Ryan's clients are novel ones, ones that you have not encountered before, and it's my job to prepare you for them. For those situations, you do need my guidance, and my role is more of a teacher than psychologist. As far as how you deal with your family and how you present the details of your life in Miami, in my opinion, is that should be something that you decide. That way, you'll have arrived at that place yourself," Dr. Bernstein explained patiently.

"Is the reason you won't answer my questions as to how to deal with my family because Oona is paying you to advise me in situations that only have to do with her clients?" I had to know. If that were the case, then I would stop asking, as it would not be fair to place him in an uncomfortable position.

"No, of course not, Magnolia. We've talked about so many different subjects while you've been coming here. I'm surprised you think that." Dr. Bernstein got a hurt look in his eyes, making me ashamed that I'd asked him that. "It's because I know that you are perfectly capable of answering those questions on your own. By the way, there's something that I've been wanting to bring up for a while. I've come to know you a bit during our sessions, and I suspect that there is something about your life here in Miami that you're not telling me."

Max! He knows about Max! Or was he just fishing? I feared that I had underestimated the good doctor. I lowered my gaze and looked down at the floor while I thought furiously how to respond. So far, I had only omitted telling Dr. Bernstein about Max. True, I'd been deceiving him, but I hadn't outright lied to him—a fine line, in any case. Now I was being placed in a position where I had to decide how much to tell him. I decided that the best approach would be to deflect the question and not really answer him. I liked and respected Dr. Bernstein, and I certainly did not want to jeopardize our relationship by blatantly lying to him. "I'll make you a deal," I replied. "You give me advice as to how to handle my family, and I'll tell you whatever it is you want to know."

"Magnolia, I can't make a deal like that with you, you know that. But, in any case, I have my answer," he said. "You are keeping something from me. I'm not worried, though. I know I'll find out eventually. It's just a matter of time."

The conversation with Dr. Bernstein served to put me on notice yet again about the risks I was running by continuing to see Max. From my behavior, the doctor suspected I was keeping a secret from him. Would Oona? Anita?

Dr. Bernstein was very interested in hearing about my plan to open up a school to teach art. At first, I hadn't wanted to discuss that very personal subject with him because Dr. Bernstein was an excellent therapist, and I was apprehensive that he might point out to me that the truth was that I hadn't accepted Oona's offer to be able to fund such a plan, that I had other reasons. If opening up my art school hadn't been my real motivation, I, at least, wanted to fool myself and remain convinced that I'd signed on to this work for a selfless reason. However, much to my relief, Dr. Bernstein must have believed at least some of what I said because he discussed several avenues I could explore to make my dream a reality.

After ten or so sessions, I finally understood why he was interested in my plan to open the school. He'd told me about his "other life," as he referred to it. Prior to becoming a psychiatrist, he'd been a teacher in an innercity elementary school, so he knew the dismal and very limited situations there as far as choices the students had. Oona surely wouldn't have appreciated that several thousand of the dollars she was paying Dr. Bernstein had gone toward his helping me work out a plan to open my school. He was there to make me the best sports geisha I could be and not to further my personal goals; however, that didn't particularly bother me, as she was going to make plenty of money off me. Besides it was for a good cause that we were having such discussions, in my opinion.

As for Brandi's project to redo my body—that was coming along really well. Every day I could feel myself getting stronger and more flexible, with greater endurance. I had way more energy, which was a real plus. No question about it, my body was in the best shape ever. The workouts with Brandi—as well as those with the trainers who specialized in yoga, Pilates, boxing, belly dancing, etc.—had the added benefit that my mind was becoming sharper, more focused. I was getting increasingly efficient in all aspects of my life.

It was normal for patrons of Brandi's gym to come in and work out with their trainers at a specific time—it seemed that everyone there was on some kind of schedule—so I soon began to recognize the other individuals that would come in while I was there. One of my favorites was Simone, a lady in her early thirties who was such a fan of cosmetic surgery that I would have bet that she did not have a single one of her original body parts. Funny, loud, and flamboyant, with platinum-colored hair full of extensions that hung well past her waist, she cracked jokes throughout her entire workouts—which she did with her dog, a four-pound black Chihuahua called Fang—perched on her sizeable chest, which was the best money could buy. Her trainer had standing instructions: Simone was never to sweat—otherwise she would be fired on the spot. Suzanne hated any kind of perspiration, and, for a reason known only to herself, would never, ever allow herself do to become even slightly damp, regardless of the fact that she was in a gym.

Weeks before, Brandi had told me that Simone was a madam, a quite successful one, never having less than twenty girls working for her at any time. I, of course, had been fascinated and had immediately wanted to ask her all kinds of questions about the business. What exactly, did her girls do? What did they charge? What percentage of their earnings did she keep, and how much did they give her? I also wondered what Simone would say if she were to find out what it was that Brandi was training me for, and because I wanted my private business to stay private, I stayed quiet.

As I progressed in my training, Brandi increased the intensity of my workouts. Soon she had me doing things I never would have thought myself capable of, such as standing on my head during yoga, jumping rope for ten minutes, running a five-minute mile on the treadmill, doing sprints around the gym until I thought I would pass out. My legs, especially, became very toned, something that did not go unnoticed in the quietly competitive atmosphere of the gym. One day, Brandi reported that Simone had asked her about me. Apparently, one of her girls, the one with iron legs, had gotten sick, and been unable to work. Unfortunately, the timing of her illness could not have come at a worse time, as her best client—the man who paid her thousands of dollars to just wrap her legs around his neck and squeeze them until he would lose consciousness—wanted to hire her for an emergency session. Simone was unwilling to disappoint the client, so she was desperately looking for a replacement. Brandi answered by telling her I was a student, and not in the life, which was kind of the truth. I was a student geisha, so I would not be able to step in and help her out of her predicament.

Before, I'd dreaded going to the gym, feeling strange and out of place in such a luxurious establishment, but as I was able to do the workouts with more ease, my self-confidence increased, and I actually began to enjoy my time there and found myself looking forward to going.

I'd also learned to manage my overall time better, so much so that by the end of the third week, I even had a bit of free time. Thinking I might be able to volunteer a few hours a week, I began making calls, but, much to my disappointment, I found out that given my hectic, activity-packed schedule, there was no way I could honestly commit to giving the time required by the organizations I contacted. The last thing I wanted was to begin volunteering and have to drop out because I couldn't work the required hours. In addition, Oona, of course, would have had to be informed that I would be spending time volunteering, and it was highly likely she would forbid me from doing so. She wasn't investing all this money in me for me to turn out to be a do-gooder.

Oona would call and check in with me every other day; our conversations were cordial but brief and to the point. Oona was a no-nonsense boss, that was for sure. Although I was prepared for her calls and pretty much stuck to answering her questions, I would still become apprehensive that I would inadvertently let slip any kind of information about my extracurricular activities with Max. I knew I was being duplicitous, but I could not give him up. I tried to minimize the chances of that happening by only meeting him at the restaurant, a public place where I could explain my presence. Even so, I could be busted any time.

I began to look around for other ways to keep myself

occupied, as I didn't want to sit in the apartment, with time on my hands. After considering my rather limited options, I decided that I would continue to develop my interest in all things Japanese, so I signed up for Japanese flower-arranging classes. I'd always loved flowers, so when I read that a course in ikebana, the ancient art of Japanese flower arranging, was going to be offered at the neighborhood florist, I signed up right away. Classes were held on Saturday mornings, which meant that, in spite of my erratic schedule, I would be able to attend them. There were only four students in the class, which was terrific, because then Yuriko-san, the teacher, or sensei, as she was referred to in Japanese, was able to give each of us individual attention. She told us that ikebana meant "flowers kept alive" and that the Ikenobo school of flower arrangement was the oldest and most traditional of all the styles, founded by a priest in the fifteenth century. I was pleased that in Miami, a young city, such an ancient art was being taught.

From the very beginning, I'd loved the class, so much so that it became the highlight of my week. I had such a good time there that I found myself arriving earlier and earlier each time. Just walking in through the back door of the florist's shop to the room where the classes were held put me in a good mood. I loved everything about the place: the smell of the flowers, the assortment of vases waiting to be filled, even the frigid temperature the room was kept so the flowers would stay fresh. An extra bonus to the classes was that I was even able to use some of the Japanese phrases that I had picked up from the crew at the Best Language School and learn new ones as well.

I learned that it took a great deal of work and preparation to create such simplicity. Unlike Western arrangements that used dozens of different colored flowers, the Japanese never used more than a few, each carefully selected, and each having a specific use, meaning, and purpose. For me, in addition to the beauty of the flowers, the calmness and serenity was what made those Saturday morning classes so appealing.

Slowly, during those first few weeks, my life took on an order that I had never before experienced. Although prior to coming to Miami I hadn't exactly led a wild and crazy life, I had never, ever followed such a strict routine, one in which I pretty much knew what I would be doing every hour of the day. I was somewhat surprised to discover that I liked it. Maybe that was why I responded so well to the Japanese way: they had a unique sense of order, in their language, food, art, and culture that greatly appealed to me.

The scary truth, though, was that I was so comfortable with my routine that I was lulled into a false sense of security, thinking that this life would just continue ad infinitum. Soon, though, all of this would come to an end, and I knew that one way or another, I was going to have to pay the piper. But until that day came, I would continue to enjoy it.

Chapter 11

$\mathcal{I}$ was in the kitchen pouring myself a glass of white wine when the phone rang. "Hi, Oona." I recognized her office telephone number on the screen of my cell from previous times when she'd phoned. "How're you doing?"

"The reports I'm getting are that you're making great progress," Oona commented.

"Yes, that's right. Everything is going well," I replied. Although I spoke with Oona regularly, I somehow sensed that this call was different.

"I'd like to come over to your apartment tonight and meet with you. If that's okay with you." My mind immediately jumped to Max. Had I been found out? Oh, God! "If you're not busy, of course," she continued. "I don't want to put you out or anything if you've made plans."

Oona had been unfailingly polite with me in our dealings, but it was unlike her to be so overly solicitous. She knew I didn't have much of a personal life, so it was unlikely she was interrupting anything. The antenna buried deep inside my brain—the one that warned me of imminent danger—had instantly started to whirr, putting me on my guard. My heart started to pound.

Although we'd met on a couple of previous occasions, these times had always been at her office—brief and very businesslike. Just a kind of checking in, to give her updates on how I was doing, and, I suspected, for her to look me over, to see that her money was well spent.

"It'll be nice to see you."

I could hear the faint sounds of papers being moved around. "I have one more meeting at seven o'clock that shouldn't take too long, and then I'm done for the day. Probably get to your place a bit after eight."

Oona would be here in just over an hour. I was still in my workout clothes and wanted to clean up the apartment, although there really wasn't much for me to do, as the place was spotless. After that, I had to take a bath and get dressed. Whatever it was that Oona was coming to tell me—clearly this was not a social visit—I wanted to be properly attired, especially if she were going to confront me with the Max situation. If so, I'd need to feel at my best in every way to deal with it.

I picked up the few things that were lying about—some books, a glass or two, articles of clothing, a couple of DVDs of Japanese movies—and put them all back in their proper places. I would be offering Oona something to drink so I had to set up a mini bar to be ready for whatever she might want. I looked around the living room for the best place to do that, and settled on the corner of the table by the entrance.

I'd not yet had any visitors to the apartment—thank God I hadn't invited Max—so if the subject were to come up, I could be truthful and tell Oona that I'd not entertained anyone there. I began to scrounge around the kitchen for what I needed to set up a respectable bar. I came up with an ice bucket, glasses in assorted shapes and sizes, some bottles of liquor—scotch, Jack Daniel's, gin, vodka, as well as a bottle each of a red and a white wine.

Oona had been drinking Jack Daniel's when I first met her at the Miami Sports Bar, but just to be safe in case she wanted something else, I put out all the bottles that were in the apartment. After setting out the bottles of liquor, and, as she'd had her drink on the rocks, I took out some ice cubes, in case she wanted them. I added a couple each of Cokes, Sprites, Pepsis, tonic, and soda water. Then, as an extra precaution, I cut up some lemons and limes and arranged them on a small silver plate.

I remembered that there was some cheese in the fridge and crackers and nuts in the pantry, and figuring that Oona would surely be hungry after working all day, I laid them all out on a platter. Then, in case she had a hankering for something salty, I opened a bottle of olives and emptied the contents into a small silver bowl. I realized I'd just acted the way my mother and grandmother did whenever we expected company at home. I blinked back tears hard and kept on tidying up the apartment.

After finishing, I stepped back to admire my preparations. It struck me that I had carefully assembled so many things, both alcoholic and nonalcoholic, that it seemed as if I were expecting to host a huge party. It was clear I'd gone way overboard in my preparations, but at that point it was too late to start all over again and scale down. I took one more look around the living room, and only when I was fully satisfied did I begin to get myself ready.

I told myself not to feel silly for having done all I had for Oona's visit, that it was better to be overprepared than underprepared. The last thing I needed was for her to watch me as I scrambled around to find whatever it was to serve her a drink. I wanted to have her see me as cool and calm, a com-

petent hostess, and that she would realize I'd made an effort
to make her feel welcome.

Oona had certainly not struck me as the Martha Stew-
art type of homemaker, but out of the office setting, or in a
bar, she just might turn out to be one, so I wanted to be
prepared for that possibility. Back in the bedroom, I took
off my dirty workout clothes and put them in the hamper.
Then, naked, I walked into the bathroom, and started running the water for a bath. As I lay back in the tub, completely
immersed in the rose-scented, scalding-hot water, I began
to go through the different reasons Oona might have chosen
that particular evening to meet with me. I was in the fifth
week of my training, and, although I knew for sure that I
was really making progress, I felt I still had a long way to
go before being sent out to fulfill my duties as Oona's edge.
Surely she wasn't coming over to tell me that she wanted
me to start. At the same time, she'd said on the phone
that all the feedback she'd received said I was doing very
well, so the visit couldn't be because I was falling short of
expectations. I couldn't come up with a good reason for
Oona coming to see me; I would just have to wait and see
what she wanted.

I did hope, though, that she wasn't coming to personally
tell me that my setup was going to be changed. I liked the
way my life was arranged, even if the healthy lifestyle I was
leading was like that of an older person's—but I was content.
After all the turmoil of my life with Fred, there was a lot to be
said for having the peace of mind which comes from following a set routine, free from worry.

And, of course, there was the increasingly important
matter of Max. It was surprising that even though I had only
met with the man on several occasions, all of them quite

innocent, he had taken an increasingly important role in my life. Apart from my Japanese classmates, with whom I could only sort of communicate, Max was the only person outside the O'Ryan operation that I interacted with on a social level. So why did I feel guilty about Max when there was absolutely nothing to feel guilty about? I knew the answer to that, of course: Although it had not yet become physical, I was having an affair with Max, breaking the number-one rule that Oona had laid down.

I loved his personality—smart, witty and confident; his looks— tall, dark and handsome—were not too shabby, either. He was charming, but not so smooth that he seemed too practiced at it. I particularly admired the way he treated people, especially the ones who worked for him, from the bus boys to the maître-d'.

I stayed in the bathtub until the last possible moment then reluctantly eased my body out of the water and dried off. Next, I walked over to the closet, to see what I would wear for the occasion. After looking at my clothes, I contemplated which of the outfits that Stacy had chosen for me would be most appropriate. In the end, though, I decided that I would just choose whatever I would be the most comfortable in.

I put on a pair of khaki cargo pants, a black cotton T-shirt, and sneakers. After getting dressed, I combed my hair then braided it. I decided that I would not wear much makeup, but I did spray on lots of Chanel No 5. It suddenly hit me that I'd chosen to wear exactly the same outfit I'd worn on that long-ago night at the Miami Sports Bar when I first met Oona.

Less than five minutes later, the intercom buzzed, and Paolo, the Brazilian concierge, announced that a Ms. O'Ryan had arrived and was on her way up. I checked my reflection one more time in the mirror in the bathroom, made a couple of unnecessary minor adjustments, and then walked back into the living room

"Magnolia! It's wonderful to see you!" Oona bounded out of the elevator, and as she had done that first time in the office, took me in her arms and kissed me on both cheeks. "You look more beautiful than ever!" Oona had never been this openly demonstrative before. My survival skills kicked in and instantly placed me on my guard. Oh, God! What did she want from me? Was she going to hit on me? Was that why she was coming to see me in the apartment, so we could have privacy? Oona knew I did not like women sexually, but was she there to give me a trial run, to see if I could do something that went against my nature? Oh God, I hoped not.

Needless to say, Oona was wearing a suit. I'd never seen her dressed in anything but a suit—she probably slept in one. That night, Oona was wearing a silver-colored dress and jacket outfit that hit just to her knees. She had on high-heeled sandals that showed toes that were perfectly pedicured, the color matching her manicure. She had on the same pearl necklace and earrings that I had noticed on my first visit to her office. Oona was immaculately made up, as usual, but her hair seemed a bit lighter colored, a touch shorter, which framed her face beautifully and made her seem younger.

I led her into the apartment. Her eyes were taking it all in, not missing anything. "Have you been here before?" I was curious to know. She had told me the apartment belonged to a client of the firm, so it was probable that she had.

"A long time ago." Oona walked over to the sliding glass doors that led out to the terrace. "Quite a view, eh, Magnolia?"

Suddenly, I remembered my manners. "Oona, sorry,

what a terrible hostess you must think I am! I forgot to offer
you anything to drink." I was jumpy, no question about it. I
hurried over to the table where I had set up the bar. "What
would you like?"

"Just some Jack, over ice, thanks." Oona took in the
spread I had prepared. She watched as I opened the bottle
of Jack Daniel's and poured a generous amount over some ice
cubes. I handed her the glass and waited until she had taken
a couple of sips, then poured myself a glass of white wine
from the bottle that was chilling in the ice bucket. Glasses in
hand, we walked over to the sitting area.

We took our seats on the couch, a respectable distance
apart, and once we were settled, Oona asked, "No regrets
about having agreed to accept my offer to work for me?"

I sensed that she was testing me. Although I'd had
a number of conversations with her, those had mostly
been about practical matters—classes, finances, etc.—
and never about how I felt about my role or whether I had
second thoughts.

"No regrets," I hurried to assure her. "Everything is going
pretty well. I'm working hard, as you know."

"Good. That's good." Oona nodded appreciatively. "Okay,
then." She took a sip of her drink. "Next week, as you know,
your classes end. Señor Ramos has given glowing reports
about your progress; he says you're quite fluent in Spanish. He also said he was going to charge me a bit more for
your classes, because you've picked up two languages while
you were studying there. Japanese, huh? That's pretty good.
There are a lot of Japanese athletes out there, you know,
Magnolia, who need representation. Baseball players, golf-
ers... " Oona's eyes positively sparkled at the thought.

I shouldn't have been surprised that Mr. Ramos

reported on my progress in his class to Oona—after all, she was the one paying the bills. Still, I had to admit, I was a bit disillusioned to hear about it, especially when I'd considered my interest in the Japanese language to be private. I suppose I was naïve to think I could keep my personal life just that way: private and personal. How long had Señor Ramos been giving Oona reports about me? And how had Oona explained the nature of our relationship? Perhaps more important, what else did Oona know about me, I wondered? Was Oona aware of the fact that I'd developed a friendship with Mr. Tanaka and my other classmates? I hoped that wasn't so. And Simone, the Miami madam? Did she know about her as well?

"Dr. Bernstein has informed me that in his professional opinion, it is appropriate that the formal part of your sessions with him be concluded. He says that you are very bright, a good and eager student, a quick learner, so you've achieved what I asked him to teach you. You've become a sports psychologist without having had to go to college for it. I think the idea you had about using props and going to venues with clients is nothing short of brilliant, one that will work out very well and that the clients will be very appreciative of your creativity. A happy client is one that performs well in competition, as we are all very aware." Oona smiled approvingly at me. "Dr. Bernstein asked me to be sure to tell you that you're more than welcome to consult with him as needed, that he's always happy to meet with you." From the light, almost breezy tone of Oona's voice, I picked up that Dr. Bernstein hadn't divulged my confidences, for which I was relieved.

I was sorry to hear that my regular meetings with Dr. Bernstein were over; I had come to look forward to our sessions and I was actually beginning to consider him a friend. More importantly, I had come to rely on him for advice and guidance, limited as it was. I would have liked to have personally said good-bye to him and thanked him for his help. Maybe in a few weeks I could request a few sessions with him, and he might break down and give me advice about how to deal with my family. Just a thought.

"Brandi too," Oona said. "As well as the rest of the crew that's been working with you—they all think you've come so far that you're at the point where you could continue doing what you've been doing on your own."

Suddenly, what I had deep down suspected, but hadn't wanted to acknowledge, became pretty obvious. Oona, smart lawyer that she was, had personally come to see me in an informal, relaxed setting, to make sure the glowing reports weren't exaggerated. And now she had seen for herself that they were all true. I'd taken as much advantage of my training as there was to be had. I couldn't believe it was over—and so suddenly. What now?

"Wonderful," I repeated, feeling a bit numb. "Very nice of them."

"Sorry to bring up an unpleasant subject, but I don't think I can avoid it."

Here it was: She knew about Max.

"What's that, Oona?" I somehow managed to ask.

"Well, before you start working, you have to have a full medical checkup. I have to know my clients won't get any kind of diseases from you—any kind at all—I have to be able to tell them that."

I was so relieved at hearing that the unpleasant subject that she was bringing up was that I had to go for a full checkup, that, at that point, I would have agreed to have a colonoscopy, that most dreaded of exams. Max was safe! I was still in control of one part of my life.

Oona was staring at me, waiting for an answer. "I have no problem with that—a physical is fine. I haven't had one in years, so it'll be good to do."

"I'll have Anita set it up, and give you the details of where you have to go and when. She'll make all the appointments." Oona stood up to leave. "Oh, last thing before I forget, now that you're ready to start. Remember the part of the agreement about not having personal relationships with men, clients or otherwise." She headed towards the front door then turned to me. "You committed to that. You assured me that you would not be with any men, other than the clients, of course. Especially after you're checked out by the doctor."

"I remember, Oona," I assured her.

"Thanks for the drink. I'll be in touch." Oona opened the door and let herself out.

I stood behind the door and pressed my ear to it, not moving until I heard the elevator doors open and close. The clock was ticking; the physical was bringing me one step closer to having to live up to my part of the bargain with Oona. I was living on borrowed time, and I knew it.

My heart pounding, I ran to my cell phone and punched in the first number on speed dial. "Max? It's Magnolia. How are you?" I didn't wait for him to answer before continuing. "Feel like having some company?"

Chapter 12

Oona, savvy woman that she was, said she would choose my first client carefully to break me in gently. After investing so much time, money, and energy into me, the last thing she wanted was for me to get spooked by some three-hundred-pound pumped-up linebacker with "backne" who got off on S&M kind of sex.

I was in the best shape of my life. My blood pressure was so low it was almost in single digits; my cholesterol barely registered; the EKG test that was administered showed that I was so fit that I could compete with any Olympian. I was, of course, thrilled with the results. It wasn't that I'd thought I had any kind of sexually transmitted disease—unless I picked up something from a toilet seat, I was clean; it had been my blood pressure I had been worried about. The doctor renewed my birth control prescription, which was about to run out.

I had a lot on my plate. Not only was I living a secret life, one that I was hiding from my family (the calls home were incredibly stressful for me), but I also had a secret boyfriend (Max, of course, who did not know what I was doing either). How long would I be able to keep up the pretenses with all these people? I had always thought of myself as being an open, truthful person, but those days were clearly behind me.

The fact that so far I'd been able to compartmentalize my life so successfully did give me pause, but I didn't want to get too introspective. I had committed to Oona, and I would continue to do so.

In the gym, I'd become friendly with Simone. Simone was very open about what she did, and listening to her tell her stories, I would be reminded of the need for the services of those who practiced the world's oldest profession. The reality was that after my first encounter, I would be a bona fide member of that august group. As Groucho Marx once famously declared, "I wouldn't want to belong to any club that would have me as a member."

One day I summoned up some courage and told Simone what I was going to be doing for a living. She wasn't surprised at all; instead, she smiled and looked at me with total understanding. After respective grueling workouts at the gym, Simone would occasionally invite me to go grab a cup of coffee and talk about our lives in a more relaxing environment, which I really enjoyed.

The first time we met outside the gym, we sat in the far corner table at the neighborhood Starbucks to avoid any unnecessary attention. Simone saw the conflict in my eyes, grabbed my hand, and assured me that there's nothing wrong with the profession that I had chosen. "Oh, sweet darling." She took a sip of her bitter black coffee. "I am so glad you told me. I know how hard it is to be in such business on your own, leading a double life. But to be content with your decision to do what you agreed to do, you have to stop burdening yourself with all that guilt. Think of it as business. It's all that is—business. You like sex, don't you?"

I nodded like a four-year-old. "Yes, I do."

"So what's the problem then, Magnolia?" said Simone.

"You like sex and I assume you like money. Doing this will help you achieve your goal with the kids and the art. Put the two together and you've got a perfect job." She laughed. "Darling, if the thought of being an escort still scares you, think of yourself as an actress and a therapist. Because that's what you are and that what you will be doing—acting and curing athletes' damaged psyches so they can perform on the field to the best of their abilities. Tell yourself stories about the situation and then act on them. Pretend you're competing for an Oscar. The rest, the sex act, is just a formality."

It was a huge relief for me to hear Simone speak that way; it matched what Dr. Bernstein had counseled me to do. The irony that Dr. Bernstein, with all his degrees, and Simone, a madam who was basically self-educated, agreed on what the approach would be in my encounters with Oona's clients did not escape me. I still worried about not being able to deliver what was expected of me, but Simone, as had Dr. Bernstein, once again assured me that I would do just fine. After a bit more chitchat, I gave her a big kiss on the cheek and waved good-bye. I felt as if I had made my second friend in Miami: Mr. Tanaka was my first.

Five days after visiting me at the apartment, Oona called me into her office to give me a briefing on my first client: discuss his background, the reason why he needed my services, and what he hoped to accomplish as a result of my meeting with him. Oona, who in her former role as a criminal defense attorney had coached so many of her clients for depositions and trials, was very aware of the value of preparation. She needed to see for herself that I was ready for that critical first encounter.

My first client was to be a Mr. Preston Waddington Stoddington II, a competitive yachtsman from Newport, Rhode

Island, who had been represented by Oona for the past three years. Oona had repeatedly made it very clear that she was very fond of this man.

Preston was a world-class sailor; at one point he'd been captain of a yacht that won the America's Cup race—very successful and much in demand for his formidable skills. Although he was doing extremely well in his professional life, his personal life was in a shambles. Oona reported that a few months ago, Preston's wife Sofia, also an accomplished sailor in her own right, who normally competed on the same boats as he did, had left him.

It would have been bad enough that she'd walked out on him and their three children, but to add insult to injury, she left him for another woman—Samantha, a sailor on another racing boat. And not just that, but it had been the spectacular way Sofia made her exit that hurt so badly and was so humiliating. During a race, at a moment when the Stoddingtons' yacht and Samantha's veered so close on the high seas that their bows almost touched, Sofia had jumped from Preston's yacht onto her lover's, waving good-bye to him when she landed on the deck.

The story of how Sofia left Preston spread like wild-fire, not surprising considering that the community of sailors at that competitive level is very small. Although no one made any comments to Preston about it, he sensed, correctly, that his fellow sailors were laughing at him behind his back. The majority of sailors at that elite level are male, men who feel that women have no place in competitive sailing. The conventional opinion was that Preston deserved what happened with his wife and Sam.

For the first few weeks after Sofia walked out on him—or, rather, jumped ship—Preston told Oona that he'd been convinced that she would realize that she'd made a mistake, that she was straight, a wife and mother, and being involved with another woman was only a short-lived rebellion, something to add excitement to her life. After all, Sofia had married very young, at nineteen, and had had three children before her thirtieth birthday, a milestone she was facing in a month, so she had never really sowed any wild oats. In Oona's opinion, that was what was happening now.

The hurt that Preston felt at his wife's leaving was beginning to turn to anger and that anger, according to Oona, was affecting his professional judgment. Oona told me that in the three years that she had represented Preston, she had always found her client to be a calm, gentle individual, one who thought things through before speaking, and that when he did so, it was in a measured, low tone of voice. Since Sofia left him, though, the change in Preston's personality and character had been startling. Gone was the nice, sweet, gentlemanly fellow, and in his place was a thoroughly unpleasant, bitter man, someone to avoid.

There was no room for someone who was so nasty and surly in the close quarters of a yacht. Lately, though, to make matters worse, Preston's professional judgment was beginning to come into question, and he had made some mistakes, blatant miscalculations during the course of two races. The most serious of those had taken place at sea during a race between the yacht he was skippering and the one that Sofia and Sam were on. According to eyewitness reports, Preston had executed some maneuvers that placed his yacht and crew at risk. There were no second chances during a race in the high seas with boats going at high rates of speed, so this did not go unnoticed.

Oona's plan was to have me go with Preston to a spa

resort where he knew Sofia and Sam were having their beauty rest, and act all lovey-dovey with him in front of them. I was to put on the public display of affection of all time, including touching Preston inappropriately, if necessary, laying it on to the point where we would come close to being arrested for lewd behavior. I, personally, thought the whole plan sounded very junior high, but Oona assured me that it would work.

From what I could tell this first encounter was going to be an easy one. No "real" sex involved, just some heavy petting. Given that, I was not about to jeopardize it by volunteering my opinion as to how I didn't think this stood a chance in hell of working. Plus, as I had no better plan of my own, it wasn't as if I could offer an alternative suggestion. I decided that a much better strategy was to establish early on that I was a team player and agree to do everything that they had planned, and do it to the best of my abilities.

I was quite nervous waiting for Preston in the lobby of the hotel where we were supposed to meet. As he drove up in his sports car to pick me up to go to the resort together, I was so very grateful that he was sort of attractive, making my job of hanging all over him much easier. Preston was tall and slim, with expressive dark brown eyes and wavy chestnut hair that was going a bit gray. He was nicely dressed, too, in khaki pants, a white open-necked shirt that showed off his deep tan, and a navy blue blazer. He looked exactly like what he was: a yachtsman. I'm sure other women would have found him quite good-looking, but his appearance did nothing for me—not that there was anything negative about him, but he just wasn't my type.

Recalling Simone's advice about having to be an actress, I decided that in order to be able to successfully convince Sofia that I found her husband irresistible, I needed a scenario, a motivation that would allow me to throw myself with wanton abandon at him. I pretended Preston was a money-man, a banker, who was in a position to give me the cash I needed to fund my cherished project.

So as not to seem like total strangers, on the short ride to the resort where we would be seeing his wife, we chatted a bit about ourselves. As we spoke, I was relieved to see that Preston was as businesslike as I was, equally determined that the plan be successful. If he was attracted to me, he sure didn't show it; he was totally focused on Sofia. On the drive to the spa resort, we had also, naturally enough, gone over the plan, so by the time Preston gave his car to the valet to park, we were a couple, or at least I had worked myself up to the point that I was a woman in lust.

At the resort, Preston and I checked in at the front desk, where we were shown up to our suite. Once there, we got out of our street clothes, and put on bathing suits: boxy, dark green cotton Brooks Brothers–type suit with a short-sleeved white shirt on top for Preston; a bright red strapless bandeau bikini with see-through silver cover-up for me.

Once back downstairs, we headed for the pool area where Preston had said that Sofia would be; apparently, it was her new hangout place. As we waited for the cabana boy to show us to our lounges, I discreetly looked around the place. Preston was becoming noticeably nervous, so I decided we should order a couple of much-needed drinks before taking our places by the pool. Drinks in hand, we made our way to our assigned chaise longues under a palm tree. The place was completely packed with gorgeous women who looked like they'd just finished a photo shoot for the Sports Illustrated swimsuit edition. Other equally attractive but less athletic looking ones were lounging around, sipping on their cocktails.

Preston spotted his wife in the shaded area of the far corner of the pool deck. I could feel him freeze next to me. I quickly glanced over and saw that Sofia, wearing a minuscule white bikini, was stretched out languidly on a chaise longue, occasionally taking sips from a brightly colored drink with an umbrella on it. She was animatedly chatting away with another woman, who, by the intimate way they acted with each other, could only be Samantha. Preston was close to losing his composure.

"Keep it cool," I murmured in his ear. "If you want to get her back, you have got to pretend as if she is not even here. Let Sofia notice you first."

We sat on our chairs, holding hands and whispering to each other like two teenagers in love. As I did so, I was pleasantly surprised how easily behaving this way came to me, especially with a man I was not particularly attracted to. Every so often, I would discreetly glance over my shoulder to see what Sofia was doing. She had definitely noticed Preston, but it was not hard to see that she did not want to acknowledge his presence or the presence of his new fling.

I decided it was time to move things along, so I leaned over and kissed Preston on the lips as provocatively as I could to see if Sofia would react. She didn't. I did it again, this time kissing him longer. Conspicuously ignoring us, Sofia suddenly whispered something to Samantha, then stood up, and, after wrapping a beach towel around her body, sarong style, marched inside. A moment later, Samantha followed her.

Preston pulled away from me. "What do you think? Did this work? Is she leaving for good, or just going inside for a while? Can you see what they're doing?"

"Preston, stop worrying. Let's see what happens next." And for good measure, just in case Sofia was watching from inside the clubhouse, I kissed him again. "Maybe she's jealous. Jealousy is good. It means she still cares for you."

Preston was not responding to my advances in a way that was believable. It was time to change tactics. I decided that we should follow Sofia inside and get in her face. We went in and found his wife and her girlfriend getting cozy, sitting on one of the couches by the entrance to the restaurant, holding each other's hands and laughing at their own little inside jokes. Seeing Sofia behave in such manner made Preston very angry and he started clenching his jaw as his cheeks slowly turned bright pink. Bad, bad move on Preston's part, I thought, to make it so obvious that Sofia was getting to him.

"I'm hungry." I pulled his arm. "Let's get a table, and have something to eat." I headed toward the maître d' stand, and once there, requested a nice table for two by the window.

The first thing Preston did once we were seated was to ask for the wine list, and after deciding on a bottle of white wine, he ordered a couple of lobsters. I wasted no time before beginning to touch Preston in an inappropriate manner: I put my hand under the table and started stroking his thigh, flipping my hair and quietly moaning as if in pleasure. Surprisingly, Preston composed himself, and played along beautifully, responding quite nicely to my advances. He grabbed me by my neck and pulled me toward him for a kiss. I didn't resist, and enthusiastically kissed him back. Throwing a quick glance at Sofia, I noticed her staring in our direction, clearly annoyed, as she completely ignored Samantha.

We drank the wine, ordering a second bottle, laughing and enjoying ourselves. The lobsters were delicious. All the time, we kept touching each other, flirting openly. I have to admit, I was having fun.

After a while, Sofia had had enough of seeing me paw her husband—I was all over him like a cheap suit (thank God, I didn't know too many people in Miami; I would never, ever in a million years have acted that way in Minneapolis) and out of the corner of my eye, I saw that she got up and was headed for our table. We, of course, acted as if we hadn't seen her, and happily continued to feel each other up. Sofia, tall and muscular and tan, the female equivalent of her husband, stood in front of us, face purple in anger, fists clenched, so furious that I thought she would explode. We continued to pretend that we hadn't noticed her, which made her even angrier. She huffed and puffed around us but soon walked away. I kept catching glimpses of her as we went about our business of groping each other.

"I say we go to our suite right now, honey, for dessert? We can order room service," Preston suggested, speaking in a loud voice.

The man was good. "Good idea, babe." I stood up. I was proud of Preston for coming up with the plan. All this posing and constant flirting was getting to me, and I was ready to stop. Back at the suite, Preston, still nervous, popped a bottle of champagne and poured both of us a glass to celebrate our performance. I definitely needed a drink. As we sipped, we heard a knock on the door. It was one of the porters from downstairs, holding a note he had been instructed to deliver to Preston. Preston thanked him, then, after tipping him, he took the note and shut the door behind him.

Preston read it out loud: "Preston, you son of a bitch! How could you do this to me? Meet me outside in the parking lot right now!—Love, Sofia"

Preston rushed into the bathroom, brushed his teeth, and fixed his hair. After checking himself out in the mirror, without saying a word to me, he dashed outside. I followed after him, curious to see what would happen. Although, naturally, I was not sure how Sofia would respond to Preston, I had not expected her to react in such a manner—a note seemed so old-fashioned. I thought maybe she would have sent a text, confronted him in a heated manner, something along those lines. My curiosity was getting the better of me, and I decided I would watch to see what would happen.

Once downstairs in the lobby, I looked through the floor-to-ceiling bay window and saw that Sofia was yelling at Preston. He stood there like a naughty teenage boy being scolded by his mother and took it all, but I could see that he was happy. Sofia was so wound up that she finished by giving him a good slap across the face for disrespecting her by acting that way. It was all quite entertaining, really, but I could see that these two still really loved each other. After all, if she hadn't cared for him, she would have just ignored him.

Preston then grabbed Sofia as he had grabbed me at the restaurant and gave her a big smooch on the lips. She was angry but couldn't resist kissing him back. The two of them started passionately making out in front of everybody, completely forgetting those around them. After fifteen minutes of grabbing and kissing and back-and-forth yelling, Preston and Sofia took off in his fancy sports car, Sam clearly forgotten.

I have to say, I was quite pleased with myself. I had started this first assignment with a bit of a rocky performance, but it had thankfully ended as intended. I was drained after the day's show, so, once back at the suite, after having packed the few clothes I had brought with me, I phoned downstairs and requested for the concierge to call a taxi. I waited in the lobby for it to arrive, a bit nervous in case I was to run into Samantha, but, thankfully, she was nowhere around.

I was so happy to get back home that I almost kissed the floor of the entranceway to my apartment upon my return.

Once safely inside, I took off my dress, the first of the outfits that Stacy had picked out for me for this assignment and carefully hung it up. I also put the shoes and the purse into their assigned boxes. Stacy was obsessive-compulsive when it came to clothes, and I knew she'd have a fit if I did not take the proper care of them.

Next, I went into the bathroom, and started to run a bath. Although I was bone-tired—this first encounter had physically, mentally, and emotionally exhausted me—I was too wired to go to sleep. I knew a scalding hot bath with rose oil would relax me as well as cleanse me of the day's activities.

Lately, it seemed as if I had been taking more and more baths. True, the bathtub in the apartment was magnificent, but I knew it went deeper than that; I didn't only use it because I was physically dirty. The importance of water for a Catholic could never be overemphasized: at birth, we were baptized by having water poured over our heads; during the course of our lives, while entering or leaving a church, we would cross ourselves with holy water from fonts there; the priests who were celebrating Mass would sprinkle us with holy water during processions; and, at death, we would be anointed with it, to prepare us to go to meet our Savior.

As I soaked in the tub, I thought back on the evening; I was realistic enough to know that I wasn't going to get off so easily in the future. I had been very, very fortunate that the encounter with Preston hadn't resulted in my having to have sex with him. All I'd had to do was to put on a good show, not that difficult, really. I was grateful to Oona for having planned it that way. I'd passed the test. Now the real work would begin.

Sometimes, when I thought about the agreement that I had made with Oona, I was more convinced than ever that, in a kind of perverse way, it might have been because I'd met Max that I'd been able to do what I had promised. Although, obviously, Max didn't know what my life was really like, still, he'd been so very supportive of me.

And to turn the tables around: What if Max found out what I did for Oona? There was a huge difference between thinking your girlfriend had graduated with a degree in art history and was taking Spanish lessons while living in her parents' friends' apartment and one who was a high-priced call girl who specialized in servicing professional athletes. So far, I'd not had sex with a client, but that would soon change. It had to.

I replayed all that had taken place at the resort earlier that night, and decided that it had not been all that difficult to get it on with a man I had met five minutes earlier—even if it hadn't ended in sex. It had been so much easier to get into the role than I had anticipated. Maybe I'd be able to manage to deliver after all.

Chapter 13

*T*he loud ringing of the phone woke me from a sound sleep. As I listened to the shrill, piercing sound, I cursed that although I had turned off my cell, I'd forgotten to switch off the landline last night.

"Magnolia!" Oona's voice boomed over the bedside phone so loudly that I had to hold the receiver a few inches away from my ear. "I just got off the phone with Preston—Sofia is back home. He's beside himself with happiness. According to him, you were responsible for that, my dear." Oona's words came out all in a rush. "Preston didn't give me all the details of what happened. He just kept repeating that you're the best. The absolute fucking best! Magnolia, I am so proud of you! You've got a real talent!"

"Thank you, Oona," I managed to reply. "That's nice to hear."

I opened one eye, turned my head, and looked over at the clock to see what time it was. Eleven o'clock! I immediately opened the other eye to make sure I had read the numbers correctly. I hadn't slept that late since I'd split up with Fred. I had slept almost twelve hours. I must have been way more tired and stressed out than I had thought.

"You're being modest—it's terrific." Oona must have realized that she was in danger of sounding like some kind of over-caffeinated out-of-control lawyer, so she took a deep breath. "I have to tell you, thanks to you, for the first time in months Preston sounds like his old self."

"That's good. Hopefully, things will continue to work out between them." I was pleased that Oona called to tell me that my first encounter had been a success and took it as a sign that she had called me to tell me the good news right away, on the very next morning. Preston and Sofia must have had a hell of a reconciliation after leaving the resort together.

"Well, seeing as how you did so well with Preston, are you ready for another client?" Oona ventured. "I have someone who needs your help."

"Of course." I tried to sound excited. "I'm ready whenever you need my services. Just give me the details."

"I'll have Anita call you right away to give you that information. Remember, if you have any questions or concerns please don't hesitate for one minute to call me. I'll be in touch soon. Bye." Oona sounded beside herself with excitement, a trait I had not seen before.

Less than one half hour later my phone rang again. "Magnolia, this is Anita. Oona asked me to call you with your next assignment." Anita spoke in an abrupt manner, not bothering to hide that speaking with me was an unpleasant part of her job; the feeling was mutual.

"Yes, Oona told me you would be contacting me," I replied as sweetly as I could. Then, just for good measure, I could not resist adding, "So, Anita, how've you been? It's been a while since we last spoke—hope you've been well."

"Yes, well, I'm fine. Now, to get back to business," she replied.

I grabbed one of the notebooks that I had earlier placed

by the telephone and a pen and began to take notes. Anita informed me that my next encounter would be with a certain Pietr Romanov, a very popular, highly successful Russian ice skater who had broken the very lucrative two-year contract he had just signed with Super Stars on Ice, a touring company consisting of mostly former Olympic medalists. The promoter who had brokered the deal was suing Pietr, his partner Natasha, and even Oona for enormous sums of money.

Not yet being able to tell what was relevant, I pretty much wrote down everything Anita was saying. Soon, I had filled pages of the notebook, jotting all the information down so fast that I hoped I could read my handwriting afterwards.

According to what Anita told me, everything had been going well when, two months ago during a sold-out performance at Madison Square Garden in New York, while completing a spectacular, but very risky move, his signature lift, Pietr had dropped Natasha, his longtime partner, injuring her so badly that it ended her career. Her right hip had shattered, and if she were ever to walk normally again, she would need to have it replaced.

Natasha, of course, knew that accidents were part of the danger that skaters at their level risked, so she did not blame her friend and long-time partner for her injuries. As a matter of fact, she even claimed that she had been thinking of retiring—she and her husband wanted to start a family—and took her fall as a sign that now was the time to do it.

In spite of her repeated reassurances that it hadn't been his fault, Pietr still blamed himself for the accident. What had happened to Natasha had so deeply affected Pietr that he had been unable to return to the ice as a professional skater. According to Anita, my assignment was to restore Pietr's self-confidence so he could skate in public again. It went without saying that then he would be able to fulfill his contracts and the lawsuits dropped.

To make sure I clearly understood problem with Pietr, I asked Anita a few questions of my own; I had been successful with Preston, but I couldn't afford to screw up my second assignment. There was one very important question I needed answered: whether she was positive that Pietr was straight. I hated to typecast male ice skaters, but I had to be very sure of that one vital detail. Anita assured me that Pietr was straight and not just straight—he was infamous in the professional skating circles as being quite a womanizer.

Pietr was scheduled to be in New York for the next two days, and would be coming to Miami directly after that, which was when I should be ready to meet with him. She instructed me to call her as soon as I had figured out a plan to fix the skater's problem, explaining that she needed to know when and where the encounter with him would take place, so she could pass on that information to Pietr; it was her responsibility to make sure that he arrived at wherever it was that I would be meeting with him.

Yesterday, in Preston's case, the plan for getting back his wife had been laid out for me, and even though I had disagreed with it, the truth was that it had worked. This morning, however, Anita's parting words made it crystal clear that from now on I was going to have to come up with my own plan to satisfy/please/cure whatever it was that Oona's clients needed.

For the next two days all I could do was to think about how the hell I was going to get the Russian back on the fucking ice. To complicate matters, the man barely spoke any English, nor did he speak Spanish, nor, dare I say it, Japanese, which meant that whatever plan I would come up with could not involve any kind of conversation. The only break I took was to go to the Spanish Rose and grab a quick bite, as well as see Max, of course. I wasn't with him much, as he was preoccupied with a corporate group that had rented out the back part of the restaurant. Still, it was nice to be able to spend even a few minutes with him.

By the morning of the third day, I had an epiphany: I figured out how to get Pietr back in the rink and on the ice. As I worked out the details, all I could do was to thank God that I had grown up in Minneapolis, that year-round winter wonderland, a place where kids learned to skate before they could walk.

I decided that I would try out the kind of plan that I had discussed with Dr. Bernstein, where I would use props from a client's sport and arrange for the encounter to take place in the type of venue where he competed. My plan involved finding an empty skating rink that could be rented for a few hours, no easy feat in tropical Miami. The props I would use were few but pricey: a mink coat, a sable blanket (I tried not to think of the reaction of the PETA people), a couple of bottles of vodka, some brown bread, and close to a pound of caviar. Anita had the job of rounding all of that up–which, in all fairness, she did brilliantly.

My props prepared, I was surprisingly calm as I waited for Pietr at the assigned rink on the night he arrived in Miami. Pietr greeted me with a cautious and wary, almost suspicious, air, barely shook my hand, just nodding his head. As I didn't know what Oona had told him about me and my role, I could not be sure whether that was his normal attitude, or just toward this encounter. As I looked him over, it occurred to me that the skater looked like he could have been Dr. Zhivago's twin—tall, dark, and brooding—he was definitely not gay.

I'd always been attracted to anything to do with Russia. In college I had taken several Russian literature courses, and with his Slavic, chiseled cheeks, million-mile stare, and melancholic air, Pietr certainly looked the part of the main character in a novel by Dostoyevsky or Tolstoy. Thankfully, I found him to be appealing, something that would make my job significantly easier. After checking me out, he dropped the wary attitude and began smiling and winking at me.

To break the ice (ha!), predictably, we first drank some vodka, a Russian tradition. After that, as we ate the caviar, we drank some more. Then, naked under the mink coat, vodka shot in hand, visions of Dr. Zhivago dancing around my brain, I coaxed Pietr, slipping and sliding (I hadn't skated in a while) out onto the ice. The vodka must have affected me more than I had thought, for at that point I became convinced that Pietr was going to absolutely love what I planned to do with him, so much so that he would never be frightened about getting out on the ice again.

I had really thought that this moment—having sex with a total stranger—was going to be a life-changing experience for me, one that I'd dreaded, but it was surprisingly smooth and easy, almost natural. The vodka clearly helped, and the time with Pietr went by really fast, faster than I had thought possible, so I did not really have much of an opportunity to analyze it. I just lived it, powering through.

The truth was that the sex with Pietr that night in the empty rink hadn't been all that weird. Maybe it had been the vodka, maybe it had been that I was so fucking freezing that I hardly felt anything. Whatever the reason, if I were to be brutally honest with myself, being paid to have sex with

a complete stranger who was quite attractive—the fact that
he was Russian surely helped—hadn't been anywhere as
difficult as I'd feared. Pietr was actually quite sexy; he knew
exactly what to do and when to do it. It could be my imagination, but I could have sworn he smelled like gooseberries. I
recognized the scent because my Russian literature professor in college used to make a type of tea with it.

It could also be that I didn't feel dirty about what I was
doing was because I'd come up with a scenario in which I
could playact, just as I had done with Preston. In Pietr's case,
my obsession with the book Doctor Zhivago came in handy.
At certain times during the night, I had closed my eyes and
pretended that I was living in the Russia of a hundred years
ago, conjuring up images of Omar Sharif as Dr. Zhivago,
with me playing both roles of Geraldine Chaplin as his wife,
and Julie Christie as his mistress. I couldn't deny, of course,
that the vodka (and gooseberries) helped, as did the sensual
feel of the sable coat on which we lay. Pietr's English was
rudimentary at best, so perhaps our not being able to have
any sort of communication helped with the illusion that we
were in Russia.

Not exactly surprising, Pietr was amazingly acrobatic. I
wasn't sure if he was trying to impress me or if he was doing
it to keep his muscles warm, but he executed several breathtaking moves, ones that I recognized from years of taking
skating lessons. He began with a spread eagle, went on to do
a sit spin followed by a butterfly jump, and ended the brief
but passionate performance with a back flip. I was unused
to being with a man who could fold and mold his body into
countless positions without exertion. And, probably because
he was used to moving his partners around, Pietr was easily
able to place me into poses that would guarantee the fullest

satisfaction for both of us.

Pietr, experienced womanizer that he was, saved the best for last. While we were lying naked on the sable blanket, touching each other, he surprised me by sliding his index finger on the ice for a few moments, and then, once it was the desired temperature, shoving it inside me. I moaned as his icy cold hand pleasured me in a surprisingly effective way. I was about to reach the peak of my orgasm, but I knew I had to stop no matter how good it felt. I was there to get Pietr back in the rink, so it was time for me to take charge. When conjuring up a plan for the encounter with Pietr, I had consulted the Internet and read up on the sport, so I could familiarize myself with the finer aspects of ice-skating. My research had not limited to simply Internet research; I'd also contacted an individual who was in a position to give me first-hand information.

My best friend back in Minneapolis, Lindsay Pears, had been a very talented ice skater, so much so that she had a real shot at competing in the Olympics. For years, she had lived and breathed the sport, dedicating countless hours to practicing and then competing. Unfortunately, her dream was shattered when, during the spring of our second year of college, she had gone to a fraternity party and, after having been over-served of the punch that the "brothers" had concocted, had woken up, naked, on one of their beds. A few discrete inquiries were made, and not surprisingly, no one claimed to have any knowledge of what had transpired. For her part, Lindsay, deeply embarrassed at her behavior, had not pursued the matter any further. Being a staunch Catholic, she had gone ahead with the pregnancy that had resulted from the encounter, and nine months later, she had given birth to a lovely daughter, whom she named Lydia.

If I wanted to know anything about ice-skating, Lindsay was my "go to" person. I picked up the phone and punched in her number. I spoke with her at least once a week, so it wasn't unusual that I'd be calling. Still, I had to be very, very careful in what I disclosed to her as to the reason why I needed the kind of information I was seeking. Lindsay had known me all my life, so she'd spot if I were deceiving her in a minute.

"Hey, Linds. How are you?"

"Hey yourself, Magnolia! Nice to hear your voice again. How's warm, sunny Miami? I'm so jealous. It's starting to get chilly here." Lindsay went on to chat about the weather, describing it in such detail that you'd think she worked for The Weather Channel.

"Thanks for texting me the latest pictures of Lydia. She's absolutely gorgeous! Takes after her mother," I cooed.

"She's a sweetheart. Can't wait for you to see her." Lindsay suddenly turned serious. "Something tells me this is not just a social call. What can I help you with?"

Some things never change. I could never get anything past Linds. "You know I'm working for a sports agent here, right? Well, she has a kind of difficult client, a professional ice skater. I'm hoping you can clear some stuff up for me, you having been such an ice skater yourself."

"Sure. I'd love to help. So, what can I do?"

"First of all, this is confidential. You cannot discuss this with anyone. I could get fired for even talking about this with you, but I knew I could count on you," I warned her.

"I swear I won't tell anyone," Lindsay solemnly promised. "So what is it? What's the problem?"

"He likes to have kinky type of sex on the ice. That's all we know, but it's becoming a problem with his partners, so I thought if I knew exactly what kind of sex ice skaters have while on the ice, maybe my boss could find a way to cure him of it, or, at least, deal with it." Even as I spoke, I knew the explanation sounded implausible, but it was the best I could come up with.

"You're right. I am the person to consult. I've done all that—in my pre-Lydia days, of course," she hurried to add. "Well, there are ice skaters who like having what's called 'ice sex,' as that's the only way they can achieve orgasm—they're so connected with the ice and the rink. One of the things they do is to slide pieces of ice over their partner's genitals, the women over the men's penises and scrotums and the men over the women's vaginas; then, they perform oral sex right afterward. The skaters that do that enjoy the contrast of hot and cold. I never went for this, but some skaters put ice cubes in their mouths and, with the cubes there, in their mouths, perform oral sex. Sometimes, ice cubes are frozen beforehand into different shapes—for example, into penises. Lesbians use those as dildos on each other. You can also add color to the cubes, and instead of just using water, can freeze different beverages. But you have to be very careful not to put ice cubes on the private parts straight from the ice trays as doing that can cause numbness. The cubes have to melt a bit first, so they won't stick."

"I had no idea there were so many variables." My brain was on overdrive at the possibilities. "What else?"

Lindsay was on a roll. "Well, then there's nude figure skating. The skaters start off skating while dressed, but then they take off their clothes bit by bit."

"Nude figure skating? Really?" I felt like such an innocent. "Tell me, please, Linds, that that is not an Olympic sport, you know, like alternate Olympics."

"That would never happen. There's a risk of hypothermia

associated with that," Lindsay said seriously. "Then, of course, skaters during sex have to be very careful not to slice each other open with the blades. Really, Magnolia, ice sex is not for beginners, as you can see. I can give you other examples, if you want, but was that helpful?"

"Yes, very. Thank you," I replied. "I'm getting the picture of what our client might be into. I'll pass on the information to my boss, and let her handle the situation as she sees best. You've been wonderful to help me out this way." And she had been.

"Anytime, just give me a call or text. When are you coming home? We miss you."

"As soon as I can." I tried to keep my voice unemotional, but it wasn't easy.

I was homesick, there was no denying, but I did not want to let it be known, as then pressure might be put on me to come home. Lindsay began telling me the latest gossip about friends we had in common in Minneapolis. I listened without much interest, but let her go on and on as it gave her pleasure. A few more minutes of that, and I'd hung up.

Now, newly armed with information about how ice skaters had sex while in the rink, I had set about making my preparations for the encounter with Pietr. The first thing I did was to go to the bar in the apartment and check to make sure that there was a bottle of vodka there. I needn't have worried, as there were three. There were no ice trays, not surprising in such a modern place, so I added those to the list of items I would be purchasing at the hardware store.

Earlier, Anita had reported that it had been a while since Pietr had performed his signature move, the one that caused him to drop his ex-partner Natasha. Knowing I was taking a huge risk, but even so, convinced that that would be the only way for Pietr to get over his fear, I requested that he lift me in the same way. At first, Pietr made it clear that he was unwilling to do so and resisted. But by giving him physical encouragement, demonstrating that I really wanted him to do it, I managed to convince him that I was serious.

I tried not to think about Natasha as I felt Pietr's freezing hands on my naked body as he lifted me high above his head and spun me around, although I was scared shitless as to what might happen. It wasn't easy to do, but I managed to put the thought of all the vodka that Pietr had consumed out of my head and reminded myself that he was a Russian and that Russian men had a huge capacity for liquor. I urged Pietr to repeat the lift several more times, until he performed it in a perfectly smooth way. My hunch, that having Pietr safely execute the same move with me that he had with Natasha would cure him of his terror of hurting his next partner, turned out to be correct.

After completing a few variations of the move several other times, Pietr and I decided to get back to what we were doing before. It was bloody cold and I was still naked, and unless I wanted to get hypothermia, I had to warm up. The ice cubes that I'd frozen with vodka, the trick I'd learned from Lindsay, had come in handy. Pitr and I rolled around on the ice, pleasing each other in every way possible. He was a great lover and extremely well endowed.

All in all, I could not have asked for a better first real encounter. Not only was my client nice and considerate—a bonus, for sure—but he was Russian, flexible, sexually experienced, and unable to verbally communicate with me. And I got to drink lots of really good vodka and eat pounds of Beluga caviar, all while dressed in a mink coat, lying on a blanket of sable. Minneapolis was far, far away. If I'd had any second thoughts about having accepted Oona's offer (and risking freezer burn on my ass while doing it), the thought of all the money I was making helped to smooth all those doubts away.

Oona called me the next day to congratulate me on my success with Pietr. She reported that the skater had had someone who could speak English call and leave a message on her voice mail early that morning announcing that, thanks to me, his fear of performing on the ice had ended. He also told Oona not to call him back right away because he would be unreachable for the next few hours; he would be on a flight to rejoin the skating show. Having witnessed his happiness and satisfaction the night before, I hadn't been surprised to hear that Pietr was cured of his aversion to ice.

HORSERACING
Adonis Perez, 30, 5', 100 lbs. Jockey

BACKGROUND
My regular manicurist, Odalys, had just started putting on the final coat of polish on my nails when one of the cell phones, the one reserved for business calls, rang. I risked smearing my nails—comparable to committing a mortal sin—if I were to answer it, so I let it ring. Besides, I knew perfectly well who was calling me, so I was in no hurry to answer. Anita would just have to wait until Odalys had finished with the manicure before speaking with me.

For the past six months I'd had a standing appointment at two o'clock on Saturday afternoon, after my flower-arranging lessons, with Odalys, the best nail technician in Miami, for a manicure and pedicure. Unlike most manicurists, who worked out of salons, Odalys would come to her clients' homes and do their nails. She was as reliable as she was good at her job; she had only missed coming twice, and those had been during hurricane season when a Category 5 storm had been threatening Miami.

The fact that I didn't want to interrupt the routine with Odalys wasn't the only reason I avoided speaking with Anita: I didn't want to hear what she was going to tell me about one particular client, the one I knew she would be calling me about. I had read in the paper that Adonis Perez, one of the jockeys Oona represented, was back in Miami to compete in the Festival of the Sun event at the Calder Race Course, in a graded stake race worth $1.6 million.

In the nine months that I had been associated with Oona, the only client that I'd balked at getting together with had been Adonis. Certainly there had been others that I disliked: the one who had halitosis; the one who wanted to videotape our sessions; the one who farted during sex; the truly frightening one who said he wanted to kill me with sex. There were three that I didn't feel safe with, sensing that they could hurt me if they wanted to. It wasn't sur-prising that I feared them, as athletes, they were very strong and could harm me without meaningto. At times they didn't seem to be aware of their own strength; others, unfortunately, were too aware of it and enjoyed watching me protect myself. However, not wanting Oona to think I could not handle certain situations, I'd mostly remained quiet about them, though.

With Adonis, the situation was different—much different, to such a degree that I had actually made my feelings known to Oona. Since that was the one and only occasion that I'd announced my objection to a client, Oona treated the matter with the utmost seriousness. For all her faults—her coolness, her fake-heartiness, her all-around weirdness—Oona had always been receptive and respectful of my feelings. I had been so concerned about the situation that I had actually gone to her office to discuss my dilemma with her.

It wasn't that Adonis was unpleasant, or abusive, or that he beat me, or that he had disgusting personal hygiene, or anything like that. It was that, during our encounters, the way he liked to have sex with me was after we'd indulged in a long session of pony play.

Pony play! It was even worse than it sounded.

Adonis, the first time I met with him, had been quite upfront about his preferences, and left it up to me whether or not I was willing to participate in equestrian role-playing, as he so delicately put it. I was aware of what pony play was—a sexual fetish in which one person took the dominant role of the master or trainer and the other, the submissive role of the pony. During pony play, participants would dress up in outfits that corresponded to his or her respective role in regular horseback riding, with the equipment used including saddles, hoof boots, mitts, reins, and ponytails.

What disturbed me about pony play wasn't so much that I felt that it was slightly ridiculous and slightly dangerous, given all the props it entailed, but that growing up (I'd ridden all my life) I'd had a pony named Patches. I thought pony play was insulting to all horses, especially the memory of Patches. My grandparents had given me my beloved Patches on the occasion of my eighth birthday. Knowing how much I wanted a pony, my grandparents had gone to an auction of horses that were otherwise headed to the slaughterhouse, and had bought her for one hundred dollars.

Although Patches had been old, almost blind, and slightly lame, I thought she was the most beautiful thing

I had ever seen. I loved her with all my heart for the twelve years that she lived with us, until her peaceful death from old age. As far as I was concerned, after having loved such a special pony, pretending that Adonis was Patches (during pony play, Adonis took on the submissive role of the pony) was kind of mental animal abuse: for me and for Patches. I knew that not everyone was satisfied with having straight sex with one partner for his or her entire life, and I certainly had no quarrel with their experimenting until they found whatever it was that suited them. Different strokes for different folks and all that—but I personally found the whole concept of pony play particularly loathsome.

I had gone along with what Adonis wanted during my first encounter with him. However, after having to dress up in the costume and then having had to mount Adonis and ride him much the way I'd done with Patches proved to be too much for me. I decided that this pony business was definitely not for me. That first night, after leaving Adonis, I went home, soaked in a scalding hot bath for an hour, and then wrote a sizable check for a horse rescue organization, in memory of Patches.

I'd found the experience so terribly distasteful that I'd decided that I had to let Oona know how I felt. Oona, bless her heart, heard me out and told me I did not have to do anything I did not feel comfortable doing. She seemed to understand how I felt. I speculated that maybe Oona had had a horse as well, which was why she empathized with my dilemma. However, even as I spoke about my feelings, I was able to acknowledge that I sounded irrational.

The fact that Adonis, a world-famous jockey wanted to pony-play with me, Oona quite logically pointed out, had nothing to do with Patches; it wasn't personal, therefore I should not take it as an insult to her memory. Adonis kept winning races, making serious money for Oona, which made it difficult for her to side with me in that matter. Still, to Oona's credit, she did so, supporting me all the way.

I had left Oona's office feeling quite relieved, confident that I would never have to meet with Adonis ever again. Or if I did have to meet with him, pony play would not be a part of the encounter. I wanted to be reasonable. Adonis was actually quite a nice man; it was his sexual preferences I objected to, and if he wanted to have a regular, normal encounter with me, I would not turn him down. Even though I no longer had any contact with Adonis, I still followed his career, of course, as I did with Oona's other clients. Whatever his weird sexual cravings were, there was no question that the man was very talented: he had won both the Kentucky Derby and the Preakness the same year.

And so, as several months had passed without news of Adonis, I thought the matter had been settled. Until, that is, the afternoon when Anita casually mentioned the fact that Oona had lost Adonis as a client. According to Anita, Adonis had not taken the news that I refused to participate in pony play with him very well and had fired Oona as his agent.

I thought long and hard about what had happened, and decided that Oona should not have lost a client because of me and my childish prejudices; to have allowed that to happen had been so very unprofessional on my part. I was in the service business in Miami: My business was to have sex, and I would do whatever it was that was required of me to make my clients happy.

That night, I had logged onto the Internet, searching for whatever I could find on pony play. At first, I had to force myself to read the articles. Looking at photographs of certain individuals dressed as horses and others as their riders was particularly upsetting to me but after a while, I became so familiar with the different aspects of the fetish that it no longer troubled me as much. I think the fact that during the course of my research I'd come across so many other fetishes—some being really, really disturbing ones (balloons or plush animals anyone?)—that by comparison, pony play seemed almost mild.

I telephoned Oona and told her of my decision to see Adonis again and that if the jockey wanted me to indulge in pony play with him, I was willing. Oona was understandably surprised to hear that, since I had initially been so resolute. It was only when she had been absolutely certain of my change of heart that Oona had said she'd contact Adonis to give him the good news. For her, losing a client, any client, but particularly one as successful and lucrative as Adonis, had been almost physically painful, so she'd be thrilled if she could represent him again.

As my refusal to participate in pony play had been the only reason that Adonis had changed agents, the moment he had heard of my willingness to meet with him again, he had promptly fired his current sports agent and retained Oona once more. Since then, I'd met with Adonis on perhaps half a dozen occasions. I can't say that I enjoyed what we did, but I had become more comfortable with it. Perhaps more important was I had come to terms with the fact that if Adonis was to remain Oona's client, then my indulging his preference for pony play was going to be part of it. Oona, knowing how I still really felt about it, gave me a bonus every time I met with Adonis. She called it combat pay.

Still, in spite of my having agreed to continue to keep Adonis as my client, knowing what Anita was going to tell me that the jockey had returned to Miami for the race at Calder and wanted to meet with me, I avoided calling her back.

THE ENCOUNTER

"Magnolia, it's on for tonight with Adonis," Anita informed me. "He wants you to meet him at his apartment, exactly the same arrangements as before." Anita had shown surprising tact, a trait I could have sworn she did not possess on the occasions when she informed me that Adonis requested an encounter. Was she human after all?

"All right, thanks, Anita. I'll be there," I assured her.

"I don't know if you're aware of it, but he lost the race this afternoon He's not doing so well. That's what Oona told me," she added before hanging up.

I had not heard the news regarding the outcome of the race and, being kind of fond of Adonis, I was sorry he had lost. As a professional jockey, and originally, at the start of his career having had bad luck winning horse races, Adonis reported he had gotten involved with pony play in order to restore the emotional bond which he once had with his beloved horses. He explained that he needed to experience what those beautiful saddled animals felt on the racetrack. He wanted to feel it all—the weight of the rider's body bouncing on his back, the bit in his mouth pressuring his jaw, the kick of the heavy boots on his ribs, and the lashings of the leather crop on his haunches.

The first time we'd had an encounter, Adonis had dressed me up in custom-made S&M jockey attire. He provided me with a sturdy crop, rubber riding boots, and all sorts of leather restraints that were essential for our equine role play. I could tell the outfit cost him a fortune.

Never having participated in pony play before, I was

unsure what to do, so Adonis guided me, instructing me. I mounted his bare back; he neighed and asked me to give him a hard kick in the ribs. I closed my eyes, took a deep breath, and did as he ordered. It was not an easy thing for me to do. I'd never been into pain, either giving or receiving it. Even then, I was extremely uneasy doing so. Then, of course, there was the matter of Patches.

Sensing my reluctance, Adonis had taken the bit out of his mouth and asked if I was all right, if his request was too much for me to handle. It was, but I smiled and told him that everything was fine. I just needed to get myself together so I could continue. Oona couldn't afford to lose Adonis as a client again, and I couldn't afford to disappoint Oona.

I mustered the courage to kick Adonis as hard as I could without breaking any ribs; then, just as he said I should do, I pulled on the thick leather throatlatch and ordered him to crawl. It was difficult to hold on to Adonis with his naked body all drenched in sweat, as he scampered around the room on his hands and knees, neighing intensely like a horny young stallion. Still on top of Adonis's back, I crossed my legs in his groin region for some balance, and noticed his protruding tumescence. Adonis was aroused: I must be doing something right.

After hours of my lashing him and pretending that a pro jockey was my pony, Adonis asked for permission to relieve himself. I allowed him to do so then walked him to the fantasy stable that he built especially for our assignations, and, as per his request, watched him masturbate. He jerked his penis for a good two minutes before collapsing breathless on the floor. I knelt before his prostrate body and gave him a gentle kiss on the forehead.

"Thank you. I will see you soon," Adonis murmured, trying to catch his breath.

I was so exhausted that I went straight home; my muscles were aching and my head was pounding. I didn't realize how tiring and emotionally draining pony play with Adonis would be. Most of my clients just wanted straight sex, with a few sports props thrown in, to fix their damaged psyches. Adonis, on the other hand, required so much more. Vanilla sex wouldn't save him. He sought solace in riding crops and pony bridles.

That night I arrived at Adonis' place in thirty minutes, a record for me. After parking the Mercedes in the usual spot, I let myself in with the key that he had given me. Walking through the labyrinth of corridors in his huge apartment, I finally got to his bedroom. I found Adonis on the bed, still dressed in his street clothes, holding a drink in his hand. He seemed upset, not surprising since he had lost a huge race. He was, but not for the reason I would have thought. "I went to church—Saint Augustine's, you know, on the University of Miami campus—after the race and prayed to Saint Eligius. He's the patron saint of jockeys, you know." He crossed himself.

Placing my bag on the floor, I sat on the bed next to Adonis, and, after taking his right hand in mine, asked, "Is something wrong?' Adonis had never struck me as being particularly religious.

"I don't want you to think I'm crazy, Magnolia, but I knew that I had run the race of my life; I should have won. I stayed there, praying in the front row pew until I had an answer." He looked at me. "And I did get one, but it wasn't from Saint Eligius—it was from the Virgin Mary herself."

"And what did she tell you?" I couldn't wait to find out.

"The Virgin said I had to change my lifestyle, that's why I'd lost. She said Saint Eligius thought he needed to send me a

strong message—which losing the race today certainly was—
so I would pay attention," Adonis revealed.

"How are you going to do that? Change your lifestyle?"
Being Roman Catholic, I had to admit that I was having a
bit of trouble visualizing the Virgin voicing an opinion on
pony play.

"I'm sorry to tell you this, Magnolia." Adonis took both
my hands in his. "I know how important pony play has
become to you, how much you've come to like it, how much
you know about it, all the research you've done on it." Adonis
took a deep breath before delivering the bad news. "Saint Eligius told me, through the Virgin, that if I wanted to go back
to winning races, I had to give up pony play. He's the patron
saint of jockeys, and he thinks pony play goes against what
jockeys should do. It's disrespectful to the sport—that's what
he thinks I should do."

It was all I could do to keep from screaming, "Thank
you, Saint Eligius!" I managed to control myself, instead saying, "That's okay, Adonis. If that's what Saint Eligius thinks
you should do, then that's okay with me. We can't go against
what the saint's order, can we?" I smiled my most virginal
smile. "It's out of our power."

Adonis looked very relieved. "So straight, normal sex is
okay with you?"

"Normal sex is fine," I replied.

Clearly relieved, Adonis then took my hand and kissed
me on both cheeks. Although his bedroom was a far cry
from the stable, most noticeably—it had a king-size bed,
and, thankfully, it didn't smell of manure—it was still completely decorated in equestrian themes. The first thing that
jumped out was the horse-print wallpaper that covered every
square inch of wall space. The floor was covered by a luxuri-

ously thick, dark green carpet, the exact color of a pasture. The headboard of the bed was rather unique—it consisted of horizontal wooden slats, one on top of the other, resembling jumps. Framed photographs of Adonis wearing his jockey silks and riding different horses were hung on the walls. The two oversized windows were framed by thick curtains in a tan fabric with a horseshoe-design print all over.

Although, true to his word, Adonis proceeded to have normal sex with me, I sensed his heart simply wasn't into it. His penis, which normally got hard in an instant during pony play was now barely erect. Even the Viagra pill that he said he had popped just before my arrival didn't seem to help. I gave it my best—I stroked him all over, something which did not take very long as he was so tiny—but still, I could not elicit much of a response. I climbed on top of him, and rubbed my ass against his cock, a favorite act of his, but still nada. Since my previous tactic wasn't working, fellatio, I thought, would get him aroused enough for intercourse. I grabbed his limp penis and inserted it in my mouth, stroking it up and down and sucking on it like a vacuum cleaner. I hoped that doing all that would result in a response, but in spite of my best efforts, nothing happened.

I knew that if I continued to try different ways to arouse him, and the results stayed the same, the situation would only worsen. I hated to do it, but I hated failure even more, so I suggested that we try to have sex in the stall in the stable. No sooner were the words out of my mouth than Adonis sat up in bed, grabbed me by the hand, and led me into the next room. Thankfully, Adonis decided it would be best for us not to change into our pony play outfits; after all, the last thing he wanted to do right now was upset Saint Eligius and the Virgin Mary.

I bent over and grabbed onto the gate of the stall, teasing Adonis with my bare bottom. His face lit up and his penis got hard. Snorting like a horse, he entered me from behind. Having sex while naked in a stall in an apartment was not, and never had been, one of my fantasies. The sweet smell of horse manure had never been a turn-on for me. However, I have to admit, it was an amusing experience. At least, it wasn't pony play, I told myself. Adonis, thank God, was more than pleased with the outcome, so I supposed that for the foreseeable future, we would be consummating our relationship in that manner, which meant that I would be pulling straw out of my ass for months.

Chapter 14

Oona kept me very busy, so much so that I almost had no time for myself. Still I would manage to occasionally get away and meet with Max. For his part, Max, naturally enough, wanted me to spend more time with him, but I did not dare to do so, as part of the deal with Oona was that I be pretty much available to her around the clock. At the very least, I had to have my cell phone turned on, and it sure as hell would not be a good thing to receive a call from Anita setting up an encounter while I was with Max.

"You are so very mysterious, Magnolia," Max pointed out one night while we were having a late dinner at the Spanish Rose. We were sitting in my favorite booth, the very last one, not visible from the front door. "You seem so open at times, but then at others I suspect you are keeping a secret from me." He put his right hand over mine, and looked deeply into my eyes. "So, mi amor, do you have a secret life? I'm starting to think you do, the way you act sometimes."

First Dr. Bernstein thought I was keeping something from him, and now Max suspected the same. Was it just a question of time before I got busted? I was going to have to be ever more careful.

"No, Max, of course not," I protested. "I'm just busy with classes and homework and that. The dogs, too, that I'm babysitting. I really don't know where the time goes, honestly. You're busy with the restaurant, too. We both have a lot going on."

"That's true. But at least you know where I am pretty much all the time. Apart from the time we spend together here and what you tell me, the reality is that I don't know very much about you. For example, I know you're living in your parents' friends' apartment on Brickell Avenue, but you've never invited me there. I don't even know the address!" Everything that Max was saying was the truth. I could feel myself growing cold. Suddenly, he got a mischievous look on his face. "Maybe one day I'll follow your car when you leave here and surprise you there."

"No, no. Don't do that!" I blurted out. I was thinking furiously. "The reason I haven't invited you to the apartment is that my parents' friends made me swear that I wouldn't have any male friends there. Those were the conditions under which they allowed me to stay there." I hated to pile lie upon lie, but I was backed into a corner.

"Oh, you should have said that before," Max commented, nodding. "I guess we'll just have to go to my house then, if we're going to eat a home-cooked meal together."

"I'd like that very much." My relief at having dodged a bullet was palpable.

"But I still don't know where you are living in Miami," Max pointed out. "Maybe I'll have to follow you after all. Surprise you, in spite of your hosts' rules. If they kick you out, you can move in with me." He teased. Or maybe he didn't.

Well, I'd cross that bridge if that ever came to pass, I rationalized. The line of questioning that Max had pursued brought to light again the risks I was running by continuing to work for Oona. I could not keep this up indefinitely, that was for sure. Something was going to have to give. I just hoped it wasn't me.

As each situation with Oona's clients was unique, I had to come up with different scenarios to satisfy the players' needs. Some of the encounters were pretty straight-forward—just run-of-the-mill man-woman sex mostly carried out in the missionary position; others only wanted oral sex; while others had requirements that were so complicated that they required real creativity to be able to deliver the full fantasy of what was needed. Thankfully, Oona's clients were so satisfied with my services that they'd become regulars, and even the ones who were difficult turned out to be pretty decent guys, or at least they had moments when they were, which was a good thing, because I spent a lot of time with them.

By now I'd been earning hundreds of thousands of dollars, but perhaps more important, the time was flying by, so I hardly had time to think about what I was doing. My debt was wiped out. I had paid down all my credit cards, and I even had money to buy some short term CDs, even though they hardly paid any interest. The piles of hundred dollar bills in the lockbox that I kept under the bed kept getting higher, so I decided that it was time to invest some of my earnings. Plus, because of the harsh economic situation, the stock market had dropped some, but I had faith it would go up again, so I opened a brokerage account at Citibank. I was assigned a financial officer, and slowly, I began to buy stocks. Me with a financial officer!

Prior to working with Oona, the only times I'd had to go into a bank was to cover checks that I had written that had been returned. Never having invested before, in the beginning I stuck to purchasing safe stocks and bonds, only triple "A" rated, but, as I became more knowledgeable, reading the

Wall Street Journal and Financial Times, I started putting some of my money in funds. It was fun following the market in the financial pages of the newspapers. I even began watching CNBC while on the treadmill, developing a schoolgirl crush on Jim Cramer, their financial analyst, and would watch his show without fail.

Although I knew that the chances that I would actually go ahead and follow through opening an art school for underprivileged and at risk children in the near future probably were not all that realistic, still I hadn't given up thinking about it. If I were to be honest with myself, I would admit that it made me feel better about my lifestyle. I wanted to be just like my aunt Tessie and inspire students the way she had.

Still, as the time passed, other than going on the Internet to conduct research, I hadn't really done much to realize my dream. I decided that if it was going to happen, I was going to have to do a lot more than just going online, and began working on figuring out, exactly, what starting such a school would entail.

I sat down one Sunday and spent almost the entire day calculating the finances. It was a good thing that my father had insisted that I take a couple of economics courses in college, as the knowledge came in handy. As I worked the calculator, it occurred to me that Dad would not have been happy to learn how exactly I was using that knowledge. I was well aware that I would be facing lots of costs that I couldn't calculate out on my own just yet—teachers' salaries, equipment, inventory, electricity costs, insurance, etc.—but at least I could use what I did know to make some reasonable estimates. I took into consideration not only what the purchase price would be for the building—that seemed to be the easy part—but also how much I should budget to keep the school running until it could become self-supporting, through grants, foundation money, any funding source that I could find.

After having scoured the real estate section of the Miami Herald looking for commercial properties that would suit my needs, I wrote down some addresses. Map in hand, on several Sundays, I would drive out to see the properties themselves, making notes about how each would or wouldn't suit my purposes. I well knew that going about it this way was the most rudimentary kind of research, but at least I was doing something.

I had been working so much that I almost didn't notice that over five months had passed since that fateful night Monday night in August when I'd met Oona at the Miami Sports Bar. The six weeks of training, and the three and a half months of working as her edge had passed in a blur. In Minneapolis, where the passage of time is marked by the distinct changes in the weather—sometimes it felt to me that the seasons there were divided into whatever sports the residents did (snowboarding, fishing, hunting, hiking)—everyone was very aware of the seasons. In Miami, though, there were no noticeable changes in the seasons; time just passed. As it was always hot, the year was basically divided into two six-month periods: hurricane season (June through November) and the rest. When the weather didn't require a change of wardrobe, years could go by unnoticed.

I had developed a routine, one that suited my schedule as well as my personality. I converted one of the bedrooms of the apartment into a simple gym, and began running on the second-hand treadmill that I had purchased. After the workout on the treadmill, I would slather myself with sun block, then go down and swim laps in the building's Olympic-sized pool. At that time in the afternoon, the sun wasn't that strong, so I wouldn't get burned much. I was realistic enough to recognize that part of my success in working for Oona was due to my fair complexion, so I wasn't about to do anything to endanger that.

After the swim, I would head back upstairs and dig through the kitchen drawer that held dozens of take-out menus and would chose whichever I was in the mood for. It hadn't taken me more than a week to learn how long it would take for the delivery to arrive. I had calculated the delivery times almost to the minute, giving me enough time to soak in the bathtub between the time I ordered and the time the meal would arrive. Then I would have dinner out in the terrace, sipping a glass of wine, as I admired the lights of the city in the distance. A quick nap later, and I was ready to begin working.

I was perfectly aware that, at twenty-two, I was way too young to be so set in my ways, but that was the only way I could manage it. Apart from meeting for dinner with Max and the occasional meal with my Japanese classmates, I had no personal life to speak of. As much as I wished to have a normal life, I knew that wasn't possible, so I had pretty much resigned myself to like the way I was. I was making shitloads of money, and my accounts were growing at a fast and furious pace—I figured I could forgo having a personal life until later, when all this was over.

I really didn't have to work as much as I did. Oona would ask me every so often if I wanted to take a break. I almost didn't want to have time to myself, as then I would think about what I was doing and the repercussions if I were caught. Of course, Oona never exactly urged me to change my mind, because as long as I was working, she was making money. The truth was that I was basically on-call twenty-four hours a day, seven days a week—nights and holidays included. Sometimes I felt like a 7-Eleven, but that's the way it was. I was on a sort of autopilot, just going in a straight line, not looking to either side, just staring at the road in front.

Knowing that the more clients I met with, the quicker I would be able to quit and do something else with my life, which was start my school, I was basically reconciled to working those kinds of hours. However, I have to admit that the holidays, those weeks between Thanksgiving and New Year's, were tough for me. My family had always celebrated the holidays, following the same traditions year after year: caroling, going to midnight Mass, all of us going together on the day after Thanksgiving to the Humsteads' farm, choosing, then cutting down the Christmas tree. It was a special time of year for us, one we relished.

Maybe I could have spent the holidays with Max, but as I continued to play my role as a college graduate student, I would tell him that I was going home to be with my family, as a normal student would do. Being deceitful was getting more and more difficult, but that was the only way I could get around not being with him then. The holidays were the busiest time at the Spanish Rose, so for once he really didn't seem to mind. He actually seemed relieved, which kind of worried me.

I could have gone to Oona and asked her for some time off so I could go home to Minneapolis, but I decided not to do that. Not because I didn't miss my family; it was that I didn't want to have to lie to them about what I was doing in Miami. At that point, I was telling so many lies to Oona, Max, and my family that sometimes I did not open my mouth, for fear that I'd let the cat out of the bag.

When I first started working for Oona, I had to decide what I should tell my parents I was doing here that required my constant presence and after much deliberation, had come to the conclusion that it would be best to stick as close to the truth as possible. Trying to make up a complicated lie just wouldn't work for me; in one second, just the tone of my voice could give me away. However, were I to have concocted some outlandish story about what I was doing, they would have undoubtedly asked me lots of questions about my job, which would have inevitably resulted in their catching me in the lie.

I was walking a fine line and I knew it. I risked turning into the kind of person I used to loathe: selfish, opportunistic, manipulative, greedy. Although it was difficult for me to admit, I was very aware that when I'd accepted Oona's offer, I had not taken anyone else into consideration. I had done it for selfish reasons: boredom, excitement, money. And the price I would pay for that was having a guilty conscience and the risk of getting busted, so I had no choice but to live with the consequences of my actions and suck it up.

I decided to tell my family that I worked for a sports agent (true) as her personal assistant (sort of), a very demanding job that I loved, but that required me to be available twenty-four hours a day. Naturally enough, they expected me to go home for either Thanksgiving or Christmas, or maybe even both, but I told them I had to work, news that had devastated them and me; in fact, it bothered me a lot more than I could tell them.

Several times they had volunteered to fly to Miami and visit me, but I'd repeatedly claimed that my job took up so much of my time that I wouldn't be able to be with them much. Still, I was worried that they might show up anyway, surprising me, something that they were perfectly capable of doing, a frightening thought that sometimes kept me awake at night. All I could do was pray that never happened. But that possibility was always very real, yet another risk I was taking by leading the life I was.

The first six months of working for Oona had actually been okay—although I was lonely, my loneliness was offset by the fact that I was making so much money. Sometimes I had to pinch myself to believe my good luck. I began closely following the commercial real estate market in Miami. Fortunately for me, though unfortunately for current owners and investors, news reports repeatedly stated that real estate prices in Miami continued to fall. Bad for Miami but good for me. I knew that eventually they would rise again, and I wanted to get into the market before the turnaround started, which would inevitably happen. After making some calculations, I found I would have to work maybe only six more months, less time than I had planned to pay for the kind of building I needed for my school.

After a few months of study, I had familiarized myself with the commercial markets enough to feel confident I could make an informed decision as to how to proceed. I met with Mr. Vogel, my financial advisor at Citibank, and consulted with him to ask for his advice. He knew of my dream, my plan to open the school, though, of course, without being privy to the details as to how I was acquiring the funds necessary to afford it. I'd let him assume I was a trust-fund baby with a heart of gold.

Mr. Vogel had made some calculations and confirmed—my own calculations had been correct—the good news about how affordable the prices had become for the kind of building I would need for my school. He warned me that I shouldn't just focus on the actual cost of purchasing a building as the increases in the other expenses—taxes, insurance, electricity, etc.—would more than offset the decline in real estate prices. As I listened to him, I could feel myself begin to get depressed as it all seemed so out of reach, costing so much more than I'd ever imagined. Being the eternal optimist, however, I told myself that where there was a will, there was a way. All I had to do was find it.

JAI ALAI
Jairo Arriaga, 21, 6'3", 210 lbs.

BACKGROUND

I was once told by a man who'd been a police officer in Boston, that during the bitter winter nights when they were on duty, he and his fellow officers often wished 911 was an unpublished number. That was kind of how I had begun to feel when Anita would call me, to announce that one of Oona's clients wanted to have an encounter with me.

Although I had tried to not let it get to me—yoga, hypnosis, Zen, pills, etc., lately, whenever my business telephone would ring, and Anita's number would pop up in the caller ID screen, my blood still would turn just a teeny bit cold. In spite of my best efforts to control my reactions, late on that Tuesday afternoon, that was still the case.

"Hey, Magnolia, how do you feel about playing a little pelota?" Anita's tone of voice was so smug that it felt as if she was taunting me.

"Jairo?" I asked, even though he was the only one of Oona's clients who played jai alai. I hadn't yet met Jairo Arriaga in person, but, as Oona raved about him and his seemingly infinite possibilities, in a way, I felt that did know him.

"Yes, but Oona wants to talk to you personally, so I'll pass you on to her. I'm just putting you on notice that the encounter with him will take place soon—maybe tonight, maybe tomorrow," Anita explained. "Here's Oona."

"World still treating you right? If not, let me know and I'll fix it for you!" Chuckle, chuckle. Someone was in a good mood.

"Hey yourself, Oona. I'm fine, thanks." I really and truly disliked it when Oona felt compelled to act in such a hearty and jovial way. I think that for her, behaving like that, as if we truly cared about each other's well-being, made our relationship more personal and friendly. The fact was, I never felt I knew her as well I had that first night at the bar. Maybe that was for the best, but I wasn't sure.

Oona, of course, knew how I was doing; if something had been amiss, she would have heard it from Anita. I sounded cold and calculating when I thought of Oona in that way—after all, it was she who set me up in the business, who allowed me to live in the grand style I was so enjoying—as well as saving money for my school. Still, our association had been beneficial to both of us, and not just me. And she still had not told me about her hardscrabble background—in spite of my hinting that I would love to hear it, she had not mentioned it since our first meeting, an eternity ago.

"Can't complain, can't complain," she added. For some weird reason, she lately had taken to saying things twice, a somewhat irritating habit.

I waited a moment to see if she was going to bring up the purpose of the call, but she didn't, so I did. "You wanted to discuss Jairo with me?"

"I need your help with him, Magnolia." I could hear her inhale deeply. It was clear Oona was having trouble getting to whatever it was she was trying to tell me. It was so unlike her to be reticent about anything, which, of course, meant I was dying of curiosity to find out what she wanted.

"He's young, just twenty-one years old, born in Barcelona, has been playing jai alai at the Miami Fronton since last year—he's been the top scorer there for four seasons. A superstar, really." Oona apparently felt the need to refresh my memory.

I knew that jai alai existed, of course. The Miami Fronton, the huge, pink, windowless building where the games were played, was located just a few minutes from the airport, so it was impossible to miss. The moment Anita mentioned Jairo, I'd tried to recall what, if anything, I knew about the game and realized it wasn't much. I remembered reading somewhere that jai alai had come from the Basque region of Spain, and that it was a fast, dangerous game, but apart from that—nada.

"That's impressive," I said, even though, of course, I had known that already from all the times she had spoken of him. "Has he been your client for a long time?"

"Less than a year. He's very nice. Well, he seems very nice. I hate to admit it, but I can't fully communicate with him. In addition to speaking Basque, he only speaks Spanish, and, Magnolia, you know my Spanish is rudimentary at best. We use his uncle, Mario Arriaga, also his manager, as an interpreter," Oona explained.

For Oona to call her Spanish rudimentary was an overstatement. I had heard her attempts to say a few words, and my skin had crawled with embarrassment: for her, for me, and for the individuals she was torturing with language abuse. Oona was of the school of thought that if one were to speak really, really fast, and in the loudest voice possible, then one would sound fluent. Trying out her Spanish in public, all she did was to butcher the language, and mispronounce certain words to such a degree that they ended up sounding like obscenities. Behaving in such a way called attention to herself, and was so contrary to Oona's usual self-controlled manner that it never ceased to surprise me when she did that.

"Well, I guess that's okay then as long as you can understand each other," I commented. Oona was avoiding getting to the point, something that was curious, as she'd always been very direct. "Exactly how, Oona, do you need my help with Jairo?"

"What I'm going to tell you, Magnolia, is covered by attorney-client privilege, okay? You are not to discuss this with anyone, anyone at all. Do you understand, Magnolia?" Oona was almost abrupt as she warned me.

"I promise," I replied solemnly.

"It has to do with Jairo's immigration status," Oona said slowly. "That's why I need your help."

"His immigration status?" I repeated. "Oona, he may be a great client of yours, but I am not marrying him so he can get a green card."

As was the case with every single individual that had lived for any length of time in Miami, I was very aware of the problems that immigrants—legal or illegal—faced. It seemed that just about every man, woman, and child here knew enough immigration law to be able to offer legal advice to a new arrival. I wouldn't have been surprised to hear that some babies' first words were: visa, green card, lottery, or even Homeland Security. Miami was a city in which an overwhelming number of residents were immigrants or exiles. Everyone here knew someone who had either swum, walked, paid, or married someone to get here and stay here. "Visa" was not a credit card company—it was a coveted immigration status.

"No, Magnolia, I'm not asking you to marry Jairo so he can get a green card; that's already been taken care of: that's something that you needn't concern yourself with," Oona reassured me.

"What is it then?" I was curious.

Oona practiced sports law, not immigration law. My brain was in overdrive trying to figure out what Oona's interest in this was—because she did have one. Oona didn't do anything out of the kindness of her heart.

"I think I'd better start at the beginning," she said. "Two years ago, when he was just nineteen years old, Jairo came here on a temporary student visa to study at the World Jai-Alai in Miami. Apparently, there's a school here with a terrific program for amateurs who are aspiring to go pro. There at the school, Jairo became such an outstanding player that he decided to turn pro—great for him, but that meant he'd lose his student visa; he's been playing at the Miami Fronton since then." Oona took a deep breath, a sign that indicated she was going to be treading on difficult ground and that she was going to try to talk me into doing something that I might not want to do. "One thing led to another, and Jairo found himself entering into a marriage with a very nice American girl. So as you can see, Magnolia, you don't have to worry about any upcoming nuptials—my client is already married."

"Then what's his immigration status now?"

"Jairo has a hearing with INS in three months to determine if he will be granted a green card and thus be able to stay in the U.S. legally," Oona explained.

"And, let me guess, Oona, you need my help to make sure Jairo doesn't get into any trouble between now and then, is that right?" I knew, as everyone else did, that requirements for immigrants to stay in this country legally had tightened considerably. Since 9/11, one wrong step, and an individual could immediately be deported. Oona's silence confirmed my suspicions. Sensing victory, I pressed my advantage. "Seeing as how he's a married man and all that, can't have him be seen chasing girls, just before his hearing and getting into any kind of trouble, can we? And him being a newlywed, it wouldn't look too good, would it, for the sanctity of the marriage—his wedding vows and all that? Did I get that right, Oona?" I teased.

"I always knew you were smart."

THE ENCOUNTER

"Magnolia, this is going to be a first for you," Anita declared. "Jairo wants you to come to the Miami Fronton to watch him play before the encounter with him."

Jairo would not be the first client to request that I meet with him where he played. Most of them wanted to meet either at the sports facility or at a hotel, but he'd be the first to ask that I be there in the stands cheering before we got together. Usually, I kept up with sporting events by watching them on TV and through the sports pages like everyone else. I had decided early on that not being there, observing my athletes as they competed was one more way to keep from getting involved in any way with them. But going to watch this one game wouldn't hurt anything. It just meant more hours to bill to Oona, more money for me. Plus it just might be fun. "When?"

"Tonight. He's playing both singles and doubles," Anita informed me. "Doors at the Fronton open at seven."

I'd never been to the Miami Fronton before, so I wasn't familiar with the layout of the building or the rules of the game for that matter, but I was confident I could figure those out. The more I thought about it, the more I decided I was going to have a good time with this.

In any case, I was already having fun: Oona had promised to give me the equivalent of combat pay and a bonus if I succeeded in keeping Jairo out of trouble until the hearing for his green card, which, I guess, was fair enough. The kid must have been really important to Oona for her to lay out so much cash on his behalf. God only knows what the marriage must have cost. Green card spouses are expensive; they put dowries to shame.

Oona told me that Jairo had made it to round two of the Florida Cup, apparently quite an achievement, and the fact that he had done this before his twentieth birthday had made it all the more meaningful. A player named Joey had long been considered to be the greatest American jai-alai player ever, and now people were starting to refer to Jairo as the next Joey.

Just as Oona had advised, I tried to put out of my mind the circumstances surrounding Jairo's marriage, but somehow I kept coming back to it. A marriage like that was illegal, and it was best that I had as little knowledge about it as possible, especially since I suspected Oona had been instrumental in facilitating it. For this much risk, Jairo had better be the Muhammad Ali, Lance Armstrong, Michael Phelps, and Babe Ruth of jai alai; otherwise, it sure as hell was not worth it. After 9/11, Homeland Security, understandably, did not fool around.

It was a well-known fact that such a marriage was extremely risky for all concerned. To begin with, if it were judged by the authorities to be a fraud, then the foreigner applying for the green card would not only be immediately deported, but also legally barred from entering the United States for the next five years. And, for the American spouse, well, the penalty to that individual was quite severe: it would result in a one-way ticket to jail.

"Where am I supposed to sit at the Fronton, and how do I meet up with Jairo afterwards?" I needed to know the details.

"Well, I can see you've never been there before. You'll sit in the court-view clubhouse area, and not general admission. But if you want to have dinner there, you can. The food's not bad. I'll call you back with details," Anita told me, then hung up.

The doors to the Miami Fronton opened at seven o'clock, giving me a couple of hours at home. Since I had no knowledge of jai alai, I didn't know how to calculate when to be there, but, if the doors opened at seven, then I would be there at seven, first in line, waiting outside for them to swing open.

I decided to use the time before meeting Jairo to conduct Internet research into the world of jai alai and found out that it was, indeed, a very old game that had been invented more than three hundred years ago in the Basque region of Spain. Jai alai means "merry festival" in the Basque language and was first played outdoors, using the walls of churches as courts. The Guinness Book of Records declared jai alai to be the world's fastest game because the ball moves at speeds in excess of 180 miles an hour.

The more I read, the more fascinated I became with the game. It could be quite a dangerous sport; in 1968, a player died after having been hit by a pelota—the rock-hard ball made out of Brazilian rubber and covered by two hand-sewn goat skins. The pelotas, which were three-quarter the size of baseballs, cost $150 each, and took such a pounding during a match that they had to be replaced every fifteen minutes during a game. As each ball was made by hand, no two were identical, increasing the challenge of the game, since no two bounced alike.

Anita had told me that Jairo was reluctant to disclose what exactly he had in mind for us to do that night, that the only thing he had let her know was that he wanted me to watch him play. She said he'd asked for my cell phone number, so he could call me after his last match and give me more information. Anita had given him my business number and said I should expect a call from him on that cell at around midnight. I had to admit that I was intrigued by the mysterious arrangements. It piqued my curiosity.

The Fronton was located in a very shady neighborhood of Miami, so I was pleased to see that there were security officers milling about the building, increasing the chances my car would still be there when I came out. I drove around until I saw an empty spot as close to the building as possible, under a bright light.

I stood in front of the ticket window and read the list of prices for the different seats. As the best seats in the place cost the grand sum total of five dollars each, I decided to splurge and buy one. It didn't exactly take a genius to figure out that the Fronton made its money from gambling and not from ticket prices. Once inside, I headed to the Court View clubhouse seats, passing the betting windows with signs over them proclaiming that the betting would stop once the game began. As it was early in the evening—just a few minutes past seven o'clock—the Fronton was not filled.

I made myself comfortable, and began to watch the game that was in progress. I'd seen in the program that Jairo wasn't scheduled to play until the second match, for which I was grateful, because it not only gave me time to familiarize myself with the game, but, more important, to place a bet on him. How could I not? Reading the program, I could see I would have lots of opportunities. There were thirteen games tonight, each lasting between ten and twenty minutes—and Jairo was listed as playing in almost all of them. I saw he had played in the session that had taken place for the matinee that afternoon as well—busy guy.

How on earth would he have any energy left for a romp after midnight? True, he was twenty-one years old, but playing so many games in both day and night sessions was sure to be grueling. I loved men with stamina; it would be interesting to see how he managed.

I could see that the Fronton was open on three sides, with the fourth wall facing the audience. Although the players were dressed in different-colored shirts—their team numbers on the back, and their individual numbers on the front—all had on white trousers and red sashes, or fajas, around their waists. I recalled from my reading that during play it was important that the ball be in constant motion, and that motion be fluid at all times. If that didn't happen, then the point went to the opposing team. It didn't take me long to get the hang of the game, and soon I found myself yelling along with the other spectators. As I didn't know any of the players, I cheered for the ones with the best butts.

As soon as the first game was over, I hopped out of my seat, and headed over toward the pari-mutuel windows to place my bets on Jairo. I looked up at the board, where the odds on the different players were posted. As I wasn't too sure how to interpret the figures, and looking at all those constantly changing numbers was not especially helpful, so I gave up, and went to stand in line. I decided that I might as well live dangerously and go for broke, so I bet on Jairo to win all his matches, which seemed only fitting. Oona was betting on me; I was betting on Jairo; Jairo was betting on staying in this country. It was high-stakes all round.

Having placed my bets, I headed back to my seat. I still had a couple of minutes before the next game, so I flipped through the program book where the different players' statistics were listed. Jairo's win/loss record was impressive, but more impressive still were the official photographs of him—one formal, the other showing him in action. This client was a hunk—all 6'3", 210 pounds of him—from his piercing blue eyes to his olive skin to his longish black hair to his devastating smile, the Basque was a true heartthrob—a lady killer—with a great ass.

Walking onto the court, Jairo looked every bit as good as the pictures. He immediately placed the ball in his cesta, and, in one practiced motion, threw it against the wall and started playing with just the kind of fluid motion I'd read about. From where I was sitting it was difficult for me to get as good a look at him during the games as I wanted, but I could see enough to appreciate his moves. His agility was astonishing; in hot pursuit of the pelota, he would climb the sides of the court as if he were a mountain goat.

The longer I watched, the more easily I was able to understand the strategies of the players. To my surprise, I found that I was thoroughly enjoying myself in a way I didn't usually when I was working. Finally, at a quarter to twelve, an announcement was made over the loudspeaker that the last game was about to start, the signal that, according to what Anita had said, Jairo would be calling me soon after to set up the meeting.

I waited until the final results had been announced—Jairo's team had won the last game—before going to window to collect my winnings. I'd worked the numbers out throughout the evening, and calculated that I won several hundred dollars by betting on Jairo across the board, but I was greatly mistaken. Imagine my surprise when the clerk gave me just over three thousand dollars! Clearly that was double-dipping—winning at jai alai and being paid to meet with the star player later. Yet one more reason to love the game!

I had just finished putting away the last of the hundred dollar bills when my cell phone rang. "Magnolia? Jairo here." His voice sounded just like I thought it would—low, sexy, accented.

"Congratulations on your performance tonight, Jairo. You were amazing." I was almost grinning.

"I hope you bet on me and made lots of money." He chuckled.

I chuckled back. "Yes, as a matter of fact, I did. Muchas gracias."

"Tell me where you are, and I'll come out to meet you." Jairo was speaking to me in English, which surprised me a bit. But then I remembered hearing that he'd been taking lessons because he needed to speak English to pass the immigration test.

I looked around where I was standing, and gave him a couple of landmarks. Less than a minute later, a young man came running toward me, moving so fast that all I could see was a blur. He pulled me close and kissed me on both cheeks.

"Magnolia, you are just as beautiful—no, more beautiful, than Oona said." His face beamed with pleasure as he spoke.

"Thank you." I took a step back so I could see him more clearly. Jairo was, if anything, better looking up close. He was casually dressed in blue jeans, a blue-and-white striped shirt, and loafers—and his hair was still damp from the shower, a delightful turn-on.

"Let's go." Jairo took my arm and began to guide me towards the entrance of the building. "I thought we could go back to my apartment. I'm staying at one very near here—very small, but it's okay. We can have something to drink, eat something, and get to know each other." His blue eyes locked on mine. At that point, I would have followed him anywhere, any time.

The building where his apartment was located was just a couple of blocks away, so it didn't take more than five minutes to get there. We each parked our cars—he in the residents' lot, I in the visitors'—and met back again in the lobby. Although we rode up in the elevator in silence, we couldn't stop smiling at each other in anticipation of what was to come.

Jairo's apartment was unremarkable: small and sparsely furnished with rental furniture. What was fascinating to me was the array of tools of the trade that lay around—everything that I imagined a jai alai player would need: pelotas, cestas (wicker baskets), fajas, helmets. Almost immediately after entering the apartment, Jairo went into the kitchen, and returned with an opened bottle of wine and two glasses. We sat on the sofa, and drank the wine, Spanish, of course, as he showed me the different items of the equipment he used while playing, explaining how they were used.

We finished the wine at exactly the same moment that Jairo finished telling me about the equipment. Quicker than I would have thought possible, we divested ourselves of our clothes, and ended up naked on the twin bed in his bedroom.

Amazingly enough, Jairo was even more spectacular naked than he had been clothed.

All the athleticism that Jairo had showed on the court earlier that night paled in comparison to his skill in the bedroom. His body was so flexible that he could have gotten a job at the Cirque du Soleil as a contortionist. Not just that, but it was obvious that somewhere along the line he had studied female human anatomy to such a degree that he knew every nook and cranny of a woman's body and used that knowledge in such a way as to be able to extract the most pleasure possible while performing the sexual act. He was rough yet, at the same time, quite gentle. I was extremely turned on by him. He stroked my ass and played with my hair while entering me, one orifice after another.

My slight apprehension about Jairo being exhausted from playing all those matches turned out to be completely unfounded, and instead of tiring him out, they had served to build up his stamina. The man was completely indefatigable. Jairo was like the Energizer Bunny—he just kept on coming and each time it was as strong, as powerful as the first. And I wasn't complaining.

And it wasn't just that Jairo played my body like a Yo-Yo Ma played his cello; he used the tools of his trade as props while he doing so. During the course of my career as Oona's edge, I'd participated in some S&M, but I'd had no idea how many uses a sash could have, and I sure discovered them once Jairo skillfully tied me up with it. It wouldn't be easy later to get the red-dye stains off my wrists and ankles, but just then, I didn't particularly care.

Jairo and I had just woken up from a post-coital nap when he suddenly sat up, reached over and turned on the lamp on the bedside table. He then opened the top drawer and looked over at me. "You like to play?" Jairo took out three rolled-up red sashes that were inside the drawer and dangled them before my eyes. "Okay?"

This encounter was becoming more interesting than I had anticipated. "I like." I had no doubt that Jairo would put the sashes to good use. I watched as he proceeded to take out a large, sharply pointed peacock-type feather and a pair of scissors that he placed next to the sashes. Clearly, he had done this before.

"You submissive, okay?" Jairo began unrolling one of the sashes.

"Yes." I watched as he made his preparations. "Safe word?" I wanted to make sure that I would be able to walk away uninjured.

"Pelota."

Dr. Bernstein, having anticipated that some of Oona's clients might be devotees, had spent an entire session discussing bondage sex, so I would be familiar with it. Fred and I had dabbled in it back in Minneapolis, but after having been enlightened by Dr. Bernstein as to the various forms it could take place, I had quickly realized that we had been rank amateurs. The goal of bondage is to restrict movement of one partner while delivering unusual and intense stimulation as the sex act is performed. Although, naturally enough, bondage could range from the very mild to the hardcore, there were similarities in them. For example, all types of bondage required the usage of a "safe" word, one that had been previously agreed to by both parties that indicated that whatever was being done to the submissive partner should be immediately stopped. "Soft" and "hard" limits should be set beforehand, so that the parties were clear on which boundaries should not be crossed, the "soft" limits denoting acts that a participant would not do under normal circumstances, but that were acceptable while enjoying bondage sex, and "hard" ones stating the acts that were absolutely never permitted.

Jairo was becoming increasingly aroused as he laid out the sashes on the bed. I was curious as to how he was going to tie me up, seeing as how we were lying on a twin bed without any bed frame. I suspected that for all his preparations, Jairo may not have been an experienced as he wanted to appear, or, perhaps it was that he was good at improvising. The fact that he was using sashes from his jai-alai uniform indicated that he was not into hardcore bondage; in that case, he would have been equipped with cuffs or used the kind of Japanese ropes that true aficionados tended to favor. Or, it could have been that he was so into the sport that he incorporated all aspects of it into his life, resulting in the use of fajas. If I'd known beforehand that Jairo was into bondage, I would have brought my bag filled with items we could have used. After having conducted research on the best kind of equipment, I had decided I liked Paul Seville's selections the best, especially the black leather paddle, although I did have some of Coco de Mer's toys, too. I made a mental note to bring my bag the next time I was to meet with Jairo, now that I knew he was into bondage.

"Turn around," he ordered. "Close your eyes."

I did as he said, and soon found myself being blindfolded by one of the sashes that he'd taken out of the drawer, an indication that maybe he did know what he was doing. Next, he tied my hands with a basic wrist tie behind my back, probably with the second sash, but thankfully not too tight. I was reassured by the knowledge that the scissors were close by in case there was a need to cut the sash quickly.

Having seen the peacock feather earlier, I assumed Jairo

would soon stroke me with it, but I was mistaken, for he began to lightly spank me instead with his hand. At first, I could feel my cheeks becoming warm; then, as he increased the intensity of the spanking, the burning set in. He had clearly done this before, as he knew exactly where to place his hands to extract the maximum pleasure. I was about to call out "pelota," the safe word, when Jairo changed gears and began touching me with the feather all over, beginning with the soles of my feet, and ending behind my neck. I had never enjoyed being tickled, but this was a different kind of sensation, and I found myself really getting into it, anticipating where Jairo would touch me next. That I was blindfolded increased the sensuality of it.

And so it went, alternating from the spanking to the feather for the next few hours. By the end of the session, the bed sheets were soaking wet with a combination of sweat and body fluids. Again, I was in awe of Jairo's stamina, for, after I'd played the submissive, it had been his turn, and he had been equally enthusiastic in that role. By then, I had stopped counting how many sashes he kept in the bedside drawer, nor did I care that all this had taken place while we were cramped in a twin bed.

Dr. Bernstein had described bondage in pretty explicit terms, but his explanation, although it had served to enlighten me about the practice, had clearly not prepared me for the real-life episode that I'd had with Jairo, an enthusiastic practitioner of the sport during that memorable encounter. I was a bit surprised, though, that Dr. Bernstein had not mentioned that roles could be reversed—that a dominant could take the role of submissive and vice versa in one session. Or it could be that doing so had been pretty unique to Jairo, with his stamina. In any case, it had been a pretty amazing introduction to this dual, alternative form of practicing.

And the things he did with that cesta! I knew that for the next couple of days, I'd have to pick bits of wicker out of my skin, especially in hard to reach places. I, however, was not about to complain about any damage to my body. It had been well worth it, and I would wear the scars and stains, if there were to be any, as proud mementos of that most astonishing night.

As I lay on Jairo's bed battered, bruised, and breathless, I watched dawn break outside. I stopped speculating about why Oona was going out on such a limb for Jairo. I was more than happy to be a part of whatever they were doing, especially as I hoped to continue offering my services.

Instead, I turned my thoughts to Jairo, who was sleeping peacefully next to me. Being with him that night convinced me that Jairo Arriaga was going to be a credit to his newly adopted country, and it was going to be my patriotic duty to see that he would safely make it to that immigration hearing. I determined to meet with him on a regular basis until then—this time bringing my bag of toys so he would enjoy the experience to the fullest—and then afterwards, to make sure he didn't get his permission revoked. It would be the least I could do.

Chapter 15

It was a hot, sunny afternoon in April when, after having met with Mr. Vogel, my financial advisor at Citibank, for the second time to consult with him about opening my school, the harsh reality hit me that it wasn't going to be as easy as I had thought. Boy, had I been naïve! Mr. Vogel, in the time between my first meeting with him and this one, had begun looking into all that it entailed. He had wasted no time in setting me straight, and he had begun the meeting by listing in detail all the expenses I would incur to operate it, even implying that the cheapest part of my plan was purchasing the building—the operating costs were going to be almost prohibitive.

Mr. Vogel had clearly done his homework. He had written down on a pad for me some of the expenses I would be facing: teachers' salaries, furniture, supplies, several kinds of insurance costs—property, flood, wind, malpractice, etc.—many licenses, such as occupational, fire, etc., and security costs—and, those were just a few. Finally, he had advised me to set up a meeting with an official from the Small Business Administration, the organization equipped to give me the best guidance.

After the meeting, I stood there, outside the bank building, stunned. I'd so been looking forward to discussing

with Mr. Vogel the date at which I could stop working for
Oona and begin to concentrate on my school. Doing what
I had been doing was taking a toll on me, resulting in what
I've become: secretive, deceitful, and frankly, a person I did
not like.

The fact that I was weary of working as Oona's edge
pretty much nonstop for close to a year shouldn't have come
as a surprise to me, but it wasn't so much the encounters that
had gotten to me: it was the lies that I'd had to tell that had
convinced me I had to stop. Maybe by opening my school, I
could shake off some of the dirt that was sticking to me. We
Catholics believe in redemption. I fervently hoped I could
make up for what I'd been doing by dedicating myself to
helping others.

I could fool myself by pretending that the skills I had
picked up during my training would serve me well for the
rest of my life: learning to speak Spanish as well as Japanese,
psychology sessions, physical training and workouts, learning tricks and pointers from a stylist. The harsh truth was,
though, that I could have just as easily enrolled in classes,
and done it on my own; it would have been very expensive,
and taken longer, true, but it could have been done.

As time passed, the glamour of living in a fabulous
apartment, wearing beautiful clothes, meeting talented athletes and making piles of money, of course—was beginning
to wear thin. I appreciated all that, truly I did, but the price
I was paying of continuing to live that way was becoming too
high. However, if I were to be brutally honest with myself, I'd
have to admit that I enjoyed all the benefits from living the
high life. Luxury was addictive.

There was no denying that I took great pleasure from
seeing the money in my Citibank accounts pile up. By then,

partly due to Mr. Vogel's conservative stewardship of my money (as well as Jim Cramer's recommendations), I had just over a million dollars invested, and that did not include the four hundred thousand in hundred-dollar bills in the safety deposit box, money that I did not intend to touch. I felt the old "hate the sin, but not the sinner" saying seemed true as it applied to me and my lifestyle. I missed having a normal life. I wanted to be with my family, to have friends, to get a dog.

Max also had his own troubles. His lease on the restaurant space was running out, and the landlord was quadrupling the rent, something that might force him to close the Spanish Rose. His landlord, a very nice, helpful man, had confessed that one of the reasons he had to raise the rent so high was that because his property taxes were going through the roof, and his insurance, due to all the hurricanes, had become prohibitive. The number of empty tables at the Spanish Rose was becoming more and more noticeable as the customers stayed away; eating out had become a luxury, not a necessity.

Max's story, sadly, was not an isolated one. The state of the economy was severely affecting Miami. The Miami Herald would chronicle on a daily basis how Miami was suffering: real estate was in the toilet; the cost of doing business in Miami-Dade County had increased to the point that businesses could no longer afford to keep operating; tourism that accounted so heavily for its revenue had dried up. Every so often one could see glimmers of a turnaround, but it was glacially slow.

The last time Max had brought up the very painful subject of the precarious status of the Spanish Rose, he'd looked so forlorn, with his brushy, dark hair all tangled and wild, his tie and collar pulled a little loose, that I suspected he'd been up all night, trying to find a solution to the predicament.

"I can't let my father down and have the restaurant fail," he said. Sitting there in the booth across from him, I thought he was going to cry.

Max had only two months to solve the problem, so most of his time lately had been spent desperately trying to discover new options and weigh them against each other. The three banks where he had applied for loans had turned him down, making it a very real possibility that he could lose the Spanish Rose. For him, it wasn't only his income that was at stake: his honor was on the line, as well. I would have given anything to have been able to help him financially, but I couldn't see how I could do that without a lot of explaining. And even if I were to come to his aid, it would be a short-term solution, and I wasn't even sure he would accept the offer. All I could do was to listen to him, and try to console him.

The financial realities that Mr. Vogel had pointed out to me didn't necessarily mean putting off my dream of the school forever; I would just have to postpone it for now until I could generate more income. In the meantime, I'd have to find some other way to start doing some of what I wanted, coming up with an enterprise that would take less start-up money. I was sure I'd think of something, maybe take over an existing school, maybe help with the expenses of another. Surely there was a school that needed the kind of financial assistance I was ready and willing to give. I would just have to do some more research.

I missed my family so much that it had become a constant, physical pain. I resented not being able to see them, not being able to talk honestly with them about what I was doing; I missed just physically being around them. I wanted to hang out with girlfriends, friends I could confide in. I missed having a boyfriend, someone I could openly do regular things with, like going to the beach, movies, restaurants without worrying about getting caught. My one outlet was on the occasions that I would meet up with my classmates from the language school, but I could hardly think of them as either a girlfriend or boyfriend. I wanted to get a dog.

I had Max, but not really, as he did not know about my true life. Our relationship centered around the Spanish Rose, something which normally was fine with me, as the last thing I wanted to do was to be out somewhere with him and have a client, or, God forbid, Oona, or even Anita, see me with him. Our relationship had progressed to the point where it had become sexual, something that had been inevitable. We were two adults who enjoyed being with each other, and who cared for each other. It had happened in November, on my twenty-third birthday. Max had invited me to his house to celebrate, the first time I had been there. No sooner had I walked in the door of a beautiful two-story house in the southern part of Coconut Grove then we headed for the bedroom, and the experience had been just as I had imagined it. Max had been both passionate and tender with me. I however, had to keep my performance as natural and straightforward as possible—it wouldn't do to show off the tricks I had learned to please a man while working for Oona. No bondage, pony play, or costumes. The last thing I wanted to do was to give Max any reason to question why I was so experienced, how I had come to acquire the knowledge.

After our first lovemaking session, Max's and my relationship had clearly moved to a deeper level. I honestly didn't think I could handle it if he were to find out what I really did for a living if our relationship continued. One day I probably would have to tell him, of course, but until then, I would keep it quiet as long as absolutely possible.

I realized that the one pleasure I did have was my continuing and still surprising friendship with Mr. Tanaka and his crew. After that first dinner we had together, we'd meet a few times to have a meal at one of the many Japanese restaurants here or to see a Japanese film in one of the two artsy cinemas in Miami that showed foreign films. Mostly, though, we would meet on South Beach, near the hotel where A Most Peaceful Place, the spa where they worked, was located. Although I would have liked to stay with them longer—because of time constraints, like me they seemed to work all the time—all we could do was to go out for a quick bite of sushi. Not ideal, but, it was better than nothing.

Unlike their Spanish, which, sadly, had virtually disappeared, my conversational Japanese continued to improve. And because every time I met with my friends, I would learn something new—a term, an expression, a colloquialism—I had become so fluent in their language that I could carry on a conversation with no problem at all. The Japanese flower-arranging classes helped a great deal, too. As per my request, Yuriko-san would address me more and more in Japanese, and I would answer her in the same language.

Mr. Tanaka and his fellow masseurs were still in Miami because their plans, through no fault of their own, had changed. They had expected to go to Buenos Aires to work in the Shiatsu massage parlor there, but the Argentine man responsible for running the business had run away with the investors' money, so the opening had been, understandably, indefinitely delayed. They had needed to support themselves while they waited for the situation to be resolved, so they all had taken jobs at A Most Peaceful Place.

A few months after they'd begun working there, Mr. Tanaka invited me to take a tour of the place, an invitation that I happily accepted. With great pride, he had escorted me through the entire location, showing me every last detail of each different massage room, which I took in with great interest.

The place just oozed serenity. When Mr. Tanaka first told me that the name of the business was A Most Peaceful Place, I had thought it quite tacky, but, after having spent an hour there, I saw that it had been most aptly named. From the moment I stepped into the reception area, it was very obvious that whoever was responsible for the design and decoration of the business had carefully chosen items that would convey peace and serenity not only to the patrons but to the staff as well.

Every wall of the spa had been painted a soothing light-green color, a shade similar to that of young bamboo stalks; the sound of running water could be heard throughout and, in the background, the soft sounds of a musical instrument I didn't recognize. When I asked Mr. Tanaka what made that enchanting sound, he had explained that it came from a very traditional musical instrument called the koto, a combination of harp, dulcimer, and lute. The few items of furniture that were in the different rooms were made from natural materials. Every member of the staff, both men and women, were dressed in cotton kimonos, with thick white socks on their feet so they could glide by without making any sounds.

And although we had spent close to an hour touring the place, I hadn't heard any voices, only the sounds of the koto—very refreshing. Mr. Tanaka had once told me that in Japan, for centuries, the occupation of masseurs had traditionally been one that blind people practiced. There were several reasons for that: it was believed that their sense of touch was much more highly developed than that of a sighted person, and they couldn't be distracted by the goings-on around them—plus, it afforded the client a sense of privacy.

On my very first visit, with every passing minute at A Most Peaceful Place, I had felt the stress and anxiety of my life lift off me as if by magic. I was hooked, and knew I would be returning, but the next time as a patron. Since then, I'd made several visits, each time blissfully receiving a Shiatsu massage from Mr. Tanaka, or, if he wasn't available, from another of my former classmates. Even though they would see me naked and would touch me all over, their doing so never felt awkward. Afterwards, we then would all go to dinner together, something that, had Mr. Tanaka and my other friends not been completely professional, wouldn't have ever been possible.

After that first tour of the place, I could not help but think again about why it was that I was so drawn to just about all the aspects of Japanese life. From the language to the culture to the art to the food to the flower arrangements, their entire way of life greatly appealed to me. Could it be that the Japanese lifestyle attracted me so much because it was in such direct contrast to my current life? What struck me most about Mr. Tanaka and his colleagues was the unhurried way in which they led their lives. Mr. Tanaka had told me that his fellow countrymen so prized beauty and order in living things that the gardeners in the parks in Japan would clean by hand each leaf and branch on the trees and bushes. The more stories like that that I heard about, the more the country fascinated to me. On numerous occasions I had told Mr.

Tanaka that I fully intended to visit his country, but that trip, given my current situation, personal and professional, would be far off into the future. Just thinking about going to Japan made me happy, making me even more determined to go.

The conversation I'd had with Mr. Vogel had upset me to such a degree that I needed to get a massage from A Most Peaceful Place to relax me. So instead of driving back to the apartment, I headed toward South Beach. Because Mr. Tanaka, bless his heart, regardless of what day or time I turned up, somehow usually managed to fit me into his schedule, I wasn't concerned that I was going there without an appointment. I felt badly for Mr. Tanaka that I was going to see him in such a state of mind, as I knew that working on someone with such stress was much harder on him because he'd have to apply much more pressure to relax my muscles.

I had been about to get on the MacArthur Causeway, the road that linked Miami proper to Miami Beach, when my business cell phone rang. Seeing who was calling, I let it ring five times before picking up.

"Magnolia." I heard Anita's voice. "I need to see you right away."

"Now? Right now?" I had been so focused on meeting with Mr. Tanaka that I especially resented her interruption. Then I thought about what she had just said: She had to meet with me? She wasn't calling to tell me that one of the clients had requested an appointment with me? What was this all about?

"Can you be at the Starbucks in Coconut Grove, the one by Cocowalk, in an hour?" Anita was insistent.

I looked at the clock on the dashboard of the car. I wasn't scheduled to have a client appointment until tonight, as she well knew, but there was absolutely no way I was going to miss my massage. "Anita, I really wish I could. But I'm working tonight, and I need this time to get ready. How about tomorrow morning?" I countered.

"All right then. Eight o'clock sharp. At that same Starbucks in Cocowalk." And she hung up before I could complain about the ungodly early hour. Anita had never, ever requested a meeting with me that way. What the hell did she want?

TENNIS
Guillermo (Willy) Santos, 25, 6'1".
Finalist, Wimbledon; Finalist, U.S. Open;
Winner, Australian Open; Winner, French Open

BACKGROUND
"Hey, Magnolia, I hope your tennis whites are clean. You'll be needing them tonight," Anita informed me.

That could only mean one thing. "Willy's already back in Miami?" The finals of the French Open had just taken place yesterday.

"No, actually, he's on the flight back from Paris," Anita corrected me. "But he called Oona just before boarding the plane to ask for your services. So if his flight is on time, he should be back home on Star Island by six o'clock. He's going to call me from the car, after he's left the airport, when he's on his way home, so I can let you know when to get there."

"He wants to meet with me as soon as he's home then, right?" It was a few minutes after four o'clock, which meant that I would have around two hours before seeing him. I could not be late for Willy. "Okay. I'll be waiting for your call."

I had been at home, taking a long, leisurely soak in the bathtub, reading a current issue of Art in America when

Anita called. I had never been particularly fond of Willy, an arrogant Argentinean tennis player, but, as he was one of Oona's best clients, I really had no choice but to show up when he asked for me.

True, he was exceptionally talented—he had either won or reached the finals of all three Grand Slams tournaments in the last year—but the fact that he felt he was God's gift to tennis did nothing to endear him to me. I was not the only person he had alienated with his behavior; throughout his career he had paid fines of hundreds of thousands of dollars to the Professional Tennis Association for his rude outbursts on the courts as well as off them. He threw rackets, insulted linesmen, spit on people in the stands, cursed using the most disgusting profanities, and yelled at reporters. Once, in the middle of a match, he had actually yanked a spectator out of his seat in the bleachers and started yelling in the guy's face.

Outrageous as he was, Willy had not been barred from playing, nor was that likely to happen. He brought fresh interest to tennis and drew in significant crowds. It was generally accepted that as long as Willy sold tickets, people would just have to put up with him. The long-suffering men and women who served as chair umpires or linesmen for his matches, however, did not enjoy his tirades; it was an open secret that they were quietly given the equivalent of combat pay when assigned to his matches.

Although Willy had never treated me badly, I suspected that he considered me to be a necessary evil. Being a normal, red-blooded male with carnal needs, he had to have sex, but given his high profile, he needed to have it with a woman he could trust, someone who would never betray him. Willy had made millions of dollars in his short career, not just by playing tennis but also by all the peripheral contracts that Oona had gotten for him. He had multiple endorsement deals with all kinds of companies, from watches to sunglasses to belts to juices. Willy's image so saturated the planet that it was impossible for a day to pass without seeing his face looking down from a billboard, or in a newspaper or on TV.

In a stroke of genius, Oona had even gotten him a deal with a baby food company. Willy appeared in numerous commercials in which he touted Babylete, a brand of cereal that suggested that if a baby was fed the cereal, then he or she could grow up to be a professional athlete, maybe even a world champion tennis player like Willy. However, it was his line of athletic clothing—shoes, shorts, shirts, warm-ups, socks, head and wrist bands, jock straps, etc.—that really raked in the mega dollars for him, and Oona, of course. And me.

Even a Willy fragrance was in the works; a company in Paris was assigned full-time on developing the scent. And if Oona were to have her way, the United States Postal Service would soon be issuing a Willy postage stamp. Oona had been working overtime to stir up Willymania and, from all accounts, she was succeeding.

If Willy was a superstar in the United States, in his native Argentina, he was a god. Whenever he went to Buenos Aires, his hometown, he was mobbed, his every move reported in the media, what he did every minute of his day making front-page news. He moved around Buenos Aires with dozens of security men around him to protect him, not from kidnappers, but from his rabid admirers.

Willy may have had millions of fans, yet he hadn't had a serious girlfriend in years. I didn't know what he was like before he was famous, but by the time I met him, he was so guarded that it was almost impossible to have a conversation with him. We were pretty much limited to speaking about the weather, but even that subject could be a minefield and I had to be especially careful when discussing it. A few months ago, he had conveyed to me that he felt I was being intrusive when I asked if he thought a particular hurricane was going to hit Miami. One night, in a moment of weakness, he had actually confessed that he wanted a steady girlfriend, someone with whom he could be himself. He'd seemed so lonely and vulnerable at that point that I almost liked him.

During one of the very few times he had confided in me, Willy had told me that there were several reasons for his not having a steady relationship. He said that after giving it much thought, he had concluded that it was mostly due to the fact that he would never really know if the girlfriend liked or loved him for who he was, or for what he was: a multimillionaire athlete, an American-Express-Black-Card-carrying meal ticket. Plus how could he be sure that she wouldn't go public with facts about their relationship? All she'd have to do is call up the National Enquirer, or TMZ or Perez Hilton or some other celebrity media outlet, or get a book deal, and every intimate detail about Willy's life would be splattered across the pages. Sometimes he would wake up in a cold sweat during the middle of the night imagining what Inside Edition or Access Hollywood would report about his private life. Quite a few of my clients worried about this stuff, but not as much as Willy.

And what if the girlfriend were to become pregnant? In spite of the many precautions Willy took, he knew that any time he had sex with a woman, she might get pregnant; and there sure were many thousand women who would not object to having a "little Willy" running around. That, he explained to me, would be her annuity for life. The first time we had sex, in spite of the fact that I had assured him numerous times that I was on the pill, he still insisted on wearing two condoms, made of such hard rubber that it was a miracle he'd been able to retain any sensation in his penis. He confessed that after having sex, sometimes he would take the used condoms with him, so the woman he'd been with could not impregnate herself with his sperm.

Because of those fears, Willy had decided he should turn to a professional for his physical needs. When Oona heard that, she'd offered him my services: sex for money, total discretion, and, most important, a guarantee that there would be no babies. It had been an offer Willy could not turn down. Still, before having had relations with me, ever cautious, Willy had insisted on meeting me.

And so last year one Saturday afternoon in late spring, in the weeks between the French Open and Wimbledon tournaments, I had gone to meet Willy at his place on fabulous Star Island. He lived in a huge, three-story rust-colored Mediterranean-style house set back from the road, with beautiful old trees planted all around it. So many fountains were placed in strategic spots on the grounds that the soothing sound of running water could be heard from every corner of the property. The house itself had a moat around it. Dr. Bernstein would have had a field day with that one.

I thought the house and grounds were enchanting and would have been thrilled to be invited to explore them both, but to my disappointment, Willy hadn't offered. Although, of course, I had watched him play tennis on television. I had never met him in person before. His image on TV did not do him justice, so I had not been prepared for how attractive and how imposing a figure Willy was. First, he was very tall for a tennis player, easily clearing six feet in height, with bronze-colored skin, light-brown eyes, and jet-black wavy hair that he wore in a ponytail. The sheer animal magnetism and raw sexuality of him was close to overwhelming, and I was certainly no shrinking violet.

From our first meeting, Willy, although very polite, had made it clear that he was looking for a no-fuss, no-muss kind of relationship, and that I was not to expect anything personal, not to get any Pretty Woman ideas. I was there for one thing, and one thing only: straight-up fornication. I must have passed inspection, as we had sex during our very first encounter, if one could call it that with the double-thick condoms he wore. I discovered that he was as businesslike and impersonal about sex as he was during our limited conversations. I really wasn't used to that, as I tended to be able to pretty much engage with my clients on every level. They were, after all, paying me to be intimate with them, so they had no trouble opening up freely.

From the very beginning, I had been put on notice that our meetings would be all business. However, I thought that as the time passed and my visits to his home on Star Island became more frequent, Willy might have become warmer, friendlier toward me. But that hadn't happened. The first time we met had set the tone for our relationship and, in the dozen or so occasions that I'd been with him, except for that one time when he'd talked about his wish to have a steady girlfriend, nothing had changed.

I have to confess that I continued to be taken a bit aback by the chilly atmosphere of our encounters. The more I saw of Willy, the more I tried to analyze him. After a while, I decided that the reason he wanted our meetings to be so businesslike was so he would not for one second confuse me for a girlfriend. I kind of liked the idea that he'd be tempted to make such a mistake. Had I been his girlfriend, he would have had to be considerate of my feelings and think of someone other than himself, something that was very difficult, if not impossible, for him to do. Not just that, but he'd have to get to know me, and let me know him—a huge hurdle. After so many years of keeping to himself, I suspected he honestly did not know who he was.

Willy was very spoiled, not exactly surprising considering how he was the center of importance in the lives of many people: his immediate family, his coaches, his trainers, his physical therapists, Oona, his bodyguards, his business associates, his attorneys, his publicist, his personal assistants (two), the live-in staff that kept up his various properties, his chef, his nutritionist, and, last but not least, his fans. As far as I could tell, Willy had at least thirty individuals on the payroll at any given time, an entourage of individuals who were totally dependent on him for their livelihood, and that number did not include any of the members of his extended family in Argentina that he completely supported. Given all the adulation he received twenty-four hours a day, it was no wonder Willy thought the whole world revolved around him.

Contrary to his public persona, where he was known for being flamboyant and over the top, in our sessions Willy was straightforward, even traditional in his sexual tastes. However, lately he had begun changing our routines in subtle ways—not by much, but enough so I could detect it. He may have thought that I hadn't picked up on the changes, though, thank God—at that point, he at least trusted me enough that we were down to one condom—but, of course, I had. After all, I was a professional, and finely attuned to every client.

The truth was that what Willy considered to be pretty daring was nothing more than departing from the usual missionary position to other rather ordinary whims. Without coming right out and saying what he wanted me to do, he would, instead, show me what his request was. Lately, his favorite position had been that I get on top of him; other times, he would only want to have oral sex (with him as the recipient). He had become so adventuresome (for him), that on one occasion, he had even playfully asked if I could tie him up using the tape that he used to bind the grip of his rackets. I have to admit, I was disappointed when he changed his mind at the last minute. Willy was such a control freak that I would have thoroughly enjoyed seeing him at my mercy.

Sometimes, though, I had trouble reading Willy and could not anticipate his moods. He kept so much to himself, that even while having sex he was unable to express his wishes. He definitely presented a challenge, so I devoted quite a bit of time to trying to figure him out. Lately, it had occurred to me that there was a definite correlation between the number of Grand Slam tournaments Willy did well in, and the increase in his interest in expanding the scope of our sexual adventures.

That Monday afternoon, I knew he had won the French Open the day before, so this encounter would give me the perfect opportunity to test my theory of the connection between his wins and his sexual exploits. I was very much looking forward to testing it out.

THE ENCOUNTER

At five-thirty, the phone rang. It was Anita. "Willy's in the car, on his way home. He's about to get on the MacArthur Causeway."

I had to get going immediately if I was to arrive at Star Island when he did. "Thanks, I'm on my way." I gathered my things and got in the elevator, heading for the parking garage.

My building had extraordinary security, and for good reason, as several of Miami's wealthiest, most prominent residents lived there. Although at times being constantly watched in public bothered me, I loved the privacy that living there gave me. During the year that I had been in my apartment, I had not met any of the other residents, which was fine with me as there was too much about my life I didn't care to discuss. I had heard that delivery people had to undergo a background check so rigid that secret service agents could barely pass it. For the individuals who were employed by the building—the administration, security guards, maintenance people, and janitorial staff—the checks were even more stringent. Given that level of service, the maintenance fees were astronomical; thankfully, I wasn't responsible for the ones for the apartment I was living in, but as far as I knew, no one had lodged any complaints. On the contrary, I had heard that there was a very long waiting list to get in.

Although Star Island was less than a mile from Miami Beach, it was not on Miami Beach proper, but rather located on the north side of the causeway, across from the ferry depot where the boats departed to Fisher Island, another luxury residential area. There were only about twenty houses on Star Island, properties worth many millions of dollars and mostly occupied by celebrities. All the houses were waterfront: on one side, they faced the channel where the cruise ships docked before heading out to sail the Caribbean Sea; on the other, the mansions, including Willy's, looked out on the waters of Biscayne Bay.

I always enjoyed driving on the causeway; the sights all around me reminded me what living in Miami was all about. Dolphins surfacing and rolling in the gentle waters of the bay; sailboats, their sails filling with wind; pelicans gracefully swooping down, beaks open, as they skimmed in search of their evening meal.

Heading east, I drove past the exits to Palm and Hibiscus Islands until I reached the traffic light that led to the bridge to Star Island. I was about to turn my blinker on to signal to turn left, when my cell phone rang.

"Hi, Anita. What's up?"

"Where the hell are you?" Anita's sounded annoyed. "Willy just called."

"Making the turn onto Star Island. I'm waiting for the light to turn green, unless, of course, you'd like me to run it and get into an accident." I let honey ripple from my voice.

"I'll call Willy to let him know you're almost there." One loud click, and Anita hung up.

Just then, the light turned green, and I crossed the bridge. I stopped at the security booth at the end of the short drive and identified myself. The guard said I was expected and raised the wooden barrier, so I could proceed onto the island. Less than a minute after leaving the gatehouse, I pulled into Willy's driveway and parked where I normally did, over by the thick hedge of ficus trees. The usual assortment of luxury cars was there: three Mercedes, two Ferraris, two Jaguars, two Hummers, and last but not least, parked closest to the house, Willy's black Bentley. For all the value he placed on privacy in his personal life, Willy did not believe in keeping a low profile in public.

The door opened before I had a chance to ring the bell, and I was escorted by Juan, the head butler, through the house and out the back toward the cottage near the tennis courts. As I walked through the property, I marveled again at how beautiful the place was.

Juan bowed toward the front door of the cottage. "Mr. Willy is there, waiting for you."

As I looked at him, I thought then, as I had done every time I had seen him, how totally inscrutable the butler's demeanor was. I had no idea what he thought of my visits to his employer, but, whatever his opinion was, he had never divulged it. Having delivered me, Juan bowed again and turned, heading back to the main house. I waited until he had disappeared from sight before walking toward the front door of the cottage. If Willy and I were to have sex there, that would be a radical change, as it would be the first time we'd ventured outside the master bedroom of his house.

On my second visit, Willy had taken me on a tour of the property. The whole place was amazing, beginning with the tile-roofed main house with its tall plantation columns, three-bedroom guest cottage, tennis courts, and enormous media building with a movie theater, a pool table, and what appeared to be every electronic game ever invented. Willy had barely spoken to me then; he had only pointed out an especially interesting detail here and there. However, as we walked through the grounds on the way to the tennis court area, it was obvious that his greatest pride was in the tennis courts.

There just wasn't one court; there were three: a regular hard court, a grass one, and a clay one. Willy explained that he wanted to be able to practice on the same kinds of surfaces he would encounter in tournaments, and so had replicated the conditions he would find when playing in courts all over the world. There were stands along side each of the courts, players' benches at the sidelines, stations for the chair umpires, and areas for the press. It was all quite impressive, and it showed how seriously Willy took the sport.

The four-room cottage at the rear of the property was dedicated to all things tennis. The main room consisted of a common area, a large space that was simply decorated with several sofas, a dining room table and chairs, a plasma television, a bar with a refrigerator that held drinks and snacks, and a computer. A real man's room. Next to the living area was the storage room for equipment: his rackets, balls, assorted nets, tennis shoes, etc. The third was a locker room with showers, dressing tables, grooming products, and other personal items, and a room for his trainer and physical therapist, with a massage table in the middle.

"Willy?" I called out, as I slowly opened the cottage door.

"I'm in the trainer's room," Willy replied. "Come on back."

I walked through several doors inside the cottage until I reached it. Willy was standing over by the massage table dressed in the white shirt and shorts that I recognized as the kind he wore during tournaments. As I got closer to him, I saw that his clothes were dirty, sweat-stained, and caked with some kind of red dirt. A stale, slightly bitter odor emanated from him, which surprised me, as Willy had always been a fanatic about hygiene.

"Congratulations on the win, Willy. I watched it on television—you played terrifically well," I said as I reached up to kiss him. It had been a grueling match and so close that I hadn't been sure Willy would win. "The French Open—what an achievement! You must be so happy." Willy had told me that that had been the one title that had eluded him, but it was the one he had wanted the most to win.

"Thanks," he said somewhat abruptly. Willy pointed to the narrow massage table with its blindingly white linens. "Take off your clothes and lie down on the table."

I did as he ordered and lay there naked, on my back,

while Willy stood silently, staring at me for such a long time that I was starting to be frightened. Suddenly, he reached for a gallon-sized plastic bottle that had been on the table by the wall, opened it, and dumped the entire con-tents—clouds and clouds of red powder—all over me, until I was covered head to toe in it. He then stepped back to look at me again.

"From Roland Garros stadium," Willy announced. "In Paris. Clay from the court that I played on and won! Yester-day." By then, there was so much dust flying around the room that all I could do was nod.

Willy stripped and lay on top of me on the massage table. We proceeded to have sex —not for a few minutes but for hours, without taking a break, on the massage table, both of us covered in red clay. All my ideas of Willy being a cold, reserved person went out the window, and I realized that I would never figure this man out, so I might as well simply enjoy the time with him.

Finally, Willy rolled off me, and sat up. "You know, Mag-nolia, in the third-set tiebreaker, when I was fighting for the match, I told myself that if I were to win, this would be my reward. I would not even shower afterward; I just dried off. I would come to you exactly as I was when I won the match and rub the clay all over you. I feared I smelled up the business-class section on the flight back, but, hopefully, the deodorant helped." He chuckled.

Touched by what he had just said, I began to smile. Hid-ing my feelings had become such an integral part of my interactions with him that I was not able to really express how pleased I was that Willy had thought of me on those critical last games of the match. Secretly, of course, I was thrilled that Willy considered me to be his reward for winning. Was that progress? It sure seemed so to me. However, instead of telling Willy that I was touched by what he'd said, I began stroking him again in the sensual way I knew he enjoyed. An admission like the one he had just made to me surely deserved some consideration, so I put extra care into my strokes.

Willy had enormous stamina, but he hadn't had much rest in the past few days. Not only had he competed in the French Open, he had played a grueling final match to win the tournament, a five-hour battle which had been decided in a tiebreaker. He hadn't rested even then, after the match, and had instead chosen to immediately return to Miami, to have an encounter with me. The man was exhausted and a bit smelly, usually a turn-off for me, but it had the opposite effect with Willy.

Wanting to show Willy my pleasure at being with him at such an important time, and remembering the occasion, a few months back, when he had wanted to have me tie him up with tape, I left Willy dozing, went into the trainer's closet where I knew the supplies were kept, and brought back a couple of rolls of tape.

"Come on, Willy, wake up. Please turn around." I gently nudged him. "Here." I lifted up my hands with the rolls of tape in them so he could see them. "Now it's my turn to decide what we're going to do."

"Magnolia, what the hell?" Willy sat up on the table and tried to push me away, but I had been faster than him, so I already had his hands tied behind his back before he'd had a chance to touch me. I had really not played fair, as the man was exhausted and half asleep; any other time, he would have been quicker than me. I was undeterred though, and took full advantage of him in his weakened state.

That night we had sex every way Willy wanted, doing things that he admitted he'd dreamed about but hadn't yet done. We started as usual with me orally pleasing him, which he got off from the most. Then, with his hands still tied up, he fucked me senseless as I was just lying under him, moaning at the top of my lungs. Willy was rough in a sort of arrogant tennis player way, but he was great. His athleticism was nothing short of astonishing.

Although on a previous occasion Willy had hinted that he might want to try getting into bondage, after watching him for a few moments as he was acting with his hands and ankles tied with the tape, I determined that he was not enjoying himself as much as he had done at the beginning. It wasn't anything he said, as, at that point, honestly, we weren't talking much; it was more than his enthusiasm waned a bit. I had an idea.

"Willy, would you like to try something a bit different?" I ventured.

"Different how? Getting tied up is already different," he mumbled. Willy was lying on his stomach, resting after our last go-around.

"Are you up for some anal sex?" I whispered. There was a kind of protocol involved in that particular kind of sex—the first time a couple tried it together, both parties had to consent and agree to whatever they were going to do. Willy, for all his bravado on the court, was really not all that experienced as far as sex was concerned, and I suspected he had never done that. Our relationship had evolved to the degree that he trusted me, but anal sex was not for everyone, so I had to be respectful. I was not asking the question out of the blue, but rather because I had noticed that Willy became ever slightly more aroused when I stroked him in the area just below his scrotum, especially when I did it in a circular motion.

"Anal sex? I've never tried that. I thought only gay people had anal sex. Or perverts." Willy frowned, and for a minute I feared I had overstepped my bounds. This was clearly unchartered territory, but that night there definitely was something different about Willy. Maybe the weeks he had spent in Paris prior to his win at the French Open had opened him to new experiences.

"Actually no. One quarter of all straight couples have had or do practice anal sex." Like Willy, I had also been under that mistaken impression, but Dr. Bernstein, in one of our sessions, had informed me of that statistic. "Do you think you might want to try it?" I asked him gently.

Willy was silent. "I heard it was painful. And dangerous. I don't want to get hurt."

"Yes, it can be, but not if it's done right," I assured him. "We can try it, and, if you don't like it, or if you're uncomfortable, just tell me to stop and I will immediately."

"You've done that before, right?" Willy was becoming curious.

"On occasion. I know what I'm doing." I got up from the massage table where we had been lying and walked over to the closet where the medical supplies were kept. I opened the door and took out the tube of K-Y Jelly I had spotted there earlier. Then, from the counter next to the table, I picked up a condom from the small pile on the corner. I reached for a couple of the pillows that had fallen to the floor, and slid them under Willy's butt, so it was elevated. Perfect. I lay down next to Willy and began stroking him the way I was doing before, concentrating on the area between his penis and anus. Soon Willy began moaning with pleasure. I kept playing with him until he was fully aroused, then, in one quick motion I opened the condom and placed it in my right index finger. Then, I applied a generous dollop of K-Y Jelly on it, and gently, very gently, began slowly inserting the tip of my finger up his ass, stopping at the first knuckle. I began to alternate between pressing and removing my finger, movements that I knew would further stimulate the many nerve endings there. By this point, Willy was having trouble controlling himself and had begun panting heavily.

While I pleasured Willy, I cautioned myself to be very careful, as it was possible to inadvertently injure him in the process. As I stroked Willy, I could see he was on the verge of having an orgasm, so I withdrew my finger, quickly turned him over on the bed, and straddled him. We both came at exactly the same moment.

And so the encounter continued, with us having sex, then napping to recover our strength until the light of dawn began filtering in through the window blinds. I was tired and sore, but quite pleased for myself for what I'd accomplished with Willy. The fact that he had trusted me to consent both to tying him up and having anal sex indicated that we'd broken a huge barrier. Just before leaving, I stopped in the bathroom of the cottage to clean myself up. I took one look at myself in the floor-length mirror, and saw that I was still covered in the red clay from the Roland Garros stadium. I looked like a native from the Stone Age, like the ones living with their tribes up the Amazon or in New Guinea who were featured in shows on the National Geographic station. What the hell was in that red clay? Some French aphrodisiac, no doubt.

Soon after dawn, I left Willy peacefully sleeping on the massage table, covered by a white sheet, the clay from

Roland Garros Stadium long worn off, but the tape marks on his hands and ankles still clearly showing. As I drove home, yawning, I wondered how our next session would be. Now that we had experimented with other forms of sexual play, would we go back to the missionary position, or would we continue on our voyage of sexual adventure? Trite as that might sound, I knew only time would tell. But the thing I did know was that we had passed a number of milestones. Willy had only worn a single condom throughout the encounter. No more doubles from now on, thank God.

Chapter 16

*E*arly the next morning, even though I was fifteen minutes early, Anita was waiting for me at Starbucks, sitting at
a table by the window with a stern expression on her face. I
saw that she hadn't ordered anything to drink, so I didn't do
so either, but instead just sat across from her.

I hadn't seen Anita outside of the O'Ryan and Associates
office in over a year, since when she had picked me up at my
apartment in Little Havana. In the unflattering light of early
morning, Anita looked slightly ghoulish. She was dressed in
a mannish, navy-blue tailored suit with thick, tan stockings,
black, low-heeled pumps, and a matching quasi-leather bag.
Her black, slightly oily-looking hair was pulled back into a
bun, and she wore no makeup, which she sorely needed. I
couldn't help but notice she had a slight moustache, and her
eyebrows needed plucking.

I was wearing my normal outfit of blue jeans, T-shirt,
and espadrilles. "Hello, Anita. Morning." I tried to find a
comfortable position, which was extremely hard to do on
this rickety chair. At that time of the morning—Miami
was not an early town—Starbucks was not very crowded.
"What's up?"

"You know, Magnolia, that I am aware of the terms and
conditions of your employment at O'Ryan and Associates,"

Anita dove right in. No sooner were the words out of her mouth than I knew why she had requested the meeting.

"Yes, I know that." I nodded.

"The other night, Tuesday, I went to dinner at a restaurant in Little Havana. My brother invited Mother and me to a place where he and his wife often go. It was her birthday, and she wanted to celebrate it there." Anita pulled up her chair, and moved closer to me. "You want to know the name of the restaurant?"

Tuesday? This past Tuesday? I felt a shiver go through me. Yes, I'd been there, at the Spanish Rose. I held myself under control: I was not about to give Anita the satisfaction of having spooked me. "There are many restaurants in Little Havana, Anita."

"Yes, that's true." She smiled as well, but her smile was more like a grimace. "But, as far as I know there's only one Spanish Rose—and you don't have an identical twin," she announced triumphantly.

Anita, realizing that I was not going to say anything, took a deep breath and continued speaking. "Well, once I realized that it was you, Magnolia, who was sitting in the booth, kissing the man with you, I asked my brother, who, as I told you, frequents there, if he recognized either you or the man you were with."

"Ah," was all I could manage to say.

"My sister-in-law told me the man, Max, was the owner of the restaurant, and that you were his girlfriend. She did not know your name, but said that she and my brother had seen you there on various occasions." Anita grimaced again, this time with a victorious look in her eyes. "With your looks, Magnolia, you're hard to miss." That last was not intended to be a compliment.

Anita had not summoned me to Starbucks just to tell me that she had seen me with Max in the restaurant, or that I had been described to her as being his girlfriend. No, she had a plan. Anita had disliked me from the minute she laid eyes on me, but it wasn't even a slight dislike. Anita envied me. She knew that Oona fancied me from day one, and that bothered her more than anything else, and like a cunning snake, she had been waiting for just the right time to strike. By my breaking the no-men clause in my agreement with Oona, she now had me exactly where she wanted me—or so she fervently believed.

"So, Anita, what do you intend to do with this information?" There was no point in denying anything.

"I want you to quit working for Oona. Immediately," Anita informed me in a cold voice. "If you don't, I'll tell Oona what I found out."

"Why not tell her now?" I wondered.

"Because she thinks so highly of you, it would crush her. And let's admit this much to each other. We both know how Oona truly feels about you. Learning how you betrayed her, how you took advantage of her generosity and her friendship, that would break her heart. Really, her self-esteem would be shattered to learn that she'd misjudged you so badly." Then Anita leaned over the table, getting so close to me that I thought she was going to spit in my face. "I couldn't have such a two-timing little shit as yourself do that to such a wonderful woman."

Finally it was out in the open. Anita was in love with Oona; she loved her so much that she was willing to cover up for me to spare her the pain of finding out that I'd betrayed her. So Anita liked women; did Oona? She must, otherwise Anita would not have acted the way she was doing.

"You know, Anita, I think you've just done me a huge favor," I announced, as I stood up. "I was about to quit anyway, and you've just given me the motivation to do it." I leaned over, and kissed her French style on both cheeks. Anita looked so shocked that I thought she would have a coronary on the spot. That had certainly not been the reaction she had expected.

I flew out of Starbucks. Until the meeting with Anita, it hadn't been clear to me how deeply working as Oona's edge was affecting me. The confrontation with Anita, although unpleasant, forced me think about how I felt about the life I was leading in Miami. For the past few months, I'd been so busy that I had not examined my feelings, but now, with what had just happened, I would have to, especially as I was going to have to plan the next chapter. I'd always known there would be an end to my life as an "edge," but I sure as hell did not think it was going to come while I was sitting on a rickety chair at Starbucks at eight o'clock in the morning.

Although it was not easy to admit it, the truth was that deep down inside, after an initial adjustment period, I had actually come to enjoy what I was doing. Sure, I was having sex for money, and that made me a prostitute, but I was an expensive, high-class one, a distinction that allowed me to feel superior to the kind of women normally associated with that profession, street walkers and escorts. I may have worn designer dresses and driven a Mercedes, but still, at the end of the day, that's what I was. There was no sugarcoating it.

The fact that I had come to enjoy meeting with Oona's clients was unexpected. When I broke down the reasons for that, though, it should not have been surprising. First of all, I was making a lot of money; second, I was being challenged to come up with appropriate and creative ways to take care of the needs of the athletes, which I enjoyed; third, these men expressed appreciation for my efforts, which made me feel as if I was contributing to their success in their respective sports.

Oona was very pleased with me, for I had increased her bottom-line significantly, but perhaps even more important for her, the hemorrhage of her clients' desertion had stopped. Not just that, but her client list increased; nothing like success to bring on more success. Oona was thriving in a male-dominated field, and I had helped bring that about. Power to women, right?

Then, as far as my personal life was concerned, that was also satisfying. My relationship with Max was going as well as could be expected; I treasured my friendship with Tanaka-san; I could now speak fluent Spanish, and passable Japanese; my body, thanks to Brandi, was in phenomenal shape. I continued to meet with Dr. Bernstein, without Oona's knowledge, sessions that I thoroughly enjoyed, especially as I paid for them myself, so I was free to discuss whatever I wanted.

Needless to say, in spite of the positive spin I put on my situation, not everything was rosy: I knew that the double life I was leading was starting to take a toll on me. I was becoming increasingly apprehensive about the risks I was taking and I had no illusions about the price I would have to pay if what I was doing came out in the open. The prospect of going to jail was a very real possibility; Miami was a small community, and I could not expect to continue doing what I was doing indefinitely. Then there was the matter of filing false tax returns. As the daughter of an accountant, I was very aware of the fact that, when all else had failed, that had been how the government finally nabbed Al Capone. I did not want to follow his example.

I missed my family greatly and was beginning to avoid contact with them, so I would not have to lie to them. If they were to find out what I'd been doing, that would destroy them. And they wouldn't just blame me for my choices; they would feel like failures for having raised a daughter who would do what I'd done. And the lies I had told them! Those they could never forgive, especially as they had been constant and creative, not a one-time deal.

Also, I lived in fear that Max would find out about the life I'd been leading. Max was a proud man, and he would feel betrayed, and rightly so. I could expect to pay a high price for having deceived him, and in such a spectacular and totally hurtful manner. Knowing how the truth would impact him, I probably should have never become involved with him, but, selfishly, I kept going. I needed him, and I had put myself ahead of him, something that I was certainly not proud of.

Although I talked a good game about volunteering and helping children, the truth was that I'd not done anything about it. Sure, thinking about it made me feel better about myself, but so far, that's all I'd done. It was time to put my money where my mouth was, to validate the reason I'd told myself I had accepted Oona's offer.

Anita had made the decision to leave the life for me; she'd not given me any choice, so she'd actually done me a favor, but she did not know that. She thought she'd buried me, and the fact that she had brought about the exact opposite made me very happy. Well, she'd never know the truth, that was for sure. It was time to change course, while I was still able to do so. The question was, what road to take? Now I felt free, much freer than I had thought I would feel, so relieved to be finished working as an edge. It was true what Anita had said, that Oona had been wonderful with me, always treating me with the utmost respect, and paying me exactly as she said she would. For that, I owed her much.

I got into my car and headed toward my apartment, but I could barely concentrate on my driving; my head was so full of plans as to what I was going to do next. I knew to the penny how much money I had made during my time with Oona; there was just under two million dollars in the safety deposit bank and brokerage accounts combined and the lock box under my bed.

I found myself heading to South Beach. Subconsciously and without meaning to, I had decided to go to A Most Peaceful Place. The massage I'd had last week after my first meeting with Mr. Vogel had been great, but I needed to see Mr. Tanaka again, talk about my plans. It was early, but I wasn't worried Mr. Tanaka wouldn't be able to see me. His first appointment, he had told me, was at six o'clock in the morning.

The longer I drove, the more determined I became to follow through with realizing my dreams, but I would just have to do that a different way and study the various options. Rather than start a new school, I could donate a substantial amount to an existing school, one that was already up and running and in need of funds; I could volunteer there; I would give money each year to an inner-city school, so it could set up an arts program along the lines of the one I'd had in my mind. The question now became: what kind of business could I start that would generate enough income so that I could continue to do that? I would have to think about that long and hard.

For now, I had to get one final encounter with an athlete under my belt so I would clear the two million dollar mark, a figure that had a nice ring to it. Just one more, and I would be done. Anita hadn't given me a deadline for resigning, after all, though if I didn't do it within a reasonable amount of time, she probably would do it for me.

I headed east to Collins Avenue, where A Most Peaceful Place was located, and parked the Mercedes at one of the many empty spaces along the building. As I locked the door, I looked at the car with sadness, for once I quit working for Oona, I would no longer have it. I headed up the path toward the front doors of the building, and as I walked, considered how I could go about making money. The one thing I could be sure of, given my previous experience seeking a job, was that I would not be using my art history degree from the University of Minneapolis here in Miami. I was pretty resourceful, so I really didn't have any fear that I wouldn't be able to come up with a viable plan, one that would give me both personal and professional satisfaction, while allowing me to make money.

I was looking forward to my new life, one without lies and secrets.

NASCAR

Waldo Peterson, 27, 6'3", 200 lbs.
Race-car driver, Homestead-Miami Speedway

BACKGROUND

"Hey, Magnolia, start your engine!" Anita positively chortled with delight. "Waldo's back in town!"

If it weren't for the fact that I was intimately acquainted with Anita's personality, I would have mistakenly guessed from her tone of voice that afternoon that she was an upbeat, positive, bubbly person. I'd found out early on that Waldo, and only Waldo, could transform Anita from Miss Crotchety into Miss Little Ray of Sunshine—that was the power of his magnetic character.

Frankly, I wasn't surprised at the metamorphosis Anita underwent whenever she discussed Waldo, especially given her predilection for women. I, also, immediately became a more cheerful person by just thinking of him. Waldo had that effect not only on women—gay or straight—but also on pretty much everyone he came into contact with. It wasn't that Waldo was exceptionally good-looking; he was certainly attractive enough, but I'd often suspected that the appeal was probably due more to his infectious personality than to any perfect features. Waldo had thick, dirty-blond hair, which he still cut himself just as he had done since childhood, so it had an uneven, chopped look. He had caramel-colored eyes framed by black lashes, and a ruddy complexion, the last a combination of too much sun, cigarettes, and beer. As Waldo was always either laughing or smiling, he was constantly showing off a perfect set of pearly white teeth. He just oozed such happiness and goodwill that it was a pleasure to be around him. He was quite tall for a race-car driver, and after speculating how he did so, I finally asked Waldo how he was even able to get inside the car. He didn't give me an answer and, instead, always a good sport, he just told me it would be easier to observe.

One afternoon in late summer, Waldo and I had gone to the Homestead-Miami Speedway so I could watch him get into his car. Much as a contortionist might have done, Waldo actually folded his body into sections before entering the car. Immediately I knew why, instead of just giving me an answer, he'd thought it best to demonstrate his technique in a way I would understand. Waldo had just moved his body in a similar fashion to the way he did while we were having sex—it was quite erotic, actually, watching him manipulate it that way.

Waldo Peterson was what was referred to as a "good ole boy" in the best sense of the term. He had been born in the back hills of North Carolina, in Rooster's Beak, a town with so few residents that it didn't even rate a stoplight. According to Waldo, no one really noticed they didn't have one, since they wouldn't have had any use for it—not exactly the kind of community you'd expect to breed a NASCAR star. No one in Rooster's Beak had enough money to buy a car and, even if they were to have owned one, there were no paved roads to drive on or gas stations where they could fill up, no mechanics, and no stores stocking parts, so it would have pretty much been impractical.

Besides, as Waldo so eloquently put it, the only traffic that used to come through town consisted of the small, stripped-down pickup trucks that were used to transport the barrels of moonshine around the county, and those only made the round trip from the stills which were hidden in the hills to the distribution points along the creek, and back. The making of moonshine whiskey was Rooster's Beak's only industry, and one in which every resident was involved.

I always loved hearing Waldo tell his stories about what it had been like growing up there, but I especially enjoyed listening to him after he'd had a few too many beers, when his accent became even more country and the stories more outlandish. Had he not chosen to be a race-car driver, I was convinced he would have been a very successful stand-up comic, that's how gifted a storyteller he was. Sometimes the stories were so incredible that I suspected he might be making them up. Well, he might have been making up some of them, but what was real was how talented a driver he was.

In one of the few serious moments we'd had, Waldo confessed that sometimes he'd thought the reason he had become a race-car driver was because he'd grown up without a car. His father and five older brothers had been arrested on numerous occasions for their illegal activities and had served time for them. For generations, the Peterson family had owned an operated one of the more successful moonshine whiskey operations in their part of the county—not necessarily illegal, but their aversion to paying the significant taxes they owed on profits was something the law did not take kindly to. Although Waldo was allowed to work in the family business, they wanted to protect him, the baby in the family, from the same fate. So, to limit his exposure, he had been forbidden to even ride in one of the trucks that carried the liquor. Waldo would walk, instead, to and from the still halfway up the mountain.

Waldo really enjoyed telling me the story of the first time he'd ridden in a car. He said it had been at the age of fifteen, when he had been arrested by a couple of deputy county sheriffs as he stirred moonshine at the family still. He had been taken to the station in a squad car, not exactly a luxurious vehicle: the back seat was made of hard plastic, and the windows were locked in the up position, which not only kept it stiflingly hot, but kept the assortment of smells trapped inside. The doors had no handles, something that was irrelevant, as he was handcuffed. The clear bulletproof divider between the front and back seats had kept Waldo from checking out the front part of the squad car, something he said he would have enjoyed doing.

Still, in spite of the less than ideal circumstances of his first car ride, Waldo reported that he had been in heaven. All he'd had to do, he said, was inhale the different smells of that squad car—gas fumes, leaking oil, stale cigarettes, old vomit, hopelessness and despair—and he knew he was home.

The reason Waldo had been picked up was because it had been his turn to stir the brew his father and uncles had made as it cooked, one of the steps in making moonshine whiskey. When the cops descended on the still, they had caught Waldo with a giant spoon in his hand, moonshine dripping from it. While on the ride to the station at Rooster's Beak, Waldo volunteered to the officers that the ride in their police car was the first time he had ever been in a motor vehicle of any kind.

Waldo was familiar enough with the law to know that because he was fifteen years old, he would have to go before a juvenile court judge to determine what would happen to him. There was no such judge in Rooster's Beak, so that meant he would have to be transported to a neighboring county, requiring another car ride, something he found himself anticipating with joy. He told me he was the only guy in the holding pen who was actually looking forward to going in front of a judge, even though he was in very real danger of being sent away to a boys' home for three years until he was an adult, to be rehabilitated. But even knowing that, Waldo, ever the optimist, didn't feel bad about the fix he was in. Something was sure to work out; it always did.

The cops had taken a shine to him, and after learning about his newfound passion for cars, had given him Car and Driver and NASCAR magazines to look through while in jail. Waldo devoured the first set of magazines, reading them so fast and with such obvious pleasure that the officers gave him others. It was while incarcerated that Waldo decided not just that he wanted to pursue his interest in cars, but that he was going to aim much higher than that, and set his sights on becoming a NASCAR race-car driver.

The charges against him were dropped. It was a first offense, and everybody he met liked him so he caught a huge break, and he walked out of court free to pursue his dream of being a race-car driver. It had been during the time he had spent in jail that Waldo had first heard talk about NASCAR racing and that one of the greatest NASCAR tracks in the United States was in his home state of North Carolina. So with fifty dollars, which represented his grandma's entire lifetime savings that she slipped to him on the day he left Rooster's Beak, he headed out for the NASCAR track at Concord, North Carolina. Coincidentally, he managed to hitch a ride there in the squad car of the very officers who had arrested him.

Waldo, though uneducated, had a healthy amount of street smarts and endless ambition. Once in Concord, he figured out that, rather than beginning his NASCAR career by boasting of how he intended to become a driver himself, it would be a better strategy if he hung around the track doing odd jobs and picking up information. The first thing he learned was that there was serious money to be made as a NASCAR driver. That year, in 1992, the driver with the most points was Alan Kulwicki, driving a Ford, who took home winnings adding up to almost a million dollars. To a skinny, gangly, fifteen-year-old kid from Rooster's Beak who was sleeping in cars and eating leftovers that restaurant owners were going to throw out, earning a milion dollars a year by doing something he loved was simply unimaginable.

Waldo told me that NASCAR started in Wilkes County, North Carolina, two counties over from Rooster's Beak.

Apparently, the fellows that made moonshine in the mountains needed fast cars so they could outrun the officers of the law, so the very enterprising residents of Wilkes County dedicated themselves to adapting cars they had into faster and more maneuverable vehicles.

Fifteen years old, Waldo didn't even have a driver's license; still he continued to hang around the track, getting to know the drivers and their crews. He was extremely likeable, and a pleasure to be around, so much so that one day, one of the drivers took pity on him and offered him a job as his gofer. Waldo had a reputation for being hardworking, eager, and reliable; soon he found himself actually driving his boss's car, not racing, of course, but moving the car around as needed. By the time he got his driver's license, Waldo told me that he'd been driving cars worth hundreds of thousands of dollars for years. He was so busy that he wouldn't have bothered with the formality of taking the driver's test, an omission that he was forced to correct when he was stopped for speeding at Watkins Glen in New York State.

Although Waldo's road to the top had not been an easy one, he'd traveled it with style, grace, and good humor, with the result that he'd become the most highly regarded driver of his generation, a role model for thousands of boys and girls who aspired to be race-car drivers. He was generous with his time and money, and the fans loved him.

Waldo realized early on that he needed help in managing not only his career, but also the significant sums of money he was earning. By the time he retained Oona to represent him, his endorsement deals were worth many times over what he was making with his wins at the track. Almost immediately after Waldo had signed with her, Oona had phoned to tell me to expect a new client, one that drove fast—very, very fast. Oona's clients requested my services for one or more of a variety of different reasons, mostly involving some kind of situation that needed resolving. I expected to hear about a problem that Waldo was having.

In Waldo's case, however, Oona had told me that when she asked the race-car driver why he wanted to retain my services, he'd answered, "Because I like bad girls—they're the most fun!"

Me? A bad girl? Really.

Not surprisingly, I could not wait to meet Waldo.

THE ENCOUNTER

The meetings with Waldo always took place at his home, a place that was remarkable and unique. Located in Homestead, a predominantly agricultural town south of Miami, the house was right in the middle of a one-acre section of a strawberry field. Waldo later told me that the building that he converted into his home was originally a refrigerated strawberry warehouse. On my first visit there, the first thing I noticed was that the building, a huge square concrete block, had no windows, something that I, being slightly claustrophobic, found kind of creepy. Finding a place to park my car would not be a problem, as there were over two dozen slots, twelve on each side of the large patio-garden area in front of the house.

After parking the car, as I had been instructed to do, I phoned Waldo to let him know I had arrived. As soon as he answered, he apologized that he wasn't able to personally escort me in as he was finishing something, but that he would unlock the front door, and I should go right in and make myself at home, that he would be with me in a few minutes. I couldn't recall the last time one of Oona's clients had apologized to me for anything. Naturally, I was charmed that he had done so.

Not quite knowing what to expect, I slowly let myself into the house. Inside, I found myself in an enormous room, one that had been divided into two distinct areas. At one end was what looked to be a lounge area, all done in red, with banquettes lining the walls and small round tables in front of each. A huge, fully stocked copper bar ran along the entire length of the far wall. The area to the left of the room was a bit larger, with a large stage made out of Lucite in the middle, with three thick steel poles lined up in a triangle in the center of the stage. As I looked around me all I could think about was what a hell of a party boy Waldo had to be! No wonder he liked bad girls. I was about to explore the place further when I heard a door open Waldo bounded towards me.

"Magnolia, darling! Look at you! You're just as gorgeous as I was told you'd be! No, wait, that's not true. You're better than gorgeous, you're luscious, too!" He pulled me toward him and enveloped me in a hug; he smelled sweet, in a faint kind of way, like tobacco. "Shoot, where are my manners? Leaving a lady thirsty in my house? Here, let's get you a drink."

It didn't take me long to conclude that Waldo was not a normal man: he was a force of nature. I was actually looking forward to an encounter, as being with Waldo was surely going to be fun.

Waldo took me by the hand and led me over to the bar by the far wall, indicating I should sit on one of the stools in front of it. "So, what'll it be?" Waldo looked me over in such a penetrating way that I felt as if he was x-raying me. "You look like a champagne kind of gal."

"Champagne would be wonderful," I replied. I liked to keep my wits about me at all times, so I normally did not drink, or at least, not much, while meeting with clients, but that afternoon, I broke that rule with Waldo. It was the first of many I would break, as it turned out.

Waldo opened the door of the refrigerator that sat to one side of the bar, and picked out a bottle of Cristal champagne from the dozens that were there. I watched as he expertly twisted off the cork then poured some of the golden liquid into a flute made of the thinnest glass possible.

Waldo might be a good ole boy, but somewhere along the line he had picked up some pretty sophisticated tastes. I watched him pour the Cristal with such ease, and it was clear to me that Waldo had left Rooster's Beak behind a long time ago. He handed the glass to me, and then opened the refrigerator door again. This time, however, he took out a can of Pabst Blue Ribbon beer and tipped the can to me. "Cheers."

In spite of Waldo's ebullience, I sensed that he was a private person. Given that, I began by asking him a relatively innocuous question. "Have you lived here, in this place, for a long time?"

"I bought it in 1995, right after the speedway was built," he said.

"It's a very unusual house," I commented, the understatement of the year.

"I'll take you on a tour later, if you want to see the rest." He finished his beer and grabbed another from the fridge.

We stayed at the bar, sipping our drinks, talking for hours. Sometime during that time, Waldo had gotten up, and put on some music, mostly Willie Nelson. The quality of the sound that filled the room was so amazing, so pure, that a professional engineer must have installed the system. As the day wore on, I found myself doing what I swore I would never let happen: I began to take a personal interest in a client. Work was work, and my personal life was my personal life, and the only way I could manage would be to keep the two totally separate, something I had so far managed to do with Max Martinez. Once again I thanked God for my ability to compartmentalize, a strategy that had worked for me until the afternoon I walked into a windowless concrete block house in the middle of fields full of ripe strawberries in Homestead and met Waldo.

Sitting there on the barstool, talking with Waldo, sipping Cristal while listening to Willie Nelson, I felt my resolve about not getting personally involved with a client begin to crumble. There were the obvious reasons: he was attractive, funny, smart, successful, and wealthy—but that was the case with many of my other clients, so that couldn't be the only explanation. This man appealed to me on a deeper, purer level. I, who had always prided myself on being clearheaded, was becoming confused, and I didn't like it. Even though I was having a wonderful time sitting there, talking with Waldo, I began to wonder when he would get down to business, the reason why I was there. Since Waldo did not seem to be in any hurry to take our encounter to a more intimate level, I decided that maybe he had been waiting for me to make the first move. After all, I was a bad girl, and bad girls were expected to take the initiative.

By then, I had drunk close to three-quarters of the bottle of Cristal by myself, so I pushed my glass aside and reached over across the bar for one of Waldo's hands. "A little while ago, you said you were going to give me a tour of your house." I smiled sweetly. "I'd love to see it."

Waldo sprung into action so fast that it confirmed what I had suspected: he had been waiting for me to make a move. I wanted to laugh out loud at the absurdity of that—here was a man who routinely risked his life by racing cars at speeds in excess of two hundred miles an hour, but he could not initiate physical contact with me. That shyness alone endeared him to me even more. He took me by the hand, and we walked through the main room heading toward the entrance of a long, very wide hallway. Before entering, I stood there and counted ten doors on each side, with a massive, heavily paneled door at the center of the back wall. The doors to all the rooms were closed.

"Are these rooms all bedrooms?" I wondered as I counted all the doors we had passed.

"Well, they're not all bedrooms; maybe I'll show you those later on," he said, dodging the question and letting go of my hand. "I want to take you to the room at the end, my bedroom."

With every step I took, the more curious I became. Waldo had seemed so open about everything, but quite mysterious about that. What was behind those doors? Was he hiding something? Well, I was just going to have to wait to find out.

Waldo opened the door to his bedroom, and I found myself literally in heaven! I was so overwhelmed at the sight that it took a few moments for my brain to process the sight. From the doorway on in, the entire room was draped with some kind of white, gauzy cotton material shaped like giant clouds. To enter the room, it was necessary to open a set of iron gates that were wrapped in white satin. As if those didn't provide sufficient security, the gates were guarded by a life-sized statue of a frowning, bearded man, Saint Peter, I assumed, who was holding some kind of clipboard. The stern-looking saint seemed to be stationed there to judge who would be allowed to enter the hallowed room, reminding me of the rope person at an exclusive club. I prayed I would make the cut and be allowed to enter.

Suspended from the ceiling were perhaps a dozen blond-haired, blue-eyed cherubs, their bodies loosely wrapped in filmy white cloths. At the far corner, I spotted an angel holding a giant gold harp, busy playing Baroque-style music. In the center, was a huge four-poster bed, the top of which was covered with a canopy of ivory-colored, satin fabric. The white carpet was so thick—at least three or four inches deep—that I was having trouble walking on it. The walls, which had been painted with murals in the style Michelangelo used in the Sistine Chapel, depicted different heavenly scenes.

Waldo waited until I'd had an opportunity to take it all in before speaking. "So, Magnolia, what do you think?"

"I've never seen anything like it, ever, Waldo," I replied truthfully. "Is this what heaven looks like?"

"Yes, Magnolia. You are now in heaven." He smiled, and took my hand, then led me toward the bed. Once there, he slowly began to undress me, carefully laying my clothes on the chair next to the bed. When I was naked, he turned to me and asked. "You want to know why I chose heaven as the theme for my bedroom?"

I nodded, still somewhat speechless.

"Because I might die at any moment when I'm on the track—one split second, that's all it takes. Something goes wrong and it's over for me." He smiled. "I don't want to be afraid; I don't want to be ruled by fear, to have fear affect my judgments; that's why I made this room this way, so I'm not afraid of going to heaven. I have heaven right here." He waved his left hand around the room to prove his point. He then began taking off his own clothes, which he placed next to mine on the chair.

Waldo may have been a speed demon on the track, but in bed he was slow, very slow, wonderfully slow. Some of my clients could be a bit rough, their sexual requirements served with kink on the side, but Waldo was different; he didn't need to use any props. No sex toys, no Viagra or Cialis, not even sports equipment. He was gentle and knew how and where to stroke to please a woman.

Waldo got on top of me and kissed me on the lips, with the softest touch of all. Then, he slowly moved down and took my right nipple in his mouth, then the left, his tender wet tongue, making circular movements around them. God, I thought I'd come right there and then! I was getting increasingly aroused, but Waldo didn't progress to the sex act itself. I began to suspect that he liked foreplay better than the intercourse. I was to discover that even outside the bedroom, Waldo knew how to treat a lady, even if that lady was a whore. Usually men, although they enjoyed their services, did not much care for a hooker, but Waldo looked past my profession. It was a true pleasure to spend time with him.

Waldo and I got along so well that he began requesting me more and more often. I looked forward to the visits, anticipating our pleasurable experiences in bed. After a while, I forgot that I was there for professional reasons, and we began to think of each other as friends. It was quite nice, really, a change from the way I had to behave with my other clients. As comfortable as we were with each other, still there were some secrets between us: for example, what was behind the locked doors. It had only been after I'd been there a dozen or so times that Waldo, quite unexpectedly, let me see what the secret was.

In the rooms behind the doors were the cars that Waldo

had driven when he won NASCAR races. With the opening of each new door, I felt as if I was coming closer to really
knowing this man. And not just in the biblical sense. I found
myself liking that feeling a great deal. I felt normal with him.
It had been a very, very long time since I'd felt that way with a
client, if ever.

Chapter 17

Sitting in the waiting area of A Most Peaceful Place, wait-ing for Mr. Tanaka to come out, I decided that I would start by being honest with him; I no longer wanted to hide what I had been doing. That new, open attitude would only apply to Mr. Tanaka. As far as my family was concerned, they would not benefit from my newfound sincerity. And, of course, nei-ther would Max. I could not come clean with them, not after having spent all this time telling them lies about my life. No, no confession to relieve my guilt would be forthcoming. I would have to live with the knowledge of what I had done.

Just then, Mr. Tanaka came out from the back, and after greeting me, whisked me away to one of the massage rooms in the back. "I am surprised to see you again today, Magnolia-san."

"Yesterday's massage was so good, I wanted to have another one right away," I replied.

Mr. Tanaka looked at me, then, without explanation, turned and left the room, then came back a few minutes later. "I have arranged to be able to spend this time with you," he explained. "I sense you need to discuss something important with me."

"Yes, I do. Thank you, Mr. Tanaka. I am very grateful." However, instead of giving me a robe to change into, he indicated I should sit, fully clothed, on the table. He stood a few feet away and looked me over with those piercing black eyes of his that missed nothing.

"Magnolia-san, is something troubling you?" Mr. Tanaka spoke in a gentle tone of voice. "You seem different."

This was the first time that Mr. Tanaka had ever asked me a personal question. "Oh, Tanaka-sama." I purposely used the honorific term of address. "I received some upsetting news today. Well, the news was bad in the beginning, but then not so bad."

Speaking in Japanese. I began by telling Mr. Tanaka the story of how I came to be living in Miami, starting with my having accompanied Fabulous Fred here after graduating from college in Minneapolis, and how it came that I ended up sitting next to Oona so long ago at the Miami Sports Bar. I left nothing out. Not the arrangement with Oona to be her edge, nor the description of my training, nor the stories of my various encounters with athletes. I spent the most time describing my goal of setting up the art school for inner-city children, and telling him that it was going to have to be postponed, but I had found an alternative way to realize that dream.

The only time that Mr. Tanaka showed any kind of a reaction to what I had been telling him was when I mentioned that because of my training, I considered myself to be an American version of the geisha. After I'd finished speaking, we sat in silence, listening to the soft, soothing music of the koto playing in the background. Mr. Tanaka, moving slowly, handed me the cotton robe that had been hanging on a hook behind the door, and discreetly left the room, so I would have privacy while I changed. The room that he had taken me to was particularly soothing, bathed in diffused light, with the most delicate scent wafting through the air from the trio of candles in a corner of the room. It was even more beautiful to me now than it had been yesterday.

At this point, I was physically, mentally, and emotionally spent. After exposing the secrets of my life to him, all I could hope and pray was that he would not pass judgment on me. Deep in my heart, I didn't think he would; otherwise I couldn't have ever have brought myself to say anything to him. I greatly valued his opinion, but I still had to be realistic and consider the very real possibility that his sensibilities were offended, or, worse, that he was personally disappointed in me. After all, I'd lied to him, too. Well, it was too late to worry about that now. If Mr. Tanaka turned out to be so upset by what I had told him, then that would prove to me that I'd been completely wrong about him. Might as well find out now.

Moving as slowly as if hypnotized, I took off my clothes and hung them on the hanger in the tiny closet. Next, to make Mr. Tanaka's job easier, plus to avoid getting strands greasy with massage oil, I piled my hair on top of my head, fastening it with one of the large tortoiseshell combs that I carried in my purse. Last, I put on the robe that Mr. Tanaka had handed me earlier and lay facedown on the massage table.

I had almost fallen asleep when I heard Mr. Tanaka enter the room. At that point, I was so drained that for a fleeting second I wished that he would leave, so I could sleep undisturbed. Even though my eyes were closed, I could feel his presence, standing at the top of the bed, near my shoulder.

"Mr. Tanaka, I'm sorry I wasn't honest with you before. I should have been, but I was so ashamed of the double life

I've been leading, of keeping secrets from you." I began to cry. Not wanting to look into his eyes, I continued lying facedown. "I didn't want you to think badly of me. That's why I kept quiet. Friends don't keep secrets from each other, and you've been a wonderful friend to me all this time. I have not honored our friendship. Please forgive me."

After a moment, he leaned slightly towards me, as if bowing, then he spoke, in a voice so low I almost had trouble hearing him. "Magnolia, child, please don't worry yourself about that. We all make mistakes; no one is perfect. I suspected from the first time I met you, at the school, that you were carrying a burden, that you were keeping a secret. It was your decision to tell me when you felt you had the need. I sensed you would, in your time, so I am not surprised to see you here today."

"Thank you for understanding." The relief I was feeling was overwhelming. I sat up, and took his hands in mine.

Mr. Tanaka stroked my hair. "It's all right, Magnolia. I am just happy that you came to me with your problem. You say you want to help children who are disadvantaged, a very noble goal, one you should continue to work toward."

"Yes, I fully intend to do that. After all, that's a big part of why I did what I did." At least I hoped it was. I had been quite conflicted and not thinking clearly, and going to see Mr. Tanaka had been a wise decision, very cathartic. I was feeling so much better, really I was.

Mr. Tanaka looked at me, then said, "I have an idea about how you can solve your problems. I know how you can get the money you want to earn to go out on your own, doing what you want." I had told him earlier that I had to come up with a couple hundred thousand dollars to cross the two million dollar mark, the sum I needed to stop working for Oona. Mr. Tanaka hadn't commented on that, nor had he asked why I felt I had to do that; he just accepted what I said.

It took a moment for his message to sink in. "Tanaka-san, what are you saying?" I stayed sitting up. "What is your idea?" I sat up on the bed, and looked at Mr. Tanaka, who had stepped away from the table and was now busy pouring hot massage oil into his hands.

"I need for you to lie back now, and relax, Magnolia, so I can begin your massage," he replied.

I knew Mr. Tanaka well enough to be sure that if he told me that he had been able to figure out a way to help me with my dilemma, then he had. He was a man of honor, and friendships were important to him. I had certainly not expected Mr. Tanaka to help me, only to listen sympathetically to my story.

"I thought about what you told me, about your goal for the children. When I left the room, I went to our Shinto shrine here, to pray for guidance, to see how I can help you achieve what you seek." Knowing how spiritual my former classmates were, I shouldn't have been surprised to learn there was a shrine in this building. "I spent some time there, praying. After a few minutes, an idea came to me, and I made a telephone call. This is what took me so long to return." Mr. Tanaka gently laid me back on the massage table, and began stroking my body with his hands.

"You prayed for me?" I was so touched at hearing this that I almost began crying again.

"Yes, Magnolia-san. You have been our friend here, our only friend, really, since we came to Miami." His hands were starting to work their magic on me, and I felt the stress slowly leaving my neck and shoulders. "You have honored us by speaking our language and learning about our culture. You need help, and in my own humble way, I am in a position to give it."

"Tanaka-sama. I happily accept your help." At that point, I was so relaxed that I almost couldn't coordinate my facial muscles enough to speak. "What is it? What do you have planned for me?"

He didn't reply. Instead, he just kept massaging my body. I thought he had forgotten that I'd asked him a question, when he answered, "You said that in your employment with the lady lawyer you were responsible for the peace of mind of her clients, all athletes?"

Mr. Tanaka was using such delicate terms to describe my job that, for an instant, I had trouble understanding their meaning. "Yes, Tanaka-sama, that's correct."

"You will do the same for a very special, longtime client of mine, but, this time you will only do it once, and it will be the last time that you will ever need do this work. And you will be in Japan."

"In Japan!" I bolted up on the table. Had I heard correctly?

"Yes. In Japan, in Tokyo." Mr. Tanaka gently pushed me back down. Even though the light was dim in the room, I could see enough to know that Mr. Tanaka was beaming with happiness. "You will fly to Tokyo, meet with Fukuy-amasama, the champion sumo wrestler of Japan, a Living National Treasure. You have to make him happy by helping him to solve a problem. For that, Magnolia-san, you will be paid all the money you need to stop working the way you are doing. I guarantee it," Mr. Tanaka added, triumphantly. "Finally, Magnolia-san, you will achieve your wish of going to Japan!"

A sumo wrestler? What kind of a problem could one of those giants have? I didn't care. I could deal with whatever it was. "Thank you, thank you," I kept repeating.

I lay stunned, moved by Mr. Tanaka's kindness, and flooded with hope. Mr. Tanaka kept on talking, going over the plans, over and over again; but all I could hear were the magic words "stop working for Oona, and realize my dream." And what was, at this moment, most incredibly thrilling: I was going to go to Japan! And to be with a Living National Treasure! What an honor. It was beyond anything I could have imagined.

Deep down inside, I'd always known that I had met Mr. Tanaka and his colleagues at the Best Language School for a reason, and now that had been revealed. Our business concluded, Mr. Tanaka then continued giving me a massage, his hands working their usual magic, so that, at the end, I was so relaxed that I had almost fallen asleep. My last thought before drifting off was to hope that during the course of this last encounter—doing whatever Fukuyamasama, the Living National Treasure of Japan, wanted me to do—he didn't roll over and crush me. I'd read somewhere that sumo wrestlers weighed over five hundred pounds. If that were to happen, I thought sleepily, I really did not care because I'D BE IN JAPAN!

SNOWBOARDING

Achilles Porter, 22, 5'11", 170 lbs. Professional snowboarder; Olympic bronze medal winner; 2002 winner, multiple competitions

BACKGROUND

"Hey, Magnolia, your favorite snowboarder is in town, recuperating from an injury. This time, it's not a tear in his ACL; it's his Achilles' heel that let him down. He fell during a competition and shattered the heel of his right foot. Get that? Achilles' heel?" Anita laughed at her own joke. I did not join in her laughter.

Achilles had once told me that his mother, a nurse, loved the stories of Greek mythology and thought that by giving her son that name, she would be able to protect him from being hurt. Unfortunately, Achilles' mother's fervent desires to keep her son injury free were just that, desires. Achilles was forever getting banged up; it went with the territory of being a snowboarder.

"Anita, I don't think the fact that Achilles is injured to be particularly amusing, and, I'm sure that neither does Oona," I pointed out.

Taking the cue from me, Anita immediately adopted a more serious tone. "He's supposed to be laid up in bed recovering from his operation, but he's not following doctor's orders to stay off his foot. He's been told he's not supposed to put weight on it, but he's doing whatever he wants."

"How badly is he hurt?" I hoped the injury wasn't a career-ending one.

"Well, I can't tell you exactly, but was serious enough that he needed an operation. The orthopedic doctor worked on him for hours. Oona's quite worried."

Oona, for all her tough guy bluster, was a bit of a softie when it came to certain of the athletes that she represented. Although she tried to hide that she preferred some more than others, I knew that those athletes she particularly liked received special treatment, and Achilles was one of those select, fortunate few. I suspected that Oona sometimes thought of the snowboarder as the son she'd never had, which brought out the limited amount of motherly instinct that she had.

"So where do I come in?" I asked her.

Anita hadn't called me to give me a medical report on Achilles' heel just for the hell of it. My services were needed, and they were needed in a hurry. Achilles hadn't been following his doctor's orders, and I was being brought in to amuse him during the rest of his convalescence, something that was fine with me. I'd always liked Achilles; we'd always had fun. He was hot looking, very sexy in that outdoorsy, wild-man kind of way, and most surprisingly for someone so young, a very accomplished lover.

Oona had initially offered my services to him not because Achilles had any fetishes that needed to be satisfied or special needs that had to be met, but as part of the representation package. Oona wanted to present herself as edgy enough to be plugged in with a new generation of athletes in a sport that was gaining importance by leaps and bounds. She had quite correctly calculated that by making it known that an on-call snow bunny was part of the deal, the young snowboarder would be intrigued and sign with her.

It was a well-known fact that just about every sports agent in the country had been actively courting Achilles after the 2006 Winter Olympics in Torino where, at eighteen years of age, he had won a bronze medal. It hadn't taken long to see his potential as a moneymaker. Achilles was the embodiment of the perfect all-American boy: tall and clean-cut, with white-blond curly hair, blue eyes, straight white teeth. Even his family was all-American: Achilles was the youngest of four children of a firefighter and a pediatric intensive-care nurse.

Achilles had made it known that after the Olympics

were over, he wanted to turn pro, which was like dangling raw meat in front of a carnivorous pack of agents, especially as he announced that his goal was to make lots of money, not just for himself but also for his family. Achilles was a sports agent's wet dream come true, and as Oona was like a shark, always moving, always looking for ways to stay ahead of the curve, she'd seen that snowboarding was a sport that was poised to explode. Achilles, with his talent and telegenic good looks, was the perfect athlete to allow her to accomplish that. Not only could he snowboard, but all he'd have to do was to turn on his winning charm and he could have sold an igloo to an Eskimo. After signing Achilles, Oona confessed to me that she used to go to sleep at night with visions of endorsement deals dancing in her head.

According to Oona's research, snowboarding was the fastest-growing winter sport in the United States, increasing at such a fast pace that it was expected to overtake skiing in popularity within a decade or so. Of course, the fact that all those snowboarders would need to purchase equipment to be able to enjoy the sport was something that had to be taken into account, and which would, naturally, translate into big bucks.

Once considered an activity predominantly pursued by crazy young men, a lifestyle more than a sport, really, the perception of it changed drastically when, in 1994, snowboarding was declared to be an Olympic sport. It had finally gone mainstream, gaining legitimate acceptance, and not just as a passing fancy of some underground types, young hotdogs. Snowboarding took off as fast as the snowboarders that competed.

As if any more proof were needed to see that the sport had reached mainstream America, Playboy magazine, to celebrate its fiftieth anniversary, commissioned Burton, one of the top manufacturers of snowboards in this country, to create a board for that very special occasion. The Playboy Custom 58 with its Rabbit Head at its base, of which only seven hundred boards were produced, was considered to be one of the best boards ever designed for an all-around snowboarder.

When Oona first heard about the Playboy snowboard, especially that the company had produced one made out of solid gold and the bunnies were out promoting it, well, her brain had instantly gone into overdrive, and she spent hours coming up with different schemes as to how she might be able to snag a similar gig for Achilles.

Within months of having signed him, Oona had nailed down an agreement with one of the biggest manufacturers of snowboards for Achilles to develop a line of boards under his name. Achilles was given almost unprecedented creative freedom: he picked his own artist to draw the logo, selected the materials for the board to be made out of, chose the bindings, etc. His snowboards were an instant success, selling out the first batch that were manufactured. As far as Oona was concerned, the Achilles 2008 may not have been the Playboy Custom 58, but it had come mighty close to it.

Achilles had turned out to be an even better client than Oona had envisioned. He was hardworking and energetic and would cheerfully comply with just about all that was asked of him. However, there was one aspect of her association with Achilles that was deeply troubling to Oona: when on a snowboard, this client was totally fearless, and would constantly take risks, without regard to safety.

Oona, of course, understood that this kind of behavior was what had made Achilles such an outstanding snowboarder; he could not win as many competitions as he had, especially the Olympics, by playing it safe. Still, Oona would cringe at the thought of how a truly serious injury would damage her client: physically, emotionally, and financially.

The legions of fans, as well as the executives who managed Achilles' endorsement deals, knew that athletes who competed in such risky sports as snowboarding had a higher likelihood of becoming injured, so they would bear with him for a while when he needed to recuperate from any injuries. However, human nature being what it was, they also expected that those periods of time when Achilles was out of commission to be brief, and that their beloved star would be back on the slopes performing his signature daredevil stunts.

Oona was well aware of the harsh reality that the memory and loyalty of the public—and, of course, of the executives who sign endorsement deals—were quite short. All it would take was for Achilles to be sidelined with an injury and out of the spotlight for a few months, and he might be relegated to the back burner of snowboarding history. There was always a younger, equally attractive and talented athlete waiting in the wings to take the injured one's place.

Achilles had been hurt on other occasions, but this time, the injury to his heel was such that, unless he followed his doctor's orders to stay off his foot, it could permanently affect him. And yet in spite of having received repeated warnings about how serious the situation was, Achilles had claimed the doctor was overreacting and continued to basically do whatever the hell he wanted.

Oona had witnessed Achilles' fall. She had been on a rare vacation, watching Achilles compete in a minor event in a small town near Vail. Racing down a black diamond slope, going at a million miles an hour, Achilles had been performing his usual daredevil maneuvers when something had gone terribly wrong. Achilles had gone down hard; his ankle bent at the wrong angle. Thankfully, the Ski Patrol arrived within a matter of seconds. Oona had watched helplessly as Achilles was carried down the mountain on a stretcher between two rescue skiers; it had been clear that the accident was quite severe.

Although Achilles could have received excellent care in the town's hospital, Oona had immediately chartered a plane and had flown him back to Miami on a private plane. There, not only would Achilles be under the care of the experienced doctors at Jackson Memorial Hospital, but perhaps most importantly, Oona would be able to supervise her prized client's convalescence.

Oona had planned everything out so carefully; however, what she hadn't expected was Achilles' refusal to listen to medical advice. In the beginning, she had been quite patient with him, thinking that part of the reason why Achilles was acting this way could be attributed to his youth: at twenty-two years of age, one tended to think of one's self as invincible, and therefore nothing permanently bad can happen.

Or it could be that Achilles' refusal to follow doctor's orders stemmed from the fact that, as he loved Miami and had always had such a good time here, he didn't intend to sit in the apartment that Oona had arranged for him at an assisted living condominium, a place for patients who were recuperating from surgery, and not step out on the town? Whatever the reason for Achilles' behaving so recklessly, it had to stop. There simply was too much at stake if he were to not heal properly or hurt himself again.

That's where I was to come in: Nurse Magnolia, on the job to make sure my patient was well behaved. I'd assumed many roles during the years I'd worked for Oona but playing a modern-day Florence Nightingale was certainly going to be a new one for me. I was confident that I was up to the challenge.

THE ENCOUNTER

In Minneapolis, Fred and I had been invited to a Halloween party where the guests had to be in costume, or else they wouldn't be allowed to enter the house where the festivities were taking place. But because Fred and I were chronically on a very limited budget, we had almost no money for spending on our costumes. We knew we would have to get quite creative if we were going to attend.

Fred, who had never been a fan of dressing up, was indifferent to attending the party under those conditions and announced that if I wanted to go that badly, then it was up to me to come up with some costumes. In spite of the roadblocks he'd thrown in front of me, instead of being discouraged, as I secretly suspected he intended, I was not in the least deterred. Rather, he'd succeeded in making me determined to rise to the challenge. As a result, I was more excited than ever about going to the party, and set about the task of coming up with two creative, yet inexpensive, fun costumes that would allow us to look attractive.

Because Fred and I were a couple in real life, it made sense to go for an idea which would incorporate that. I set about looking for his-and-her costumes. Looking in regular stores was out of the question, so I went to every thrift store in Minneapolis. Nothing I saw there seemed adequate; the selections were minimal, and what they did have looked cheap. Clearly, I had champagne tastes on a beer budget.

October 31 was approaching, and I still had no costumes. The ones I liked (Napoleon and Josephine; Caesar and Cleopatra; Bonnie and Clyde) were way too expensive, or they were the sort of thing Fred would never agree to (Lady and the Tramp; Popeye and Olive Oyl; Little Red Riding Hood and the Wolf). I was going to have to buckle down and come up with some creations of my own. I recalled that in a beginning psychology class in college, in a lecture on human sexuality, the professor had discussed the need that certain individuals had to dress up in costumes before being able to perform sexually. Even though I'd taken the class during my freshman year, that tidbit of information had stayed with me.

The professor had given several examples of costumes that were used. According to his research, some of the more popular ones were: Snow White, police officers, naughty nurses, Hooters girls, Pocahontas, and Marilyn Monroe. I tried not to speculate as to why Little Red Riding Hood was in such high demand.

One afternoon after classes, I had gotten in my car and had driven over to the part of Minneapolis where the city's sex shops were located, on a quest to find the perfect costumes for the party, hopefully on sale, or at least to get ideas that I could incorporate cheaply. I had driven around for a few blocks and noticed there were several shops; however, not being familiar with any of them, I had decided that my chances of succeeding would be best in one of the larger of these establishments. Of those, I had chosen the last store, for no other reason than because the parking lot was not visible from the street.

Assuming that there probably would be several surveillance cameras focused on the place, I had held my head down while entering the store. Once inside, I took a quick look around trying to find out where the costumes were displayed, but couldn't see them. I didn't particularly want to have to ask the pimply teenage kid behind the counter, as he had perked up significantly upon seeing me enter, and I did not want to engage in any chitchat with him. In spite of my best efforts, I hadn't been able to find the section with the costumes, so unfortunately, I had no choice but to go up to him and ask for what I was looking for.

"Uh, costumes are on the second floor of the store," he replied, pointing at a staircase.

I went up the stairs and headed to where he had indicated. I immediately understood why a whole floor was needed: There were rows and rows of costumes, enough clothes to fill several boutiques. Some were hanging on hangers on racks, others were folded on tables; the more elaborate ones (like Cinderella, Barbie, and Elvis) were displayed on a dozen or so life-sized mannequins scattered around the room and caught my attention, and I walked over to them to check them out. I started with a rather menacing Darth Vader, who had holes cut in strategic places; next, I moved on to Bambi (missing her backside) and her mother (ditto), to a couple of mermaids (also with cutouts on their tails), and then to devils (those, for some reason, were intact), the Tin Man (couldn't tell with him), and the late Anna Nicole Smith (very healthy looking). I walked around the floor until I came across the section with the pretty girl costumes. I flipped through the racks of outfits such as the flirty French maid, the saucy waitress, Lolita, the naughty nurse—the last, as it happened, turning out to be my favorite.

After giving it much thought and looking at the price tags, I decided to spend the measly amount of money that Fred had given me to buy our costumes on one costume for me. I would have to make an outfit for him, one that would complement mine. Although it might have seemed selfish to buy a costume only for myself, I rationalized that as I didn't have enough money for two, I really had very little choice. Besides, the naughty nurse costume—a very short, very tight white vinyl dress with snaps instead of buttons, paired with matching thigh-high white vinyl boots with four-inch heels and a perky little white nurse's cap—looked terrific on me.

As I would be going to the party dressed as a nurse, Fred should obviously wear some kind of medical-themed outfit. I came up with what I thought was a brilliant and cheap idea: Fred would go as my patient. Now that I had formulated my plan, I recalled that my friend Jenny was a nursing student at the university. The very next day, I went to see her and asked her if I could borrow the items I needed for Fred's costume from the hospital where she worked: a patient's cotton gown, an IV pole, and some bandages. I promised to return them the following day, so they wouldn't be missed.

We were a hit at the party; even Fred had to admit he'd had a good time. I kept the nurse's costume with me as a reminder of that night. Impractical as it might seem, in case I were to need it for another Halloween party, the costume had come from Minneapolis to Miami with me, where it was stored on a shelf in my closet, still in the plastic bag that I had packed it in so long ago for the trip south.

When Anita had told me my services were needed to make sure Achilles obeyed his doctor's orders, I instantly thought of my naughty nurse's costume. Although I still wasn't sure how, exactly, I would do that, the one thing I was sure of was that I was going to be able to put the costume to good use.

During my previous encounters with Achilles, I had found that, for all his wild ways on the slopes, he actually led a very conservative life. He didn't indulge in the usual vices of his contemporaries: he barely drank alcohol, he didn't smoke either cigarettes or marijuana, and he didn't fool around with groupies. His parents had clearly instilled solid values in their son—I was the only vice he had that I knew about.

The first time I'd met Achilles had been when Oona was courting him, trying to hook him in as a client. Oona had put me on notice that, as she was really, really interested in representing Achilles, I should elevate my game to make sure the snowboarder would sign with her. Oona seldom spoke to me that way, so I knew that becoming Achilles' agent meant a great deal to her. As if I needed any more pressure, Oona made it clear she felt the encounter I was going to have with Achilles might make all the difference as to which agent he would choose.

I had, of course, been aware of all the hoopla surrounding Achilles and was expecting to meet some arrogant, egotistical hotshot. Instead, I was pleasantly surprised to find him to be a really nice, unspoiled nineteen-year-old boy with very nice manners. However, what was the most surprising of all about him was what a patient and skilled lover he was. When I commented on that, he said he'd been brought up to be respectful of women, sensitive to them and their needs. He also told me that he'd only ever had sex with two girls before, an explanation for his inexperience.

Not only had Achilles surprised me with his patience and skill during our encounters, his preference as to where he liked best for us to have sex surprised me as well. I would have thought he'd want to have sex in an unusual place: someplace outdoors, maybe on a beach, or at the American Airlines Arena, or on a boat—anywhere but where he wanted. Instead of any of those, Achilles explained to me that his preference was to go to a luxury hotel, where he liked to have sex in a king-sized bed with expensive, soft sheets.

Achilles went about seducing me in a traditional manner: once in the room, he would then turn down the lights, and, after laying me on the bed, would slowly take off what I was wearing. It was only after I was naked with my clothes neatly hung up that he would allow me to undress him, and we would get under the sheets and begin foreplay, slowly, gently, deliberately. Making love like that was my personal preference also, which might explain why he was one of my favorite clients.

Achilles' private persona could not have been more different from his public one; our encounters had never deviated from the way it had been that first time. We had gotten along from the very beginning so having sex that very first night had been quite natural. We were comfortable with each other, making it seem as if he'd been a regular date, and not an appointment for professional sex.

Normally, the arrangements of my encounters with Oona's clients were made in accordance with their preferences—most athletes had definite ideas as to how/when/ where our get-togethers should take place. However, in Achilles' case that first time, as he was not yet a client, it had been left up to me to decide what would work best. I thought that a long, leisurely meal in a fancy restaurant would be absolutely the wrong way to court him; that would definitely be too stiff and formal. I had to tread carefully.

If Oona wanted to seem the perfect agent for Achilles, young and hip, then catering to his interests would definitely be the best way to accomplish that. I decided we should first go to a Heat game at the Triple A. Oona, of course, was easily able to get us floor seats. Then, after the game, we would stroll over to have something to eat in one of the many restaurants located at Bayside.

For Achilles' first visit to Miami, Oona had decided that nothing but the best would be good enough, so she'd reserved him a suite at the Mandarin Oriental Hotel, on Brickell Key, a hotel located just a few blocks south from Bayside, making it easy to drive there after dinner. My own game must have been elevated that night, for Achilles signed with Oona the very next day. We had gotten along so well that first time that we continued seeing each other every time he came into town. Achilles was great fun, especially when he would tell stories about his snowboarding exploits.

Now, though, our encounter would be quite different from those we'd had in the past. I would no longer be the carefree companion who catered to his every whim. I was on a mission and one that was not such a fun one: to make sure Achilles understood the severity and long-term implications of his injury, how there was a very real danger of his career ending. Most important, though, was that he obeyed his doctor's orders.

I took the naughty nurse's costume down from the top shelf in my closet, where it had been lying undisturbed, and placed it on my bed. Even though I hadn't worn it for almost five years, still, just looking at the dress, cap, and boots brought back a rush of emotions. I found myself blinking back tears from seeing a reminder of my old life, one from such a long time ago that it might have been someone else's.

Suddenly, reality took over, and a very practical thought came to me: I grabbed the dress and held it against my body. What if it didn't fit? It had, after all, been years since I had last put it on. With some trepidation, I undid the snaps and slid it over my naked body. Much to my relief, the dress still

fit, although it was a bit tight (the muscles that the sessions
with Brandi had developed in my body stuck out more than
the soft body I'd had in Minneapolis), but not so much that
anyone else would really notice. Or if they did, I figured they
wouldn't object. I lifted the skirt, what there was of it, anyway, and put on a white thong. I knew that tiny bit of fabric
wasn't much in the way of underwear, but I put it on anyhow,
remembering my mother's warnings; just in case I got hit by
a car, at least some of my private parts were covered.

Next, I slipped my feet into the thigh-high, white vinyl
boots, which, since I wanted to make sure they were laced up
right, took a bit longer to put on than I remembered. Last, I
pulled up my hair in a sort of ponytail at the top of my head,
securing it with the nurse's cap.

When I'd finished getting dressed, I walked over to the
full-length mirror in the bathroom. One look at myself, and I
gave out a loud gasp.

A few minutes before, when I'd first tried on the dress, I
had thought it had felt as if it might be just a bit snug. However, now that I was looking at myself in the mirror, I realized I had been delusional when I'd thought of the costume
as being that of a naughty nurse. "Slutty nurse" was a more
apt description of what I looked like: my breasts were spill-
ing out of the front of the dress, the thin white vinyl fabric
strained against my hips, the thigh-high boots were positively hooker-like, and my hair was cascading down my back
like Lady Godiva's. Well, it was too late to do anything about
it: I could either wear it the way it was or change into normal
clothes and come up with a new plan. Whatever I was going
to do, I would have to do it fast, as I had to get to Achilles. It
didn't take long for me to make a decision: I would just have
to be slutty nurse, I told myself as I grabbed a coat to wear

over this outfit.

Oona had arranged for Achilles to spend the time he needed to convalesce at an extended-care apartment over by Jackson Memorial Hospital, thankfully not too far from my apartment, so it didn't take me long to get there. Although I had no time to waste, I made myself drive slowly. The last thing I needed just then was for a police officer to pull me over for a moving vehicle violation, see what I was wearing, and arrest me for indecent exposure.

While waiting at the entrance to the convalescent center's garage for my parking ticket, I looked up at the building's ugly, square, windowless facade, and immediately knew why it was that Achilles tried to run away from there every chance he got. The atmosphere around the place was completely depressing, with the doom and gloom that surrounded it like a heavy curtain that could not be lifted.

I drove around the garage until finally, on the fifth floor, I found an empty space and parked the Mercedes there. As I walked through the long, gray corridor—gray walls, gray floors, gray ceilings—that connected the garage to the building proper, it seemed to me that the best thing about the extended-care apartment building was that it was close to the hospital, convenient for doctors' appointments and therapy sessions and the like. There was no way that such a depressing atmosphere would lift any patient's spirits. If anything, it would just make them sicker.

I was a bit apprehensive that I might be stopped by building security as I went up to Achilles' apartment, especially if a guard were to notice the outrageous boots I was wearing, but my fears turned out to be unfounded. No one even looked at me. I calmly walked up to the elevator, and when the doors opened, I stepped inside and pressed the button for Achilles' floor. Once there, I walked down the corridor until I found his door, then knocked hard on it.

"It's open! Come on in!"

Achilles was seated on the sofa, wearing only a pair of cotton boxer shorts and a T-shirt. He looked as cute and boyish as ever, with his bushy blond hair all rumpled. I guessed that Oona hadn't told him I was coming by, for he looked at me with his mouth open as he dropped the channel changer on the floor.

"Magnolia! What the hell!" he blurted out.

"Hi, Achilles, I hear you're being a very bad patient." I immediately got into my slutty nurse persona, speaking in a sweetly accusatory voice. "I'm your new nurse, here to make sure you obey doctor's orders." I slid off the coat I was wearing, and let it drop to the floor, exposing my outfit. His mouth, when he took in my costume, opened even further.

Achilles, quick study that he was, wasted no time in getting into the act. "Oh, yes, nurse, I've been bad, really bad." He then looked at me, and blinked hard, as if he was very, very frightened. "I know I haven't followed the doctor's orders. I've been a bad boy, very naughty. I should probably be punished, shouldn't I?"

I could not believe what I was hearing. Was sweet, innocent Achilles really asking me to hurt him? What happened to the guy that liked having missionary position sex in five-star hotels with thousand-thread-count sheets? Could I have been such a bad judge of character that I had totally and completely misjudged him? My professional pride was crushed. I had always thought of the young snowboarder as a nice, wholesome, all-American boy, the son of a firefighter and a nurse, for God's sake. But from what I was hearing, unless I was drastically mistaken and had misinterpreted his words, the boy was into light S&M. I vaguely recalled that his mother was a pediatric intensive-care nurse. Did that factor into Achilles' being turned on by my nurse's outfit? That was a thought I did not want to pursue.

Clearly, I had not been expecting to indulge in any such practices, so I hadn't brought my bag with the bondage equipment. I'd been following Oona's orders, coming only with the intentions of making sure Achilles understood the severity of his injury and that he followed his doctor's orders. However, from the looks he was giving me, he was clearly and most eagerly anticipating my next move. I'd played the stern mistress before, so I could do it again, no problem. But with Achilles? It didn't seem right.

"Yes, I'm going to have to punish you. I'll hurt you in ways you never knew possible, but I'm not starting until you promise to follow doctor's orders." I started to unbutton the top buttons of my uniform; to me, the sound the snaps made as they popped open seemed incredibly erotic. I climbed on the sofa, and, balancing myself while being careful not to seriously hurt him, stood on top of his chest, my boots digging into his skin. "Now, promise."

Achilles' eyes began to shine brightly. Observing him closely, noting such eager anticipation, I recognized the signs that my earlier suspicions that he had indulged in S&M before were confirmed. "I promise, I promise," Achilles was almost shouting. "Now, Nurse Magnolia! I've been a bad patient! Really bad! I need to be punished, I do! I need to be spanked."

Spanking? Achilles? Well, this sort of thing wasn't really my favorite: the guys you wouldn't mind hurting a little never turned out to be the ones who wanted it. But I knew that, for some, pain had its appeal. As I remained standing on his chest, I looked around the room for what would best serve as a spanking bench for me to administer the "punishment" that Achilles was wanting. Unfortunately, there was nothing that would do, so I would have to improvise. I carefully got back down off Achilles, and stood on the floor next to the sofa, looking sternly over him.

"Achilles, you've been a very bad patient. What happens to bad patients, ones that don't follow their doctor's orders?" I put my hands on my hips and thrust them out.

"You have to punish me, don't you, nurse? Spank me to teach me a lesson and I won't do it again." Achilles eagerly awaited the punishment I would mete out to him. "Now, nurse!" He ordered.

Observing him such a heightened form of arousal as he prepared for the spanking he so clearly craved, I thought yet again how mistaken I had been about him, how badly I had misjudged the snowboarder. True, I did not know him all that well, but never in a million years would I have taken him to be a spankophile, the kind of individual who was a devotee of erotic spankings.

"Right now." I walked over to one of the armchairs that faced the sofa and sat down. "Come over here. And, take off your shorts!"

Achilles almost tripped over himself as he took the few steps towards the chair where I was sitting. He slid his surfer shorts down to around his ankles and kicked them across the room. Not surprisingly, he wasn't wearing any underwear. "Ready, nurse."

"Lie across my knees." I commanded. "Now!" Achilles was almost trembling from anticipation. His breathing was labored, and his eyes had begun to glaze over in the way I recognized from our previous encounters that meant that an orgasm was not far behind. Achilles was in his own world now, in some kind of zone that the prospect of being spanked took him to. It was almost frightening. For some, spanking resulted in an intense sexual experience, but I had never really subscribed to it. Physical pain had never been my thing; pleasure was.

Achilles quickly lay down on my lap, his bare bottom facing me. I crossed one of my legs over the back of his knees to keep him secure, as the last thing I wanted was to injure him someplace else on his body. "Oh, nurse, please spank me now," Achilles moaned.

Like any good private-duty nurse, I did as my patient asked. While I administered the punishment to Achilles that he so desperately wanted, my thoughts kept turning to his mother, the nurse. Was this need for spanking tied up with his relationship with her? That was a question for Dr. Bernstein.

The session with Achilles turned out so well that he swore he would follow his doctor's orders. Normally, I would not have believed such assurances, but I knew that Achilles would do as I said. Otherwise, I warned him, there would not be any more spankings.

Not surprisingly, the nature of our relationship drastically changed. Out went the five-star hotels; in came the hot-sheet motels where you paid by the hour. The naughty nurse's uniform never again went back to the top shelf of the closet; as a matter of fact, I got some other medical outfits. Achilles particularly liked white coats and stethoscopes, and because he was becoming increasingly interested in expanding his horizons, I made sure to include extra bondage toys—harnesses, floggers, stud mask—that he enjoyed. And with the help of my formerly innocent young snowboarder, I enjoyed being increasingly naughtier. Come to think of it, that wasn't the only thing I enjoyed. I'd begun to really get into my role as Oona's edge.

Chapter 18

I had just finished unlocking the front door of my apartment, dropping my bag with the Tokyo airline tags still on it, when my business cell started ringing. As I listened to the song that was played during the opening credits of The Sopranos television show, what I'd programmed as the ring tone, I was tempted to just let it go to voice mail, but I knew that Anita would only start calling my other phones until she reached me.

My moment of gratitude to her for having sped up the schedule for me to get out of the life had passed. However, the thought that I would not have to deal with her for much longer made me instantly more cheerful, so I decided that it would be best if I were to take her call. Besides I was curious to hear what she had to say. I stepped inside the apartment, closed the front door behind me, and then answered the phone.

As far as Oona and Anita were concerned, I was not overly concerned that they would find out that I was not in Miami. I'd taken the precaution of telling them that I had a severe case of the flu, a terrible virus, and would be out of commission for a few days, reporting to them that I'd gone to the doctor who had told me that I had to stay in bed, resting, otherwise I would end up in the hospital. I'd never pulled the sick card before, so neither of them questioned me. They just told me to get better and to call when I had recovered. I planned to text them once or twice a day to give updates on my condition, so they would not contact me.

"Magnolia, hi, it's me, Anita. I hope you're feeling better." Perhaps because she smelled victory, she was able to summon a dash of civility from somewhere in the depths of her body. "Oona asked that I call you now to schedule an encounter with Jake the Enforcer. He's in Miami for the week. You know he has a championship fight Saturday night here at the American Airlines Arena, and he wants to set up a few sessions with you before it."

I could not believe what I was hearing. Anita sure as hell had balls, calling to schedule an encounter after she had threatened to expose me. Well, two could play the game and deal with each other as if nothing had happened between us. I was having none of it, but I was not about to let her know that I had already made plans for my life, post-Oona. I decided that the best course of action was to go along with her exactly as I always had, even though there was no way that I was going to agree to have an encounter with one of Oona's clients, regardless of how important he was.

"Oh, Anita, good. I'd love to. I've always been fond of Jake." I paused for a moment. "I have to be honest and tell you that I'm still sick. I have a fever, actually." I rustled some papers on the dining room table so Anita would think I was looking for something. "But if I stay in bed all day today, I should be okay by tomorrow." I forced myself to cough hard, doing so in such a vigorous manner that it felt as if my lungs were going to come out through my mouth, just to give her something else to worry about. "I'd hate to give whatever it is that I have to Jake—especially as he has such an important fight this week."

"Oh, so you're still sick?" Anita sounded puzzled. "It's been how many days now? Six?"

Actually, it was closer to seven. I couldn't blame her for being taken aback. I could hear the wheels in her brain whirring away, as she considered her options as to what she should do next. "Well, I am in bed, with a fever. As I said, I hope it's not contagious. I'm taking medicine—Tylenol, Robitussin—I'll take NyQuil tonight, and some other stuff." I began coughing again. "But I'm sure I'll be ready to meet with Jake tomorrow." Ever the good soldier, I pointed out.

"I don't know, Magnolia, you don't sound too good." Anita spoke hesitantly. "I'll let Oona know the situation." She hung up. I really had not expected her to show much concern for my well-being, but, still, she could have asked me if I needed anything. After all, until I was officially off the payroll, once I had the opportunity to speak to Oona and tell her of my decision, I would continue to add to the bottom line at O'Ryan and Associates and that included paying her salary.

Contrary to what I had told Anita, I greatly disliked Jake the Enforcer. Not only was he conceited, ill-mannered, and full of himself, he also liked to hurt me, which may not have been so surprising considering he was an ultimate fighter. Unlike other athletes who would refrain from having sexual experiences before a match or game to conserve their energy, Jake liked to have sex, rough sex and lots of it, claiming it gave him an edge, increasing his testosterone. I found myself having to constantly put him in his place, and even though I knew he made huge amounts of money for Oona, I had actually walked out on him once. Still I could not let Anita suspect that I hated him, otherwise she might think that I was faking an illness, so I wouldn't have to meet with him. I told myself I could not put off having the meeting with Oona any longer.

I went into the kitchen, opened the wine fridge, and took out one of the bottles of Dom Pérignon that were chilling inside. Next, I reached for one of the crystal flutes on the shelf and poured myself a full glass of champagne. Glass in hand, I headed toward the bathroom, took off my clothes, and ran a bath, making the water as hot as possible. I poured a healthy amount of rose oil into it, and then very carefully lowered my body into the steaming water. Just then, lying there and inhaling the sweet smell of the oil, taking sips from the glass of champagne that was resting on the side of the bathtub, I felt totally and completely happy. It wasn't often that I such confidence in a decision that I had made, and I discovered that I liked the feeling. Implementing my plans would not be easy, but I felt I could make my new life happen.

Half an hour later, I got out of the tub, wrapped one of the thick white terry-cloth towels around me, and headed for the living room, looking for my purse. I rummaged through it until I found the business card that I knew was there. I took a deep breath and began dialing. My call was answered on the first ring.

"Yes?" Simone's voice came through the line.

"Simone? Hi, it's me, Magnolia—you know, from the gym, Brandi's client." Simone didn't say anything; she just waited for me to explain why I was calling. Simone wasn't the one to talk much. A madam and an ex-call girl, she learned that it's best to keep her mouth shut on the phone and just listen.

"Ah, yes, of course, Magnolia from the gym. How are you?"

"I realize this might sound weird, but I'd like to meet with you, away from the gym. I want to discuss something that is best to do in person."

"Of course, honey. When and where?"

SUMO
Fukuyamasama, 22, 6', 450 lbs.
Champion sumo wrestler, Japanese Living National Treasure

BACKGROUND

I had just returned from my early morning quiet time on the terrace, having just poured myself a second cup of coffee, when one of my cell phones rang. I wondered who could be calling me at such an early hour. Normally, I would have hated such an intrusion, but the night before I had slept like a baby, the first restful sleep I'd had in months. I was ready to start the day. I walked over to the desk where I had laid the three cell phones out so they would charge overnight, and picked up the one I used for personal calls. I smiled as I recognized the number that appeared on the caller ID screen.

"Magnolia. Good morning. I hope I'm not telephoning you too early." Mr. Tanaka's voice on the telephone was just as soft and measured as it was in person. "How are you feeling today?" He was very discreet man, so it was not surprising that he had not mentioned the breakdown that I'd had in front of him the day before at A Most Peaceful Place.

"Good morning, Mr. Tanaka. No, you are not calling too early. I am much better today. Thank you for asking," I replied formally. "How are you?" I suddenly felt an urgency to know what it was he had to say, but I was familiar enough with Japanese social mores that I knew it was bad manners to rush the pleasantries.

"You recall the matter of which we spoke before? Of your going to Tokyo?"

"Yes, of course, Mr. Tanaka. I'm so very grateful for your

help." I could feel myself becoming excited.

"Oh, it is nothing, Magnolia." Mr. Tanaka, true to form, brushed aside my attempts to thank him. "I'm calling to finalize the arrangements."

"To finalize them?" I was a bit surprised. Mr. Tanaka certainly didn't let any grass grow under his feet. I'd only gone to see him the day before to discuss my predicament. "You've already discussed this with the client?"

"Yes, he and his wife are very eager to have you leave for Tokyo as soon as possible." Mr. Tanaka announced. I thought I could detect a tremor of excitement in his voice. Suddenly what Mr. Tanaka had said registered in my brain. Maybe I was not as awake as I had thought.

"He and his wife?" I repeated.

"Yes, Magnolia. This is a very confidential matter, a matter that requires the utmost secrecy. That is why you, as a foreigner with special skills, are being brought in to assist them with their predicament. Yes, they will both be your clients. Fukuyamasama and his wife, Noriko-san," Mr. Tanaka patiently explained. "He is the most important sumo wrestler in Japan, and Noriko-san, his wife, is a prima ballerina with the Royal Ballet of Japan. They are both Living National Treasures."

They were Japanese superstars, as close as can be to be deities on earth. "I'm not quite sure what my role is to be, Mr. Tanaka. Please explain what the problem is, and how I am expected to help the couple." I was trying to be as formal and respectful as possible, but the truth was that I was feeling extremely uneasy at this sudden turn of events.

There was silence on the other end of the line. Mr. Tanaka was doubtlessly pondering which would be the best way to broach such a delicate subject. I could easily picture him, wearing either his black suit or his dark-blue-and-white cotton kimono, sitting on a chair, frowning as he contemplated his options.

"Remember, Magnolia, I need your total discretion in what I am about to tell you. This is very, very confidential." He spoke in such a low voice that I had trouble understanding him. "You know that sumo wrestlers are very large men. Fukuyamasama himself weighs close to two hundred kilos—that's around four hundred and fifty pounds—he's one of the biggest sumo Japan has ever had." Mr. Tanaka's pride in Fukuyamasama's size came through loud and clear. "He's won the most fights, too. A true champion! Our Living National Treasure!"

"That's very impressive, Mr. Tanaka," I commented. "I'm honored that you chose me to help with the situation." I could not visualize what a four-hundred-and-fifty pound man would look like naked. During my time with Oona, I'd been with some pretty big men—I once had an encounter with a three-hundred-and thirty-pound football player—but the sumo's size was beginning to frighten me a bit.

"Yes, he is very impressively large. Magnolia, that's also a problem, and it is the reason why your services are needed." He explained. "You see, his wife, Noriko-san, is very small—tiny, actually."

I was beginning to see why I was needed. It was time to put poor Mr. Tanaka out of his misery and help him out. "And, Mr. Tanaka, given the differences in their sizes, the problem, I think, is that they are having marital difficulties, ones that have to do with intimacy, is that correct?"

"I knew you'd understand." The relief in his voice was palpable. "They love each other very much, but need help in the marriage bed situation. Noriko-san fears being crushed by her husband while they are having intimate relations and that she will be injured and unable to dance. They need guidance, to learn how to manage that."

It was bizarre to be speaking about a sumo wrestler and his ballerina wife's sexual problems with Mr. Tanaka, but I just kept going. "Mr. Tanaka, if I may be so rude as to ask, why do you know so much about the client and his wife's private lives?"

"I was their personal masseur for years in Tokyo before coming to Miami. First, I was his, and then, after they were married, I became Noriko-san's as well. I used to give them massages every day, sometimes even several times a day, so we came to know and trust each other. Before coming to Miami, I worked only for them. They would tell me their problems as I massaged them, and even now, I speak on the telephone every day with each of them, which allows me to know what is happening in their lives."

As I listened to him tell me about his clients, I realized there were many aspects of Mr. Tanaka's life that I knew nothing about. Coming from such a background, life in Miami must have seemed so strange to him, even moreforeign that I had suspected. "And, after having listened to me yesterday telling you about my professional life, you decided that, given my background and experience in such matters, that I was the ideal person to help Fukuyamasama?"

"Exactly!" Mr. Tanaka could not have been more proud of me than if I had just been given a four-year scholarship to Harvard. "I knew you would understand, Magnolia."

"Yes, Mr. Tanaka," I found myself saying. "I'll go to Tokyo to meet your Living National Treasures to see how I can help them." What did I have to lose? They would be paying me very well, and I'd get to go to Japan: a win-win situation. Provided I didn't get crushed, that was; besides, I'd never met even one Living National Treasure—let alone two!

"Now, I was anticipating you would say you would accept. I've been looking into flights to Tokyo, to see which would be the best way for you to get there—first-class, of course. There are no nonstop flights from Miami to Tokyo—the best connections are through San Francisco or Chicago, and either way, it's a long trip, many hours in the air."

I suddenly realized that I didn't have a passport; I had never actually been out of the country. I had a brief panic attack, then calmed down as I recalled hearing ads about companies that specialize in acquiring passports for their clients in one day (for staggering fees, of course), so, hopefully, that should not be a problem.

"Mr. Tanaka, before you make any reservation, I have to renew my passport—it's about to expire." I didn't want Mr. Tanaka to know I'd never had a passport. "But I know of a place where it can be done in one day."

"I'll wait to purchase your ticket until you tell me yours has been renewed," Mr. Tanaka agreed.

I hurried to assure him that the passport situation was under control. "I'll get the paperwork going right away, and call you the minute the passport is ready."

The minute I hung up with Mr. Tanaka I had gone online to research places in Miami where I could get a passport issued in the shortest amount of time possible, and the requirements for doing so. Thankfully, I had brought my birth certificate from Minneapolis with me, so I had the proper documentation. I took a quick shower, got in the Mercedes, and headed to Coral Gables, where the agency that issued passports in one day was located.

Suddenly, instead of being happy at the prospect of the

trip, I began to feel overwhelmed. What was I going to tell Oona? Anita? My family? I couldn't just disappear for a week, without explanation! And Max! Should I call him and tell him I was going? Show up at the restaurant? And how would I explain a poor grad student taking such a trip? I'd have to come up with a believable story, that's all. Yet one more lie, but hopefully, the last one.

My life was going to change, that was for sure.

THE ENCOUNTER

Mr. Tanaka was correct when told me that Tokyo was very far from Miami. As I lay, exhausted, smelly from so many hours on airplanes, on my bed in the Hotel Okura, I felt much as I might have if I had sprinted up Mt. Everest. I closed my eyes, and tried to calculate how many hours it had been since I'd begun my trip, which had started off two nights ago at MIA, moved on to Chicago's O'Hare airport, where I'd changed planes, and finally ended up in Narita International Airport, in Tokyo, but I gave up after passing the twenty-four-hour mark. All I knew was that I'd watched something like six movies, finished two books, read five trashy magazines, eaten over ten meals, and had dozens of drinks—mostly champagne, which I happily consumed at a steady pace, resulting in a slight hangover.

Even if it had been unbelievably long, I really could not complain about the trip. True to his word, Mr. Tanaka had booked me on first-class seats all the way, a luxury that would spoil me for the rest of my life; it would be painful to sit in the back of the plane after the pampering of first class. I was shocked when I saw that my ticket cost more than thirteen thousand dollars. The Living National Treasures must have been in dire straits to shell out that kind of money for my services.

And not only had I flown first-class, but the luxurious treatment had continued after having landed at Narita. No sooner had I cleared Customs and Immigration than I'd spotted a man dressed in a black suit holding up a sign with my name on it, who'd introduced himself as my driver, telling me that he was responsible for taking me from the airport to my hotel in Tokyo. As I followed the driver to the car, I had flashbacks to Ramón, my former driver in Miami, who dressed and bowed, much as his Japanese counterpart did.

From one of the travel books I'd read on the airplane, I'd learned that the ride from Narita to the Hotel Okura, where I would be staying, was long, close to two hours. Even though I was so excited to finally be in Japan, I'd been so tired that, in spite of my best efforts to take in all the sights, I'd nodded off a few times, and dreamed about Max.

After giving it much thought, I had decided that it would be best not to tell him about the trip. There would be too much to explain, and, of course, all the lies I'd told him, and just then, I wasn't ready to do that. Still, I was worried about his somehow learning I'd run away to Japan without telling him, but, as it was going to be a short trip, chances were he wouldn't find out. I'd keep in touch by e-mailing and texting him, so he would keep hearing from me and not worry that I was missing.

I'd expected Tokyo to be a thriving, bustling city, but the extent to which that was true had taken me by surprise: the place threw off so much energy that it almost didn't need fuel to keep it going. I'd thought that I would find some sort of old-fashioned gentility and grace in this modern city, but as I looked around, I realized how wrong I'd been. Everyone was going somewhere—the roads were clogged with traffic, amazingly polite drivers all, but the vehicles were in such close proximity in their lanes that they almost touched. At almost every intersection, police officers were stationed, smartly dressed in their uniforms, looking efficient, making sure that everything ran smoothly. From their body language, it was clear they took their responsibilities very seriously and were so focused that they looked as if they thought they were performing complicated brain surgery. The term "controlled chaos" definitely applied to the Japanese roadways.

The minute that Mr. Tanaka had told me where I would be staying, I'd begun reading up on the hotel; it looked beautiful from the pictures on the website. The place was enormous, with nine restaurants, thirty-three banquet halls, and my own personal favorite, the Powder Puff Beauty Salon. While working for Oona, I'd stayed at plenty of five-star hotels with her clients, but this would be the first time I would be staying on my own. I couldn't wait!

After arriving at the hotel, I was so tired after checking in that instead of looking around, I decided that I would go straight up to my room. The concierge at the front desk had informed me that the Sakura Organization, the outfit that had paid for my room, had requested that I be placed on the Grand Comfort Floor. When I'd asked what exactly that meant, the concierge, a young man with a most serious expression on his face, had bowed repeatedly as he told me that that was a very special floor of the hotel: the goal for the guests who stayed there was for their bodies and souls to be nourished during their visit. The concierge had gone on to explain that the hotel took its responsibility to refresh and invigorate their guests very seriously, for there was a Relaxation Nature Court for guests like me, a place where one went to heal.

My junior suite, located on the Grand Comfort Floor, consisted of a large bedroom with adjoining bathroom—a luxurious room, to be sure, but still, it couldn't hold a candle to my bathroom back in Miami, as well as an average-sized living room and an enormous walk-in closet. I had brought two photos with me: one of my whole family, the one my mother had sent out as a Christmas card and the one of Fluffy, and placed them on the night table. I kissed both and set about doing the rest of the unpacking. The few clothes I had brought looked lost hanging in the corner of the closet, reminding me that I'd had the same reaction when I first moved into the apartment on Brickell Avenue. I blinked back a few tears as I stood there, looking at the familiar clothes hanging in the unfamiliar closet. I shook my head, told myself to stop acting like a sentimental idiot: I was in Japan, where I'd dreamed of going to for so long.

The living room of the suite, like the bedroom, was decorated in Western style with elegant, traditional furniture covered in assorted shades of a soothing cream color, perfectly complementing the faint yellow shade of the walls. As attractive as the décor of the suite was, it was the queen-size bed that made me fall in love with my accommodations. The mattress was just the perfect firmness for me, not too hard, not too soft, with some sort of thick down-filled padding over it that made me feel as if I were lying on a cloud—but the sheets! Ah, the sheets! They were so incredibly soft that they must have been several thousand thread count. The perfectly square four pillows at the head of the bed guaranteed the exact support. Before leaving, I would definitely write down all the information about the bed: the mattress, the padding, the sheets, the pillows—in the hopes that one day I might be able to sleep in such a bed in my own home.

By then, it was close to ten o'clock at night, Tokyo time. I decided that I should get acclimated as soon as possible, and the best way to do that would be to order dinner from room service, take a bath, and then after finishing eating, pop an Ambien and go to bed. I would have to be fresh for what awaited me the next day. I had been informed by Mr. Tanaka that Ms. Suzuki, the young lady assigned to accompany me during my stay in Tokyo, was coming for me at eleven o'clock. The Sakura Organization was spending lots of money on me, and I wanted to make sure it got excellent returns on its investment.

I glanced through the room service menus. There were two: one for foreigners, one for Japanese, and decided that, although I was tempted to order from the latter, it would probably be safer to stick to the one for foreigners. After getting over my sticker shock ($75 for roast chicken?), I chose my meal—three courses, along with half a carafe of white wine. I called room service, and with some difficulty, placed my order. Even though I was speaking very slowly in English—I had not dared try out my Japanese yet—it took a while before the incredibly polite young lady at the other end understood what I was saying. I repeated my order several times, but after fifteen minutes, I gave up, and said yes to whatever it was she said.

Thankfully, against all odds, the meal that was delivered by room service was just what I had told her I wanted. I was hungrier than I had thought, because I ate every bit of the $200 dinner (not counting the cost of the wine) that I had ordered. No sooner had my head hit one of the four perfect pillows than I was asleep. I slept soundly and woke up eleven hours later, feeling more refreshed than I would have thought possible. I ordered breakfast and remembering the speed with which the dinner had arrived the night before, showered and washed my hair at a breakneck pace.

I'd noticed the night before that the Japanese dressed quite formally, so I decided to follow their lead, and wore a dark, two-piece gray linen Armani suit, with a pair of black leather Manolo Blahnik high heels and stockings, all, of course, chosen by Stacy. For underwear, I chose an extra sexy Agent Provocateur black lace bra and matching panties. I had read somewhere that the Japanese were very label conscious, so I figured I could not go wrong with Armani and Manolo, as well as the underwear. After putting on a discreet amount of makeup, I brushed my long blond hair up in a French twist and held it in place with a black lacquer comb.

At exactly eleven o'clock, the phone in my room rang, and the operator announced that a Ms. Suzuki was waiting for me in the lobby of the hotel. I took one last look at myself in the mirror, picked up my purse, and headed downstairs. Ms. Suzuki must have been told what I looked like, because she immediately came up to me and introduced herself. With her black hair cut in a precise bob, her porcelain-colored skin, and her severe dark blue suit, Suzuki-san was so tiny, so cute that she looked like a doll. She did not seem to be a day over fifteen years old. I knew that she had to be at least somewhere in her twenties, otherwise she would not have this job, so that could not have been.

"Larson-san? I am Suzuki." She bowed so low that she was perpendicular to the floor. Not knowing quite what to do, I also bowed. "Welcome to Tokyo." She bowed again. "I hope you had a good trip and a good rest. And that the accommodations are to your liking." Suzuki-san's English was impeccable.

"Yes, thank you very much. Everything was perfect." I

bowed again, but, this time, not as low as before. I smiled at her. "This hotel is wonderful. I slept like a baby."

"I have a car waiting outside. We can discuss the schedule in the car, if that is agreeable to you," Suzuki-san suggested.

"Yes, of course. Thank you." We bowed one more time, and began to walk toward the front entrance to the hotel. I followed her outside to the driveway, where a black Japanese car—I did not recognize the model or make—with tinted windows was waiting. As we approached it, the driver of the car, the same man who had driven me from Narita to the Hotel Okura the day before, greeted us.

"Please." Suzuki-san stepped aside so I could get into the car.

"Thank you." I slid into the back seat of the car.

Ms. Suzuki got in next to me, and off we went. No sooner had we pulled out of the driveway and onto the wide avenue in front of the hotel than I saw my impressions yesterday of Tokyo as a bustling city had been correct. Every square inch of sidewalk was occupied by a pedestrian walking at a brisk pace, but in spite of the crowded conditions, each person still had space, and no one was touched or jostled by the individual next to him or her. I was so struck by how orderly everything and everyone was.

We drove for a while in silence, me with my forehead pressed against the window, looking at the sights, much as a child might on her first visit to Disneyworld. Suzuki-san, much to her credit, did not say anything and let me take in my surroundings. I had not come to Tokyo with any preconceived ideas of what it was going to be like; I'd only had some vague notion of a big, busy city. After all, I'd seen the film Lost in Translation several times, so I did have an idea, but nothing could have prepared me for the sights and sounds around me. The samurai movies that I'd seen, as they took place in the seventeenth and eighteenth centuries, were therefore of no help.

Fifteen or so minutes must have passed before Ms. Suzuki spoke again. "Larson-san, we are only a few minutes away from our destination, so I must tell you some of the details of the arrangements that have been made for your meeting with Fukuyamasama." She reached into the black leather folder on her lap, and began rifling through the contents. A moment later, she took out one of the manila envelopes, and handed it to me. "I did not know how much you know about the sport of sumo—the history, the rules, the traditions, the wrestlers—so I have prepared this report for you to study."

I didn't want to hurt Suzuki-san's feelings by telling her that I had done some reading about the sport of sumo wrestling before coming to Japan, and that the more I'd read about sumo, the more fascinated I had become by it. I'd learned that sumo was a very ancient sport; it had begun in the eighth century, in the royal courts, and had evolved as a way for disputes to be settled, gaining in popularity until it had become known as the national sport of Japan. However, it wasn't until the twentieth century that it was standardized, with rules, regulations, and associations.

The rules in sumo were very easy to follow, possibly because there were only two people involved. A wrestler lost a bout if he was forced out of the ring, or if any part of his body, other than his feet, touched the ground. The ring, a floor that consisted of clay with thin layers of sand on top, was outlined by bales of hay, and measured fifteen feet in diameter. The wrestlers were enormous men, with weights that averaged five hundred pounds. Thankfully, they didn't have to spend much money on uniforms, as the only item of clothing they wore was a thirty-foot, ten-pound piece of silk called a mawashi that was wrapped around their waist, sort of like a thong. Their opponent would use this garment to grab and push him out of the ring. The wrestlers all fought with their hair pulled into an elaborate traditional topknot.

"Larson-san, we will not be going to Fukuyamasama and Noriko-san's apartment. He does not live in the stables with the other sumos. They have their own place. I was told to take you, instead, to an apartment in Minato-ku, a residential area of Tokyo, where you will be meeting with him," Suzuki-san informed me solemnly.

"Fukuyamasama has a very important tournament coming up in two weeks," I commented. "The Autumn Grand Sumo Tournament here in Tokyo, at the Ryogoku Kokugi-kan sumo arena. He is the only yokozuna—Grand Champion—to be competing, is that right?"

"Oh yes, Larson-san, yes, that's right." She nodded vigorously. "It is a very, very important tournament."

By her reaction, apparently she hadn't been told that the reason why I had been brought out to Tokyo was because Fukuyamasama was scheduled to compete in that tournament. Mr. Tanaka had been very clear in emphasizing the importance of the tournament, pointing out that sumos who competed at Fukuyamasama's elite level could not afford distractions.

It had been during the course of our last meeting that Mr. Tanaka and I had discussed the most effective approach to help solve the couple's problems. Mr. Tanaka believed it might be best if, at the start of our sessions, I were to only deal with Fukuyamasama, explaining that Noriko-san

might not take too kindly to having a woman, and a foreigner at that, interfere in her marriage. The Japanese were
a very private people, and marital problems were never aired
in the public arena.

Although I didn't let Mr. Tanaka know it, I was
delighted to learn that in the beginning at least, I would
be having encounters with the sumo alone, as I preferred
to deal with male clients. I'd never had a female client, so
I didn't have any experience with dealing with one and this
did not seem to be a good time to experiment. The idea of
having a threesome with a man and his wife, two Living
National Treasures on top of that, would have presented
quite a challenge.

A few blocks later, our driver turned into the driveway
of a modern-looking four-story building and stopped just in
front of the double steel doors that were located in the middle of the thick wall that surrounded the building. I watched
as he punched in the numbers of a code into the black box
to the side of the right gate. Almost immediately, the heavy
gates swung open, and we drove slowly down the driveway to
the parking garage under the building.

The driver circled the parking lot until he reached a
bank of elevators at the far end. Then, with the motor still
running, he got out of the car and opened the passenger door
where I was sitting. Apparently, I would be the only person
getting out.

Suzuki-san turned to me and, indicating the last elevator on the far right, solemnly announced. "That elevator will
take you to the apartment where Fukuyamasama is waiting
for you." I must have looked confused, because she added,
"It's all right, Larson-san. Each apartment has its own elevator. I'll be waiting down here for you."

I picked up my purse and the slim black leather attaché case that I had brought with me and got out of the car.
I walked toward the elevator and stepped inside; the doors
closed, and as Suzuki-san had said it would, whisked me
up four floors. And then, just as quietly as they had closed,
the doors opened, and I was looking into a small vestibule-
style room.

"Welcome, Miss Larson, someone will be with you in a
moment. Meanwhile, please be so kind as to take off your
shoes," a woman's voice called out.

Being familiar with the Japanese custom of removing
one's footwear before entering a home, I bent down and took
off my shoes, thanking God I'd had the foresight to wear
stockings. I then slipped on the pair of white cotton slippers
that were to one side of the door.

A tiny, exquisitely beautiful Japanese woman dressed
in a simple dark blue kimono came toward me, walking
so gracefully that it looked as if she were gliding. Her eyes
downcast, she motioned I should go with her. I followed
her until we stopped in front of a pair of sliding doors that
seemed to be made of the lightest of bamboo. My escort knelt
on the floor, opened the doors a couple of inches on each side,
and motioned I should enter the room and sit at the table in
the center of it. The floor of the room was made of tatami
mats, the woven straw flooring materials used in traditional
Japanese rooms. I waited for my eyes to adjust to the dim
light before walking where she indicated. I noticed that the
only furniture in the room was a very low dark red lacquer
table with four cushions covered in beige brocade fabric on
the floor surrounding it. I walked toward it and sat down on
one of the silk cushions, then gently placed my purse and the
black leather envelope on the floor next to me.

I looked up and saw that standing against the wall right across from me was a very large man who could only be Fukuyamasama. I looked around and saw that the two of us were alone in this spare, dimly lit room. The sumo was like a mountain that had been there all along but because it was so dark, and he was so still, I hadn't been able to see him.

Fukuyamasama was dressed in a plain gray cotton kimono with a black sash around the waist, the thick white socks on his feet the only other item of clothing he was wearing. It was strange, but even though he was enormous, larger even than I had expected, he somehow did not give the appearance of being fat. I could see muscles peeking out of the sleeves of his kimono. Fukuyamasama had a broad face, tiny black eyes, and a mouthful of teeth. His well-oiled, jet-black hair was arranged in the traditional sumo's topknot. He was enormous, true, but there was something appealing about him.

After we smiled at each other for almost a minute, I decided it was time to take matters into my own hands, and indicated the tea in the middle of the table, a questioning look on my face. He watched every move I made as if deciding what to do, then, a minute later, joined me, sitting on one of the cushions across from me. The man was so very graceful in his movements that it was difficult to believe he was as large as he was. I smiled at him as I served him tea from the simple green porcelain pot on the table, then poured my own cup and drank from it.

"Delicious." I tipped my cup of tea toward my host.

The sumo nodded. As we continued to sip, I wondered what would happen after we had finished. A minute later, much to my surprise, the sumo spoke. "Hai."

Hai was "yes" in Japanese, so I guessed that meant we

were making progress, that I had passed inspection. Encouraged, I reached down to the floor where I had placed the thin black leather attaché case next to my purse, and laid it flat on the table.

"May I?" I could tell he was curious.

"Hai."

I reached into the case for the item I had prepared back in Miami, on the day I had spent while waiting for my passport to be ready. Researching the history of sumos, I had been surprised to learn how intertwined their history was with that of Japan, so I'd begun looking for drawings of these wrestlers from their earliest days. I also discovered that geishas dated almost as far back as the sumo in Japanese history, so I then began researching drawings of those lovely, accomplished ladies as well.

Seeing the drawings of sumos and geishas together gave me an idea as to how I would be able to help the two Living National Treasures, so I had printed out drawings of both. Even though it had been quite time-consuming, through the magic of Photoshop, I'd blended the two types of drawings until I was able to come up with images of enormous sumos having sex with tiny geishas. After much manipulation of the images I was able to come up with a series of sumos and geishas having sex in just about every position imaginable. I had chosen the best thirty of the series, then headed to my local photo store and had them printed on good-quality paper. Even though it had been prohibitively expensive to do, I'd had to expedite them as well, so they would be ready in time before my departure. The prints had turned out so well, that I had ordered two other sets. I'd left those back in Miami.

Very carefully, I took out the first of the photos, the one

that I had thought would be most appropriate for easing into our encounter (I was saving the most acrobatic for later) and laid it facedown on the table. I could see I had piqued the sumo's interest. We both sat there, not moving, just staring at the back of the photo, until, finally, Fukuyamasama reached for it, and slid it, still facedown, until it was right in front of him. The tension in the room was thick with anticipation. The sumo looked up at me, an unspoken question in his eyes.

"Hai." I gave him permission.

He turned it over. The Grand Champion's reactions were incredibly quick because it took less than a nanosecond for him to realize what it was it he was looking at. From the expression on his face, it was clear he thoroughly approved of what was in the photograph: a very erotic image of a geisha riding the sumo, straddling him as if he were a horse and she were Lady Godiva. He got up, walked over to the wall to the right side of the room, and slid it open, revealing a closet. I watched as he bent down and opened one of the drawers and took out what looked like a thick bedroll, a futon-like item, but very large, and carried it back to the center of the room. He then moved the table and cushions where we had been sitting against the other wall. Once the room had been cleared, he unrolled the futon.

Fukuyamasama picked up the photograph and showed it to me. "We do this one." He spoke in Japanese.

"Hai." Thrilled that this was going so well, I began to take off my clothes.

Much to my surprise, I discovered that the sumo, for all his size, was an amazingly agile lover. He had learned early on how to mold and fold the different areas of his body in such a way that he was able to both give and extract the most satisfaction possible. As we tried out different positions, I could tell why Noriko-san was apprehensive about being smothered because the man was so huge, that I myself, even though I was a pro, was at times, a bit frightened. Still, he was so aware of his size that he was extra gentle and very considerate.

Fukuyamasama had enormous stamina, and because of that, we were able to try out five different positions per session. The difficulty and intricacy of what we were doing kept increasing; by photo number twenty, the sumo was sweating bullets, and his body had become quite slippery. The champion, however, was undeterred by that, and was becoming extremely interested in copying what the sumo and geisha were doing in the photos. I admired the way he wouldn't hold back one iota. Knowing how important weight was to the wrestlers, I could only hope that he was not dropping too many pounds as a result of our rigorous exertions. Satisfying the sumo was such hard work that, in spite of how much I ordered from the Hotel Okura room service menu, I was burning more calories than I could consume. As a result, I was dropping weight like crazy. Brandi would have been proud of me.

I was so exhausted from our sessions that I would almost fall asleep in the bathtub each night waiting for room service to arrive. Unfortunately, I was kept so busy that I hadn't had any opportunity to check out the city, but that did not bother me as much as I thought it might have. I slept so soundly that I had to set two alarms to wake up every morning, otherwise I would have been late to meet Suzuki-san. The sumo was certainly getting his money's worth with me.

It was on day six, my last day, that Fukuyamasama had a surprise for me. We had just laid down on the futon when the sliding door opened, and a tiny woman walked in. Noriko-san! I had immediately recognized her from her photographs.

Oh, my God! What kind of a surprise was this? But then I noticed the happy expression on her face, and I relaxed. Contrary to my fears that she would feel like a betrayed wife, she seemed very pleased to see me there. I saw that she was carrying a rolled-up picture or painting in her right hand. With the graceful walk and stick-straight posture of a ballerina, she came to the futon, knelt at the end of it, and after bowing to her husband and me, she unrolled the picture she was holding. I saw what seemed to be a very old and genuine antique print of a sumo and two geishas cavorting, having quite graphic sex. At first, I had trouble believing what she seemed to be proposing, but it only took me one look at the mischievous expression on her face, and I knew exactly what she wanted. Her husband and I were only too pleased to comply.

That final session with the three of us was something for the record books, at the very least deserving an entry into the Guinness Book of Records. More important, though, than the show of our incredible athletic skills and endurance was that Noriko-san was now able to see how it was possible for a small, slender woman to safely have a satisfying sex life with a man who weighed more than four times what she did. Contrary to Mr. Tanaka's warnings about how shy and reticent the ballerina was, judging by her eager participation in the last session, I suspected that Noriko-san would have been happy to have joined us earlier. It had been when I had witnessed the two Living National Treasures play out the scene of that first print, Lady Godiva and the horse, that I realized that what I was witnessing was the Japanese version of pony play! Who would have thought?

After my last session with the sumo and his wife, secure in the knowledge that they would be put to good use, I'd left the photographs with them. The only regret I'd had about being with those two wonderful people was that I'd not been able to practice my Japanese with them to the extent that I would have wanted to. For reasons known only to themselves, they had instructed me to address them primarily in English. The truth was, I couldn't get too upset about that, as what we had done had not required much conversation.

Chapter 19

With my heart in my mouth, I picked up the phone again, and punched the number on the speed dial. I'd only been back in Miami for a few hours, but I could not delay in making the call. "Max? Hi, it's me, Magnolia."

"Oh, hi, Magnolia. I'm so glad to hear your voice. I hope you're feeling better, and not so busy," Max replied. "I've missed you."

"You, too." I swallowed, and took a shaky breath. "I was wondering if you were going to be around tomorrow. I'd like to come to the restaurant and discuss something with you."

"Is something wrong?" No sooner had my words registered in his brain than Max went on high alert. "What is it, Magnolia?"

"Max, don't worry, it's nothing all that important. It's about my future." I stumbled over my words, my nerves getting the better of me.

"Can you make it tonight, instead? Can you come to the restaurant?" Max was insistent.

"Tonight? I don't know!" I thought for a moment. No, I had to get this over with. "I can be there within the hour, Max."

"I'll be here. See you then. Bye." Max hung up, almost as if he didn't want to give me an opportunity to change my mind.

I went into the kitchen and rummaged through the fridge, searching for something to eat. I settled on some frozen fettuccine alfredo that only needed to be heated up. I had learned early on to always have something on hand that I could easily fix for an occasion such as this. I looked pale and tired so I applied some makeup to liven myself up a bit. Unlike previous occasions of going to meet Max, when I was filled with anticipation, I was not looking forward to seeing him. However, if I was going to honor my promise to myself that I wasn't ever going to live a lie again, I had to tell him the truth about who I was, and what I had been doing.

From the very first time I had laid eyes on Max, on the night I'd met Oona, I had instinctively known that he, too, would be an important person in my life. As time passed, although we had really seen so little of each other, the feeling got stronger. I didn't think we'd made love more than a dozen times; however, it was not until this moment, when I was about to come clean and almost certainly lose him forever, that I felt the full impact of how very important he had become to me.

Max was waiting for me near the door of the restaurant. He greeted me warmly, kissing me on both cheeks, and after asking me if I'd like anything to eat or drink, he led me to our usual table in the back of the room. On the way there, he told Bobby, the maître d', that we were not to be disturbed.

Max waited until I had made myself comfortable. "So, Magnolia, what is it that you'd like to discuss with me?"

I looked into his dark blue eyes, took a deep breath, and replied, "Max, there are several things about me and my life that I have not been completely open about with you. But first, I want to tell you how much I love you, how you mean the world to me, and that if I am to lose you because of what

I am about to tell you, well, my heart would be broken, but I would understand."

Max took my hands in his, and squeezed them. "Magnolia, I'm so happy to hear you say those things. I, too, love you with all my heart; you, too, mean the world to me." He smiled at me, and for the first time, I allowed myself to hope that maybe his reaction to my news was not going to be as bad as I'd feared. "I've never told you that before because at times you've seemed remote, reserved, so mysterious, and so I didn't know how you'd respond." He leaned over and kissed me lightly on the lips. "Whatever you're going to tell me can't be all that bad. I'm listening; go ahead."

"That night, the night I first met you, when I came in alone to have dinner, before coming here, I had met a woman at a bar. She made me an offer," I began.

And with that, I told Max the whole story of how I became to be Oona's edge and the kind of life I had been leading since that day. Max listened to me for close to an hour without saying a word. Some things he had known about, such as the Best Language School and my fascination with Japan, my education and family, but the important information about Oona and all aspects of that relationship, he had obviously been in the dark about.

When I had finished, Max just sat there, looking at me, with a shocked, stunned expression on his face. By that time, the dinner crowd had left the restaurant, so it was relatively quiet. Finally, after what seemed like an eternity, he spoke. "Well, Magnolia, that's quite a story. I can certainly see why you felt you were going to lose me after what you've just told me." My heart sank—this did not bode well; I could see how it was going to go. I began blinking back tears. At the same time, I saw his face darken with fury.

"What kind of a man do you think I am? You came in here, telling me how you are a student, a 'good girl' who volunteers her time with children, a family person." Max moved farther away from me, as if he couldn't stand to be near me. "What am I supposed to do?" He was speaking in a hoarse whisper, so as not to be overheard. "Forgive and forget? Is everything you've told me a lie? Are you really from Minneapolis? Hell, are you a woman, or have you had a sex change? Is that a lie, too?"

"I know you are upset." I tried to reassure him. "I understand; it wouldn't be normal if you weren't." I reached over and tried to take his hand, but he brushed me off.

"Normal? What the fuck does that mean? The woman I love, I just found out, is a hooker who fucks professional athletes. Please tell me I'm wrong, Magnolia." Max stopped speaking and stared at me. "If that is your name."

"Yes, Magnolia is my real name." I nodded miserably.

As I looked at him, all I could think of was that my working as Oona's edge had not been worth it. True, I had made a lot of money—but at what price? I had sold myself and destroyed the man I loved, and, more important, who loved me. For what? Money? Thrills?

"I don't know you anymore. You look the same, but I don't know what's inside you." He shook his head slowly. "I mean, I was thinking of asking you to marry me. I saw you as such an innocent, a traditional girl, that I felt I should move slowly and carefully." Max hit the side of his head with his hand. "What an idiot I've been!" He began to walk away, then stopped, and turned to me. "What were you thinking? Was I just a toy to you? Someone you could use to get away from your seedy, disgusting life?"

"No, Max! I love you. I've loved you from the moment

I walked in here that first night and sat in this same booth, and you came over to ask how my dinner was." Tonight was the first time I'd ever declared my feelings for Max, and, figuring that since I had started, I might as well continue. I knew I was being cheesy, but I was fighting for my life— for Max.

Max just listened to me, taking it all in. He shook his head again, turned, and stood up. I watched as he walked to the entrance to the restaurant and then go outside. I sat in the booth, incapable of moving.

Ten minutes must have passed before I was able to function enough to get up from the table. Slowly, as if sleepwalking, I made my way through the restaurant and out the front door. Max was nowhere to be seen. Once outside, I walked over to the square wooden box where the valet kept the keys, opened it, and looked for mine. They weren't hard to find, as, at that late hour, the keys for the Mercedes were the only ones there. I was about to take them when I saw that there was something hanging from the hook next to them. There wasn't much light in the parking lot, so I picked up my keys and the small item next to them, and walked over to the street light to see what it was.

I almost fainted when I saw what it was that I was holding: a beautiful, perfectly round diamond solitaire ring on a platinum band. Oh, my God! Max! Then a frightening thought occurred to me. When had he placed it there? Before or after the talk? Of course it was before; he'd told me he was thinking of asking me to marry him. What a fool I had been!

I slipped the ring on the third finger of my left hand; it fit perfectly. Ever the optimist, I thought that once Max cooled down, maybe he would reconsider our relationship. After all, I rationalized, he hadn't taken the ring back after having walked out of the restaurant. That was a good sign, no? The Catholic Church taught us that where there is life, there is hope. Well, we were both alive, so there was hope.

BOXING
Benny "The Ice Man" Castillo, 28, 5'10", 195 lbs.
Title Contender, Heavyweight Division, International
Boxing Federation

BACKGROUND
For the past ten minutes, I'd been standing in the kitchen, sifting through a drawer full of takeout menus, trying to decide what to order for dinner that night. Chinese from Dim Sum? Japanese from Sakura? Cuban? Mexican? French? Just as I was about to make my decision, the phone rang.

"Magnolia?" Anita was on the line. She had the kind of voice that not even a mother could love. "I assume you've been reading the sports section of the Miami Herald."

"What part of the sports pages, exactly, are you referring to?" I was annoyed that Anita had interrupted my search through the menus.

"Boxing. Benny's defending his heavyweight title two weeks from Saturday. The fight's in Vegas, at Mandalay Bay, but he's been training here," she enlightened me.

"Then he's been training at the same gym as always, the Knockout Club?"

"That's right. Maxie, his trainer, called Oona, and asked for you to work your magic. It's the same situation with Benny, and you're supposed to take care of him the way you always have. But, Magnolia, it's a huge fight; the purse is worth millions, and it's for the title, of course." Anita was putting me on notice.

"Sure, no problem. Tell Oona not to worry. I'll take extra good care of Benny. I always do," I hurried to assure her.

"Will you deal with Benny directly, or do you want me to set it up?"

"You set it up, please. Just let me know the details." I went back to flipping through the menus.

Although I was fond of Benny, I hoped Anita would not set up the meeting for that night. I had just returned from a ten-mile run and had been looking forward to a long, leisurely soak in the tub while waiting for my dinner, and a session with the heavyweight was not my idea of a relaxing night. Besides, there was always the possibility of getting hurt. Benny did not know his own strength, and every so often, without meaning to, he would punch just a bit too hard.

Apart from the few times when he had inadvertently hit me, I enjoyed the time Benny and I spent together, but he was the kind of client who left me exhausted, both physically and mentally. He was very demanding, and I'd had to come up with different ways of entertaining him as holding his interest was not an easy thing to do. And the schedule was rough. We usually got together at the Knockout Club, a boxing gym, between two o'clock in the morning after the cleaning crew had left and five o'clock, when it opened again. I had to keep my energy up the day before and all night, which I found difficult.

Even though I was used to large, strong, athletic men, Benny Castillo was no ordinary client. He had mostly been nice, sweet, and gentle during our encounters, but because I had attended several of his fights, I had personally witnessed what damage his powerful hands could inflict. The truth was that I was both attracted to and frightened by his sheer physical power, and with reason, as with him the line between pleasure and pain was murky. Benny had no fear, and would take on bouts against heavier, more experienced opponents, fights that he would win. He was called "The Ice Man" because he had such a powerful right jab that when he connected, the other fighter would stand, as if frozen, before collapsing to the floor.

For all the trappings of his success—the huge house, expensive cars, bling, flashy women—Benny had had a rough life early on. Born in San Juan, Puerto Rico, he had moved with his family to the Bronx when he was six years old. He descended from a long line of boxers: his father, Benny "The Hook" Castillo, Sr., had also been a heavyweight, as well as his uncle and two cousins. His grandfather, Benny the First, had been the most famous cut man to have come out of Puerto Rico, and his half-brother, Benito, had reigned for years as the best corner man ever before getting stabbed, at the age of thirty, outside of a strip club in a fight over one of the women who worked there. The half-brother had never been too smart, something that fighting over the honor of one of the stripper-hookers confirmed.

Benny's father had also died young as a result of a blow to his head during a title fight. After the deaths of her husband and brother, Benny's mother was determined to make a new life for herself and her son, and had left Puerto Rico for good. Señora Castillo's plan did not exactly work out as she'd thought it would; a couple of years after their arrival in New York, Benny was off to the nearest boxing ring, determined to carry on the family tradition. One look at young Benny sparring in the ring, and the scouts came calling.

The legendary trainer, Maxie Feldman, had seen Benny's potential early on and had taken him on as one of his boxers. As a result of Maxie's careful nurturing, Benny had slowly, but steadily, risen up through the ranks. The only thing that Maxie had not been able to control had been Benny's preoccupation with ring girls. Fighting required total concentration; boxers could not afford to be distracted while in the ring.

Oona had told me she considered Benny one of her best clients, not only was he kind, generous, and followed her advice to the letter, but unlike many athletes, he had never had to be bailed out of jail. Of course, the fact that Benny kept winning and making piles of money for her also made him even more attractive.

And now at twenty-eight, Benny was poised to claim the heavyweight title of his division. If he continued to train and perform the way he had been doing, the belt was his. But Oona and Maxie knew better. They were aware of the threat that the ring girls presented, but now most alarming, was that lately the problem had been intensifying.

It had been Maxie who had first noticed Benny's increasing attraction to ring girls and at first, he had dismissed it. Several of his other boxers had also fallen for ring girls, not really surprising, since they were chosen for their raw sex appeal. A lot of them had been recruited from strip clubs or were out-of-work actresses or "models." During bouts, Benny would sit on the stool between rounds, and instead of listening to Maxie's advice as to how win the fight, would stare at the girls as they paraded around the ring, carrying the signs announcing the rounds. Maxie feared that his preoccupation with the girls could dash his chances of becoming a world-class champion. True, Benny had won his most recent fight, but just barely: the win had come as a result of a split decision, too close for comfort.

I'd met with Benny for the first time at his house in Key Biscayne, just before he had been scheduled to fly to Los Angeles for an International Boxing Federation bout at the Staples Center. He'd made it obvious from the minute that I had entered his house that he neither wanted nor felt he needed my help in any way and was only meeting with me because Maxie and Oona had insisted he do it.

In spite of Benny's dismissive attitude, I could tell right away that he'd been attracted to me. It wasn't just the way his eyes ran up and down my body and the way he shifted his compact shoulders. He kept running a hand over his wiry black hair as if he were primping, preparing for action. Oona had put me on notice that Benny was going to be reluctant to talk about the ring girls, as, in his world, admitting that one had a problem was seen as a weakness. Drugs and alcohol were commonplace, but women—that was tantamount to suicide.

Benny, having finally opened up to me, told me that at the beginning of his career, attraction to ring girls had not been a problem. His fights had taken place under such spartan conditions that there hadn't been any ring girls; the rounds had been called by an announcer using a scratchy-sounding microphone. However, as time passed and Benny had begun to win, his fights had taken place in more upscale establishments, more high-end, and those included having beautiful women as ring girls. That first day I had stayed with Benny for hours, discussing the various aspects of his attraction to the girls, from when it had started, to how he felt it could be brought under control, not leaving until I had felt confident that I understood the situation well enough to be able to help. Dr. Bernstein would have been proud of me.

It seemed Benny had developed a crush on a ring girl

who had worked the very first professional fight he had fought in. He had taken a terrible beating—blood everywhere, broken nose, split lip, cut over his right eye, etc.—and she had run over to hug him. His blood had gotten all over her, and she hadn't minded, something that had earned her his undying admiration.

But Adrianna Montez, the ring girl who had captured Benny's young heart, had been the wrong choice for him. She had explained to Benny that she was in her first year of college, working toward a nursing degree, and had taken the job as a ring girl to help make ends meet. It was her childhood friend, Rita, a real hell-raiser, who had gotten her the gig, and, although it paid well, Adrianna hated working there.

Coming from a strict, overprotective, devout Catholic, Nicaraguan family, Adrianna was not comfortable with the rough-and-tumble atmosphere of the boxing world. For starters, she felt completely naked in the skimpy outfits she had to wear; she disliked the drinking, smoking, and swearing that went on, as well as the casual violence of the sport. But, as she desperately needed the money, she had been forced to overlook those things. On the plus side of being a ring girl, though, because the fights took place in the evening, the schedule allowed her to go to class during the day.

Adrianna wasn't hardened like a lot of the other girls that hung around the fighters. To Benny, she seemed a pure, ethereal beauty in the midst of the ugliness of the boxing world. He told me that from the moment she ran to hug him, all bloody and sweaty, he had fallen head over heels in love with her. His love for her was gentle and respectful, never pushy or demanding. In spite of the fact that his career was taking off like a rocket, Benny never became conceited or arrogant. He, who was used to groupies, junkies, sluts, and whores, courted her in a quaint, old-fashioned way. Flowers in hand, Benny would come to her house in Hialeah, sit in the living room with her, and visit with her entire family.

Benny thought their relationship was progressing nicely until the day that Adrianna told him she was not going to see him again, that the boxing world was just too vulgar and violent for her. That word "vulgar" had especially hurt him. Not just that, but Adrianna was quitting her job as a ring girl. At first, Benny did not believe her, since he had observed her at the fights, and she had seemed to handle the situation well. Plus, he knew she needed the money. But if she hated the job, he said, then she should marry him, and let him pay for school if nursing was what she wanted. The sad truth, though, was that she didn't want to marry him. After much prodding by Benny, Adrianna finally admitted the real reason she was breaking up with him was that she was interested in a young man she'd met at school who was studying to become a doctor, and who had gotten her a job at the medical library there. Adrianna was determined to go the respectable route.

Benny was brokenhearted and tried to get Adrianna to change her mind, but she stood firm. It soon became obvious that Adrianna's days and nights with anything related to boxing were over, and that included him. Benny, who had so devotedly and carefully courted her, felt he'd been had. Bent on revenge, he then proceeded to have sex with each and every one of the other ring girls who had worked the fights with Adrianna. The girls, who had long had a crush on Benny, were more than happy to oblige. They had hated Adrianna, and had considered her to be a stuck up goodie-two-shoes.

Soon, however, normal sex with the ring girls failed to satisfy Benny, so he began to have kinky sex, threesomes, group sex, even indulging in dangerous sex games, activities that took up so much of his life that his boxing was in danger of suffering. He had become a ring-girl addict.

At that point, Maxie was so worried about Benny that, if there had been a twelve-step group therapy session for ring-girl addiction, he would have sent him to the meetings. Not knowing what to do—none of his boxers had ever had the problem to this degree before—the trainer hadturned to Oona for help. Oona, naturally enough, had then turned to me.

After that conversation, I had gone back to my apart-ment, and logged on to my computer, digging up all the information I could find on boxers and ring girls, not stop-ping until I had formulated a plan. Two days and nights later, at two o'clock in the morning, I had met Benny at the Knock-out Club for our first encounter. A second two-night session followed a week after that.

A month later, Benny won the fight at the Staples Center. This time there was no split decision, no contest; a clear win by knockout in the third round.

THE ENCOUNTER

The Knockout Club was located in a converted warehouse off U.S. 1 in South Miami. During the day, the area was bustling with activity, but at two o'clock in the morning, the neighbor-hood was deserted.

Although I had met other clients late at night in dodgy neighborhoods, this was by far the scariest, as it was consid-ered to be one of the highest crime-rate areas of Miami, and I always breathed a sigh of relief when I would safely arrive at the block where the gym was located. I drove slowly as I approached the gate at the center of the ten-foot-tall chain-link fence that surrounded the parking lot of the gym and tried not to focus on the fearsome rows of concertina wire that ran along the top of it.

I dialed Benny's number. "Benny, hi, it's Magnolia. I'm here. Please open the gate for me."

No sooner had I ended the call than the fence swung out, so very smoothly, almost as if by magic. I drove into the parking lot, and parked the Mercedes in the slot next to Benny's Porsche. We only had three hours alone in the gym, so there was no time to waste, and I quickly took the duffle bag, which held my props, from the back seat. The outside door that led from the parking lot into the reception area of the gym was open, so I was able to get inside without having to wait to be let in.

On my first visit to the Knockout Club, I had been in shock at how big, bright, and intimidating the place was. Brilliant light illuminated every square inch of the room with half a dozen wide-screen televisions hanging down from the ceiling. The walls were all mirrored so the boxers could check themselves out from every angle. The cavernous room was divided into three distinct areas: at the far corner, suspended by industrial-sized hooks from steel beams in the ceiling, hung thirty or forty black leather bags; in the middle was the weight area, filled with all kinds of top-of-the-line equipment; at the near end of the room, were three regulation-size rings.

That night, as always, rap music blared from the enormous, black wooden loudspeakers at the four corners of the room. I understood the cultural importance of rap music but was not particularly fond of some of the lyrics in the songs. Though not much of a feminist, I didn't like listening to women being referred to as "hos" or "bitches" on a regular basis. I didn't view my mother or both grandmothers as either one. Almost as much as I disliked the way women were described, I disliked all the referrals to violence. At our first meeting, I had asked Benny why he always played that kind of music. He reported that it was because of the hard "easy to punch to" beat, and anything by DMX or Kid Rock worked the best.

I opened the door to the gym and was almost knocked over backward by the pulsating beat of the DMX song that blasted from all four corners of the room. Knowing how that kind of music adversely affected me—after thirty minutes my head would begin to throb—I was grateful that I had taken the precaution of swallowing four Advil Liqui-Gels before leaving home. The bright fluorescent overhead lights weren't going to do much to help my head, either.

Benny was coming out of the men's locker room dressed in his fighter's outfit, a dark blue satin robe, the hood partially covering his head, with "Ice Man" written in gold sequins across the shoulders. Under the open robe, his chest muscles bulged. He had on dark blue satin trunks with yellow trim and, on his feet, yellow boots laced up with gold thread. He looked terrifically menacing. As Benny walked towards me, the gold tassels at the top of his shoes swung around. A lot of women would pay to have my job—well, at least for this night.

I picked up the duffle bag from the floor. "Same routine tonight?" I gave him a light kiss on the lips. Benny wasn't much of a kisser; he liked to get right down to business. His focus, as well as his short attention span, might have been explained by the fact that his life was measured in three-minute increments, the amount of time each round lasted during a fight.

"To begin with, yes." Benny got a mischievous look in his eyes as he added, "Then I thought we'd try something a little bit different."

I thought about what Benny had just said. This would be the first time we had ever deviated from our normal routine, the one that helped him win that decisive fight, which made me a bit apprehensive. I didn't particularly want to mess with success, nor did I want to get hurt. "So should I wear something different or the same as always?"

"Same as always is fine for now," Benny replied. "I'll see you in the ring."

"I'll be right there." I gave him a little wave and headed for the women's locker room. He still had his obsession with ring girls but, thanks to me, it was now under control—as long as we met regularly, that was. I had devised a plan to deal with that, and he had been so pleased by the results that he had not wanted to deviate from it at all.

Well, I'd find out soon enough what Benny had in mind, I told myself, as I changed into the first of twelve ring-girl outfits I would be wearing that night. The costumes I wore during my encounters with Benny were so minimal that they made the Hooters girls seem overdressed. After changing, the costume being only a couple of wisps of fabric so it really didn't take long to put on, I laid out the other eleven outfits on the benches lining the walls of the room, so they'd be ready when I needed them.

To successfully carry out the plan I had devised for Benny, it was vital that I be able to accomplish several tasks in a very short amount of time, so I had to be very quick. I had less than a minute, the time between rounds, to make the round trip from the boxing ring to the locker room and back. Not just that, but I also had to change from the costume I was wearing and into the next one. Last but certainly not least, I had to thoroughly clean myself off, so I was fresh for the next bout.

Even though the door to the women's locker room was made of thick wood, I could hear the three-minute bell as it went off, signaling that Benny was ready and waiting for me. I took one last look at myself in the mirror and gave a final adjustment to the tiny bits of fabric here and there on my body. Then I picked up the first of the large, white poster boards from the stack I had placed neatly on one of the white benches by the costumes, the one with a large number "1" written in big, black, bold ink in the middle, and opened the door to the gym.

As he always did, Benny had turned off the fluorescent overhead lights and turned on the spotlight that illuminated the middle ring, creating quite a dramatic effect. Carrying the poster board, I slowly made my way toward the ring. I climbed the three steps that led up to it, then, bending down, parted the ropes enough so I could fit through them, and stepped inside. I was once again surprised at how small the ring was, something that couldn't be properly appreciated by watching a fight on television, or even, for that matter, in person.

Holding the poster board high over my head, I made the first of the circles I would take around the ring. I felt sexy, and exposed. I had barely started on the second turn, when the theme from Rocky blared over the loudspeakers, Benny's cue to make the important march into the ring. Sure enough, less than five seconds later, he bounded from the locker room, arms held high over his head, fists pumping the air.

Like a good ring girl, I waited at the ropes, ready to part them, helping him to enter. Benny took the obligatory victory lap, his game-face on, my cue to hold the poster board up high as I could over my head. The fun and games would begin momentarily. When the music ended, Benny headed for his corner and sat down on the stool, the signal for me to hit the bell for the three-minute count for the first round to begin.

Benny's difficulty had presented a challenge on several levels: not only was he venting his anger at Adrianna, he was also having sex with multiple partners, as well as being distracted during the fights by the girls with whom he was having kinky sex. I came up with what I thought was a brilliant plan: Benny and I would have sex that would last exactly as long as the round that was being announced took. That would keep him aware of the numbers, the rotating of girls. For example, if round six was about to start, I would parade around the ring holding the poster board on which the number "6" was written, then Benny and I would have sex for six minutes. We would continue in this way until we reached round twelve, which was how long Benny's fights were scheduled for.

I would have one minute, the amount of time between each round, to run back to the women's locker room and change my costume, clean myself off, and switch the poster board to the one that corresponded to the following round. It was an exhausting routine, but one which had worked. By the time we would reach round twelve, I was almost comatose with fatigue. Benny, because of all his training, was barely winded. I learned that although I could not physically exhaust Benny, I could make sure that his obsession for ring girls was satiated. I didn't think it would have taken a genius or, Dr. Bernstein, for that matter, to figure out that his focus on ring girls all went back to Adrianna, the virgin girlfriend who had betrayed him.

Benny and I had sex multiple ways, from the straight-forward missionary position (round twelve) to his tying me against the corners with the wraps that boxers use on their hands inside the gloves in order to protect them (round six) to his tying my hands over my head with wraps, and then hanging me from one of the hooks where the bags were suspended from the ceiling (round ten), and so on.

Benny and I were lying in the center of the ring, soaked with sweat, after the twelfth round, when I turned my head, opened my eyes, and said, "Benny, you mentioned earlier that you wanted to try something different tonight."

He sat up and looked me over. "You're not too tired?" At that point, just breathing was a workout, but I was not about to reveal that. Benny had been so inspired that I swear he must have been trying out for the boxing/sex Olympics. I just shook my head. "Oh, good." Benny got up. "You know who Mike Tyson is, right?"

"Of course."

Benny got a wicked look in his eyes. "Mike Tyson used to call boxing 'the hurt business.'" He held out his hand to me, helping me to get up from the canvas. "Well, I want you, Magnolia, to hurt me some."

"Hurt you?" I repeated, not really understanding. He hurt others; they rarely hurt him. "But you have a fight coming up." I never understood this need to be punished. I didn't want to hurt Benny, especially as we would be doing this again tomorrow night.

"Not seriously, not so hurt that I need the fight doctor to tend to me; just enough, just enough. I'm sure you know what to do." He was right about that. After tightly wrapping my hands protect them, he handed me a pair of twelve-ounce red gloves and watched as I put them on.

"Now what, Benny?" I held up my gloved hands.

"Here." He led me to one of the bags, hanging from a steel hook, next to the ring. Then, carefully, he took the bag down, and wrapped his own hands up. I watched as he swung from the hook. "Hit me, Magnolia, hit me hard."

As I pummeled Benny, I imagined I was hitting my ex, Fabulous Fred. I thought about how he'd left me alone and penniless, in a new city. The harder I hit Benny, the more he liked it. We had to stop because my hands hurt, and not because I'd hurt Benny. I'd helped Benny with Adrianna, and he helped me finish off Fabulous Fred.

I must have done "the hurt business" right, for Benny canceled a repeat performance for the next night. However, being the gentleman that he was, he still paid for it. I must have hit him harder than I knew, because from what Oona reported, he never looked at another ring girl again.

Chapter 20

*E*ven though I'd been back in Miami for a couple of days, I was still suffering from a severe bout of jet lag. The time I'd spent in Tokyo had been exhausting. I hadn't rested at all, and the trip back, although I'd flown first-class, had taken forever. In the beginning, I'd tried to fight it and had taken Ambien to get back on a normal schedule, but although I'd popped enough pills to knock out a horse (hell, an entire stable of them), I could not get back on track, time wise. The bits of rest I did get, I was only able to do in short spurts.

Max had not contacted me. The more time passed, the more worried I became. Although I desperately wanted to do so, I resisted the temptation to drive past the Spanish Rose to try to catch a glimpse of him. I had not known what to do with the ring that had been hanging on the hook in the valet box next to my car keys. Every so often I would take it from the pouch where I kept it in my purse and put it on my finger. I seldom wore jewelry, so it felt kind of weird to have a ring on my finger, but I was sure that I could get used to it.

For the first time in years, I had free time. Thankfully Oona and Anita still thought I was deathly ill, so they did not bother me. I was still living in the apartment. It was weird, not being busy. I decided that I would put the time to good use, and just as I had done when I'd debated whether or not to accept Oona's offer, I decided to make lists. And just as I'd done the first time, I took out a yellow legal pad, sat down at the dining room table, and made a list of what I wanted to do with my life.

In spite of Anita's assurances that she would not jump the gun and go to Oona first, I did not completely trust her to keep her word; besides, I owed it to her to meet with her and tell her personally that I was going to stop working for her. Oona always got to the office early and was usually at her desk by eight o'clock, so I waited until a few minutes past before making the call.

I punched in Oona's private office number on the phone. She answered on the first ring. "Magnolia, honey. Are you feeling better?"

"Much better, thank you. Listen, Oona. There's something I'd like to discuss with you, not over the phone. When would it be convenient for me to come by your office to see you?" I tried to sound casual, so as not to alarm her.

Oona was quiet. "How about you come just before lunch, say at around twelve o'clock? How's that?"

"Perfect. I'll see you then." My hands were shaking as I hung up the phone.

The next few hours passed glacially slowly. Finally, it was time to leave for the meeting with Oona. I had a very strong sense of deja-vu as I parked the Mercedes in just about the same spot I had done with Fabulous Fred's Taurus, that first time we had met, what seemed like centuries before.

"Magnolia Larson to see Ms. O'Ryan, please," I introduced myself to the receptionist.

"Oh, yes, Ms. Larson, Ms. O'Ryan is expecting you." She smiled at me. "I'll just let her know you're here, and I'll take you to the back, to her office."

As I followed her, admiring the way the gray, two-piece suit she was wearing flattered her body, I could not help but notice that she, too, like the previous receptionist, had on killer high heels and stockings. Must be a dress code, I thought. No one would put those on those voluntarily. Oona ran a tight ship, that was for sure, or it could be that they took their cue from the way she dressed.

"Magnolia!" Oona came out of her office to greet me. She kissed me on both cheeks as usual. "As beautiful as ever."

I could feel my eyes begin to water. "Hi, Oona. It's good to see you. How've you been?"

"Fine, fine." She stepped aside so I could enter her office. "Come on in. Would you like some coffee, water, anything?"

I shook my head. "No, thank you. I'm fine." I headed toward the couch where I had first heard Oona's pitch for me to become her edge. Oona's office looked just as it had back then. Actually, Oona looked exactly as she had, too. That day, she was wearing a smartly tailored, khaki-colored two-piece suit, which was the exact same shade as her eyes and that, thanks to Stacy's tutelage, I recognized as being high-end Armani Black Label. On her feet, Oona had on black leather Christina Louboutin heels—I could see the telltale distinctive red soles on the bottom. On her wrist, she was wearing a thin gold watch with a black strap. The time that had passed had certainly not left any kind of noticeable mark on her.

"What is it that you wanted to see me about today?" Oona smiled at me. "Although, I have to tell you, I suspect I have a pretty good idea. I know you better than you think I do, Magnolia."

"Oona, you know how fond I am of you, and how grateful I am for all you've done for me." In spite of my intentions to remain composed, the tears began flowing down my cheeks.

Then, just as she had done that time before at the Miami
Sports Bar, Oona reached into her purse and brought out a
clean white linen handkerchief, and handed it to me.

"Let me help you out, Magnolia. You want to stop working as my edge. You're twenty-three years old, and you've
been doing this for a year and a half. It's time for you to
resume a normal life."

"Yes, Oona. That's right." The relief I was feeling at that
time was palpable. I'd been dreading this conversation, but
Oona was making it easy for me.

"Of course, I knew that day was coming." Oona reached
over and patted my hand. "I know you weren't going to do
this forever." She smiled at me. "Frankly, I'm surprised you
lasted over one year, I really am." She wagged her right index
finger at me, as if scolding me. "But I wasn't about to tell you
that! No, sir!"

"Really? You didn't think I'd last a year?" That was news
to me.

"Magnolia, you excelled at this, you were brilliant, really,
very creative with your ideas, much more so than I thought
you would be. I've told you on several occasions how I loved
the outfits you would wear for the encounters, and how
you thought of meeting with clients in their correspond-
ing venues. But, gifted as you were, I knew this wasn't what
you were meant to be doing for very long. I figured you
would stop when you felt you could no longer give it your all.
You'd become too much of a professional to do this job in a
half-assed way."

"I'm so relieved you understand, that you're not angry
with me for wanting to leave earlier than I had agreed." Oona
still had the ability to surprise me. "Thank you so much for
all you've done for me. I know I've made money for you, but,

what you've given me is more than I ever expected."

"You're very welcome, Magnolia. You helped me a great deal, too. We had a good run, didn't we?" Oona was surprisingly generous with her praise, an attitude I very much appreciated.

Now that the conversation that'd I'd been dreading was over, I could relax. I stayed in Oona's office for another hour, just talking to her, reminiscing about the past eighteen months. Oona was unbelievably generous telling me to stay as long as I needed in the apartment, just to let her know when I moved out. Most importantly, she wanted to make sure I knew I could come to her anytime in case I ever needed any help.

I had been about to leave her office when I turned to Oona and said, "The first time I met with you here, in your office, you told me that you'd had a rough upbringing. I asked you to tell me about that, but you wouldn't. Now that I'm not going to be working for you any longer, do you think you might tell me about that?"

Oona shook her head. "Ah, Magnolia. I should have known you hadn't forgotten that. I should have never hinted at how humble my beginnings were. I only did it so you'd understand that I didn't come from money and that I'd had to fight for everything I have." Oona stood up and walked to the bay window. She looked out at the view for so long that I wondered if she had forgotten I was there. Then she turned towards me and looked at me right in the eyes.

"Magnolia, I knew perfectly well what we were doing together was illegal. It's certainly nothing I'm proud of, and if we were to have gotten caught, what would have happened to us wouldn't have been pretty. I took as many precautions as I could to avoid that, but, still, in spite of my being extra cautious, it was risky. You, yourself, probably wouldn't have gotten into all that much trouble except for the possible tax evasion situation, and even then I knew you were careful. I would have protected you at all costs. You have to believe that."

Oona walked to her desk, opened the humidor on it, and took out one of her prized cigars. I watched as she brought it up to her nose and smelled it. I'd had no idea when I'd asked him the question about her background that she would get into her feelings about our endeavor. I, of course, was fascinated by this glimpse into Oona's mind. She was the most private, reserved person I'd ever met. After a year and a half of working for her in a most intimate way, I honestly did not know much more than I had that first day. I still did not know if she was gay or straight, although as a result of my conversation with Anita at Starbucks that morning a couple of weeks before, I knew Anita prayed she was gay.

"The clients never knew that they were paying directly for your services. I would just pad their bills enough to cover your fee, your five percent. Although you were living in luxurious circumstances and were getting an education—learning Spanish, meeting with Dr. Bernstein, having a stylist dress you, training in a world-class gym—all those things—well, they were just props, really. The truth was that I was pimping you out. I was no better than the pimps with their flashy clothes, flashier jewelry, and pimped-out cars who lived off the earnings of the women they controlled. Sure, I have a fancy office, I dress well, get three-hundred-dollar haircuts, live luxuriously, but at the end of the day, I am just like those guys, and it isn't anything I am proud of. I can tell you that now that you're leaving. When I saw that I was in real danger of losing my clients, I became more determined than ever to stay at the top of my game. I'd worked too hard and for too long to slowly slip into oblivion, to become a joke, one of those ambulance chasers, the kind of lawyer that advertises on bus benches and the backs of phone books or mail fliers, scraping for business. I was a woman in a man's world, and did not want to be held up as a failure to other women who might want to enter this business. I wanted to be an example of what could be done by a woman and not one of what could not be done. I'm certainly no trailblazer, but I did not want to discourage women from becoming sports agents because I could not make it in the field. Take my word for it, Magnolia, I've known some lawyers who were at the top of the profession, living large, charging six hundred dollars an hour, and, then they are no longer in demand. They get old, or are not as sharp, or start taking long lunches, maybe they get a reputation for hitting on the secretaries or paralegals in their offices, and, the next thing you know, they're calling around, asking for referrals."

Oona was looking at me in a way that told me she expected an answer. I hurried to reassure her. "Oona, really, that doesn't sound like something you would do. I can't see any of those things happening to you. Just because a few athletes switched agents, that didn't mean you'd end up as an ambulance chaser." Seeing her this way, vulnerable and sensitive, I realized that I was genuinely fond of her. I'd always liked her, even as I feared her a bit, but I had developed an affection for her.

As I spoke, I wondered what can of worms I had opened by asking Oona that one question about her background. It occurred to me that I had learned more about Oona during the past few minutes than I had known in the past eighteen months. And she still hadn't answered me.

"I didn't know what to do, I'd racked my brain, but I couldn't think of anything, anything I could do to stop the decline. And then, Magnolia, you came into my life. And everything changed." Oona smiled at me. "That afternoon at the bar I knew Fate had placed you in my path to stop what was happening."

"I talked too much, Oona, that was for sure," I admitted. "But then, remember, I'd had four rum and Cokes with you," I reminded her.

"That, too." Oona chuckled. "I don't know how I knew it, but I was sure you'd accept my proposal. You and I are alike in many ways, Magnolia. We both go after what we want and, we both have pride. You didn't want to have to go back to Minneapolis a loser, and I didn't want to slowly sink into oblivion. Our scheme worked out very well, don't you think? I realize that doing what you just did for the past year and a half has to have affected you. I know you paid a steep personal price for that, but you did what you did very well. And remember, Magnolia, you helped those men; they came to you for help for their particular situations, and you helped them. Don't forget that. You had sexual relations with them sure, but you were like a sexual therapist too. Remember Dr. Bernstein and all he taught you."

"I guess that's right," I agreed.

Oona was making me feel as if I was a combination of Mother Teresa and Dr. Phil. It was a classic Oona performance—half truth, half bullshit. Still, I appreciated her doing it.

"Oona, about your background," I ventured. "You haven't told me about it."

"Ah, Magnolia, what am I going to do with you?" Oona sighed in mock exasperation. "Well, I won't bore you with the whole story, really, there's not much to tell. I'll just say

I was not born with a silver spoon in my mouth, unless you count the spoon my mother would use to cook her drugs that lay on the floor of the trailer where we lived for the first two years of my life until the Department of Children and Family Services took me away. The story does not get much better from there. When you had a start in life like I did, Magnolia, there's no way you're going to go back to that. No more trailers for me; the hellhole where my mother and I lived in was the last I ever expect to enter. Ever!" Oona's eyes shone with anger. What a terrible story. No wonder she didn't want to talk about it. And it certainly explained a lot as to why she had been willing to risk so much to remain successfully. I guess I would have, too.

I stood up. "Oona, thank you for answering my question. I'm sorry if I upset you, really I am. It must have been horrible for you. I understand why you did what you did." I leaned down, and kissed her lightly on the lips, the first time I had ever done so.

Oona looked at me with such surprise one would have thought I'd touched her private parts. She stood up and embraced me. "Magnolia, you are a special person. A very nice person, too. I'm going to miss you."

As her words registered, I hoped that she would never, ever find out about Max and how I had broken the agreement. After hearing her high opinion of me, I knew that could only have devastated her. I was getting out at just the right time. I picked up my purse from the floor where I had placed it earlier, and began walking toward the door. "Good-bye, Oona. Thank you for everything. Really, I mean it."

"You have some money coming your way. I'll courier it to the apartment for you, just like I always do with your earnings." Oona had always made it very clear she did not want to leave a paper trail of our association. Nor did she want to know what I did with the money. I knew exactly what I was going to do with it. It was going to go into the safety deposit box at Citibank, along with the rest of it.

I took a deep breath, and said, "One last question." Oona groaned, but nodded, giving me permission. "Once I'm gone, are you going to get another girl to be your edge?"

"Ah, Magnolia." Oona shook her head. "You got to ask one question, one that I answered already. Not sure you get another."

"I guess it's best I don't know the answer to that." I opened the door. "But if I had to guess, I'd say that yes, you will. Maybe even two."

"I'll let you lose sleep speculating." Oona walked over to me and hugged me tightly. "I'll miss you, Magnolia. I really will. You will always hold a very special place in my heart."

"I'll miss you too, Oona." And it was true. I could feel the tears begin to well up in my eyes.

We vowed to try to get together in the future, joking how we'd return to the Miami Sports Bar and meet regularly there. I think, though, that we both suspected that was not likely to happen. Ours really, at the end of the day, had been very much a "time and place" kind of relationship, and it would probably be best that it stay that way. No question about it, I thought as I walked for the last time down the long hallway of her office toward the front door, Oona had been a class act all the way.

FOOTBALL
Buck Malone, 27, 6'2", 210 lbs.
Miami Dolphins, Second String Quarterback

BACKGROUND

"Magnolia?" I recognized the number that appeared on the caller ID screen of my cell phone. Anita. "Are you busy tonight? Buck wants to meet with you."

I had been working practically nonstop for the past couple of weeks, so I was quite tired and had been looking forward to spending a night at home catching up on my reading. However, for Buck, I would gladly change my plans. "Buck? Tonight?"

"Yes. Tonight," Anita replied.

"Same arrangements as always?" I felt compelled to reconfirm, even though I knew what her answer would be.

"Yes—everything's the same," Anita snapped.

"Sure, I'm happy to meet with Buck." I said.

"Okay, I'll tell him it's a go."

I'm not supposed to have favorites, but I have to admit, Buck Malone had always been at the top of the list of the athletes I liked the most. Although he'd been living in Miami for the past eight years—he'd won the Heisman Trophy his senior year at the University of Miami—Buck had never lost his farm-boy personality—not surprising, as he was originally from a small town in Iowa. According to Buck, Waves of Wheatville was not even really a town, more like a "group of farms located within a hundred miles of each other," united by the one stoplight in their midst.

Buck, who had played second-string quarterback for the Dolphins for the past two years, was one of the most popular players on the team. Polite and soft-spoken, he seemed genuinely unaffected by the adulation he received in Miami. Lately, for some unexplained reason, Miami seemed to be caught up in a frenzy of "Buck Fever," and he was mobbed wherever he went. Even though the Dolphins hadn't won a single game for the past two years, no one seemed to place any blame for that on Buck; he was just that likeable.

Our first sexual encounter had taken place a year before, but unlike most of my other clients, who wanted to get straight down to business, Buck had insisted on getting together with me to talk prior to our encounter. After much discussion, we decided to meet at a Starbucks in Little Haiti, a place he thought it would be unlikely for him to be recognized.

During that first conversation, Buck had told me he'd been a virgin when he reached Miami, something that I'd found hard to believe. Not only was Buck gorgeous, he was smart and funny as well, the whole package. He had explained that there were so few girls to date in Waves of Wheatville that he knew if he had sex with any of them, the news of how it had been would get around in no time. Still, as a red-blooded all-American boy, he had to try.

The big moment was to be with Marcia Olsen, one of his classmates at Waves of Wheatville High and, predictably, the head cheerleader. When the time came for them to have sex in the back of his old beat-up red Chevrolet pickup, Buck had been so nervous and freaked out that he hadn't been able to perform. He tried everything, he said, from techniques he had read about in Playboy to those he had heard about from his friends, but all in vain. Nothing. It was just as he'd feared. His body just would not respond to his commands, something that had never happened when he played football. He had simply not known how to react.

Tall, good-looking, well-built, and the captain of the football team to boot, Buck knew that he was expected to be a huge stud, but the truth was, nothing could have been further from the truth. Buck was just an average guy. The pressure on him was so intense that he simply could not perform. He felt his life was over.

That night, Buck had covered up his inability to rise to the occasion by telling Marcia that he had gotten hit so hard on the field playing that afternoon at the homecoming game that he was in too much pain to do anything. Marcia, whom he had known since nursery school, was just as innocent as he was, so she didn't question his story. If she was disappointed at not having consummated their relationship that night, she hadn't let on. That failure, however, continued to haunt Buck, and he would relive the scene in the back of the Chevy over and over again which, of course, only made matters worse.

"Buck, I realize this is going to be very difficult for you, but can you describe to me in detail what, exactly, happened that night with Marcia?" I asked him as gently as I could. It was hard to believe that this hunk of a man sitting across from me would have trouble performing sexually. It was even more bizarre to be discussing his impotence while sitting in a Starbucks in Little Haiti, but it had to be done if I was to help him.

"Do I really have to?" He was speaking in a voice so low I could barely hear him, especially over the loud shouts of the Haitian patrons speaking Creole. Buck immediately began to blush, not just a light pink color but a dark red stain that soon covered his entire face and neck. It was such an unexpected reaction that it took all my self-control to stop myself from laughing. He looked so miserable that I wanted to reach over and tell him to forget it and change the subject. But that wouldn't have solved his problem.

"Yes, so I can help you," I pressed him.

Buck took a deep breath as he struggled to regain his composure. "Marcia met me at Lookout Point over by the dam right after the game. We had played our rivals, the Iowan Pirates, and won 28 to 3. I made four touchdowns myself. Marcia, holding a pair of huge pompoms, was still dressed in her cheerleading outfit and had brought the bag of equipment they use for cheers during games. At first, seeing her in her cheerleading outfit excited me, really excited me." Buck gave me a look like a little boy who was being naughty. "Really, really excited me." I got the point.

"So what happened then?" I prompted him.

"Marcia and I had talked about going all the way. She had been looking forward to it as much as I had, and we'd agreed that the night right after the game seemed to be the perfect time. We started fooling around in the back of the truck. To prepare, I had put some towels down and all to make it soft—and everything was fine. I began to take off her little blue-and-gold cheerleading top, then the bra, and, the more I took off, the less excited I became. I mean, Marcia had always gotten me excited, she used to drive me crazy, especially when I used to see her at the side of the field during the games, dancing and prancing around! For years, my fantasy had been to have sex with Marcia while she was dressed in her cheerleading outfit!" Buck started blinking his eyes quickly, and I feared he would break down. Fortunately, he composed himself.

"Don't know why I couldn't perform that night. It would have been perfect; we were seniors, we had won the game, she had thought up new cheers, it wasn't too cold, and there was a full moon!" Buck shook his head. The whole experience was incomprehensible to him. "And, we were alone at Lookout Point, and Marcia wanted to do it!"

Buck confessed that he had been affected by that night for years afterwards. His experiences with the girls at the University of Miami had been equally disastrous. Every time he started to fool around with a girl at UM, a picture of Marcia in her Waves of Wheatville High cheerleader uniform would pop up in his head, with the same results. Much to his distress, it was the same situation with women after he graduated and joined the Dolphins.

The result was that, even though Buck had certainly done quite a bit of fooling around with women, he was still, unbelievably enough, technically a virgin. I listened carefully to Buck's story, and decided that really, it wasn't brain surgery to figure out what didn't allow him to perform. I didn't need a consultation with Dr. Bernstein to come the conclusion that all of Buck's troubles had stemmed from that fateful night with Marcia, that the nightmarish experience in the back of that Chevy would surface every time he tried to have sex. His fantasy had come true; he had actually managed to be alone with Marcia, who had been ready, willing, and able to have sex with him, but for some deep, dark reason, he hadn't been able to act.

Because of random drug testing in the NFL, taking erectile-dysfunction pills like Viagra and other little helpers, although not on the banned-substance list, was completely out of question for Buck, as he couldn't bring himself to do so. Straight, traditional sex hadn't worked for him before, so I had to get creative in order to be able to help him, and I did it with a certain amount of pleasure since I was attracted to him.

THE ENCOUNTER

That night, as I drove the final blocks on my way to the Sun Life Stadium in Miami Gardens where the Dolphins played,

I concentrated on the plan I'd come up with to help Buck. It was close to two in the morning, so traffic was light.

As soon as I reached the entrance to the stadium, I turned onto one of the lots on the north side, and drove all the way until I was in front of the ticket windows. I parked the Mercedes and picked up the bag I had placed earlier on the seat next to me. With the motor still running, I looked around to see if anyone was lurking nearby—the stadium was not located in the best part of town—before getting out. It didn't take long before I spotted who I was looking for.

"Hi, Moose!" I called out. Moose, one of the Sun Life Stadium's longtime security guards, was standing at his assigned spot in front of the gate. He was expecting me.

"Hello, Magnolia." Moose took out an impressive set of keys from the waistband of his uniform. Then, with a serious look on his face, he motioned that I should follow him.

Although my profession sometimes required that I dress in some pretty unusual get-ups, the one I had on just then was one of the weirdest. I had thought I was past being embarrassed but I was wrong. That night, I was wearing a blue-and-gold uniform of a head cheerleader at Waves of Wheatville High, which I had bought online from the uniform supply store that sold them to high schools. The sports teams of the school were called the Golden Wheats, so it was almost inevitable that the members of the cheerleading squad were referred to as "The Kernels."

Maybe it was the fact that I myself had been a cheerleader at my high school that caused me to feel awkward. I was actually having flashbacks. I would never have guessed that, five years after graduation, I would be wearing a cheerleader's outfit, not even one of my alma mater, for a mission like this. The uniform itself consisted of a cropped top and short skirt in an icy blue background with gold trim, colors that, according to Buck, were chosen because they represented the sky and wheat fields of Iowa. I wasn't just wearing the uniform but the whole damned get-up: pompoms, shoes (with yarn balls tied to the laces), white socks, my hair done up with accessories, and even a cheer lanyard (whistle attached) hanging around my neck. Additionally, I was carrying a cheerleader's bag filled with extra stuff—a megaphone, a water bottle with the school logo on it, a couple of towels—plus, my sex toys. The latter, of course, was not exactly part of a cheerleader's official equipment.

"Thanks, Moose. Is he here yet?" I hadn't seen Buck's car in the parking lot.

"Got here a few minutes ago. He drove straight onto the field." Moose led me on a long trek to the east end zone of the stadium, the only area that allowed access for large vehicles needed on the field.

The coach had taken Buck's predicament so seriously that he had pulled the necessary strings to allow him to use the stadium at night for the encounter. God only knows what he'd said to the officials who were in charge of operating the stadium to get permission to do so, but that was not my business: my job was to make sure the Dolphins' star player was playing at his best. For myself, even though I was getting paid to do so, I really just wanted to help the guy.

I scurried alongside Moose to keep up with his fast pace, and, a few minutes later, we reached the opening that led directly onto the field. Even though the stadium was pretty dark, it was still possible to see by the low lights reflected from the parking lot. As before, Buck was waiting for me, standing next to his red Chevrolet pickup, wearing the uniform he'd had as the quarterback of the Waves of Wheatville High football team. My outfit matched his colors exactly and the effect was that we looked like the yin and yang versions of each other.

"Hi, Buck," I called out as I walked towards him. It was crucial that I immediately get into character. "Great game. Four touchdowns! Wow!"

"Hey, Marcia, thanks." Buck reached out for me and began to touch my body all over. "I really like that new cheer." I swear he smelled like crushed wheat. "The one where you twirl around with the pompoms."

"How much did you like it, Buck?" I kissed him. "Show me how much, pretty please."

I prayed that he would not ask for a demonstration of the cheer, but if he were to insist, then I would do it, of course. In preparing for our encounter, I had practiced some of the cheers I managed to remember from my own days as a cheerleader. It had been a disaster, as in my zeal to do the cheers correctly, I had shaken the pompom so vigorously that I had pulled a muscle in my back. On my sofa, pumped full of Vicodin, lying on a heating pad turned on to a setting so hot I swear my back was in danger of being fricasseed, I had come to the conclusion that no one over twenty should even consider being a cheerleader. It wasn't that I lacked flexibility—after all, I had performed some pretty amazing acrobatics with some of my clients, but the sad reality was that I was no longer a high school athlete—something my body kept reminding me.

"Oh, Buck, I thought of you the whole time I was shaking my pompoms. Really, I did." I began rubbing my hands over his body. I could feel him responding nicely to me through all the padding he was wearing. "I'll show you how much I liked it, if you want."

"Show me, Marcia. I want to see how much you liked it." Buck let go of me and walked over to the back of the truck and with a practiced movement of his right hand, he lowered the back panel, motioning for me to hop on.

One of the few things I could clearly recall from my cheerleading days was that a cheerleader should, first and foremost, always have a smile plastered on his or her face. The smile should never ever leave the face, even when executing a particularly difficult stunt, or lying on the ground, in pain with every bone in the body broken and smashed to bits. But even though my old cheerleading manual covered just about every topic which had to do with the sport, (moves should always be tight and rigid, claps should be snappy, arms held at shoulder height) it did not go into such practical details as how that smile should be maintained when performing oral sex on a player.

Marcia, because of her height and strength, was what was referred to as a "base" in cheerleading terms, the foundation from which the flyers are thrown. Base is sometimes considered to be the most difficult position in cheerleading. I had been a flyer, much easier, but in my role as Marcia, I had to learn how bases performed.

I took Buck's hand and hopped onto the back of the Chevy. For his part, just as he had done back at Waves of Wheatville, Buck had made certain preparation for the tryst. I could see that several layers of towels lined the bed of the truck. Buck and I kept kissing, both becoming more and more excited. However, instead of allowing him to undress me, as had happened with Marcia so long ago, I took the initiative and began taking off Buck's football uniform. Unfortunately, in spite of my best efforts to keep him aroused, what had happened with Marcia happened with me: Buck was losing his erection. He began taking off my uniform, but that didn't help, either. In frustration, he kicked the wall of the truck bed, his cleats ringing out against the metal, the sound echoing across the stadium.

I had an inspiration: I would put our uniforms to good use because I strongly felt that they were going to be the key to our success, so I put mine back on then did the same to him. Now that we were both fully dressed, we began making out again. In no time Buck's erection was back, harder and stronger than before. But as I didn't know how long that would last, I began to play with my cheerleader props: I rubbed my pompoms all over his face then tied his hands with the lanyards as I blew the whistle softly in his ears, interspersed with cheers for his team. My plan worked: Buck was able to retain his erection, and we finally were able to consummate the sex act, even if we had been fully clothed. Buck even had a kind of orgasm—not an earth-shattering one, more like heavy breathing, but one nevertheless. I felt as if I had won the Super Bowl. The reality was, however, that it wasn't any four touchdowns; but he did score.

At the end of that first night, I decided that for the next three or so more sessions (I'd have to go back online to the uniform supply store and buy a couple of more uniforms if I could), we'd take off a few pieces of clothing, and, hopefully we finally would be able to have sex with both of us naked. My goal was to transition from the back of the Chevy to a bed, and if that worked, I would consider him cured.

Although I was pleased to have been able to help Buck with his problem, I have to confess that a part of me was already a little bit sad at the thought that I wouldn't be seeing him much anymore. Although I would miss him, I sure as hell was not going to miss wearing a Waves of Wheatville High cheerleader's outfit, having sex while fully clothed. That scratchy polyester cloth rubbed my skin raw in certain delicate places of my body. Still, I knew I would think nostalgically about those hot, steamy nights at the end zone of the Sun Life Stadium.

Buck was not the kind of man who would normally use the services of a call girl, so it was unlikely I would see him ever again in the professional sense after he was fully cured. For all his success on the football field and the fact that he lived in such a fast-track city as Miami, Buck was, at heart, a homebody. He would probably marry a hometown girl like Marcia, and have a big family. And that's the way it should be, given his background and tastes. He was a simple man with simple tastes who should and would lead a satisfyingly simple life, once his Miami experience was done.

Chapter 21

*A*fter leaving the O'Ryan and Associates office, I drove to the same Starbucks in Coconut Grove where the fateful meeting with Anita two weeks ago had taken place. After much soul searching, I had come to the conclusion that I wanted to personally stop being a call girl, but that didn't mean I wanted to get out of the business altogether. While on airplanes traveling to and from Tokyo, I'd had plenty of time to come up with a plan as to how to make money, one that I had finessed.

Even though I was early, Simone was waiting for me, sitting at one of the tables by the window. Just like anyone working in the life, Simone followed one of the golden rules: be on time, so for her, as for me, punctuality was key. Time is money, etc. I liked that in her. Simone wasn't alone, though. She had brought Suzanne, whom I recognized from the gym. We greeted each other and proceeded to the counter to order our coffees. Three black, no sugar, no milk, no nothing. Not exactly the kind of customers that Starbucks courted.

As we waited for our coffees, I had an opportunity to look over the two women. Simone had on a pair of shock-ing-pink skin-tight bolero pants with a white, see-through cropped top and four-inch-high silver pumps. On her overly tanned face, she had on enough makeup for two people. She was wearing gold dangle earrings that hung so low they hit her shoulders. Her bottle-blond hair cascaded down to her ass. She was hard to miss.

Suzanne, thankfully, was dressed more conservatively, in jeans, a tank top, and ballerina flats, but she, too, attracted attention with a body that was any straight man's wet dream. I'd heard that she was the best in the business, with a mind like a steel trap and a waiting list of client— just what I wanted. I had met her in the gym a few times and had liked her tremendously. In addition to being sexy, she was warm, welcoming, and witty, sort of like a girl-next-door, but one that was intimately familiar with sex toys. Although I had not expected her to attend this initial meeting, I was going to suggest to Simone that she be part of the plan I was about to propose, so I was pleased to see her there.

After getting our coffees, my guests and I headed for a quiet table in the corner of the room where we could talk undisturbed. I couldn't do anything about the stares we attracted; we weren't exactly inconspicuous, but at least we would not be overheard. After having exchanged a few pleasantries, I laid out the plans for the business that I was planning to start: an exclusive call-girl service, a high-class brothel that would operate out of a building, a warehouse that I intended to buy in downtown Miami. Because I would own the building, we would be able to exert control over almost all aspects of the business.

"But, ladies, this is not just going to be a run-of-the-mill operation. This is going to be different, innovative, a concept that, as far as I've heard, has never been tried before here or in any other place in the U.S." I had Simone and Suzanne's rapt attention, so I continued. "When I was planning this business, I researched the different kinds of brothels that had been operated successfully in the past, brothels that had offered services that were surprising and unusual to their clients."

"This is really interesting," Simone commented, smiling. "And, Magnolia, what did you come up with?"

"I discovered that in pre-Castro Cuba, in Havana, there had been an exclusive and extremely expensive brothel called Casa de Las Americas. This brothel was different from the many others that existed in Cuba because there, at the Casa, each girl came from a different country. A client could have sex with a girl from France, Egypt, Brazil, wherever in the world he wanted. What was unique, too, was not just that the girls who worked there had different nationalities, but that they would dress in their native costumes and speak in their language as well as follow the sexual practices their particular country was known for. For example, the girl from India would practice Kama Sutra. Total cultural immersion."

Suzanne looked thoughtful, then said, "Let me see, Castro has been in power, what, over fifty years? So the Casa closed down fifty years ago." She looked first at Simone, then at me. "Do you know how many new countries have come into existence in the past fifty years? In Africa alone, there must be dozens!" she pointed out.

"That's true. There's no way we can do that, have a girl from each country in the world on the payroll, but we can have girls that learn all about that country, teach them how to best represent each nation, and offer to have sex with the clients as if they really did come from that particular country, following the sexual practices of the countries they are assigned to." I had devoted quite a bit of time thinking about that.

"I can see it working quite well once the business is set up, if we do it right." Simone was nodding her head. "How many girls would be needed to operate a business this way?"

"Well, obviously, the number would have to be adjusted as needed. To begin with, I calculate twenty-five would be a realistic number," I replied. "Now that I've told you a bit of what I have in mind, why I asked you to meet me here today, is this business venture something that might interest you?"

They both said, "Yes."

"Good." I let out a deep breath. "I was hoping you'd say that, so I've already started the ball rolling. Last week I sent away to the Florida Department of State, Division of Corporations for papers that are necessary to incorporate. We're going to describe the business as some kind of a theatrical enterprise, and to make sure it's done right, I'm going to consult with a lawyer about how best to set it up. It has to be legal—well, as legal as possible, filing the correct paperwork, getting the necessary inspection of the building, that sort of thing—we don't want to be shut down. I assume, Simone, seeing as how you've operated your business for years without any trouble, you know how to go about it, right? Who to offer a little something so they look the other way?"

"I know who to contact so we're left alone. That's not a problem." Simone took a sip of her coffee. "It's going to cost, though, to buy protection for a brothel, I'm warning you. Miami is pretty corrupt, so we may have to pay off quite a few individuals."

"It's the cost of doing business, but we'll make it back, I'm sure of that," I agreed. "We can budget for that." Sadly, I would not be able to deduct those costs as a business expense from taxes, but that's the way it was.

"What would our roles be in this?" Suzanne asked. "You didn't say."

"Simone would be the administrator. She would handle the day-to-day operations: make payroll, pay bills, invoice clients, and the like. And you, Suzanne, I think you would be great at overseeing the girls and being in charge of the clients, making sure their wishes and desires are taken care of. Of course, you both would be partners with me on this. Since I'm bankrolling this venture and taking the risks, I think it only fair that I own sixty percent of the business, and you would have twenty percent each. I couldn't expect you to work without having a stake—we're all in this together. Naturally, I can't tell you yet how much you would make, but I figure it would be enough." Remembering how Oona had set me up as her edge, I continued. "In the beginning, until we start making money, I would pay you each a salary; we can discuss the amount later, but, I assure you, ladies, it would be fair, some figure we could all agree with."

As far as they were concerned, they were to think of me as being the deep pockets, a hands-on type of investor. It hadn't been easy to think of a business that would allow me to earn sufficient income to subsidize my art school. After considering several different business ventures, even looking into franchises, I had decided to stick with what I knew, a type of escort business that supplied high-class call girls to its clients. The trick was to stand apart from the other businesses, to have an edge, which was why I'd come up with the concept of the Casa Miami.

The economy may have tanked, but men were still men. They wanted to have sex with lovely ladies, and that had not changed. In the end, all I was doing was taking advantage of a business opportunity. There was a void, and I intended to fill it. Of course, the fact that I knew Simone had greatly influenced my choice in deciding the kind of business I wanted to be involved with. She was already well established, with a large clientele; from having had several conversations with her about her business, I'd learned that her overhead costs were preventing her from making significant profits. Also, she was getting tired of coming up with creative ways of raising cash to expand, so she was thinking of getting out of the business altogether. I was thrilled that she and Suzanne had agreed to come on board.

"What time frame are you thinking of, Magnolia?' Simone asked, quite logically.

"First, I have to interview a couple of lawyers—I have their names—to see which one would do the best job of representing us. That should not take more than a day or two. I've already found a building that would work to operate this kind of business out of, but I have to finalize the sale, something thing I didn't want to do until I was sure you would agree to work with me. After that, I have to hire a reasonably priced contractor to remodel it so it suits our needs. I have to discuss expenditure projections with my financial planner, figure out what the start-up costs are going to be, and plan accordingly. Obviously, I would not disclose the nature of the business; only the lawyer would know that. Right now, I have to make a checklist of all that needs to be done."

"So, maybe six months?" Suzanne suggested. "There's a lot to organize."

"Six months?" I laughed. "No, more like six weeks. A lot depends on the contractor. We'll be up and running fast, I promise. I'm going to work on this nonstop."

We discussed the business a bit more, batting ideas around until we all were clear on the concept. Before going our separate ways, we agreed to keep in constant touch. They made me promise that I would ask them for help if I needed any. I was pleased that Simone and Suzanne had accepted the terms and conditions that I had laid out. The truth was, I was being very generous, just as Oona had been with me, a great incentive to work hard. After leaving Simone and Suzanne, I went back to the apartment and began working on making the deal a reality.

The next afternoon, after stopping off to see Mr. Vogel, I headed for one of the office buildings in downtown Miami, where I had an appointment at the real-estate offices of the realtor with whom I had been dealing. Although I tried to act very cool, inside I was very, very excited. In my purse, secure in the zipper compartment, was a cashier's check for a million dollars, which I was going to hand over to the Realtor to pay for the building I had seen earlier in the week, one that was perfect for the Casa Miami to operate out of.

Once I'd come up with the idea as to the business I wanted to get into, I had done research to see what buildings were available that would accommodate our needs, and I'd found one building, a ten-thousand-foot warehouse in Midtown Miami, an area just north of downtown that was being revitalized. I'd called Sam Clement, the listing agent, to set up an appointment to see the building; the walk-through hadn't taken more than thirty minutes, as the building was vacant, and I knew exactly what I was looking for. Mr. Clement had told me that the building was about to go into foreclosure, the owner was a victim of Miami's current economy, so I had made a low ball offer—cash, two weeks closing— one that had been instantly accepted. And, as I didn't need to take out a mortgage, the deal had been closed without problems.

Mr. Clement told me that this had been the fastest and easiest deal he had made in his twenty years in the business.

Just as he had promised, the paperwork had been completed by the time I'd gone to his office—all that had been required was my signature on several documents, and, of course, the check to the title company. It had all been so quickly and efficiently done that I'd only had to be there for less than an hour. After returning to the apartment, I spent the rest of the afternoon sketching plans for how I wanted to lay out the place. I'd visualized the setup so often in my mind that it really hadn't been at all difficult to draw what it was that I had imagined. I didn't stop working until I'd gotten the plans to perfectly depict my vision for the place.

That night, I celebrated by soaking in a steaming hot, rose-oil-scented bath for an exceptionally long time, all the while drinking an entire bottle of champagne, with the keys to the warehouse on the ledge next to me. It had cost me a lot—emotionally, physically, and financially—to realize my dream, but in the end I felt that it had been worth it. Except, of course, for Max. Losing him still caused me pain, but there was nothing I could do but hope and pray the situation would change. The proceeds from my association with Simone and her crew would allow me to set up the program for inner-city children that I'd so long dreamed about, which would go a long ways toward making me feel better about life. The following morning, even though I had a slight hangover, I'd gone to meet with Jason Eddis, a recommendation from the Realtor, the best and, most important, fastest contractor in Miami, to give him the plans for the building, so he could start the renovation and remodeling process. We'd spoken on the telephone a few times, so he knew what needed to be done, and had begun to make the necessary preparations for when he could start the actual work.

Jason, having been in business in Miami a long time,

knew how to expedite the approval process for the necessary permits, and once they had been approved, the work could start immediately after that. As we weren't changing anything structurally, the entire scope of the job could be completed within a month, so I could realistically plan to move into the place in six weeks or so. The business would occupy the front part of the ten-thousand-square-foot building, and I would live in the back.

Even though Oona had told me I could stay in the apartment on Brickell as long as I wanted, I could not do that indefinitely. I was eager to make a clean break and start fresh, and I sure as hell could not do that living in the apartment; still, it wouldn't be easy to leave the place, my home for close to two years. I would miss the view most of all.

After having finished with Jason, I had gotten back in the Mercedes and headed west, on the 826, the Palmetto Highway, toward the Miami-Dade County Animal Services Shelter. Once there, I parked the car, and went inside. The shelter had the ability to break even the most hardened individual's heart. The people that ran the pound did the best they could with their limited resources, but it clearly wasn't enough. As I walked through, I tried not to focus on the pair of cats prominently displayed in a cage on a table in the middle of the lobby with a sign on top that read, "Please adopt me."

I asked where the animals scheduled for euthanasia at the end of the day were kept, and was told that area was a bit removed from the rest of the building. I walked down that hall several times, trying not to look too much while passing the two dozen or so cages, not stopping until I had picked out two dogs: the biggest, ugliest, mangiest ones, who had no hope whatsoever of being adopted—a male (with only one ear, and with one eye partially shut) and a female (she'd had puppies—her tits were hanging down to the floor). The mutts were considered so unadoptable that they hadn't been treated medically, nor had they ever been bathed or dipped. I could easily see the ticks on them. Resources at the pound were very limited.

The staff there could not believe I would actually want that particular pair, but when I opened my purse and took out the wads of cash to pay for the fees, including a sizable donation—they became instant believers. I left the dogs, Oona and Waldo, to be de-liced, de-flead, treated, and neutered. I was told they would be ready for me to pick them up in three days. I could hardly wait.

BASKETBALL
Vaclav "Stretch" Dostynovicz, 22, 6'11", 200 lbs.
Miami Heat, Forward

BACKGROUND

I had been taking a long, leisurely afternoon nap, having the most wonderful dream, when I was rudely awakened by the ringing of my business phone. In my dream, I had been in an apartment in Paris, lying naked on a couch that had been placed in front of a set of those fabulous double windows that the old buildings there have. The late afternoon sun had been streaming in, casting the room in that special, blue-tinged light Paris is famous for. The room was large, perfectly square in shape, with dark wooden floors and very high ceilings adorned with intricately carved moldings.

Across from me were seven men—the best known of the French Impressionist painters of the late nineteenth and early twentieth century: Monet, Renoir, Pissaro, Sisley, Degas, Cézanne, and Manet. Three were sitting, four were standing, and all were looking at me intently as they painted me. I had been about to get up from the couch to look at their canvases, to see how each of them saw me, when the phone rang, shattering my dream.

It was Vaclav, the only one of my clients who ever called me directly. "Magnolia, hi, it's me. How are you?"

What a reality check! Within less than a minute I had gone from being painted by the Impressionists to speaking with one of the most gifted and most immature players in the NBA. Vaclav's timing had never been great. He usually called at inopportune moments (when I was on the treadmill watching Jim Cramer, my financial guru, or in the pool doing laps) but that afternoon it was particularly horrible. Five more minutes, and I would have satisfied my curiosity.

"Ready for your big day?" The Miami Heat had a huge game coming up that night; they were playing against the New York Knicks, a rivalry that went back years.

"I'm ready. The game is no problem." He spoke in his thick Czech accent. "We will win for sure. Absolutely." We spoke a little longer and made a plan to meet after the game.

I closed my eyes and willed myself back to that elegant apartment on Paris's Left Bank, but I couldn't do it. Those seven men were my absolute favorite painters, why I'd majored on the Impressionists in college. I would have given anything to see how each of those Grand Masters would have painted me.

Going back to sleep proved to be impossible, so I began to think about my date for the evening. Vaclav Dostynovicz was the youngest player in the Miami Heat's roster. I was quite fond of him, but he was so very childish that it was often difficult to deal with him.

Oona, knowing how trying Vaclav could be, had filled me in on his background. Young as he was, Oona said, the boy had traveled a long and winding road, from a one-cow village in the Czech Republic to Miami. Vaclav was discovered by one of the coaches of the University of North Carolina's basketball team while on a trip with his family to the Czech Republic. Apparently, the coach's wife's family had been from one of the villages outside Prague, and they had gone there so she could meet her Czech relatives. Unfortunately, or fortunately, as it had turned out, the car that the coach and his wife had rented for the drive to the village had a flat tire, and he had been forced to walk a few miles to the nearest town to get help. Leaving his wife by the car, he had set off by himself on the long trek to the town they had passed earlier.

Walking on one of the country roads, the coach spotted Vaclav, who had been taking time off from milking his family's cows to shoot baskets at a hoop that was nailed to the side of the barn. Playing alone, he was hitting the basket from every angle possible, not missing any shots. The coach had stood there, transfixed, watching him in awe. Vaclav hadn't noticed a stranger observing him the whole time that he had been practicing.

The coach, who by then had been there over an hour, knew he was seeing the next basketball superstar in action. After all, one did not come across on a daily basis a seven-foot-tall kid who could shoot like this. The coach did not approach Vaclav directly, but instead, once he reached the village, had gone straight to the bar where the only telephone for miles around was located and had placed a collect call to the head coach at UNC, describing to him what he had just witnessed. The head coach listened intently, and trusting the other man's judgment, had told him to sign Vaclav up on the spot. The coaches from UNC knew that once the other colleges learned of Vaclav's existence, their window of opportunity to sign him would be gone. This had to be stealth recruitment.

The coach, with the help of an interpreter, explained to the astonished teenager and his family that he was offering to bring Vaclav to the United States, to a place called North Carolina, where he would be a student at one of the best-known universities in the nation. Within two days, Vaclav, who had never ventured more than fifty miles from his family's farm, was on his way to Prague to apply for a passport so he could travel to the United States. One day later, after discovering that the consular officer at the American Embassy in charge of issuing visas was a graduate of the University of North Carolina. Vaclav had been granted one. Had the officer been a graduate of Duke University, UNC's archrival in basketball, the story might have turned out very differently. And Vaclav may have still been waiting for his U.S. student visa.

Clutching an overnight bag with all his worldly possessions, Vaclav had landed at the Raleigh-Durham airport in North Carolina less than a week after the coach had discovered him. Although he was exhausted, lonely, confused, and smelled slightly of manure, he was very excited and ready to begin a new chapter in his life.

It only took a couple of weeks for him to become accustomed to his new world in North Carolina. His teammates, however, took a bit longer to get used to the Eastern European farm-boy-turned-ACC basketball player. Although he was quite intelligent, Vaclav had little formal schooling; not just that, but he had never traveled anywhere outside his village. His formal education had consisted of classes in a one-room shack taught by a single teacher, a young man responsible for the education of dozens of children whose ages ranged from three to seventeen. The teacher was able to come only during certain times: when crops were neither being planted nor harvested, and when the roads had not been washed out by the torrential spring rains, a timeline that eliminated most of the school year.

Vaclav was miserably unprepared for the rigors of freshman year at the UNC. Fortunately, though, he absorbed knowledge through every pore of his seven-foot-tall body. He had an iron will and an insatiable desire to succeed, and aided by the army of tutors that the coaches had arranged to help him with his studies, he was able to do well academically.

Vaclav wasted no time in showing off his natural skills on the court and was appointed a starter from the very first game he played in. It was clear from the warm and enthusiastic reception he received that the fans loved him from the very beginning. His teammates, who admired his skills on the court, were astounded by his actions off it, and understandably so, for Vaclav stood out, even among ballplayers, as quite a Don Juan.

Apart from basketball and academics, a large part of Vaclav's foray into American life had consisted of his seeing how many girls and women he could have sex with in as short a period of time as possible. Apparently, in his village, the young men and women were expected to be celibate until marriage, so the fact that American girls had so much sexual freedom was incomprehensible and totally appealing to him. And it wasn't just that. Vaclav soon found out that, because he was a member of the UNC basketball team, he had special status on campus, which meant that, basically, he could have almost any girl he wanted. And there were plenty of those.

The Czech was not only uninhibited on the court and in his social life, he was even more so in his private life. He seduced girls who were too young, who were friends, who were roommates, who were sisters. Once he had used them up, he would toss them aside. The coaches knew that the administration would have no choice but to expel Vaclav if the word got out officially about their star player's exploits off the court. Three girls had already been persuaded that it was in the best interest of all concerned to keep quiet about Vaclav and his sexual practices. Nothing had slowed him down. Vaclav was not even particularly discriminating in his taste in women. Basically, all they had to have was the right chromosome count for him to be interested in them.

Pro ball teams were as interested in him as he was in sex. NBA coaches had so vigorously pursued him from his first game on that it was a miracle that he hadn't gone pro immediately, but he'd done as agreed and stayed on to graduate. Now, though, the coach who discovered him feared that, far from the protected world of UNC, Vaclav would get into the kind of trouble that he wouldn't be able to get out of so easily. A few months before graduation, the coach contacted his old friend, Oona O'Ryan, to see if she would agree not only to represent Vaclav but also to take him under her wing.

Oona, who had been following Vaclav's career from the first time he had stepped on the court at UNC, had salivated for years over the possibility of representing the young Czech. The instant that Vaclav had turned pro, Oona had flown to

Chapel Hill to meet with him. They immediately clicked, and on the day of Vaclav's graduation from UNC, with the ink on his hard-earned diploma barely dry, he was on his way to Miami, to play for the Miami Heat.

It didn't take long for the stories of Vaclav's exploits with the ladies in Miami to reach Oona's ears. He'd started off by hitting on the Miami Heat dancers, a real no-no. Then he tried to work his way through the staff and the administration of the Heat organization; he had even tried to hit on the team doctor, something that had not been appreciated. Oona had been very annoyed. She had known about the boy's exploits at UNC, but that had been as a college player. Oona had assumed that Vaclav would have grown a bit more discreet at least, but apparently his penchant for hitting on anything in a skirt had only intensified. In the NBA, things were different; much was on the line, starting with money and reputation, and Vaclav's behavior, unchecked, was certain to have serious consequences, legally and financially.

Oona knew she had to get her star client under control, but she had to do it in a delicate way so as not to alienate him. Vaclav was young and immature, a bit of a hothead, and he might just walk away if he was called out on his behavior. There were plenty of teams and agents that would be more than happy to have him, problems and all.

One morning, after hearing that Vaclav had offered one of the Heat dancers five thousand dollars to have sex with him, Oona realized she had no choice but to act fast before any more damage was done and had consulted with me on how to handle the potentially explosive situation. I had never before seen Oona so concerned about any player's behavior. In addition to potential lawsuit—sexual harassment, battery, bribery, etc.—Oona was worried about the possibility of paternity suits. There was also the fear of the consequences if her client were to contract a sexually transmitted disease, potentially ruining not only his health but his career as well. Vaclav was footloose and fancy-free, taking social and health risks far beyond those of the other players, and there was no reason to believe he would suddenly become careful in his sex life.

Oona and I put together a plan for me to engage Vaclav sexually so that his urges would be satisfied in a way wouldn't get him into trouble. I was to satisfy him, but at the same time remain enough of a moving target that he would not lose interest in the chase. The plan wasn't completely without risk: if Vaclav couldn't have me, if I played too hard to get, he wouldn't hesitate to move on to someone else, someone more amenable, an easier conquest. I had to play my cards just right. After much discussion, we came to the conclusion that Vaclav, who considered himself to be attractive to all women, would not like it if his agent had to act as his pimp, so we decided that I was to pose as someone who worked in Oona's office, perhaps as a publicist, not as someone who was paid to have sex with the clientele.

One afternoon, after practice, Vaclav and I were suddenly face-to-face for the first time. He had come to Oona's office to sign some papers, and I had been the one to bring the documents to him in the cushy spare office with a ten-foot-long sofa and a lock on the door. The plan Oona and I had arranged worked brilliantly: less than ten minutes after meeting me, Vaclav had asked me out, and, less than twenty-four hours later, we'd already had sex. The boy from the Czech Republic was hooked.

THE ENCOUNTER

"Hey, Magnolia, baby!" Vaclav yelled as he came bounding out the door to the player's locker room of the American Airlines Arena to the limousine where I had been sitting, waiting for him. At twenty-three, I was only a year older than Vaclav, yet sometimes I felt as if I were his mother. I felt quite protective toward him; he was so eager, so trusting, that I actually felt slightly guilty deceiving him.

"Hi, Vaclav!" I called out, watching in admiration the easy grace with which he moved. While it would have taken me probably a hundred steps to reach the car, with his giant strides, it had taken Vaclav less than ten. He didn't as much walk as glide over the ground. It always amazed me that he could coordinate all the muscles in his almost seven-foot frame so they worked well together, and made his style of moving—walking, running, or shooting baskets—seem so effortless.

Being only five-foot-five inches tall, I had often wished to be taller. But watching Vaclav, I also saw the problems that the truly tall faced in everyday life, and I began to be grateful that I was of normal height. For example, Vaclav, to avoid hitting his head, had to bend down to enter some rooms, as the doorframes were too low for him. He could hardly ever shop at regular stores, as they did not carry his sizes, so he had to special order most, if not all, of his clothes.

He and I seldom went out in public, because the few times we had tried, it turned out badly. At his great height, naturally, he stood out from the crowd, so it was close to impossible to go anywhere unnoticed; also, as one of the most popular Heat players, he was instantly recognized. The one time we went to the movies was torture. Not only did he not fit into the seat, people kept coming up to him to greet him or make comments on the game he had just played, even giving him advice on how he should play the next time. The two times we'd gone to restaurants, we'd been constantly interrupted. To his credit, Vaclav was accommodating, at least when he was with me.

In the end, Vaclav and I had decided it was just easier to stay indoors whenever we would meet. We would end up at his apartment, downloading films (Vaclav was a real movie buff), ordering takeout, and then of course, having sex—lots of it. Although in the beginning, Vaclav was quite apologetic that we always stayed in, but as the time passed and he saw how happy I was to do so, he relaxed and never suggested going out again.

I, of course, was quite relieved at that, as the more we would go out, the more the chances would increase that one of Oona's clients would recognize me and perhaps blow my cover. After all, we'd patronized several of the restaurants that other athletes did; Prime 112 on South Beach was a favorite so I always ran the risk of being seen. One chance encounter with any one of my numerous clients and I would have lots of explaining to do. Then, once Vaclav figured out what I really was, who knew how he would react—betrayed, angry, manipulated—and the truth was, he'd have a perfect right to have felt that way. Even though he may have been childish and immature, Vaclav would be personally and professionally devastated if he was to find out that I was being paid for my services. By not going out in public, and by my insisting that I'd rather be alone with him than hang out with his friends, we avoided taking that risk.

Of course, it wasn't that I imagined he would disapprove. After all, this was the guy who had offered one of the Heat dancers thousands of dollars to have sex with him, but

then he hadn't had any kind of personal relationship with
her; he had barely known her and the offer he had made
her had been strictly for sex. With me, the situation was
different: he had met me in an office setting, as a person
with professional responsibilities. I had been assigned to
be his publicist, so he had known me before asking me out.
It was clear from the way he treated me that Vaclav
onsidered me from the start to be someone who had girlfriend potential.

On this particular night, Vaclav seemed to walk with a
bit of extra zip in his stride and, rightfully so, for he had been
instrumental in winning the game. From the first minute
on the court, he had played brilliantly, aggressively blocking
dozens of the Knicks' shots, resulting in numerous turnovers,
giving his teammates the ball, and allowing them to score.
He had proved to be a valuable asset to the Heat roster during the first season he had played with the team, and he had
become invaluable in the second. He was the Heat player the
opposing teams had come to admire and fear the most. The
Heat was on a mission to win their second NBA title, and
Vaclav wanted to help them achieve that goal.

Coming out after the game to greet his fans was one of
Vaclav's favorite parts of being a member of the Heat team.
He was genuinely affectionate with them: warm, friendly,
approachable, and seemingly unspoiled — a rarity among the
elite athletes of pro sports. He never passed up an opportunity to greet people and pose for pictures with them. Not surprisingly, this refreshing attitude endeared him to everyone,
and he was fast becoming one of the favorites, if not the most
favorite player, of the team. At least, his jersey outsold his
teammates by a factor of four.

Heat fans, and there were many, knew of the location

of the players' locker room, and they would wait there on Biscayne Boulevard before and after games, hoping to get a glimpse of the players as they entered or exited the arena. If a fan were to be truly lucky, then he or she would get one of them to autograph a program or maybe even manage to have a photograph taken with one. Given all the crazies out there, the security around the players was understandably tight, but every so often, it was still possible for the spectators to get close.

That night, before joining me in the limousine, as he usually did, Vaclav first headed out to greet his public, standing as close to them as the police allowed, which wasn't all that near, as security had been ramped up, normal for a playoff game. The game that night was the all-important fifth game of the playoffs, so the chance of crazed spectators was higher. No sooner had this crowd spotted Vaclav than the chorus of "Hey, Stretch! Great game! You rock!"

I watched as Vaclav played to his audience, making victory signs, pumping his arms up and down, clasping his hands over his head. It was clear that he loved the adulation, and it was well deserved. Through the combination of hard work, determination and luck, Vaclav sure had come a long way from milking Bessie in his native village. Before getting into the limo, he thanked the police officers for providing security then signed a few programs for them. He even posed for a couple of photographs with the officers and told each of them that he'd see them at the next game.

Once he was inside, I gave him a quick kiss on the lips, much as a girlfriend would have done. "Congratulations on the game—you played terrifically well."

"Thanks. It was a good game, but tough. Two more to go, and we're in the finals!" He shook his head as if he could not believe his good luck. He kissed me again, a bit longer that time, and took one of my hands in his. "Is there something special you'd like to do tonight?"

I assumed we would do what we always did whenever Vaclav and I got together, which was to go to his apartment on South Beach, the penthouse at the Icon, one of the fanciest buildings there, and then order out from a restaurant in the neighborhood. Now that the Heat was in the midst of the playoffs, going anywhere was going to be more impossible than ever and not even a consideration.

"It's your choice, Vaclav. We should have a victory dinner to celebrate your terrific win tonight." As far as I was concerned, the only question was which restaurant to order from. "You decide. I'm happy to do whatever you want."

"You mean that?" By telling him I was agreeable to doing whatever he wanted, I meant I was happy to order our dinner from whichever restaurant he chose and then have sex any which way he wanted. I felt a flicker of apprehension flow through me as I waited for him to give me some idea what he wanted.

"Good. Then let's go to your place," he suggested, looking at me slyly.

"My place?" God, no!

"We always go to my apartment," he pointed out. "I have never once seen where you live, so that is what I want to do. Go to your apartment."

I was so terrified at the prospect of having one of my clients in my apartment that I was on the verge becoming nauseated. The time I had been dreading had arrived. I had always been so careful, but now Vaclav had succeeded in backing me into a corner so that I really had no choice but to allow him to see where I lived. For two years I had managed to avoid having anyone come over. My apartment was mine alone, my zone of privacy, my sanctuary, one place where I could go and shut out the world and pretend I was just a normal person. I could not believe that of all the men who had asked to see my home and, at one time or another they all had, amazingly enough, Vaclav, the seven-foot-tall, twenty-two-year-old Czech farmer would probably be the first to do so.

Still, I had to try to get out of it. "Oh, of course, Vaclav, you know you're always welcome in my home." Even though my heart was beating a million times a minute, I smiled as gently and sweetly as I could manage. "But your place is so much nicer than mine. I'm only a working girl, you know."

"Oh, Magnolia, don't worry about that; if you had only seen my family's home in the Czech Republic, you would not warn me like that." He took my hand. "I want to know all about you. You sometimes are very mysterious. I think seeing how you live will answer this mystery." He kissed me. I kissed him back with as much enthusiasm as I could muster. Unfortunately, Vaclav took that to mean that I agreed with his plan. "Good, I'm happy that's decided." He stopped kissing me long enough to ask, "Now, what is your address, so I can tell the driver?"

Reluctantly, I gave him the name and address of my building, and as I did, thanked my lucky stars that he wasn't yet all that familiar with Miami, otherwise he would have instantly recognized the name and began to wonder how I could afford to live there. His excitement at the prospect of going to my apartment increased the closer we got to my building and he kept kissing me. Meanwhile, my mind was racing along at a million miles an hour, planning what I was going to say to him once we arrived there. After claiming to be a simple working girl, how the hell was I going to explain the fact that I lived in a multimillion-dollar penthouse apartment in the fanciest building in Miami on a publicist's salary?

Once the security guard at the booth at the bottom of the hill had properly identified me, the arm of the wooden gate lifted, and we proceeded up to the second and then the third set of security guards before being allowed to go all the way up to the lobby. The guards at my building were used to having celebrities come by, so no one gave Vaclav a second look. We walked through the opulent foyer towards the elevators. Once inside, I swiped my security card on the panel. Although he had been watching my every move closely, Vaclav had not said a word, so we rode up to the penthouse floor in silence.

When the doors of the elevator opened again at my floor, he politely stepped aside, allowing me to walk out first. I took out another security card and swiped it at the box to the right of the door. We heard a sharp click, and after I inserted the front door key in the lock, the right panel of the double doors opened. Now it was my turn to step aside and let him pass.

"Welcome, Vaclav," I began turning on the lights in the apartment. "Please come in."

Vaclav entered and looked around the place, taking it all in. Once satisfied, he headed over to the terrace, and looked out over the lights of the city. "Beautiful view."

"Yes, it is beautiful, isn't it?" I walked over to where he was standing and put my arms around him. Given that I was more than one and one half feet shorter than him, the buckle of his belt pressed into my chest as I held him, not exactly an ideal position for me, but, as my intention was to distract him, I wasn't about to move around to get comfortable. I wanted to do everything in my power to prevent him from concentrating too much on how I could manage to live the way I did. We stood a while longer in front of the doors to the terrace, admiring the view. I pointed out a few of the landmarks, but Vaclav didn't seem to be particularly interested.

"Are you hungry?" I began stroking his arm. I would have preferred to rub his chest, something that I knew he liked when I did it in bed, but standing up, it was awkward. "If you want, we could order something, and while we wait for the delivery to come, maybe you'd like to have something to drink?"

"A drink would be fine, I'm not so hungry now. I had something to eat at the player's dining room after the game. But if you're hungry, please, let's order out. You decide from where. You know me, Magnolia, I can always eat." Vaclav smiled at me.

I went to the kitchen and took out a Corona, his favorite drink, handed him the bottle. "Would you like to drink it here, or outside? Wherever you like."

It was really, really strange to have a guest in my apartment. Apart from Encarnación, the Nicaraguan cleaning lady who came three times a week, and the once weekly visit from Odalys, the manicurist, no one ever came there—the way I liked it.

"What I'd like, Magnolia, is to see the rest of your apartment." He set down the bottle of beer on the corner of the coffee table.

I took him by the hand and led him to the bedroom. He paused in the doorway, taking in every detail of the room, nodding his approval. I had the feeling it was the kind of place he expected, which was a surprise. Maybe, after all, Vaclav was the right client, a safe one, to come here.

It was the bathroom, with the pool-sized Roman tub, the cherubs, and the erotic frescoes on the wall that totally caught his attention. "Do you want to take a bath with me now?" I nodded. "You live in a wonderful, very beautiful place, Magnolia. You are very fortunate."

"I know, yes, I am very, very fortunate." Very, very true.

Vaclav turned his attention to choosing the bath oil. I was pleased to notice that he picked the rose oil, which coincidentally, was my favorite. He had set the temperature of the water so hot that, almost immediately, the room was filled with steam.

He pulled me to him. "Let me help you take off your clothes." Without waiting for an answer, he began to unbutton my white silk blouse. I felt my own desire stirring, and for once it was real. Vaclav, always before so fast, was moving slowly. Deliciously slowly.

Then he stripped off his own clothes in the blink of an eye. Less than a minute later, we were luxuriating in the bathtub, the hot water scented with the oil of rose petals. For someone who had grown up in a one-cow town in the Czech Republic, Vaclav had a hell of a way with bath oil. Vaclav began to massage the concentrate directly onto my skin, not stopping until every inch of me was covered. I must admit, I had never thought to apply the bath oil on my skin. After that, he passed the bottle to me, and indicated that I should do the same to him. Because he was double my size, it took twice the amount of time and oil to cover him that it had taken for him to do it to me.

Once we were all oily, Vaclav began to massage me, but this time it wasn't to cover me in oil, instead it was to get me sexually aroused, something he achieved almost instantly. I had never known that the contents of that little bottle of rose oil could produce such erotic results. Neither, by the way, would I ever in a million years have suspected that Vaclav—farm boy that he was—had it in him to be so imaginative.

That night, we made love so many times, and in such diverse positions, that it was necessary to refill the tub several times. We didn't stop until we ran out of rose oil—and it had been a very large, nearly full bottle. After our bathtub adventure that night, I knew I would be able to avoid ever having to go out and be seen in public with Vaclav ever again, as for the foreseeable future, we would stick close to the water.

The question of how I could afford to live the way I did never came up. Maybe Vaclav felt all Americans lived like that. And it was kind of nice having a gentleman around, even if he did take up a lot of space. I even felt like a real girl-friend, if just briefly.

Chapter 22

I'd worked so hard that first week after my meeting with Simone and Suzanne, getting the Casa Miami ready to open, and had accomplished so much in such a short amount of time, that I actually found myself at loose ends. I decided that it was time for me to go back home to Minneapolis to see my family. After all, I hadn't spent any time with them since I'd moved to Miami, and a visit was long overdue. And there wasn't anything preventing me from going. I may still have been involved in peddling flesh, but now I was a businesswoman.

I was pretty apprehensive about going home. However, I shouldn't have been worried as to how my family would feel about me because they received me with open arms. Five minutes into the visit, and I felt as if I hadn't been away at all. It was great to be back in Minneapolis; I spent almost the entire two weeks of my visit hanging out with my family and friends.

The one sad part of my trip was to learn that Fluffy, my beloved dog, had contracted arthritis, so was not as mobile as she had been before, but that should not have surprised me, for she was close to twelve years old. I had to carry her on and off my bed, but I did not mind, as I was very happy to be with her. Although Fluffy, my first dog, would always be the canine love of my life, I was looking forward to spending time with my new ones, Oona and Waldo.

Before going home, I'd been worried about how I was going to deal with questions about my life in Miami, but, thankfully, those only a few came up a few times, and I was able to handle them quite easily, deflecting specifics and only answering in generalities, talking about the beaches that I visited, the sports I played, the restaurants that I patronized, and the like with enthusiasm. At times, I felt almost as if I was working for the Chamber of Commerce. My family, thank God, had never been especially nosy, so my answers had satisfied them. They were just happy to have me home. For some reason, the guilt I feared would emerge as to what I had been doing for the past eighteen months never emerged. I described my imaginary job in generalities.

However, happy as I was to be back home, to my surprise I discovered that I missed Miami terribly: the beach, the palm trees, the sun. I especially missed Mr. Tanaka and his crew, and all things Japanese, even my flower-arranging classes. My family was pleasantly surprised when one Saturday night when we had gone out to dinner at a Mexican restaurant, that I was able to order our meal in perfect Spanish. They were floored when, two days after that, I'd done the same at a Japanese restaurant.

By the end of the two weeks, I was ready to get back to Miami. I was eager to see how the construction was going, to check out the progress that Jason had made. He had been giving me updates, and sending photos, but I wanted to see it with my own eyes. I couldn't wait to pick up Oona and Waldo, who were boarding in the private section of the pound. Mostly, I wanted to get on with my new life. Max, sadly, had not attempted to contact me while I was gone.

Once back in Miami, I plunged right back into setting up the business, which I had named Casa Miami. Peter Mullins, the lawyer I had retained to represent us, had advised that the best way to register the company with the Division of Corporations was as a modeling agency. We needed to have a cover story as to the nature of the business, one that had to be plausible, in case we were to get busted. In addition, all employees had to actually do some modeling, including me, so we would have a paper trail to back up our claims. It wasn't perfect, to be sure, but at least it was something.

Much to my surprise, I'd found that I was in demand for modeling gigs ranging from businesswoman and young mom to lingerie and bathing suits. Because I was only five-foot-five, I was too short to do any catwalk jobs, but I was fine for catalogue work. Although I was flattered to have been asked, I said no to the ones that required me to be scantily clothed. Regardless of my profession, I was still quite modest. Also I did not want to risk having my family or friends back home seeing me that way. Being the owner of a modeling firm, and an occasional model, was quite respectable even by Minnesota standards, so I didn't mind stating that on public records.

I heard via the grapevine that the Spanish Rose would soon be closing; Max's days as a restaurateur would be coming to an end. Although I was sad to see the Spanish Rose close, I was happy for Max. He had lived up to the promise he had made his father, and now he was free to do as he wished.

I thought about Max often in different ways. I remembered that on several occasions he had told me he liked dogs, especially big, ugly, rescued ones, and that once he was able to give up working the crazy hours at the Spanish Rose required, he wanted to go to the pound and save a couple. I held out hope that maybe one day soon he could meet Oona and Waldo. He also said he really liked Japanese food and Japanese flower arrangements, as well as getting Shiatsu massages. We had all those in common, so who knew, maybe it would be our karma that we would get together again.

BASEBALL
Leonardo "Lefty" Ortiz, 41, 5'10", 215 lbs.
Miami Marlins, First Baseman

BACKGROUND

Why did the telephone always have to ring while I was running on the treadmill? I was on mile three of the five I was running every other day on this machine. Not only that, Oprah had just started. Knowing that Anita would not give up until she reached me, I stepped off the treadmill and took her call.

"Hi, Anita, what's up?" I had been running hard, so I was panting a bit.

"Lefty wants to see you. Tonight." Anita also dispensed with formalities. "Big game today—the Yankees—World Series."

"I'm available. Just text me the arrangements. Thanks." I went back to running. I glanced down at the numbers displayed on the panel of the treadmill and was pleased when I saw that the entire conversation with Anita had taken less than a minute, so I had not lost that much time. I looked up at the television, but, unfortunately, Oprah had just gone to a commercial break. I would use the time to think about Lefty.

Even though he wasn't one of my regulars, I was very fond of Lefty, a forty-one-year-old Dominican who had played for the Marlins for years. Lefty was quite rough around the edges—I don't think he had gone to school past the sixth grade—but he had always treated me with the utmost courtesy and respect.

I had heard that Lefty had a wife and seven children in the DR, but even though it sounded harsh, that part of his life really did not concern me. I was paid to worry about the here and now of my clients, and not what happened back home. If I were to spend time thinking about my clients' personal lives, it would affect my performance, and then I would be useless.

Lefty was one of the oldest players in the major leagues, the reason why Oona had called me in to meet with him. On the field, Lefty was still the same kind of player he had always been, steady, reliable, and solid, but the sad truth was that he was beginning to feel his age. Pancho Morales, his best friend and longtime first-base coach, had been the one to notice that Lefty had begun to make comments about how old he was. To Oona, who had been Lefty's agent since he signed with the Marlins a decade ago, it wasn't surprising that it had been Pancho who first noticed the change in his old friend.

Pancho and Lefty were inseparable. They had come from the same one-stop town in the Dominican Republic, and as boys barely out of diapers, they had played ball together on the town's only baseball field. Against their family's explicit wishes, they had left their hometown together as teenagers and run away to the capital, Santo Domingo, to find fame and fortune in the baseball fields there. They didn't exactly find what they had been seeking, but they had been able to make their way to New York City.

For years, they played in the minors in the U.S., but only Lefty had been able to turn pro. Pancho's career had ended abruptly one lazy Saturday afternoon in a dusty town in South Carolina, before a grand audience of fifty spectators. In the middle of a game, needing to get to a bathroom in a hurry, he had attempted to steal from third base to home and had twisted his right ankle so badly that, ever since then, he walked with a limp. Although the accident had happened almost twenty years before, the friends still debated whether getting proper medical care that day would have allowed Pancho to be playing still alongside his friend.

Life had been good for the next twenty years, even though Pancho's accident had drastically changed their plans: instead of both being players, now only Lefty would play, and Pancho would be his coach. The adjustment to their new reality had been easier to adapt to than either man expected. Lefty played for some great teams, and Pancho went with him, coaching him and helping him with his game. However, it had been the last ten years, living in Miami, while Lefty had played for the Marlins, that they had been the happiest, which made his sudden preoccupation with age all the more surprising.

Everything had seemed fine until Lefty began making increasingly frequent comments about his advancing age. He would complain about the stiffness in his body when he got out of bed in the morning: his creaky knees, his failing eyesight, and the cricks in his neck. Normally, Pancho would have laughed those off, but lately the situation had become worrisome as Lefty was complaining more and more openly, even to the team doctors, trainers, physical therapists, and, worst of all, the other players.

So far, Pancho had been able to make jokes out of Lefty's gripes to the teammates or the staff, but he was afraid, and rightfully so, that he would not be able to forbid Lefty from making all those comments about his condition much longer. If Lefty kept pointing out his age, the Marlin's organization would begin to take notice, and take a long, hard look at the future of their first baseman.

Lefty's contract was up for renewal, and if the Marlins thought he wasn't up to the job, they wouldn't sign him again; if he made his age an issue, then it certainly would become one. There were plenty of young, hungry players chomping at the bit to take Lefty's place, ones whose contracts would cost fraction of what the organization was paying him. Replacing him would be no problem at all.

Pancho had dealt with the situation as best he could, telling his friend to stop making such comments, pointing out the repercussions if he continued to do so. Lefty, though, at his forty-first birthday party, had started up again, discussing his age and his aches and pains. At that point, Pancho had no choice but to turn to Oona for help. After all, if the Marlins were to release Lefty, then Pancho, as his coach, would be badly hurt as well.

Pancho's decision to discuss Lefty with Oona hadn't been easy. First of all, there was no denying that Lefty was indeed now forty-one years old. Nothing and no one could change that. Next, there was the fact that he felt disloyal in discussing his friend's situation with the American agent. Pancho and Lefty had been brought up to solve problems within the family. And, although they were both close to Oona, she was still, after all, a stranger. And a gringo.

After much discussion and soul searching, Pancho and Oona decided that the way to get Lefty to forget his age was to wow him with his sexual prowess, which was where I came in. Oona told Pancho about her plan to unleash me on Lefty, something that Pancho had instantly agreed to. After all, if Lefty could prove he was still a tiger in bed, well, then, he wasn't an old man, was he?

My job, as Oona later explained to me, was to make Lefty feel young again by making him seem like he had the sexual powers of his teenage years, as if that was the easiest thing in the world to do. If I could only bottle and sell that ability, I could be a multimillionaire—the hell with working as an edge! I would peddle my secret on my own infomercial TV channel—no HSN for me. I'd become richer even than I'd planned to become.

THE ENCOUNTER

"A car will come to collect you at nine o'clock tonight," Anita informed me when she telephoned me a couple of hours later. "The game will have ended hours before, and the stadium should be empty—you'll be meeting him at Marlins Park, like always. Nine o'clock pickup, there shouldn't be traffic at that time. You'll be there at around nine-thirty. That should give you plenty of time."

"Nine o'clock pick-up to go to Marlins Park. Fine, I'll be ready." I hung up.

It was just seven o'clock then, so I would have a couple of hours before meeting Lefty. Knowing that Anita would be calling to give me the information and not being sure how much time I would have to get ready after that, I'd gone ahead and had a bath and dinner, so all I had left to do was get dressed. When Anita telephoned, I had been in the kitchen, washing the couple of dishes I had used to fix my dinner. I finished cleaning up and headed back to the bedroom; there, I lay on the bed and switched on the TV.

By then it was a few minutes past seven, I had missed the start of the seven o'clock shows, but that didn't matter much to me as I was going to watch Law and Order. I was such a faithful fan that I had already seen most of the episodes that were shown at that hour. I loved Law and Order and all the spin-offs to such a degree that I would even watch the reruns.

As soon as Anita had told me that Lefty wanted to meet at the new Marlins Park that had just been inaugurated, I knew precisely how he wanted our encounter to work. Lefty may have been a terrific baseball player, but as far as his imagination was concerned, as it related to sexual matters (in spite of his seven children), he was pretty much of a dud. I had known, of course, that baseball had been the center of his life, but I hadn't realized how completely true that was; it was nothing short of a miracle that he had children at all. Sex with Lefty always involved some kind of interaction with baseball equipment. We always met at night with the lights off after a game, and Lefty always wore his Marlins uniform.

The first time we met, Lefty requested that we have intercourse on the bench in the Marlins' dugout. Although, of course, I'd agreed to it, it had been quite unpleasant on several counts; it had been tricky to retain my balance on the bench, plus, the bench was caked with chewed bubblegum, some of which had stuck to me. Even though the park was just a few months old, the dugout already also stank disgustingly of old sweat, dirty socks, dried spit, and other things I didn't dare think about. The second time, we did it in the batting cage; the third time, we were lying on the pitcher's mound. Although I was happy to oblige Lefty's every whim, I have to confess that the encounters with him took a toll on my body. Back at the apartment, I would have to scrub my whole body raw to get totally clean. It was close to impossible to get the damned red clay off of my skin, especially my ass.

As I was getting dressed, I wondered exactly where in the stadium it was that Lefty had in mind for our encounter. For our previous dozen or so encounters, Lefty and I had met at Sun Life Stadium, the venue the Marlins had shared with the Dolphins. However, as of this past March, the team had its own venue, Marlins Park, located at the sight of the old Orange Bowl in the heart of Little Havana. The state-of-the-art stadium was very controversial, as it had been primarily built with taxpayer money, a boondoggle that caused intense anger among the Miami community, one of the very few issues that had united the residents. That, and there was no parking, adding insult to injury. However it had been financed, and despite the mistakes made in its construction, there was no mistaking that the place was truly amazing, with its retractable roof, swimming pool in the style of a South Beach hotel, and two 450-gallon aquariums filled tropical fish located on either side of home plate.

Four primary colors dominated the venue: green, red, blue, and yellow; yellow was used in the area between first base and the right field foul pole, Lefty's realm. The Marlins' dugout was on the third-base side. In the time it had been inaugurated, only a few games had been played in the park, but already the dugout had the kind of lived-in feel that it had taken years for the former one to achieve.

Although the place was huge (it seated just under forty thousand spectators), we were running out of new places for sex. I, of course, would have been happy to help Lefty out and come up with some possibilities where we might have our encounter in the new stadium that he might not have considered, but as he had not asked, I had not volunteered. Early on, I had learned that Lefty was a "slam, bam, thank you, ma'am" kind of guy, so I didn't know how my suggestions would have been received. Athletes' egos were quite fragile, so I had to tread carefully. I would have preferred going to a hotel and having sex on a regular bed, but I knew that was not an option. Baseball was Lefty's life, personally, professionally, and sexually.

At exactly five minutes to nine, I left the apartment and headed downstairs. I was dressed in a short, tight khaki cotton skirt with a black sleeveless T-shirt on top, and sneakers—quite sporty, though not exactly the kind of outfit I'd have liked to wear, but one which best suited the occasion.

The limousine that Anita had sent was already parked in the driveway, waiting for me. I waved to the driver as I walked toward the car, and was pleased to see that it was the same one who had driven me out there to meet Lefty other times. We exchanged greetings; I hopped in the back seat and made myself comfortable for the short trip to the stadium.

Just as he had done on the previous occasions, the driver entered the property through the gates designated for the Founders' Club Seats. We zigzagged to get to the gate where I was to meet Lefty. As instructed to do, the driver had called ahead to let Lefty know we would be arriving in a couple of minutes, so he would know when, exactly, to expect me.

Because of the super-tight security around the stadium, there was no way I would have been able to step onto the property unless someone was there to let me in. We drove up to the main gate, but, surprisingly, Lefty was not there yet, which was unusual, waiting to greet me. I was not all that worried; if something were wrong, someone would have surely notified me. I sat back in the seat of the car to wait for him.

A full fifteen minutes passed before the back door to the

building slowly opened, and Lefty came out, dressed, not in his usual Marlins uniform, but in a pair of blue jeans and an open-necked white cotton shirt. As he approached the car, I was a bit shocked to see how slowly he was walking, as if he were in pain. I hadn't watched the game that Lefty had played in the afternoon, so now I wasn't sure if he'd been hurt then. But to my untrained eye, it sure looked as if something had happened to him. Was that why he wasn't wearing his uniform?

"Hola, Señorita Magnolia, thank you for coming to visit with me." Lefty opened the door of the car, letting me get out. He took a step back and inspected me, his eyes taking in every square inch of me. "You look very beautiful, as always."

"Thank you," I replied, with a smile. "You look well yourself," I lied. Even in the low lights of the stadium, I could see that there was some sagginess under his eyes, maybe a hint of it at his jaw line.

We headed towards the building. As we walked, I couldn't help but notice how stiff his gait was. Maybe it was true what Pancho had feared: that his friend's age was really creeping up on him. I reminded myself that I was there to make sure he felt like a young man again. I had done it previously, so I was sure I would be able to do it again. However, the truth was that Lefty had never been this stiff before or been wearing civilian clothes either (which made him seem less like an athlete and more like a middle-aged man.) Given that, making him believe he was a young stud again might take more skill on my part. I was confident that I was up to the challenge, but was Lefty?

Slowly, almost painfully, Lefty escorted me through the Founders' Club seats until we were at the very edge of the field. As before, I was in awe of the building, and, even though the only illumination was by the light of the full moon, it was possible to admire it.

"I'm sure you're wondering where I've planned we will be having our delicious rendezvous tonight." Lefty spoke in such flowery phrases it was difficult to keep a straight face. Even though it was really cheesy, still, it was kind of sweet. "Because," he continued, "I feel my days as a baseball player are numbered." I opened my mouth to protest, but Lefty held up his right hand to silence me. In the moonlight, I could see the threads of silver in his brushy black hair, something I had not noticed before. He said, "Tonight I want our meeting to be exceptionally meaningful. It will be my birthday present to myself."

Lefty took me by the hand and led me onto the field. We had only taken a few steps when he turned around and declared, "Please forgive me, Señorita Magnolia, if I'm not at the top shape tonight. We just played a very, very tough game: twelve innings, eleven to ten. We won, against the Yankees. You watched it?"

"No, I'm sorry, I wasn't able to." I felt badly, admitting that.

"That's too bad," he commented, a bit sadly. "It was a great game. Anyway, I played a little bit too hard—against the Yankees, everyone does—and I'm stiff; these are old bones and muscles, you know."

"You're certainly not old, Lefty, not the way you play, not the way you make love to me." The last thing I wanted then was for him to become maudlin, not good to set a romantic mood. I took his hand and changed the subject. "Speaking of making love. What did you have in mind that was so special?"

"First base, of course, Señorita," Lefty replied, as he steered me towards the right side of the diamond. "My home: first base."

I should have guessed, I thought, as we walked in silence to the first base. There I kissed Lefty a few times, first softly, then more vigorously, and began to take off my clothes. I tried not to wince at how the rough surface of the base felt on my soft skin as I lay down on it. Although Lefty had been watching me very closely as I had taken off my clothes, he hadn't become aroused in the least. Not an auspicious sign.

Now it was Lefty's turn to undress. Naked, he lay down on top of me. Nothing happened. Nothing! I considered my dwindling options. I had to fix this situation without seeming to have noticed there was anything wrong. Lefty, of course, knew what was happening, or rather, not happening, well enough. He didn't need for me to point that out to him.

I began stroking him, kissing him, fondling him, but in spite of my best efforts, still nada. I got up on top of him, and tried to work on him that way, a sure fire way to get him going. I didn't want to get frustrated, but close to half an hour had passed, and Lefty was just not responding.

Nothing I was doing was working, so I decided to try another angle, something that was familiar to him. "Do it like last time, Lefty; just like the last home run you hit," I ordered him. "Exactly like last time, just the way you always did. The way I love." Speaking like a radio announcer, in the same fast, staccato speech they used in calling a game, I started telling Lefty how wonderful he was, how terrifically he was playing with me, how skilled he was, carrying on to the point that you'd have thought I was a real announcer. For that was what I was doing.

As we began to make love, a sudden transformation came over Lefty. The stiff, painful movements of just a few minutes before were replaced by some rather inspired, almost acrobatic, moves. He wasn't doing it like last time at all; he was doing it like never before.

I hardly ever spoke while having sex, unless requested by my client, but that night I realized that, as Lefty was reacting so well to my running commentary, I should continue as if he was playing in a real game. So far, thank God, it was working. Throughout his lengthy career he had played in so many games that he reacted instinctively to my calling the plays. I mean, it wasn't as if it this was the World Series or anything like that, so I didn't have to be that accurate, but it was good enough.

My plan worked beautifully. The more I called the game, the more enthusiastic Lefty became, and the more inspired his lovemaking became. After a while I, too, got into the spirit, so I was able to relax a bit and started having fun. Along with my other juices, my creative ones began to flow, and I even developed a reward strategy for Lefty. When he stole two bases, I rewarded him with an especially inspired round of oral sex; a hit allowing him to get to first base earned him a full body massage; second base, I got on top of him, and rubbed myself all over him; third base, I did a lap dance, and so on. I was the one who decided what the rewards for getting on base would be. The three home runs that he hit ended in some rather prolonged orgasms.

By the time we got off the actual first base on the field, hours later, our skins were raw, close to bleeding. Neither of us, though, was about to complain.

"Lovely señorita," he said, in his hopelessly old-fashioned way, as we parted. And, of all things, he kissed my hand. His eyes no longer looked baggy and tired at all; as a matter of fact, they positively sparkled.

Maybe it was the session on first base, maybe it was because we were in the new stadium, or it could have been the fact that I'd been determined he would revert to the athlete he had been twenty years before; whatever the reason, by the time we left Marlins Park that night, Lefty Ortiz had become a changed man. He'd drunk from the fountain of youth (me!)—and it showed, even though he still talked like somebody's grandfather from the eighteenth century.

I heard that two weeks after our encounter on first base, Lefty had signed another four-year contract with the Marlins. Maybe next time, he'd make it to the World Series. By then, I should have learned how to properly announce a game!

Chapter 23

*J*ason Eddis, the contractor, had been as good as his word. Six weeks to the day I had hired him to do the job, he had telephoned me to tell me that the living quarters of the Casa Miami building were ready for me to move into. Although Oona had assured me that I could stay in the apartment on Brickell Avenue as long as I needed to upon my return to Miami from Minneapolis, I'd moved out, and had spent the last two weeks in a short-term rental in South Beach, in a townhouse that allowed dogs. Waldo and Oona, although in the beginning had been understandably skittish and mistrustful of me, had slowly begun to allow me to interact with them. Of course, I would bribe them with food and treats, which hurried the process along. Many walks, toys, and trips to the beach helped, too.

I'd used the time to prepare the setup for Casa Miami: making sure our licenses were in order, meeting the girls that Simone and Suzanne had chosen, picking the appropriate insurance carrier so we could be up and running as soon as we passed all the necessary inspections the county required. The day the Certificate of Occupancy arrived, we began to move in. I still had lots to do: choosing the décor, buying furniture, ordering lights, and the like.

Max, still, had not surfaced. Every so often I would take

the ring out of the pouch where I kept it, and would put it on. It still fit perfectly. The ring, a perfectly round diamond on a platinum band, was absolutely gorgeous. Although I was not all that familiar with the price of diamonds, I could tell it was very expensive and purchasing the ring had been an expense he could not have easily afforded. I hoped that the diamond had not belonged to his late mother, and that he had had it reset so he could give it to me. Even though I knew I should not keep the diamond, I was reluctant to return it, as it was the only link I had to Max.

Simone and Suzanne had chosen well in the young ladies they had contracted to work at the Casa Miami. I'd asked on several occasions where they had found them, but they would not disclose the information, telling me that it was not necessary that I know, which was true. As long as the girls could satisfy the clients, that's all that really concerned me, and Simone and Suzanne had assured me that they could. I suspected their reluctance to inform me had to do with the girls' immigration status, so I did not press it. After all, if we were going to get into trouble with the law for the kind of operation we were running—the modeling facade was a bit thin—the least of our troubles was going to be because we were employing undocumented workers. Still, I wondered where they had found young ladies who hailed from places such as Myanmar, New Zealand, Cape Verde, East Timor, Niger, Vatican City (!), Laos, Armenia, etc. We would be offering an eclectic group that was for sure. Hopefully, the girls were familiar enough with the sexual practices of their countries of origins that they could offer a perfect sexual experience; after all, that was our niche. I would have to garner that information anecdotally, as I would not have a way of learing it firsthand. Mostly, though, that was Simone's responsibility, as she was in charge of the girls.

Getting the actual building set up was not as complicated as I would have thought. It actually went quite smoothly, thanks mostly to Jason and his team. My living quarters were ready before anything else. I had partitioned the northwest section of the building for myself and Waldo and Oona, and although my space was not large, twelve hundred square feet, it was very well laid out, so it gave the appearance of being spacious. Jason had set aside an area for the dogs in the back, like a mini dog park, so they had an enclosure in which to run and play.

The offices were located in the front part of the building, facing the street. The rooms where the young ladies would entertain the clients were in the middle of the building, divided into twelve sections, each representing a geographical area of the world. The rooms were decorated according to the countries represented, all luxuriously done.

Simone and I, always looking for how to increase our business even before we had been up and running, had discussed ways to do so. We had come up with ideas such as having the girls have sex with clients in different containers of water (Jacuzzis, wading pools, under waterfalls, in hot tubs) or offering a culinary sexual experience (whipped cream, sushi, pasta, cheeses, chocolates) with items placed on the girls' bodies, or decorating the rooms like film sets, so they resembled banks, airplanes, lawyers' offices, churches, hospital rooms. The possibilities were endless. It was fun coming up with the different scenarios.

Busy as I was, I could not get Max out of my mind. Late on the night before Casa Miami was scheduled to open, I was lying on my bed, exhausted, sweaty, and smelly from moving furniture around, with Waldo and Oona snoozing next to me, snoring gently. I looked at the ring that Max had given me that I had placed on my hand an hour earlier. I kept twirling it around, thinking what I should do.

Two months had passed since the nightmarish meeting at the Spanish Rose had taken place. Max had not contacted me during that time, nor had I reached out to him. I wondered if he thought of me, the way I could not get him out of my mind. Well, there was only one way to find out. What was the worst that could happen?

I picked up my cell phone from the bedside table, and began typing a text. "Hey Max, I've been was just wondering how you are doing." I waited for a minute then continued typing. "I have two dogs now. Rescues. From the pound. Magnolia." Taking a deep breath, I hit "send."

Nothing. I had just about given up, when, thirty minutes later, my phone beeped, indicating I'd received a text. "What did you name them?

Acknowledgments

It is to my family that I owe the most thanks, especially to my daughters, Sarah, Antonia, and Gabriella, staunch supporters of my various endeavors, however unorthodox those might be. I am eternally grateful to them for their unquestioning and unconditional love and encouragement, even though they probably don't understand my motivation for doing what I do. Magnolia, however, is the furthest out there that I've ever gone, yet they've backed me all the way.

My sister, Sara O'Connell, my brother, Carlos Garcia, and my nephew, Richard O'Connell have always been very supportive, and for that, I am indebted to them. To the men in my daughters' lives, Andrea Macario, Ruben Millares, and Danny Renaud, thank you for taking care of my girls and for putting up with me—no easy task.

I have been so fortunate to have such wonderful friends, especially Brian Antoni, Tom Austin, Dr Scott Hall, Michael Daly, Ruth Latterner, Peter Raben, and Luis Santeiro, to name a few. As for the team that worked with great enthusiasm to make Magnolia a reality, I thank Mitchell Kaplan who believed in the book so much that he published it, as well as Books & Books Press, Ausbert de Arce, Petra Mason, Elizabeth Smith, John Dufresne, and Jessica Jonap.

Thanks also must go to the baby-faced, angelic-looking dominatrix who explained in detail the exact nature of her profession, giving such vivid descriptions that I could almost imagine myself in her world; to the saleslady at the sex-toys shop in New York City, for demonstrating proper spanking techniques and allowing me to try out the merchandise, even though my bottom was sore for a bit afterward; and to the elite athletes who gave me a glimpse into their world.

Last, I would be remiss if I did not thank my four dogs—Frost, Wanda, Charlotte, and Brian—for the hours they spent with me in my office, keeping me company and encouraging me.